SHATTERED MIRROR

ALSO BY IRIS JOHANSEN

SHATTERED MIRROR

IRIS JOHANSEN

ST. MARTIN'S PRESS ☙ NEW YORK

SHATTERED MIRROR. Copyright © 2018 by IJ Development, Inc. All rights reserved. Printed in the United States of America. For information, address St. Martin's Press, 175 Fifth Avenue, New York, N.Y. 10010.

www.stmartins.com

Designed by Omar Chopra

Library of Congress Cataloging-in-Publication Data

Names: Johansen, Iris, author.
Title: Shattered mirror / Iris Johansen.
Description: First edition. | New York : St. Martin's Press, 2018.
Identifiers: LCCN 2017049578| ISBN 9781250075864 (hardcover) |
    ISBN 9781466887244 (ebook)
Subjects: LCSH: Duncan, Eve (Fictitious character)—Fiction. | Facial
    reconstruction (Anthropology)—Fiction. | Women sculptors—Fiction. |
    GSAFD: Suspense fiction. | Mystery fiction.
Classification: LCC PS3560.O275 S532 2018 | DDC 813/.54—dc23
LC record available at https://lccn.loc.gov/2017049578

Our books may be purchased in bulk for promotional, educational, or business use. Please contact your local bookseller or the Macmillan Corporate and Premium Sales Department at 1-800-221-7945, extension 5442, or by email at MacmillanSpecialMarkets@macmillan.com.

First Edition: April 2018

10 9 8 7 6 5 4 3 2 1

SHATTERED MIRROR

CHAPTER

1

The lights in the lake cottage sent out a cozy glow that lit the banks of the lake and made that house of death appear welcoming. Everything about the place and property spoke of beauty and a deceptive invitation that made one think that all was well with this world.

Because *she* was there, Rory Norwalk thought, as he moved a few steps closer, his gaze on the cottage. She was the heart of the house, the one who destroyed the balance, who had ruined everything when she could have saved. She claimed that she was a mender, a fixer, but Norwalk knew that was all lies.

He was the one who would fix what was broken. Eve Duncan only interfered and made a mockery of what was true and right. But that was going to stop; he couldn't permit it any longer.

Laughter . . .

He stepped back in the shadow of the trees as a Jeep drove up into the driveway.

It was the father and the son. It was the little boy who had laughed. He laughed a lot; careless, joyous laughter that was as deceptive as this house. How could he be joyous when he lived with that woman who was so evil? Because he was evil, too? Norwalk had suspected it and was almost certain that the boy, Michael, would have to be fixed.

"Stay here," Joe Quinn told his son as he got out of the car and started up the porch steps. "I'll do it, but you'll owe me, Michael. She told you not to do it again."

"He wouldn't listen," Michael protested. "I tried, Dad. Just explain so that she won't get upset. Okay?"

"No, it's not okay. But I'll call you in after I break it to her." He'd reached the porch, and he looked back down at the little boy in the car. "You sit there and think about what you're going to say to your mother. And you start off with telling her that you're not going to do it again."

"But I may have to do it again," the little boy said quietly. "I can't lie to her."

Joe Quinn sighed. "No, you can't. We'll think of something." He disappeared into the house.

Leaving the little boy alone in the car.

The boy was not often left alone, Norwalk knew. He was only six, and his mother was very careful since they lived on the lake. And Joe Quinn was a police detective, and he was wary of everything and everyone.

Was this moment of abandonment meant to be a sign to Norwalk? It was not why he was here, though he'd mentally already accepted that down the road it must be done. He was very quick, and children were so gullible. It would only take a few moments. He instinctively moved faster through the trees, his gaze on the boy in the Jeep.

But the boy was no longer in the Jeep.

He'd gotten out of the vehicle and was standing on the last porch step. He was dressed in jeans and a navy-blue sweatshirt and his legs were slightly parted. The light from the porch light was burnishing his red-brown hair as if it were a copper helmet.

Helmet? Why had that word occurred to him, Norwalk wondered. It was because the boy's bearing looked almost military, he realized. He looked like a soldier guarding a fortress. Ridiculous.

As ridiculous as the idea that the boy was looking directly to where Norwalk was standing under the trees and could see him. It was pitch-dark, there was no way he could be seen.

But that little boy *knew* he was there.

And he was not afraid.

Norwalk instinctively faded farther back in the trees.

Oh, he had been right to judge that Michael Quinn would also have to be taken out before that cozy house would be cleansed of all that was broken.

But not right now.

Just a little longer, Sean. I'm just as eager as you, but we have to keep to the plan, don't we?

And all good things came to he who was willing to wait.

"Lord, you smell good." Joe slid his hands around Eve's waist from behind. "Fried onions and bacon. Is there any scent more appetizing?"

"It depends if you're hungry." She turned around and went into his arms. "Not exactly an alluring perfume if the aim is seduction."

"Is that the aim? If it is, you must have gotten the reconstruction off today."

She nodded. "This afternoon." She chuckled. "But since when did work stop us?" She leaned back, and her gaze narrowed on his face. "And since when did you decide to pussyfoot around instead of coming out with what you're thinking?"

He sighed. "I was trying for mellow and soothing. I promised Michael I'd do my best."

She went still. "Do your best to do what?"

"Break it to you gently."

"Joe."

"He has a few bruises and a swollen lip."

"What?" She pushed him away. "Who?"

"Same kid."

She swore beneath her breath. "Same reason?"

He nodded. "He did what you told him to do. The kid wouldn't listen. Boys aren't usually receptive to persuasion or reason at that age."

"He's a bully."

"And a head taller than Michael. I saw this Gary Walden when I picked Michael up from soccer practice tonight."

"That's the third time that he's come home with bruises. The soccer coach should have stepped in and stopped it."

"Probably didn't know about it. Michael wouldn't complain. You know that."

Yes, she knew very well that Michael would keep his silence. Her son would quietly take whatever came his way and try to work his way through to a solution. That had been the way he handled problems from the time he was a toddler. Only this time the punishment he was taking was because of *her*, dammit. "Maybe I should talk to this Gary's mother."

"Which might make it worse for Michael."

And that was why she had been avoiding doing that. "Kids can be savages."

"Absolutely," Joe said. "And TV and pop culture have led them to think that to latch onto something out of the ordinary and make fun of it is the way to go. But Michael will get bigger and stronger." His lips tightened. "I've signed him up for a karate class. And a few more lessons in karate from me will even out the odds in the meantime. The problem will go away."

Her lips twisted. "And this Gary will no longer tell Michael his mother is some kind of a ghoul who collects skulls for a hobby?"

"Not where Michael can hear him." He smiled. "Come on, you're the foremost forensic sculptor in the world. What difference does it make what that kid says?"

"It matters if it hurts Michael."

"It doesn't hurt Michael," Joe said. "You know that, Eve. He's only worried that it will upset you." His hand reached out and touched her cheek. "That's why he wanted me to break those damn bruises to you. He only wants to make certain that nothing ever hurts you." He leaned forward, kissed her gently, and drew her close. "That's what we all want. You know how smart Michael is. So give him a little time to work this out for himself."

"He's only six, Joe." Her words were muffled against his chest.

"Going on thirty. You've always known he's not like other kids."

Yes, she'd known from the time Michael had been conceived that he was wonderful and special and he had never disappointed her. He was superintelligent and had the sweetest nature on the planet. But that didn't mean it wasn't her job to keep on protecting him. She had lost her daughter, Bonnie, who was only seven when she had died after being taken. It had nearly broken her heart. Michael was almost that age now, and whenever she thought about it, the fear returned. Block it. It wasn't fair to Michael to live anything but a full and joyous life. "Yeah, I know. But maybe I'm not quite as grown up. I need a little bolstering on occasion." She pushed him away. "Okay, I suppose you left him outside until you paved the way for him?"

Joe nodded. "In the Jeep. I told him I'd give him a call when you were ready for him."

"I'm always ready for him." She headed for the front door. "Watch the potatoes for me, Joe?"

"Sure." He turned back to the stove. "Tell him, I did my best."

"He knows that you would." She smiled back at him. "And you'd better be quick about getting him very good at that karate. I don't know how many of these sessions I can take."

"An eternity," he said softly. "I know you, Eve."

He was right, she thought. There were no limits for her where Michael was concerned.

She went out on the porch. "Okay, Michael. Come out and face

the music. Your father has given me the lowdown and he tried to—"
She stopped. Michael was not in the Jeep, and there was something
about the way he was standing on that bottom step that was . . . odd.
"Michael?"

He turned and gave her a radiant smile that lit his entire face. "I'm
coming, Mama." He turned and ran up the stairs. "I was just looking
out at the lake. It's pretty tonight, isn't it?" He hugged her. "I'm hungry. Can we eat before you yell at me about Gary?"

She held him close for an instant. "That might be possible." She
released him and opened the front door. "I thought you might want
to stay out here on the porch and have it out first."

"Nah." His smile took on a hint of mischief. "I know Dad made
sure that you wouldn't be too mad at me. He's a guy, too. He knows
about these things." He glanced at the lake and woods, then turned
and headed for the door. "I don't want to stay out here. I'd rather go
in with you and eat supper . . ."

"Okay, talk to me," Eve said as she cuddled Michael closer
to her on the couch after supper. "I told you that if you couldn't handle
Gary yourself, you were to go to your teacher. Why didn't you do it?"

"He would have got in trouble."

"Exactly."

"And he didn't hurt me that bad. He was just scared."

"He didn't act very scared," she said dryly as she touched his
bruised cheek. "And your dad said he's much bigger than you."

He nodded. "But he's still scared."

She looked down at him with narrowed eyes. "Why?"

"Because I'm not afraid of what you do, and he is," he said simply.

She stiffened. "That ghoul name he called me?"

"His dad was killed in a car wreck last year. Gary's all confused,
and he doesn't like to think about it. I make him think about it. All
those skulls that you work on bother him."

"No, *I* make him think about it." Her arm tightened around him. "I was wondering if it was my fault. I didn't know about his father. Maybe I should go talk to his mother."

He shook his head. "It would only make her feel bad. Sometime, Gary will let me talk to him about you. Then it will be okay."

"But it's not okay now. And what can you say to him that will make it okay then?"

"I'll tell him that you work on those skulls to bring those people home. That they're lost, and you have to help them." He looked up at her. "That's what you told me that first time I asked you. Remember?"

"I don't remember you asking me." She smiled. "But maybe you did. You always seemed to understand my work and why I was doing it." She did remember Michael coming close to her worktable when he was only a couple years old and touching the skull of a young girl she was reconstructing. There had been such gentleness, such intensity of thought in his expression that she had been stunned. Then, after a moment, he had smiled and gone back to his toys across the room. "I don't like the idea of waiting around until this Gary comes to his senses on his own. I may have to take action if you won't."

He nodded. "I know. But I think it's going to be okay. He doesn't like what he's doing to me. It scares him almost as much as the stuff he won't ask me about your skulls and the people who are dead like his dad."

And how had Michael realized that? Eve just had to accept that he did. She had stopped trying to understand where those flashes of deep understanding came from. Even before the moment of his birth she had known that Michael possessed a kind of psychic connection with her, and who knew what other depths he might have? She didn't believe he wanted her to know, or maybe he didn't know himself. Either way, most of the time Michael appeared to be just a bright, happy six-year-old who was perfectly content in his life. It was only with her and Joe that he let his guard down and was totally honest.

She hoped. There were moments when she wasn't certain that Michael was entirely open even with them. It didn't matter as long as she knew that Michael loved them both, they could work on every-thing else. "It's bad for Gary to think he can hurt you. I don't want him to turn into a bully or you a victim. So you'll try one more time, then I'll have a talk with him." She held up her hand. "Not his mother. Okay?"

Michael nodded. "He's close to it, Mama. It's the death thing. He's missing his dad. It scares him."

"Then we'll try to explain and make the fear go away." She gave him a kiss on the forehead and got to her feet. "Now go take your shower and get to bed."

He grinned as he jumped to his feet. "Soon as I say good night to Dad." He headed toward the back of the house. "And tell him that you didn't yell too much at me. He'll want to know." He turned back. "Did Cara send me that CD of her last concert that she promised me last week?"

She nodded. "Morning mail. It's on your nightstand. You can play it through once. Just once. Then you turn it off and go to sleep."

"Once is enough. After that, it will play in my head until I fall asleep. It does that to you, too, doesn't it, Mama?"

"Yes." Cara Delaney was Eve and Joe's ward and one of the most magnificent violinists Eve had ever heard. She was only eighteen and a student at Carnegie Tech in New York, but she had already been a guest artist at several venues, and this CD was the one from a benefit concert at the university in Phoenix. She had been with them since before Michael was born, and Eve could not have wanted a more devoted or loving sister for her son. The two talked every week on the phone, and when Cara managed to come home, they were practi-cally inseparable. "She texted me and said she might have a break next week or the week after."

"She's coming home?" His face lit up. "That would be great. When will she know?"

Eve shrugged. "Soon. She's trying to arrange things. We'll know when she does. She asked if Jane was going to be able to get away at the same time. She might be trying to coordinate her time with Jane's." But Jane MacGuire, her adopted daughter, had a schedule that was almost tighter than Cara's. She was an artist and her agent had her constantly making public appearances at galley exhibits in London. "I don't think she has a chance. Jane's supposed to be in Paris all this month."

Michael looked disappointed. "Maybe."

Eve nodded. "Maybe. But at least we'll have Cara. You know Jane gets here whenever she can."

"Yes. I just miss her." He turned and started back down the hall. "It would be nice . . ."

More than nice, Eve thought. She believed in family and having Jane and Cara out in the world and not being able to see them as much as she'd like brought a constant ache. But she was being selfish, she couldn't have everything. Life was so incredibly good these days with Joe and Michael, and the occasional visits from Cara and Jane were like additional jewels in the crown. So she would accept what she was given with thanks and enjoy every single minute.

She flipped open her computer on the coffee table and checked for recent requests from police departments around the country. She usually did that on the day she sent the latest reconstruction back to its originator. She had a tremendous backlog of requests, but if anything appeared urgent that couldn't—

"Be back in ten minutes or so." Joe had come out of the bedroom and was slipping on his jacket. "Just want to check on something."

"Check on what?"

"A bear."

Her eyes widened. "What?"

"Michael thought he saw a bear earlier tonight in the woods on that west bank."

"He never mentioned it to me."

"But you were too busy giving him a lecture. He probably didn't have time." He headed for the door. "And it's probably nothing. It was pretty dark out there. I don't know how he could see anything."

"But you're checking it anyway."

"He hit me where I live." He smiled at her. "He asked if maybe I should tell you that you shouldn't go around the lake until I was sure." He opened the door. "What could I say? Be right back."

Eve watched the door shut behind him.

A bear?

Strange. Yet there had been that moment when she had first seen Michael on that bottom step, and she had been aware of a tense . . . alertness.

A bear? There had been no bear sightings in this area for the last couple years.

Michael had thought something was wrong and had not spoken to her but gone to his father and told him he should protect her.

She could hear Michael's shower running now.

He had finished with what he had wanted to do with Joe and was going about his life.

Yet he had thought something was wrong . . .

She instinctively moved toward the front door.

And that wrong must not touch Joe.

Whenever Joe went into the woods, he was always armed, but she didn't like him to be alone out there.

She stood on the porch, her eyes straining toward the west bank.

The beam of a flashlight.

Joe.

It was moving over the trees, down to the ground, around the bank.

"Joe," she called.

He froze. "Go back inside, Eve," he called. "I'll be right there."
He paused. "Lock the door."

She stiffened. That last order was scaring her. Joe never took action
without reason. She was tempted to go to him.

No, Michael was in this house. Someone had to be here to protect him. That was the unwritten rule she and Joe lived by. One of
them must always be there for Michael. Tonight that was her job. She
went inside and locked the door.

Come on, Joe . . .

She went to the window beside the door and looked out on the
porch and the woods beyond.

She could still see the beam of Joe's flashlight bouncing, moving
through the trees.

And now Joe was coming back toward the house, she realized
with relief. But the flashlight wasn't aimed straight before him, it was
focused on the ground.

He was tracking.

And whatever he was tracking was heading straight toward this
house.

She opened the door again as he reached the driveway. "What is
it, Joe?"

"Well, it's not a bear, unless it wears size twelve tennis shoes," he
said grimly. He was moving across the driveway, the beam focused
on the soft earth bordering the gravel. Then he stopped, his gaze on
the ground beside the passenger door of the Jeep. He flashed the beam
inside the Jeep and slowly, carefully opened the car door. "What the
hell," he muttered. "Weird."

"Tell me," Eve said.

"It's a box on this passenger seat." He carefully examined the box
before he took it out of the Jeep and placed it on the porch step. "It's
wrapped in some kind of gold foil. Like I said, weird."

She started across the porch. "I want to see—"

"Stay where you are. I want to check it out first." He strode toward the Toyota. "I'll get that portable bomb-detector kit that I keep in my trunk and see if that box is giving out a reading."

Joe had been trained in bomb disposal when he was in the SEALS, and Eve knew he still made a habit of carrying a portable unit with him as a detective with the Atlanta PD. He had used it more than once in past years.

She shivered as she looked at the glittering gold-foil box. Beautiful and glittering, and Joe thought it might be deadly.

But now he had the small mobile unit and was listening with the stethoscope to hear if there was anything that signaled a timer switch. "Nothing." He looked at the edge of the box. "It's not fastened." He was placing the end of the water hose under the edge of the box and backing across the driveway to the water spigot. "Get back inside. I'll turn on the water full force and blow this lid off as soon as I'm a safe distance."

"And how do you know that it's safe?"

"Inside," he said curtly. "Michael."

She went inside and slammed the door. Michael, the one unassailable argument. No matter what happened to either of them, Michael must survive. Her hands clenched on the drapes at the window as she watched Joe unwind the hose as he headed for the spigot.

She held her breath as she saw him connecting it to the spigot.

Then he turned on the water full force.

The lid of the box blew a foot in the air and then fell back onto the container.

No explosion. Just water pouring in a wild fountain over the gold box.

Joe jerked the hose aside and came back toward the box. "No C4." He was looking down at the contents of the box. "I don't know what the hell it is."

"Maybe some kid's idea of a practical joke?" She was coming down the porch steps now. "I feel a little foolish cowering inside."

"I don't," he said. "Whoever was out there in the woods was there for a while, and he wasn't a kid. That's called stalking. And there are other people besides that kid, Gary, who think what you do is kind of scary." He was examining the interior. "Or, what's worse, that they don't think it's scary at all." His fingers were carefully exploring something. "There's a flat surface on the top that's glittering in the light . . ." He leaned closer and muttered a curse. "It's a mirror."

"What?" She came down the rest of the stairs and looked inside the box. It was a mirror that occupied the entire upper diameter of the interior of the box. It was glittering, framed in gold and perfectly reflected her face.

And that reflection mirrored both her bewilderment and fear. Fear. It was only because this entire episode was so unexpected and bizarre that she was feeling this shaken, she told herself. It would probably turn out to be the practical joke that had been her first thought.

"That's only the top layer, Joe." She moistened her lips. "What else is in the box?"

"I'm working on it." He was gently prying the frame of the mirror away from the sides of the box. "I'll have it in a minute . . ." Then it came free and he lifted it out.

Glittering mirrored shards fell down into the box.

"Double mirror," Joe said. "This side seems to be broken. It must have been cracked and, when I lifted, it broke entirely." He reached down to pick up one of the broken shards. "It fell on this black—" He inhaled sharply. "Holy shit."

Eve saw it too. The black velvet cloth had shifted to one side, uncovering something else equally black and very familiar to Eve. "It's a skull." She pulled the cloth completely away. Blackened. All flesh gone. "Burned. Someone burned this skull."

"It's the real thing?" Joe asked quietly. "Not just a good replica from a party store?"

"It's the real thing." She turned away as she saw the bullet hole in the temple. "And there's nothing that even hints at a party. Bring it inside. I need to look at it."

Joe didn't move. "I could take it down to the precinct. It's not really your problem. You don't have to be involved. Forensics will have to go over it anyway."

"I *am* involved." She looked back at him, and added fiercely, "How could I not be? He delivered this skull to *me*. He went to a great deal of trouble on this presentation. He brought it to my home." She gestured to the woods. "He stood there where my son could see him. Do you think that doesn't make it my problem?"

"It makes it *my* problem," Joe said. "I was hoping that I could keep you out of it." He picked up the box and carried it up the porch steps. "Not going to happen."

She nodded and held the door for him. "Put the box on my worktable and call Forensics and get them out here for testing right away."

"I'll do it while I take a look around the property." He placed the gold-wrapped box on her worktable in the studio area. "Lock the door behind me." He headed back toward the door. "I don't have to tell you not to touch anything until Forensics gets through with the initial investigation."

"Just get them here soon." She followed him to the door. "Be careful." She kissed him quickly. "And I'm not about to do anything with that skull until I make sure Michael is okay and safely in bed. I don't like the fact that he was the one who sent you out there."

"A bear," he reminded her.

"Maybe." She closed the door and locked it. Then she headed across the living room toward the bedrooms. She carefully averted her eyes from the gold box on her worktable as she passed by her studio. Beautiful gold paper covering a horror of blackened skull.

But skulls were never a horror to her, the horror was when monsters reached out to make them that way.

Michael's nightstand lamp was on, and she paused a moment in his doorway gazing at him. His eyes were shut, but she knew he was not asleep. Clean and shining and beautiful, wonderful and yet also full of wonder.

She saw Cara's latest CD on top of the CD player on his nightstand. His photo of Cara was beside it. It was a picture he had snapped of her with his phone camera down at the lake. Cara was dressed in shorts and a white shirt and sitting cross-legged with her violin in her hands. She was smiling, her long dark hair pulled back in a ponytail and her brown eyes were shining with affection and humor. Eve had always loved that photo and searched out a frame for Michael when he had brought the picture to her. It showed more than the Cara who had a certain dark exotic beauty inherited from her Mexican father and Russian mother. It showed the depth, the spirit, the clean intensity of the young girl. And the heart, she thought, definitely the heart . . .

"Mama?" Michael opened his eyes that were so like the rich, tea color of his father's. "You came to say good night?"

"Among other things." She crossed the room and sat down on the bed beside him. "Don't worry, I'm not about to lecture you anymore. That's over." She took his hand. "Bear, Michael? Why didn't you tell me?"

"You would have gone out to see for yourself."

"I guarantee I wouldn't have confronted a bear without protection."

"But Dad *is* protection, isn't he? No need for you to have to do it."

She shook her head. "And you think we all have our places and duties? Sometimes it doesn't work like that. So come to me and tell me if you see a bear."

He smiled. "I'll tell you."

But he didn't say when he would do that, she thought ruefully. And anyone would think she was crazy to suspect him of avoiding that commitment. He was only a child.

"I want you to do that," she said quietly. "It will make me unhappy if you don't."

He hesitated, then nodded. "Then I have to do it." He burrowed close to her. "Good night, Mama."

"Oh, I'm dismissed?" She smiled down at him. "Okay, I'll accept it, Michael. But there's another thing I wanted to tell you. A few of the people your dad works with are coming over soon. They may make noise. I'll close your door, but I didn't want them to startle you. There's nothing to be afraid of."

"I won't be afraid of them." His face was muffled against her. "Don't you be afraid, Mama."

She stiffened. "I won't. Everything's okay, Michael."

"No. Not now." He rolled back onto his pillow and pulled up his blanket. "Maybe soon . . ."

She sat there, gazing at him. "Soon?"

He smiled. "Cara's coming. That should make it better."

"She always makes things better. Did you play her CD when you got to bed?"

"No, I'll do it tomorrow."

But he'd been so eager to play it Eve knew. Though she knew she would not be playing it tonight either. "Tomorrow will be good, too." She kissed him on the cheek and stood up. "You can look forward to it." She headed for the door. "Remember, if you wake up, it's only the people from your dad's work."

"I'll remember."

She stopped at the door. "A bear. It was so dark out tonight. Clouds. No moon. Why did you think it was a bear?"

"I only told Dad it *might* be a bear."

"Why?"

He was silent. "Big, still, hungry, full of darkness. A bear could be like that, too, couldn't it?"

Too?

She could feel a chill go through her. "I suppose it could. Good night, Michael." She closed his door behind her. She stood there a moment while she recovered from that sudden icy fear.

Full of darkness.

Whatever Michael had seen or sensed out there had been full of darkness. In that moment, darkness had reached out and touched him. All his life she had been trying to see that he was only surrounded by joy and sunlight. That he would never be drawn down into the darkness that would mean he would leave her as Bonnie had done.

No!

She would not *have* it. Never again.

Yet that darkness had come, wrapped in gold and mirrors, and it had called Michael toward it.

But she would fight it with all her strength.

And she would not let it come near him.

"They want to take the skull back to the lab," Joe told Eve in a low voice. "In case they decide to do some more tests."

"No." She glanced at the four techs who were gathered around the skull. "They've taken DNA, tooth impressions, X-rays, made an impression of the skull itself. Taken samples around that bullet hole, done a dozen other forensic tests. They're done, Joe. The skull is *mine* now. I'm going to do the reconstruction."

"A reconstruction may not be necessary if they can get another form of ID."

"It's necessary for me." She added jerkily, "It was necessary for him, or he wouldn't have delivered her to me."

"Her?"

"Female Caucasian from what I can tell. Forensics hasn't let me get close enough to determine anything positively. I certainly can't judge age or if this skull suffered additional trauma other than that bullet wound in the temple before he burned her."

"You might run into a fight trying to keep her," Joe said. "Forensics will want to be in control."

"They can have control of the box. They can have the mirrors. They don't get the skull. I'm ready for a fight."

"I can see that." His eyes were searching her face. "Would you care to elaborate?"

"I've been sitting here watching all those experts working on that skull, and I've been thinking of that man standing out there in the woods with that box in his hands. You said he must have stood there a long time." She met his eyes. "That means he was there when you and Michael drove up."

"Yes."

"And you left Michael in the car."

He went still. "Are you blaming me?"

"No, don't be ridiculous. Michael was within calling distance. The property is usually safe. How could you know . . . that . . . he was out there." Her voice lowered. "What I'm saying is that he saw Michael. And when he brought that skull to the house, he didn't put it on the porch or in front of the door. He put it on the passenger seat of the Jeep where Michael was sitting when you drove up."

"Son of a *bitch*." Joe was swearing softly. "Why didn't I put that together?"

"You've had a few other things on your mind," Eve said. "I've just been sitting here looking at that skull."

"And thinking that putting that skull on Michael's seat was a warning."

"Or a prediction. Either way, I'm not letting that skull leave the house until I know who she is, maybe not then. He wanted me to have it, and he took a lot of trouble to do it. Perhaps it means something to him. Maybe he'll come back for it."

"That's the last thing I want to happen," Joe said. "I've already started to think about how to keep you and Michael safe."

"I'm not worried. Like Michael says, *you* are the protection. You'll just take extra precautions."

"Damn right I will."

"Then go and tell those forensic people they can't have my skull. As you said, it may be a fight."

"Screw it." Joe turned away from her and headed back to her worktable. "Possession is nine-tenths. In this case, it's a big number ten."

CHAPTER

2

E ve took the black velvet cloth off the skull and started to set it up on the dais. "I'm surprised they left the cloth. It's evidence," she told Joe over her shoulder. "Those forensic techs weren't pleased when they stomped out of here."

"They took a sample. I'll call and ask them if they want me to bring it to the precinct in the morning." He checked his watch. "Which is only about six hours away." He watched her work on the skull placement. "I know you're eager, but you're not going to start it tonight?"

She shook her head. "Tomorrow morning." She stood back and wiped her hands on her towel. "Maybe after Michael goes to school. He takes my reconstructions as a matter of course, but he's never seen me work on one that's been burned and blackened like this. It might shake even him a bit."

"I doubt it." He put his arm around her waist. "But use your own judgment. Now come to bed. You need your rest."

She let him lead her back to their room. She had to ask it. "You think *he's* gone?"

"I know he's gone. No footprints after they disappeared when they reached the main road. He probably had a car hidden there. And

when I sent Forensics on their way, I took another look around."
He opened the bedroom door. "No one outside. The alarm is on,
and you have me to watch your back." He smiled. "And all your
other exceptional physical attributes. Now get undressed and let me
hold you."

"I'm on it." She was already undressing. A moment later, she was
in bed and cuddling close to him. He felt so good, so safe.

No darkness here . . .

"Your breakfast is on the bar. It's eggs and sausage," Eve told
Michael as he came into the living room. "Then you need to hurry
a little. You're not taking the bus from down the road. Your dad is
going to take you to school today, and we don't want to make him
late for work. Okay?"

"Okay." He'd crawled up on the stool and was eating his breakfast. "Why?"

"Just a change from the school bus. Everyone needs a change."
She gave him his orange juice. "He'll be picking you up, too. Or I
will if I'm not busy."

"But maybe you will be busy." His gaze had wandered to her
studio worktable across the room to the black-draped skull. "I didn't
see that yesterday. You have a new one?"

"Yes."

"A kid?"

"Not this time. I think it's a young woman."

"You don't do many of those." He finished his eggs. "Why?"

Because children were so much more vulnerable than grown-ups.
But she didn't want to say those sad words. She modified them. "When
you're grown-up, you can take better care of yourself."

"But she couldn't. Why not?"

"I don't know. I'll try to find out. Done? Go brush your teeth."

He nodded and jumped off the stool, his gaze still on the black
velvet cover on the skull. "May I see her?"

Caught. Eve gazed at him in a quandary. She'd wanted to avoid this. "You may want to wait until I get a little farther along. She was in a fire, and it's a bit—it's not like some others you've seen."

"I want to see her. May I?"

She nodded. She had never tried to hide what she did and couldn't start now. She went over to the worktable. "Sure. Come and meet her. But don't say I didn't warn you."

"I won't." He followed her and rested his arms on her worktable. "Are you going to give her a name like you usually do?"

"Yes."

"But you haven't given her a name yet?"

"Not yet." She pulled off the black velvet cloth, her gaze narrowed on his face to gauge his reaction. "I haven't had time to think about it."

She breathed a sigh of relief. No fear. No horror. Only intense interest and something else . . . "I told you that it wasn't the same."

"None of them are the same." He was reaching out to gently touch that blackened cheekbone. "She never wanted to be the same . . ." His finger went to the gaping hole in the back of the skull. "It's gone, Mama. Why?"

How to delicately explain that her brain had exploded and blown away the skull? No delicate way. Don't explain. Generalize.

"It was the fire, Michael. This kind of thing happens very often when there's a fire."

"But you'll fix it?"

"Yes, I'll fix it."

"You'll fix everything." His gaze shifted from the skull to Eve's face. "I think she'll be beautiful, Mama."

"So do I." She gave him a swat. "Now go brush your teeth. You have to be out of here in five minutes."

"Okay." He was hurrying across the room, but he stopped as he started down the hall. "Sylvie."

She halted in the act of replacing the cloth. "What?"

"You should call her Sylvie."

He disappeared into the bathroom.

Eve's phone rang when she had barely started the initial measuring on the reconstruction.

Cara.

"Don't you dare tell me you're going to have to delay coming," she said when she answered. "Michael was over the moon when I told him."

"No, I still haven't got the exact date, but I think it will be next week, if that's okay," Cara said. "But that's not what I wanted to talk to you about." She hesitated, then burst out, "Have you heard from Jock?"

Jock Gavin. Cara hadn't spoken about him the last few times she'd called, but Eve had known he was always on her mind. Cara's bond with Jock had started when she was only eleven, and he had saved her life. They had both led tortured lives filled with fear and loneliness and somehow when they'd come together, the child and the young man had become best friends, almost soul mates. But that did not mean that the relationship had been without friction. "No, not since last Christmas when he came here for that one day. Why? Haven't you heard from him?"

"No." Then she said in a rush, "Three months. Not for three months. He doesn't answer my calls or my emails. What does he think he's doing? Doesn't he know I worry about him?"

"I can see how you'd be concerned. But you know that no one can take care of himself better than Jock."

"How am I supposed to know that? Whenever MacDuff doesn't need him, he's climbing mountains or going off on round-the-world cruises or trekking off with one of his CIA buddies and trying to get himself shot."

"He's restless," Eve said soothingly. "MacDuff may be his best friend, but they have separate lives. MacDuff is Laird of MacDuff's

Run and is becoming occupied with all that goes with it. Jock will always be there for him, but he's exploring other avenues."

"Away from me," Cara said jerkily. "He won't talk to me."

Eve could sense the hurt, but she felt helpless to heal it. "That's not like Jock, and you know it." She paused, then probed. "Something's behind it?"

Cara was silent. "He's angry with me."

There it was. "Why?"

"I told him that I'd cleared all of July to spend the month with my grandfather in New Orleans."

No wonder he'd gone ballistic. Eve was upset herself. "And you didn't tell me?"

"I was going to do it next week. I knew you wouldn't like it, and I wanted to tell you face-to-face."

"No, I *don't* like it. Imagine that. Sergai Kaskov is head of one of the most powerful Mafia families in Moscow. I don't want you anywhere *near* him whether or not he's your grandfather. Just being around him is dangerous for you."

"I made him a promise, Eve," she said quietly. "He didn't ask much considering what he gave me in return. He didn't have to save you when you were carrying Michael and fighting that poison. But he did it, and you both lived. I barely knew him, but when I asked, he gave that to me."

It was hard to argue with her when she brought up that terrifying period in both their lives. Eve had been given a deadly poison by Kaskov's daughter, and he'd given her the antidote that had saved both her life and Michael's. "In exchange for one month with you every single year. That's not all that generous."

"Yes, it is," she said softly. "We have Michael. I have you, Eve. What's one month?"

"Ask Jock," Eve said grimly. "He thinks you could be the target of rival Mafia families, or that Kaskov might hurt you himself. When you started these damn visits four years ago, he asked me to stop you.

Jock never asks anything of anyone. Do you think it didn't mean something to him?"

"He shouldn't have done that."

"It didn't do any good anyway. You wouldn't listen to me. You've visited with Kaskov for the last three years. And now you have another one coming up? How long is this supposed to go on?"

"I don't know. I thought he'd get bored with me. It's not as if we interact very much. He conducts his business, and we eat meals together. I play for him in the evening. That's all that goes on."

"Evidently he's not bored if he continues to set up these visits."

"No." She paused. "It's the music. He loves my music. And he likes the idea that someone from his family is able to play well."

"Play well? You know that you're extraordinary, and I don't like the idea of Kaskov basking in your glory."

"Glory? It's all about the music, Eve."

"Maybe not to him," she said. "And it can't go on. Jock isn't going to permit it. You do know that during every visit, Jock was nearby monitoring what was going on?"

"He told me that he'd be there. I told him not to do it."

"You were afraid that one of your grandfather's goons might decide to take Jock out? Does that tell you anything?"

"You know I wouldn't have let that happen."

"It's Jock who wouldn't have let it happen," Eve said dryly. "No one has much of a chance against Jock Gavin. But he may be through with that holding pattern if he's that angry with you, Cara."

"If he'd just let me talk to him, I can make it right."

"Maybe not this. Perhaps he's taking a step back to make a statement."

"You mean to punish me? I can't believe he'd do that," she said unevenly. "He knows how much he can hurt me. He's my best friend. He's everything."

"Then think about how much these visits have been hurting him, where he has to stand by and do nothing."

"I have to keep my promise."

Stubborn, and so damn honorable that Eve wanted to shake her. "Then you should be prepared for an explosion in the near future."

"Not if I can talk to him. I *will* talk to him. I called Jane and asked her to tell him to call me. If that doesn't work, I'll call MacDuff. He loves MacDuff. He listens to him."

"And you called me. You're pulling out all the stops." She knew how determined Cara could be. If something was important to her, then she would keep on fighting until she got her way. And there was no one more important to her than Jock Gavin. "Think about it, Cara. There's such a thing as compromise."

"I did compromise. Only one month, Eve. And Michael is alive, and so are you." She drew a deep breath. "You and Joe took me into your home and your lives, then Michael came along, and he was . . . magic. Do you know what that means to me? Maybe you could have found another way to save yourself and Michael, but I only saw one way. Don't be mad at me because I took it."

"I was never angry with you." Eve was unbearably touched. "Joe and I love you. You're a member of our family now. I just want you to stop trying to take care of all of us and start living a good life. You worry about Kaskov and Jock and Michael, Joe, and me. And you work so hard on your music at that school. Do you even have any friends there?"

"Not much time. Lessons and practice. They keep us pretty busy."

"That's what you've been telling me for years."

"It's true." She added, "But you'll be glad to know I've made one friend this quarter. Housing Admin gave me a roommate because the residence halls were overcrowded. They've even been sending us around to different events together."

"What instrument?"

"No instrument. She's a soprano. Wonderful range."

"Encouraging. Now tell me you do something together that doesn't involve music."

"We went ice-skating two weeks ago."

"That's a start. What's her name?"

"Darcy Nichols. She's a couple years older and she's nothing like me. Blond, blue-eyed, so gorgeous that people stop on the street and look at her. Way more sophisticated than I'll probably ever be. She's smart, funny, and she used to be on some Disney show when she was a kid. It ran for years. *Golden Days*. Did you ever see it?"

"No, but then I was a little too busy for Disney."

"Me, too. But I think she was pretty famous while the show was running. Anyway, she never acts as if it was a big deal. She kind of pokes fun at herself. Let's see, what else can I tell you about her . . . Oh, she likes swimming and movies and rock stars. Is that good enough for you, Eve?"

"If it's good enough for you. Do you like her?"

"I do like her. She works hard, she's honest." She paused, then said slowly, "At first, I wasn't sure about her. She kind of took my breath away. She takes everyone's breath away. She kind of . . . sparkles. She operates at top speed, and she's curious about everything around her. I guess I was a little intimidated."

"Not you."

"She was different. But, as I got to know her, I realized she might not be all that different. I think she may be a lot like me."

"In what way?"

She was silent. "She has nightmares, too."

Eve didn't speak for an instant. Cara hadn't mentioned those nightmares for a long time. When a small child she had been hunted by a cartel enforcer who had killed her sister and the woman who had raised her. It was no wonder that she'd been plagued by nightmares. Eve had hoped that their frequency had lessened after Cara had come to them. "Not something I'd want to have in common. Do you still have them?"

"Sometimes. Not often." She added, "I'm fine, Eve. I get better all the time. Now who's worrying?"

"I just want you to have all the things you missed while you were on the run."

"You've given me everything. I have the music. I have people who care about me. What else is there?" She changed the subject. "And everyone probably has nightmares. I just didn't know because I never had a roommate before. But I woke up several times in the past couple months when I heard her crying out."

"Did you ever talk to her about them?"

"No, that would have been an intrusion. She has a right to her privacy."

"But you're tempted."

"I had my friend, Elena, to help me through my nightmares while I was on the run. Darcy seems to have no one. I think she's . . . hurting. Sometimes it hurts me to see her . . ."

That's all Cara needed, Eve thought, a roommate with emotional problems that she'd struggle to solve. But didn't everyone try to solve the problems of the people they cared about? It was part of life. "Then you'll do whatever you have to do. You have great instincts."

"Do I? You and Jock don't always seem to agree with them." She chuckled. "But even when you shoot me down, you do it with infinite kindness." She changed the subject. "So it's okay if I come home next week? If it's more convenient, I might be able to change my classes and come this week instead."

Eve's glance shifted to the skull in front of her. Talking to Cara had brought home to her that life was difficult and filled with problems, but with effort they had a chance of being solved. The ugliness that had been done to this young woman and the silent threat of her being deposited on Eve's doorstep might not be as easy to resolve. She was once more feeling that sudden sense of urgency again. "No, next week is just fine, Cara. No hurry."

After she had hung up the phone, she sat there an instant, looking at the ruin of that scorched and blackened face. What had driven this monster to try to destroy whatever beauty of form and soul this woman had possessed? "It doesn't matter," she whispered. "He couldn't do what he intended to do. We won't let him win." Then she picked up her measuring device again. "I'll try to get through this boring stuff quickly, but it has to be done. Then we can get down to bringing you back to the way you should be, Sylvie . . ."

CARNEGIE RESIDENCE HALL
NEW YORK CITY

"You're going to be late," Darcy Nichols said over her shoulder as she ran past Cara on the way to the stairs. "The bus for that Wounded Warrior Concert in Connecticut leaves in ten minutes. You know Madam Gallono will *kill* us if we don't show up there on time."

"I won't be late." Cara was hurrying after her. "And if I am, all I'll have to do is slip in behind you and no one will even notice me." She chuckled. "You know how to grab and hold the spotlight."

"True." Darcy glanced over her shoulder with a brilliant smile that had a hint of mischief. "Only a few months together, and you've learned how to make use of me. Everyone thinks that I'm the lightweight, and you're so serious and dedicated, but you've got them all fooled."

"Yeah, I'm clearly a master manipulator," Cara said as she followed Darcy down the stairs. "I wouldn't have been late, but that call just took longer than I thought it—"

She stopped short.

She'd reached the turn of the stairs and come in view of the reception area below and saw the man who stood there by the desk.

"Jock?" she whispered.

Darcy had stopped, too, her eyes widening. "Who on earth is that?" she murmured. "My God, he's fantastic."

That's what everyone thought when they first saw Jock, Cara thought. Fair hair, tan, perfect, almost Grecian features, shimmering gray eyes. Strength and grace and that quiet stillness that hid so much. When she had first seen him when she was much younger, she had thought he looked like the prince from a fairy tale. These days she hardly noticed what he looked like on the outside because there was so much inside. But this was Darcy's first sight of him, and she was getting the full impact.

"That's my friend, Jock Gavin," Cara said.

"And you never told me about him? Introduce me. I believe I may be in lust."

"You don't have time." Cara was meeting Jock's eyes as she finished walking slowly down the stairs. Her heart was plunging. Fear. She was so afraid of what was to come. No smile. And those gray eyes were cold. "You have a bus to catch, Darcy."

"So do you."

"I'll get there some other way."

"And you want me out of here," Darcy said shrewdly. "I would, too, if I were you. I should have known. You're such a workaholic, it would take someone like that to get you to sit up and take notice." She smiled and gave Cara's arm a quick squeeze. "Don't worry. I'll cover for you. You were joking, but I really can make black look white or gold or whatever. Just make sure you get there. See you in Connecticut." Then she was dashing across the reception area and out the front door.

Cara braced herself, then was walking to the reception desk toward Jock. "You didn't have to come to see me. A phone call would have done the trick. Or even an email. All I wanted to know was that you were alive and well. Would that have been too much?"

"Aye," he said coldly, his slight Scottish accent making the word even more clipped. "The way I was feeling, I had to block you out entirely. I couldn't take any more, Cara."

"You can take anything. I know how strong you are." Even to herself her voice sounded uneven. She paused, then forced herself to say the words she'd been preparing. "If you don't want to see me anymore, then that's different. But you shouldn't have just walked away from me. You're important to me. You're my best friend. You should have known I'd come after you. That's all I wanted to say to you if you'd answered my calls." His face was so hard, but she forced herself to go on. "But you didn't, and that's an answer in itself, isn't it?" She couldn't take this any longer. She was hurting too much. She walked past him toward the front door. "All you had to do was make me understand. Evidently, that's what you came to do. Thanks for making it clear. Good-bye, Jock."

His hand was on her arm. "You're not going anywhere. I came here to talk to you. I'm going to do it."

She shook her head. "I have to get to Connecticut. I have a concert. It's an obligation."

His lips twisted. "And I know how you feel about obligations." He took her violin case. "I hired a limo for the day. I knew this wasn't going to be a quick fix, and your place here in this residency is like a nunnery. I'll drive you to your 'obligation.'" He nudged her toward the gray limo at the curb. "Just give the driver the address, then lean back and stop looking at me like that. I've had enough for right now."

She hesitated and got into the limo. She gave the uniformed driver behind the plastic divider the address of the auditorium in Fairfield, Connecticut. "Quick fix?" She didn't look at him. "Is it going to be a fix at all? I thought maybe you'd decided I was getting in your way. I know how busy you've been lately."

"And that's why you've been bombarding me with calls and emails? Do you have any idea how hard it was for me to ignore them? You never give up."

"No, I don't. I had to be sure. Did you expect me to let pride get in my way after all we've been through together? I had to make you tell me." She still wasn't looking at him, her eyes fastened on the plastic shield separating them from the driver. "So tell me, Jock. You decided that I wasn't worth the trouble? That I'm just a kid who wandered into your life and brought you nothing but headaches and now you want out? Because that's what I've been thinking for the last three months."

"Look at me."

"You told me not to look at you."

"Look at me."

She looked at him.

The hardness and cold was gone. There was only weariness. "You're the one who should want out. How many times have I told you that I interfere with your life? You have your music, you have Eve and Joe and Michael. You're only eighteen. You have your whole life in front of you. I just get in your way."

"How could you get in my way when I hardly ever see you?"

"I seem to manage," he said dryly. "There's no one in the world as loyal and steadfast as you, Cara. I saved your life, so you think it belongs to me? It belongs to *you*. Only to you, Cara."

"You bet it does. So I should do what I want to do with it." She made an impatient gesture. "And you know that's only the tip of the iceberg. You became my *friend*, and there's no one who knows me like you do. Everyone I loved had been killed, and I felt so alone inside. And then you were there, and I wasn't alone anymore. I can't even talk to Eve the way I talk to you." She paused. "Even though you don't feel you can talk to me."

He went still. "I talk to you all the time, Cara."

"About me, always about me, never about you."

His lips twisted. "I'm quite sure Jane and Eve have filled you in on my background. It would be their duty to warn you against me."

"Of course they told me. But not because they thought there was any chance of your hurting me. They know you, Jock. It wasn't your fault. You were younger than me when that terrorist, Reilly, brainwashed you and tried to make you into an assassin."

"He didn't try, he succeeded," Jock corrected without expression. "I was the ultimate assassin."

"And you ended up in a mental hospital where MacDuff found

you after you tried to commit suicide." She repeated, "It wasn't your fault."

"There could be endless philosophic discussions about that statement. MacDuff prefers that I don't explore them. Let's just say that I am what I am."

"And that's good and shining inside," she said fiercely. "I've always known that."

"You can't know. And you've never asked me anything about that time."

"I was waiting for you to tell me."

"You would have waited a long time. I'll never take you down to that particular hell, Cara."

"Then that's okay. As long as you know I'd go with you if you asked me."

He nodded slowly as he reached out and took her hand. "Oh, I know that, Cara. That's what this is all about. I thought I'd take another shot at stepping away, so you wouldn't be tempted to follow me."

She could feel the painful knot inside her loosen and begin to dissolve. It was going to be all right. This was the Jock she knew. Her hand tightened on his. "I thought you might be angry about my going to New Orleans with my grandfather."

"That was part of it. I had to go and check something out anyway, so I decided I'd take the opportunity to see whether if I expressed my displeasure in the cruelest possible form, you might change your mind."

"I made my grandfather a promise."

"And I'm tired of hearing that," he said tersely. "But evidently I'll have to try to give you a reason other than the fact that the entire situation makes me crazy. So I'll tell you what I've been doing for the last three months."

"Besides avoiding me."

He smiled faintly. "I'm not going to be forgiven for that, am I?"

"No. It hurt too much."

"So did the idea that you were going into the mouth of the lion again." He made a motion as she opened her mouth to speak. "Let me get this over with. You know I've never liked the idea of your being in New York alone while you were going to school? I've told you often enough."

"Yes you have. But it's not as if the school isn't safe. Juilliard was superstrict, and when I transferred to Carnegie Tech, it was the same. Carnegie Tech is the best music academy in the country, and you said yourself the living quarters are like a nunnery. Eve and Joe believe I'm safe there."

He shrugged. "Maybe if you were anyone else, you would be safe. But you're the granddaughter of a Mafia kingpin who wields a hell of a lot of power both in Russia and Europe. He's a criminal, and there's nothing stable about criminals. Because of his power, he's made enemies galore in the other crime families and of the people he's victimized. Any one of them would be delighted to get their hands on you so they could hurt Kaskov in the most personal way possible."

"You've said that before, but I've gone to this school for years, and no one has made any move on me yet."

"No, they haven't." He paused. "Not yet."

She stiffened. "That sounded menacing." She tried to smile. "Is there supposed to be some dramatic John Williams music playing in the background?"

"It's like you to connect everything to music. This *is* menacing." He grimaced. "And you're probably not going to like it. I've had someone keeping an eye on you since you've been here."

"What?"

"I told you that you wouldn't like it. Jim Stanton is very good, unobtrusive, and he never takes chances with his clients. It made me feel better."

"And a waste of your money."

He grinned. "I have lots of that commodity these days. I didn't consider it a waste if it made me happier about your situation." He looked at her warily. "It's not as if Stanton interfered with you in any way. You didn't even know he was around. He was just there in the background."

"And not necessary." She shook her head. "You act as if I should be angry with you. Am I supposed to bristle because you've attacked my independence? I know how easy it is to kill people. You turn your head, and someone you love is dead. If I thought that someone was trying to hurt you, I'd hire a Stanton to watch you if I could afford him."

He flinched. "Please don't do that. I have a tendency to act instead of ask questions."

"I just hate that you wasted your money."

His smile faded. "You've forgotten that 'yet' accompanied by your John Williams music. About the time you were blowing my mind about going to New Orleans to visit Kaskov, Stanton was giving me a report. He said that you were being shadowed. At first, he wasn't certain. Whoever was doing it was very good. And even after he caught a glimpse of the tail and confirmed, he couldn't be certain how long the surveillance had been going on. But he must have realized pretty quickly that Stanton had made him, and the surveillance stopped."

Cara was feeling her heart pounding. Someone watching. Someone waiting. All through her childhood, she'd been on the run, changing cities, changing schools because there might be a threat behind her. Now it was suddenly here again. "And nothing since then?"

"Not that he's been aware of. He watched and waited, but he didn't see anyone following you."

"Then it could have been anyone. Maybe some pervert who likes schoolgirls."

"Except that Stanton said he was exceptionally good at what he was doing." He made a face. "And prepare for another John Williams moment. Stanton got uneasy after a week or so and decided to check something else. He managed to get into your quarters to have a look around."

She frowned. "Now that's not cool, Jock."

"No, it wasn't. Because he found out that the room had been bugged."

She stared at him, stunned. "Why? For goodness sake, I play the violin, and I talk to Eve and Michael. Why would anyone want to listen to me do either of those things?"

"You've forgotten. You also harass me," he said dryly. "Though I haven't given you the opportunity recently. And listening to you play is a treasure in itself, but I'm not sure that's why he'd bug your room. I'm going with the idea that since he no longer had direct access to you, he wanted to know everything he could find out by other means." He looked down at her violin. "Like this concert. How were you going to get there?"

"There's a special bus from the school."

"Easy to watch. Easy to access."

She moistened her lips. "Maybe. But there are other performers almost everywhere I go."

"Almost." He muttered a curse. "I'm scaring you. I don't want to do that. Or maybe I do. Because I've spent the last few months in Moscow trying to tap every contact I have to see if there are any rumblings about Kaskov. Or if there's any talk about any of the Mafia families who have been particularly vocal about what kind of mayhem they'd like to practice on him."

"And what did you find out?"

"Nothing conclusive. Which made me frustrated and mad as hell and sent me back here to see if I could find out anything more from Stanton."

"And to let me know that I was harassing you." She looked down at their joined hands. "You did scare me. It brought back too many memories."

"I know it did. But you're not alone now. I'll never let anything happen to you." He added grimly. "Just stay away from Kaskov. Don't go to New Orleans."

"You said you didn't find out anything in Moscow. Maybe it doesn't matter if I go to New Orleans or not."

"And maybe it does." His lips tightened. "You said you were frightened, but you're still not saying that you're not going to go."

"I have to think about it. I'm a little . . . shook right now," she said. "So stop trying to bully me into doing what you want."

"Cara."

"I have to think." She leaned forward. "There's the auditorium up ahead. Are you going to stay and listen to me?"

He didn't answer.

"Don't shut me out again," she whispered. "It didn't work, and it hurt both of us."

He hesitated, then he lifted her hand up to his lips and kissed her palm. "I wouldn't miss listening to you play. You're right, it didn't work." He released her hand as they drew up to the curb. "That sign says it's sold-out. Can you smuggle me in the stage door?"

"Yes." She looked out the window. "There's Darcy, she'll help. She just smiles, and everyone bends over backward."

"That's your new roommate?" His gaze followed Cara's. "I can see how that might happen. She's absolutely lovely. Wonderful features."

Cara nodded. "The complete package." Darcy's long blond hair framed high cheekbones, square jaw, and wide-set blue eyes that were riveting. In her white, tea-length gown, she had definite star quality. "And she has a superb voice. Though the reviews almost always mention her face and figure as much as her voice. It's not fair. I guess I'm lucky."

"I guess you are." His eyes were twinkling as he got out of the car and held out his hand to help her. "It's wonderful that you're so ugly that it doesn't interfere with the music."

"Well, it's true. Oh, I'm not bad-looking, but it's difficult for—" She saw his face and she slapped his hand away. "Stop smiling. And you'd have just as bad a time as Darcy does. You're just as beautiful and you'd see how—"

He made a face. "Beautiful?"

"You know you are. There's no other word for you. You're above and beyond. You just smile and women go into a tailspin. Now come on and I'll introduce you to Darcy. She thinks you're hot. You dazzled her when she saw you in reception. I have to make it right for not introducing you then. It wasn't the time."

"No, it wasn't the time," he said quietly. "That seems to be our mantra, doesn't it?" He didn't wait for an answer but stepped forward as he reached Darcy and held out his hand. "Hi, I'm Jock." His smile was totally charming and lit his face with warmth that was close to radiance. "Cara tells me if anyone can sneak me into this concert, it will be you. What can I do to persuade you to do it?"

CHAPTER

3

H ey, you're making good progress."

Eve turned away from the depth markers she was placing in the reconstruction to see Joe standing a few yards behind her, looking at the skull. "Not as fast as I'd like. It took a while to close up that hole in the skull and make it look perfect."

"And everything has to look perfect for Sylvie?" He smiled. "Not that you're not a perfectionist anyway, but you're being more than usually obsessive with this one." His smile faded. "Not that I blame you. I wish that I could dig in and get my hands on answers like you're doing. Three days, and we still haven't been able to trace your Sylvie through dental records or DNA. We extracted DNA from one of the molars, but there's no match on any database we can find. So we'd have to rely on finding a family match, which throws us back to finding who the hell she is."

"No leads on where she was burned? It was very thorough and must have taken a long time. A crematorium?"

"We're checking. No records from any local funeral homes that might have ordered it done. But records can be falsified, bribes can be made to crematorium employees to do the work."

Eve looked back at the reconstruction. "I don't believe he'd pay someone else to do this. He'd want to do it himself."

Joe's raised his brows. "A hunch?"

"I guess it has to be one. But he wanted to completely destroy what she looked like, what she was. If he went to all that trouble, I think that he'd want to make sure that he'd done it." She paused. "Or perhaps that he wouldn't miss the pleasure it would give him. I can see him sitting there watching the flames, planning the presentation in that damn gold box."

"I can, too." He stepped behind her, his hands on her neck, his thumbs massaging. "How long before you get to the final stages?"

"Maybe tomorrow night." His thumb pressure felt wonderful. She hadn't realized how tense she was until Joe released it. She'd been working very fast in spite of the care she'd been taking. "I'll try to stop when Michael gets home from school and be with him until it's his bedtime. You've been carrying the full load with him, Joe."

"Neither of us has been complaining. Sometimes I feel as if he's condescending to keep me company." He chuckled. "Except we both have such a good time. If you like, I'll take him to a movie tomorrow evening."

"On a school night? Sylvie is important, but so is Michael. I won't cheat him." She turned her head and pressed her lips to his hand on her neck. "And I won't cheat you, Joe."

"Have it your way. I know you will anyway. Then I'd better let you get back to work now." His hands fell away. "But you won't mind if I take Michael over after supper tonight? I've been working on his karate. He's been doing pretty well."

"And how's he been doing with Gary?"

"He doesn't talk about it. But no more bruises." He paused. "And when I've been at the soccer practices, I've noticed a certain watch-fulness in our bullyboy. I don't know if he can figure Michael out."

"No one can," Eve said. "You just enjoy him."

"Well, I'll make sure that Michael will be able to get both enjoyment and satisfaction from anyone who throws a punch at him from now on." He brushed a kiss on her temple. "Trust me."

"I always do." Her gaze went back to Sylvie as she heard Joe leave. There was no question she'd have to work most of tonight if she was to break for the hours she'd designated for Michael tomorrow. But she'd planned on it anyway. The nose and the mouth were always so difficult because the depth was never really possible to calculate. She had the cheekbones and the chin, but that mouth . . . Sometimes she had to leave it for the final sculpting phase and hope that the subject would let her know which way to go. But if she did additional measuring on the mid-therum region, it might help.

"We're getting there, Sylvie." She started measuring that space below the nasal cavity. "I can already see it coming together. It may not be clear to you, but it will once we start the final sculpting. That's when you get to give me your input . . ."

CARNEGIE RESIDENCE HALL
NEW YORK CITY

"You don't talk to me about Jock," Darcy turned in her bed to look at Cara, who had just slipped into her own bed a few feet away. "Why not?"

Cara sighed. She had been waiting for this. She had managed to put Darcy off for the last few days because their individual schedules were both so busy. But tonight, Jock had taken them both out to dinner at Marea's, and she had been aware of Darcy's curiosity rising as the evening had progressed.

"Why should I talk about him?" She punched her pillow and settled herself more comfortably in bed. "You should be able to judge Jock for yourself. We've seen him a couple times since the concert, and you seemed to get along. And you talked to him more than I did at dinner tonight."

"That doesn't mean he paid more attention to me. You sat there and smiled and listened, and I could see that he was aware of every motion you made." She wrinkled her nose. "If I didn't like you, it might have upset me. I'm too vain not to resent not being the center of attention."

"Imagination. You *were* the center of attention. Jock even mentioned how beautiful you were."

"Yeah, and he's been charming and fascinating and made me pretty dizzy. All that sex appeal in that gorgeous facade is almost irresistible. I hope you know how self-sacrificing I'm being not to find a way to take him to bed."

Cara felt a ripple of shock. "Are you?" Then she recovered. "Why should you be? That's up to you and Jock, isn't it?"

She chuckled. "But that rocked you a little. I can see it. I've never made a secret that I enjoy sex as long as it doesn't interfere with my studies. You've always been cool with it."

"Don't be crazy. You're twenty years old. Your choice. Why shouldn't I be cool with it? It's none of my business."

"But Jock *is* your business, so it made you blink. That's why I said it. I wanted to see if I could ruffle you a bit." She smiled mischievously. "And crawl under that wall that you've built to keep me from finding out what I want to know. I'm not like you. I have a tendency to barge in where angels fear to tread. While you're thoughtful and sensitive, and you care about feelings and all that business about allowing people 'their space.'"

"I've always thought those were good rules to follow." Cara added, "And I haven't noticed that you're all that insensitive. You're just . . . curious."

"No." Darcy's smile vanished. "Not all the time. I pick and choose." She was silent; and then, when she did speak, it was with an awkwardness that Cara had never heard from her. "I don't have many friends, Cara. Those I do have, I have trouble keeping. Oh, I have plenty of acquaintances and people who call themselves my friends. It's not the same."

Cara frowned. "Why not? Surely one thing leads to another. Everyone here at school thinks you're wonderful."

"Oh, I am wonderful," she said mockingly. "It doesn't even matter that I'm a has-been actress at twenty. I'm a double threat. I have a terrific voice, and I'm probably in the top five percent as far as looks are concerned."

"Two percent."

"Whatever. It depends on what you're looking for. It draws people to me, but it's no guarantee they'll stay. I was megafamous, and some people just like to warm their hands at the embers. Oh, I'll be famous again, and everyone knows it. So life with me turns out to be a kind of competition. It's always been that way. My mother, everyone with whom I came in contact over the years, even the guys I have sex with . . ." Her lips twisted. "It's been a long time since I was with anyone who I was really close to. Anyway, when the academy moved me in with you, I thought it was going to be the same problem. Everyone knows that you're going to be a superstar, so I was bracing myself. But it wasn't a problem and I . . . liked you. I felt safe with you."

"Safe?" Cara laughed. "Well, I'm definitely no threat to you."

"You are, but it's not important to you." She shrugged. "But I decided I don't want to lose you, so I had to know what to do to keep that from happening. That's why I kept asking you all those questions. Of course you'd only go so far, then you shut me out. You're friendly and warm, but you're very private. And that's okay. Everyone has secrets. I just want to know enough so that I don't step on your toes." She made a face. "You're looking at me as if I'm certifiable. I could have kept all this to myself, but I have this honesty thing. And you're smart, so you'd see through me eventually."

"I'm not sure about that," she said dryly. "Because you have me completely confused. In my world, that's not how friendships are developed."

"In my world, it is," Darcy said quietly. "I like your world much better. That's why I'm trying to be honest with you. I just want to understand you and how you react, so that you won't end up walking away from me. I thought I was close to it once you told me about your Eve and the rest of your family." She shook her head. "But I'm having trouble placing Jock Gavin in the scheme of things."

Cara was staring at her in disbelief. This conversation was becoming increasingly bizarre with every moment. "So you think that going to bed with him will help you do that?"

"No, but putting the suggestion out there might have." She drew a deep breath. "No way. I made a mistake. I realize that would definitely be a wrong step. Forget I said anything."

"That's hard to do."

"I was just experimenting, and I sometimes leap before I think. I'm backing off from Jock."

Cara moistened her lips. "I told you that's not necessary."

"I disagree. Though I doubt if it would have gone anywhere anyway."

"Of course it might." She tried to smile. "You're the two percent. Why do you think I'd mind? He's my best friend. I've known Jock for years, and do you know how many dozens of women he's had in that time?"

"No." Darcy paused. "Did you count?"

Cara's hand clenched on the sheet. "It had nothing to do with me."

"Not then, but maybe now? I'm not taking the chance." She made a face. "I've sort of bungled this. What do you expect? I'm a blonde, for heaven's sake. And I told you I wasn't all that clever. I'm sorry."

"Stop that, we both know that's just part of your act. You're only as dumb or smart as you choose to be. You just don't understand this."

"Right, I don't understand anything about you and Jock. That's why I'm bowing out. But I thought I did understand about sex since

I seduced my voice teacher when I was only sixteen. I just thought I was seeing the signs. Maybe I was wrong." She reached over and turned off the lamp, plunging the room into darkness. "Good night, Cara."

It took a moment before Cara managed to reply. "Good night."

"And you'll forgive me if I was out of line? It's not often I feel as if I can trust someone. It went to my head. I promise I'll watch myself from now on." Her voice was completely devoid of its usual lightness. "Sometimes I have a habit of getting carried away in the moment and saying the wrong thing. It's a mistake that's cost me dearly."

There was no doubting Darcy's complete sincerity. "You just . . . surprised me. You've never showed me this side of you. I told Jock you were the complete package. I had no idea you were—"

"Oh, I am the complete package." Her tone was flip again. "Just throw in a dash of vulnerability and a tiny scoop of annoying persistence along with it." She paused. "So we're okay?"

"We're okay." Cara was still bewildered. "But we might need to talk again."

"We can do that." She turned over on her side. "I'll just be more careful next time . . ."

Darkness.

Only the lights of the street below filtered in from behind the drapes to fall on the two beds in the bedroom. Darcy had fallen asleep a couple hours ago, Cara knew. But she was still lying here staring into the darkness, wide-awake.

"*You don't talk about him to me,*" Darcy had said.

And that had been the beginning, Cara thought.

But it was how it had ended that had left her stunned and confused.

Not then, but now?

I thought I did understand about sex.

I just thought I was seeing the signs . . .

The signs that Cara wanted to have sex with Jock who had been the center of her existence for all these years? To be one of those women who went to his bed and had him inside her in that most intimate way possible?

Her body was heating, tingling, at the thought, she realized, robbing her of breath as the tension started as she imagined his hands—

Wrong. All wrong. He was her best friend. That was her place in his life. She had value to him in that role. She was not one of the women who passed in and out of his existence, then faded away.

The mere idea of that happening filled her with panic. She wouldn't be able to bear that isolation from him. They were so close, so . . . complete . . . together. She couldn't let this crazy physical response destroy it. That's not what he wanted from her. She wasn't one of the dazzling 2 percent like Darcy. Hell, she was only eighteen and still a damn virgin. No competition. She had no desire to be competition. She wanted him to be her friend.

Not then, but now?

Dear God, she was lying to herself. Yes, she wanted what they had together now. But her body wanted something entirely different.

And how long had she been lying to herself? There was no telling. Probably as her body had matured and changed through the years, so had the need for sexual intimacy with him. But she had known what a terrible threat that could be for their relationship, so she had buried it, smothered it, never let it come to the surface.

Which is what she had to do again, she thought desperately. She had to keep what she had with Jock or he would eventually leave her, and she would be alone again.

She could do this. Evidently, she had buried that sexual response even from herself. It was only Darcy's probing that had brought it to the surface. When she next saw Jock, she would see that she was back to normal. Maybe, in time, it would go away entirely.

But it was not going to be easy. It would be better if she didn't lie here thinking about Jock or any of this sex business. She would get a glass of water and go over and sit on the window seat and watch the traffic on the street below. She always found the sound of traffic strangely soothing.

She needed soothing.

She tossed her blanket aside and headed for the bathroom.

She was acutely aware of the softness of the carpet under her bare feet as she crossed the room and the feel of her nightshirt rubbing against her bare breasts as she breathed in and out.

Heat. Throbbing. A clenching that she had never—

Stop it. Ignore it.

It was only that she had just discovered what was happening to her that made it so difficult to dismiss . . .

Darcy screamed!

Cara jerked upright on the window seat, her gaze flying to Darcy's bed across the room.

She was tossing and turning, eyes closed, tears running down her cheeks.

Nightmare.

Cara had told Eve that it would be an intrusion to let Darcy know that she was aware of those terrible dreams that seemed to come so often.

But Darcy had never screamed like that before. And it could be that Darcy had been as disturbed as Cara before she had gone to sleep, and that had sent her spiraling down. Who knows what caused the phantoms of the mind to attack?

To hell with not intruding.

No one knew better than Cara how painful it was to face those phantoms alone. She was on her feet and across the room in a heart-beat. "Wake up, Darcy." She was on the bed, gathering her close and rocking her back and forth. "It's all over. It's gone. It's fine. Wake up now."

Darcy was pushing her away. "It's not fine." The tears were still pouring down her cheeks. "It will never be fine again." She was sobbing. "Not here. Empty. Always be empty . . ."

Cara took her shoulders and shook her. "Open your eyes, Darcy. Do you *hear* me? Wake up!"

Darcy slowly opened her eyes. "I hear you." Her voice was slurred. Then she shook her head to clear it. "How could I help it? You're almost shouting. What's wrong with you anyway?"

"Not a thing," she said, relieved. She sat up and swung her legs to the floor. "But there was something that was wrong with you. You just had a bad dream. But it's over now." She got to her feet. "I'll get you a glass of water. Why don't you grab a tissue and wipe your face? I'll be right back."

She went to the bathroom and stood there, letting the water run for a few minutes. It wouldn't hurt to give Darcy a little time to re-gain her composure before she had to face someone who had seen how vulnerable she could be. Then she filled the glass and took the water out to her.

Darcy had turned on the lamp and was sitting up in bed. Her eyes were still red, but she was no longer crying. "You didn't have to do this, you know." She took the glass and took a sip. "It's not as if I need anyone to—"

"I know you don't," Cara interrupted. "It's probably embarrass-ing you, and that's too bad. But I know about nightmares, and I couldn't let it go on. I've had too many of my own." She smiled. "It hurt me to see you hurting. So just consider that I did it for myself."

Darcy nodded slowly. "I'll try not to bother you again." She tried to smile. "Evidently, I cause you trouble whether I'm awake or asleep. I wouldn't blame you if you put in a request for a new roommate."

"Why? Most of the time we get along fine. We can get through this." She looked her in the eye. "You told me that everyone has secrets. What's more secret or personal than a nightmare? You just have to promise to be there for me when I have mine." She paused. "And let me choose what other secrets . . . or information I want to share with you."

She was silent. "Oh, I'll be there for you when you have to fight off the nightmares, Cara." Then she smiled. "Now that last is going to be difficult, but I'll work on it. You may have to slap me down occasionally."

"I can do that." Cara took the empty glass and set it on the nightstand. "Now can we try to get to sleep?" She got into bed and pulled up the covers. "It seems like a long time since we came back from dinner . . ."

A time that had been filled with changes and uncertainties. Nightmares and revelations that had given her a new view on Darcy Nichols.

And one stunning self-revelation that might become a terrifying nightmare of her own.

The light in the cottage was burning bright.

Eve Duncan was working late on the skull as she had every night since he'd given her the gift, Norwalk knew. Was she coming close?

According to his research on her, she must be very close. Even when she was working at a steady pace, it seldom took her more than five or six days to complete a reconstruction. When she was driven, sometimes only three or four.

Norwalk smiled. And you're driven, aren't you, Eve? I did that to you.

It was exhilarating having that much power over a woman who possessed so much power herself. He would have more power soon, but for now this was enough. It was according to plan, and the plan was everything.

But the front door was opening, and Joe Quinn was coming out as he had every night since Norwalk had given the skull to Eve Duncan.

Too bad. He was very far away from the cottage and was having to watch it through binoculars, but he knew he would still have to leave now that Quinn was on the move. Quinn was painstakingly thorough as he'd noticed the night he'd dropped off the box with the skull. And he was an ex-SEAL and not someone Norwalk wanted to deal with right now. Quinn would search the entire area thoroughly before he'd go back to Duncan and his son.

. . . And that blackened monstrosity of a skull that was now ruling that house because Norwalk had willed it so.

"You're going to work on Sylvie tonight?" Michael asked drowsily as Eve tucked him into bed. "I'm glad . . . she's been waiting for a long time."

"By the time I get them, they've all been waiting for a while." Eve pulled his blanket higher around his throat. There was nothing more wonderful than a glowing, beautiful child who was just on the edge of slumber. "Do you know once I did a reconstruction on a woman who was over two thousand years old?"

"You never told me that. Neat."

"It doesn't matter how long they've been waiting. It's still my job to bring them home."

He nodded, his eyes closing. "But Sylvie is kind of special, isn't she?"

"Maybe. But it could be because she's the one I'm working on tonight."

He shook his head. "You don't like what he did to her . . ."

"No," she said softly. "Neither do you. I remember, you did tell me to fix her."

"She's already fixed inside . . . You need to match it . . ."

He was asleep.

Beautifully asleep.

She leaned closer and touched that warm, silky cheek with her index finger.

Strange, she felt as if that mystical strength that belonged to all children and Michael, in particular, was pouring into her from that featherlight contact.

Whimsical nonsense. But she had learned a lot about whimsy since Michael had come into her life. Accept it. Enjoy it.

She got to her feet, leaned forward, and brushed a kiss on her son's forehead. "Sleep well," she whispered. "Tomorrow."

She turned out his lamp and glided toward the door.

A few minutes later, she was standing before her worktable, gazing down at the reconstruction. It was at the last stage before the actual final sculpting, and every feature was crude, sometimes appearing unfinished. It wasn't unfinished, every measurement was correct, only waiting for the clay to take on life.

Eve sat down on her stool. "Here we go, Sylvie. Michael says he thinks that you're fixed inside, and I pray that's true. But now we have to do our part. Are you ready?" Her hands moved to the forehead that was now no longer blackened but smooth and flesh-toned. "I am. Let's make you as beautiful as Michael thinks you are."

She held her breath and her fingers started to move on the clay.

That's right. Don't start out too fast.

Sensitivity.

Delicacy.

The clay was cool. It would get warmer as she worked with it.

It was getting warmer now as her fingers moved faster.

Time to stop thinking.

Help me, Sylvie.

Faster. Her fingers smoothed, molded.

See, I told you it would come, Sylvie.

Her fingers were moving of their own volition now.

Ears. Generic. She had no idea whether they had long lobes or had stuck out.

Smooth.

Mold.

Mouth. She knew the width, but not the shape. She made the lips closed and without expression. She'd come back later if Sylvie came through for her.

Smooth.

Mold.

Fill in.

Eyes. Terribly difficult. Study the shape and angle of the orbits. The size of the eyeballs was all pretty much the same. She could make them protruding, deep-set, or somewhere in between. The angle of the orbits and the bony ridge above would help her decide. They were ready for work, but not now.

They were always the clincher as far as she was concerned, and she saved them for last.

Nose. Not too long. Delicate.

More smoothing along those cheekbones.

Smooth.

Fill in.

Build up a little more around the mouth, there's a major muscle under there.

Smooth.

Mold.

Almost ready to let loose.

Check those measurements one more time.

Nose width. Okay.

Nose projection. Okay.

Bring the top lip down, it's usually thinner than the bottom lip.

Deepen those cheekbones. Why?

Just do it.

Smooth.

Mold.

This is it, Sylvie.

Tell me.

Yes.

Her hands were working feverishly now.

More shaping to the nostrils.

The jaw wasn't quite right.

Change it.

Smooth.

Mold.

Fill in.

Don't look at the face.

Just do what she was supposed to do.

The eyes now.

The shape, the tilt.

Now the other one.

Are we almost finished, Sylvie?

Smooth.

Mold.

Fill in.

Almost through. I can *feel* it.

Her hands flew over Sylvie's face.

Smooth.

Mold.

Done!

She sat back and tried to catch her breath.

Don't look at Sylvie right now.

Get her eye case and choose the eyes.

She gazed down at the glittering glass orbs. She almost always chose brown because that was the most common color.

She placed the brown eyes in the orbital cavities.

Not right . . .

Okay. That was purely a personal and creative choice. She'd leave it for right now and come back to it later. It was dangerous to stray too far from what was common when you were trying to ID a subject and bring them home. She and Sylvie had gotten this far together, and she wasn't going to do anything that would tip the balance and—

She inhaled sharply.

She was looking at the finished reconstruction for the first time.

Good Lord, Sylvie. Why would anyone do that to *you*?

She reached out and gently touched the high cheekbone, then the mouth. Sometime during that reconstruction she had parted those lips. Sylvie appeared much more vulnerable and alive than with them tightly closed.

Vulnerable. Yes, that was the overwhelming affect Eve was receiving as she looked at the reconstruction. Beauty and wistfulness and vulnerability.

But weren't all of her reconstructions vulnerable? All victims, all prey of the monsters in their midst. Why was the idea of what had been done to this woman making her ache with sorrow? It didn't really matter why, Eve thought wearily. She was tired and on edge and emotional, but the important thing was that she had done her job.

"Welcome back, Sylvie," she murmured as she got to her feet. She arched her back to rid it of stiffness. "I told you that he wouldn't get away with doing that to you. Now we just have to do the computer photos . . ." She turned off her work light over the pedestal. "But that can wait until tomorrow . . ."

A few moments later, she had shed her clothes and was slipping naked into bed beside Joe.

His arms were immediately around her. "You're finished?"

"I think so. Except for the final photos." She nestled her cheek into the hollow of his shoulder. "I just don't feel . . . finished. I want to do . . . something for her."

"We will. As soon as you give me the photos, I'll shoot them through every database I can access."

"I know. And we'll ask the TV stations to run the photo, too. We'll do everything possible to ID her." She was silent. "I'm just afraid nothing will help, and whoever did that to her will get away with it. I promised her he wouldn't."

"Well, then, we'll have to make sure you keep that promise." He brushed his lips on her temple. "But not tonight. You're tired, and she'll forgive you if you get a good night's sleep."

"I'm not that tired." She suddenly turned over in his arms. He was warm and strong, and she could feel the love like a living force between them. She wanted to forget that aching sadness she'd felt when she'd looked at the final reconstruction. "Unless you are."

"Never." He pulled her over on top of him. He kissed her, long, deep, hot. "Not in this lifetime or the next, Eve."

"She *is* beautiful, isn't she, Mama?" Michael was standing by her worktable gazing at the Sylvie reconstruction when she hurried out of the bedroom the next morning. Joe had let her sleep late, and she had only woke when she'd heard Michael's voice in the hall. "I told you she would be."

"Yes, I remember." She came to stand beside him. "And you had remarkable judgment considering what I had to work with. It just goes to show you that if you work past the ugliness, you can usually find something special."

"What happens now?"

"The photos I always take, so I can find where she belongs."

"May I have one?"

"I don't see why not. Why?"

"That way she'd kind of belong to me, too." He reached out and touched Sylvie's lips. "I think she wants to belong."

Trust Michael to have sensed that same vulnerability of which Eve had been so poignantly aware. "I'll make sure you get one." She dropped a kiss on the top of his head. "Have you had your breakfast?"

He nodded, his gaze still on the reconstruction. "Dad made me pancakes." His finger went up to the right eye. "Why did you put in the wrong eyes?"

"What?"

"It's the wrong color. They should be blue."

"Brown are more common."

"They should be blue." He turned, and his arms slid around her waist as he hugged her. "Make my photo with blue, okay?" Then he was running across the room to pick up his canvas bag from the couch. "Dad's waiting in the car, I just ran back for my book bag. Bye, Mama."

"Bye."

She watched the front door slam behind him.

Then her gaze shifted again to Sylvie.

She should really keep the brown eyes. It was practical, and the odds were they were correct.

They're wrong. They should be blue.

Oh, what the hell.

She went to the drawer in her desk and pulled out her eye case.

CARNEGIE RESIDENCE HALL

NEW YORK CITY

"What the hell's wrong? You're too quiet, Cara." Jock was frowning as he stopped at the bottom of the stairs in the reception room. "I don't like it, dammit."

"Maybe I'm tired." She smiled with an effort. Lord, she'd tried to avoid this. But Jock was always conscious of her every mood. She'd hoped that Darcy would be able to join them again for dinner, but she'd had a voice lesson already scheduled. So Cara had been forced to face Jock by herself. Ridiculous to feel this strain after all the years of being together. But it seemed as if just trying to pretend an emotional change had *not* taken place was making it more acutely obvious that it had. It would be okay, she assured herself. She just needed a little more time to make the adjustment. "Or maybe you're too sensitive. You've been on edge since you got here. I've only seen you for a few hours a day, and the rest of the time you're running around with that man Stanton or on the phone." She moistened her lips. "Maybe it's good that I'm leaving for home day after tomorrow. It will give you time to decompress."

"Not long." His lips tightened. "Not if you're set on going to New Orleans the week after. You haven't given me your word that you'll call Kaskov and cancel."

"And I won't. I still have a week to decide." She shrugged. "And maybe you'll be able to find a reason why I shouldn't go in that time. I haven't seen any sign yet that anything Stanton told you had anything to do with my grandfather." She took her violin case from him and turned toward the stairs. "Until then, I'm not going to think of anything but being with Eve and Joe and Michael. I can't tell you how I'm looking forward to it. It's been a tough quarter for me."

"And I didn't make it any easier."

"No, you didn't," she said. "But perhaps I didn't react as reasonably as I should have done. I have to realize that you have a life that has nothing to do with me. I'll try to do better."

"What?" He was frowning again. "That's pure bullshit. Since when have you ever been coolly reasonable? There's nothing cool about you, Cara."

"Then I can't blame you for feeling that being around me is sort of overwhelming." Everything she said appeared to be upsetting him, and that was the last thing she wanted. She was only trying desperately to give him his space so that he wouldn't think he'd have to take it. She'd better get away from him before she completely blew it. She quickly started up the stairs. "Good night, Jock. Will I see you tomorrow?"

"You bet you will," he said grimly. "I'll be close as glue to you until I put you on your flight to Atlanta."

"That's nice, I'll miss you when I'm at Eve's."

"Will you?" His gaze was narrowed on her. "Then why do I feel you're trying to escape?"

She was ruining everything. She stopped on the steps and turned to smile at him. "Why would I do that? You've always been my best friend. You always will be."

It was true. She stood there looking down at him as all those years of caring and friendship flooded back to her. That was enough. That had to be enough. "See you tomorrow." She turned and ran up the stairs.

She didn't slow down until she had reached the second floor. She stopped and took a deep breath before she started down the hall toward her suite. Now she was glad that Darcy had not been able to join them. Darcy's eyes were far too keen, and though she'd been trying to stifle that curiosity that was so inherent, Cara had no desire to have it focused on her tonight.

She just wanted to take a shower and crawl into bed and try to convince herself that she hadn't been as obvious as she feared.

She took out her key and unlocked her door.

No light.

She reached for the wall switch. She'd thought she'd left the lamp in the bathroom on. Maybe Darcy had come back and turned—

Brutal hands on her throat, jerking her into the room!

Pain.

Her violin case dropped from her grip and she reached up to desperately grab at those hands.

He cursed as she bent back his index finger.

Move.

Get away!

She tossed one arm out and knocked the lamp on the hall table to the floor.

Crash!

She reached for the violin case and slammed it into his stomach.

More cursing. Low, full of venom, full of hate.

Then the case was torn away and skittered across the room.

And his hands closed on her throat again.

Fight him . . .

They pressed tighter, digging.

She couldn't breathe . . .

Darkness.

CHAPTER

4

Darcy's face above her . . .

Darcy's hand, bathing her throat with a cold cloth.

"Awake?" Darcy gave a sigh of relief. "Jock said you'd regain consciousness soon, but I wasn't too sure. I don't know about this kind of thing. You scared me."

"Jock?" It hurt to talk. She cleared her throat. That hurt worse. "He's here?"

She nodded. "He just left. You roused a little, and he knew you were going to be okay. He ran down to the street to meet the EMTs."

"You called an ambulance?"

"Jock did. I'm glad. I was too shaky to do much of anything. And I wasn't about to argue with him about anything in his present mood."

Cara couldn't blame her. Jock could be totally lethal and intimidating when anything triggered a slip back into the man he'd been all those years ago. Evidently what had happened here had provided the trigger. She looked around her. She was lying on the couch in the sitting room. But the entire room was in chaos. Overturned chairs, drawers opened, and the contents scattered all over the floor. A broken lamp on the floor by the front door. "What happened?"

"I was hoping you'd tell me," Darcy said shakily. "I came home from class and the front door was wide open and you were lying on the floor." She looked around the room. "It looks like a robbery, doesn't it? The bedroom is just like it."

"My violin." She sat upright in alarm. "Did they get my violin?"

Darcy shook her head. "No, it's over there against the wall. Maybe they were on their way out, and you surprised them."

Cara breathed a sigh of relief. She didn't have anything else of value, but her violin was a gift from her grandfather and was worth a small fortune. To her, it was priceless. "No 'they.' It was only one man. I remember hitting him with the case. But he lost his biggest score if he didn't take the violin." She looked at Darcy. "Did you lose anything?"

"Not that I've been able to tell. I haven't had much time to look through my stuff." She put another cold cloth on Cara's neck. "It doesn't matter. I'm just glad that you weren't badly hurt."

"So am I," she said dryly as she gingerly touched her throat. "He was very strong."

Darcy nodded. "Your throat is turning three colors even as we speak. Did you let him in?"

"Why would I do that?" She was frowning. "The door was locked. I had to use my key."

"That's crazy. How could that happen?"

"I have no idea. Maybe the police can tell us."

"A skeleton key." Jock was standing in the doorway. "Not all that difficult. Or a bumper key that opens ninety-five percent of the locks around town. I would have had no trouble."

"I'm sure you wouldn't," Cara said hoarsely.

"Shut up. You sound like a frog." He was suddenly beside her. He gently tilted her head up to look at her throat. He muttered a curse. "The EMTs should be up here in a few minutes to take you to the ER. Just keep quiet until they come."

"I'm not going to the hospital," Cara said. "I have a few bruises. Otherwise, I'm fine. I won't spend all night being checked out."

"The hell you won't."

Her jaw set. "No. If I did, they'd probably call Eve, and she'd just worry."

"And nothing must make Eve worry," he said dryly. "Not even an attack that could have killed you."

"It was a robbery." She veered in another direction. "How did you get here?"

"I called him," Darcy said. "When I found you, I panicked. He told me to call 911 and get someone to help you, and he'd be here as quick as he could. He was here in seven minutes." She swallowed. "Thank God. I was scared to death."

"So was I," Jock said curtly. "That seven minutes was too damn long. You have to go to the hospital and be checked out."

Cara shook her head. "I'll make a police report and have them check to see how he got into our suite. I won't go to the hospital."

Jock stared at her in frustration, his fists clenched, and turned on his heel. "When the EMTs come, have them check her out as much as possible, Darcy. I'm going to do some checking around the residence myself."

Darcy nodded. "I can handle it from here. I just have to be pointed in the right direction. I'll make certain those EMT guys will give her a going-over that will make her wish she'd chosen the ER." She smiled at Cara. "Sorry. I told you I hold on to friends when I find them. I can't afford to let you do anything to sabotage me."

"Whatever." Cara wearily closed her eyes again. "I just want this to be over."

"Oh, it's over as far as you're concerned," Jock said curtly as he headed for the door. "For me, it's just begun."

Jock didn't return for over three hours. In that time, Cara had undergone one of the most rigorous and thorough checkups to which she'd ever been subjected. Darcy had been gorgeous, tearful, and helpless, and the EMTs had fallen all over themselves to turn those tears into smiles. After they had left, Cara had a visit from a police detective who had taken her statement; and then the building supervisor had come to express her concern and assure her that nothing like this had ever taken place at any of the academy's residence facilities before and would never happen again.

Darcy had stood beside Cara, letting her answer the police queries but after ten minutes had sent them on their way, the supervisor had received only five minutes before she'd been whisked out of the suite. Then she'd helped Cara undress and get to bed after tidying up the chaos in the bedroom. She gave Cara the painkiller the EMT had given her to soothe her throat and made her a cup of tea and honey.

"Wasn't I magnificent?" Darcy smiled triumphantly at Cara as she plopped down on her own bed. "Though I have to admit I had to be, to make up for falling apart when I found you looking like a broken doll sprawled on the floor." She sipped her own tea. "No one ever expects me to rise to the occasion, so I really had to work at it."

"You were wonderful," Cara said in perfect truth. It was hard for her to swallow, but the hot tea felt amazingly healing. "Thank you."

Darcy nodded. "You know, I like gratitude. I don't believe I've ever earned it before and it's . . . refreshing."

"Happy to oblige." She reached up and rubbed her temple. "And you shouldn't have felt guilty about relying on Jock for help. He knows about things like this . . ."

"I gathered that when he showed up like Han Solo ready to cut down Darth Vader."

"Wasn't that Luke?"

"I always liked Han Solo better. Anyway, your Jock was electrifying."

Cara nodded jerkily. "He always is."

Darcy's gaze was narrowing on her face. "But you don't like it?"

"Not for me." She could see that Darcy's curiosity was aroused, but she wasn't about to explain that she couldn't bear the thought of Jock's being pulled back into the lethal whirlpool that had almost destroyed him all those years ago. She had been fighting his protective instinct since she'd first met him, and one of her nightmares was to be responsible for having that happen. "I should be fighting my own battles."

"Well, from what I saw when Jock left here, he may not be seeing it that way." She finished her tea and stood up. "Finish that tea. Maybe you can grab a quick nap before Jock shows up to check to see if I've done my duty."

"You've done it." Jock was standing in the doorway. "But you can go the extra mile if you'll search through the rest of the suite and make certain that nothing has been taken." He strode forward. "And then start packing up a suitcase for Cara."

"What?" Cara straightened in bed. "Why the hell should she do that?"

"You're going to visit Eve, remember?"

"I was intending to pack myself tomorrow."

"You'll be on a plane tomorrow." He glanced at Darcy. "The extra mile?"

She nodded as she headed for the door. "I earn points and avoid being involved in the storm I see on the horizon. I can live with that."

Cara was scarcely aware Darcy had left the room. She was staring at Jock. "I won't leave tomorrow. I have a class. I'm scheduled to leave the day after tomorrow."

"Not any longer. You're out of here." His lips were tight. "I'd send you out tonight, but you'd probably balk because you'd think Eve would worry if she knew why you were coming early."

"Yes, I would," she said. "It was a robbery, Jock."

"The hell it was. There are five suites on this floor. Why was yours the only one that was targeted?"

"Maybe someone heard about my violin. I had it with me, or he might have meant to take it."

"And then ran out without taking it?"

"I knocked over the lamp and it broke. The noise might—"

"Stop arguing!" His gray eyes were glittering in his taut face. "It's all too pat. There's a doorman downstairs, but he saw nothing because the entry was made through the basement. The door to the street was jimmied open, and the alarm was disconnected. This place has decent security facilities, and that alarm system wasn't easy to take down. But it *was* disarmed, and the exit stairwell was used to come to this floor. Not to any of the other four floors in this building. *This* floor. Then the door to your suite was unlocked, the furniture and drawers made to appear that they'd been ransacked. Then the door was locked from the inside, and he stood there waiting." He took a step closer. "Are you getting the picture?"

She was getting the picture, and it was chilling. A man there in the dark, waiting for someone to unlock that door and come in, so he could attack.

"I see that you are," Jock said. "Well, so did I. I don't know why you weren't hurt more than you were. Maybe you're right, and that lamp's breaking startled him enough to panic him. Or maybe it was only meant as a warning so that he could prove to Kaskov he could kill you at any time." He repeated through set teeth, his eyes blazing. "*Any* time, Cara. That time could have been tonight."

She couldn't look away from him. His intensity was overpowering. But no more than the scenario he had crafted for her in those incisive words. "I may have been targeted. But it doesn't have to be because of Kaskov's enemies. It could still be a robbery that was blown."

"Kaskov."

She nodded slowly. "Or because of Kaskov." She swallowed. "I'll have to consider that as an option. But now that I'm aware that it might be a possibility, I can take precautions and I—"

"I've been taking precautions for years, and this still happened. Stanton was prepared for an attack from the outside, not this. It was too bold, too direct."

That strong hand reaching out, biting into her throat and jerking her into the darkness.

"Yes, it . . . was bold."

"And Stanton didn't stop it. *I* didn't stop it. I swore you'd never be in danger again, and I didn't stop it."

"How many times have I told you that you're not responsible for me?" She tried to smile. "I can see why you might have felt like that when I was younger. Everyone always feels as if they have to take care of kids. But I'm eighteen, and I have to take care of myself these days."

"Oh, do you? Think again, Cara." He lifted her chin, his gaze on the deep, mottled bruises on her throat. "He knew exactly what he was doing. He wanted to hurt you. And if he'd dug his thumb just a little to the left, he could have killed you. Do you think I'd allow him to get near you again?"

She stiffened. "Allow? You don't *allow* me to do anything." She glared up at him. "Because that would mean I'd have to give you permission to go back to doing what you did all those years ago. I won't do that, Jock."

"I don't need permission to keep you safe. I can't do anything else." He touched the dark bruise on the hollow of her throat. "I realized that a long time ago." He smiled recklessly as he stepped away from her. "And I never really moved far away from what Reilly made me. It's just been waiting in the dark like the man who did this to you." He held out his hands, palms up. "Were you aware that I know twenty-two ways I can kill a man with my bare hands? Give me a weapon, and I'm damn near unstoppable. Why should I waste all that talent?"

"No, I didn't know that," she said unevenly. "You didn't tell me because you knew it would hurt me. But now for some reason you want to do that." She reached up and touched her swollen throat. "Did you think this wasn't enough?"

He stared at her for a moment. "Low blow, Cara. You know that's the opposite of what I want."

"Then you didn't go about it the right way. Start over."

He was silent. "Lord, you're tough. Ordinarily, you'd have me on my knees because I'd hate the idea of hurting you."

"And so you should, Jock. I'd never do anything to hurt you. Friends don't do that."

"You do hurt me." His voice was suddenly soft, persuasive. "The idea of your staying for even one extra day here hurts me. I trust Joe Quinn. I know he can take care of you. I want you out of this city."

"I'll think about it."

He shook his head. "Not good enough. I'll take you to the airport at noon tomorrow. You can tell Eve you managed to get away early." He paused. "If you don't, I'll call and tell her what happened tonight. I was planning on discussing it with Quinn in the next couple days anyway. But then it will be his decision if he wants to tell Eve. Or it may give you the chance to break it to her gently."

She stared at him in frustration. He'd called her tough? He knew that she wouldn't want Eve to know there was a threat when she still had a year to go to finish at the academy. "I'd have to miss a class."

"Miss it. For once, that violin takes the backseat." But she could see that he knew he'd won. "Enjoy being home. I'll spend the next few days checking for more fingerprints down in the basement and scanning for video cameras on the block. We think we've found one good print at the alarm in the basement. Everything else both down there and in the suite was wiped clean. Very professional. He must have had to take off his gloves to get into the alarm box and made one mistake. I'll start trying to maximize on that mistake right away. Then I'll make sure when you do come back that even Quinn would approve of the security measures for this residence building."

He had made his plans and wrapped everything up to his satisfaction, she realized with exasperation. "You're very pleased with yourself. Is there anything else I can do to make you happy, Jock?"

"Yes." He looked over his shoulder as he reached the door. "You can find a way to erase my memory of you lying crumpled there on the floor when I wasn't sure whether you were alive or dead."

He was gone before she could reply.

She didn't know what she would have said anyway. There would not have been any erasing for her if it had been Jock who had been lying unconscious. And she knew that it was that sight that had pushed Jock over to this explosive edge. Not that he'd had any right to practically blackmail her so that she would leave tomorrow. He still thought of her as a child who sometimes had to be coerced into doing what was good for her. He should know she had never had to be coerced to protect herself. She had known that life was precious and could be taken from her in a heartbeat.

As she could have had it taken from her tonight. She reached up to touch her throat as the memory of that hand crushing her throat came rushing back to her.

Her heart was suddenly beating hard. She was struggling to breathe.

Calm down.

It was over.

Tomorrow, she would be with Eve and Joe, and Michael would be smiling at her, and everything would be right again.

Tomorrow. Suddenly, she was glad that she would be leaving then and not waiting. After feeling perfectly safe here for the years she'd been at school, one night had made her feel uneasy and afraid.

It was only temporary, she told herself quickly. Jock would make certain no attack could ever happen again. And it probably wouldn't have occurred again anyway. She didn't really know what was happening. It was all guesswork.

But getting home would be a wonderful break, and she would be fine when she came back here.

"Hi, want another cup of tea?" Darcy had stuck her head in the room. "I overheard you talking, and I'll bet your throat is sore again. Jock should know better." She made a face. "I would have told him so before he left, but I was chicken. He didn't seem in the mood to appreciate any criticism."

"No, he isn't."

She tilted her head. "So, are you going to leave tomorrow? If you decide you don't want to do it, we could gang up on him."

"He made me an offer I couldn't refuse," she said dryly. "And I wouldn't want you to have to take any fire for me. You've done enough tonight."

"Hey, what are friends for? But you've got to promise not to repeat it. That was scary. I was ready to head for the hills."

"But you didn't, and I appreciate what—" She stopped. She'd thanked Darcy, but it was suddenly hitting home to her how frightening that experience must have been for her. Coming home in the dark and finding what might have been a dead body in the living room? And then having to rally and try to do what had to be done in an emergency like the one she had faced.

I was ready to head for the hills.

Of course she had been. And now Cara was going off and leaving her alone in this place where it had all happened. What if he came back? He'd gotten into the residence once. And even if Darcy was safe from attack, she would still be alone and afraid.

Nightmares.

Darcy was gazing at her quizzically. "You're looking at me as if I've broken out with measles, and I'd never do anything so unattractive. What are you thinking?"

Cara said slowly, "I was wondering if you could postpone your classes for this next week. And I was wondering if you could exist without the constant adulation of the masses . . ."

LAKE COTTAGE
ATLANTA, GEORGIA

"Cara arranged to get an extra day off, and she's coming in today instead of tomorrow." Eve turned to Joe as she hung up the phone.

"And she asked if it was okay to bring her roommate, Darcy, with her." She smiled. "As if we'd object; I'm grateful that she's taking time out of her practice to make friends. And she told me before that she liked this girl."

"Then I suppose we'll be able to put up with her," Joe said with a grin. "What time will their flight arrive?"

"At 3:35 P.M. Delta. Do you want to pick them up or shall I?"

"Neither. I have to pick up Michael at soccer, and you have to finish Sylvie today. I'll ask Officer Haverty to swing by the airport on his way home. He lives out this way."

"I can do it, Joe."

"Yes." His gaze went to Sylvie's reconstruction on her worktable. "But you wanted to finish the final computer workup on her today, didn't you?"

"I could do that tomorrow."

"Forensics is getting a bit pushy about having something to show for the way they bent the rules and gave the skull to you before all the paperwork was out of the way."

She made a face. "You're getting nagged?"

"They'll deny it once they get their hands on the reconstruction. Then the nagging will be represented as being only a gentle reminder."

She nodded. "I'll finish it today. You'll be able to take her in tomorrow." She stood there, gazing at the reconstruction. "I just wanted to make certain that I'd done everything I could do for her."

"You always do," he said gently. "Let her go. She's ready, Eve."

"I know." She lifted her shoulder in a half shrug. "It's probably the way she came to me, what had been done to her. That gold box was like a terrible mockery, and so was that broken mirror. I wanted desperately to make her right again." Her lips twisted. "And find a way to punish the bastard who had done that to her."

"And you've done your job. Now let me take it from here." He kissed her and headed for the door. "Try to finish Sylvie up before Cara gets here. You deserve to relax and spend a little family time with her and Michael." He looked over his shoulder. "You're still keeping the door locked when I'm not here?"

She stiffened. "Of course I am. When that son of a bitch delivered the skull, I told you I wouldn't take any chances Why? Have you seen any reason why I should?"

He shook his head. "No sign. He's nowhere close, but I'll be glad to get the reconstruction out of the house in case he's keeping an eye on it."

She frowned as her gaze shifted back to the skull. "Should I be worried about Cara's coming? I thought it was safe as long as you kept an eye on the perimeter."

"It is. But it wouldn't hurt to tell Cara not to take her friend hiking in the woods by themselves." He paused. "And, I think we should tell her about our special delivery."

"Well, if we don't, you can bet Michael will. He's been practically considering Sylvie as one of the family since I started working on her." She nodded. "Okay, we'll follow his lead and make Sylvie a family affair."

ATLANTA AIRPORT

"This is exciting," Darcy said as she grabbed her suitcase off the luggage claim. "Do you know, I've never been to Atlanta? I've hop-skipped over most cities in the U.S. on publicity tours, but we missed Atlanta."

"I'd never been here either before Eve and Joe brought me. I grew up principally in California," Cara said absentmindedly as she watched for her own suitcase to come around. "I bounced around from town to town there while I was on the run."

"On the run?" Darcy repeated. "Why does a kid have to go on the run? Hmmm. Very interesting."

And Cara should not have said that. She knew that Darcy always picked up on any tidbit of information that caught her attention. "It wasn't all that interesting." It had been a horror story. "And I prefer to forget it."

Darcy nodded and held up her hands. "Not a subject for sharing. I'll back off. See how good I'm being?" She glanced at the colorful scarf Cara had tucked around her throat. "And didn't I lend you my Hermés scarf to hide your bruises? But it's not going to fool anyone for long. It's June, for heaven's sake."

"It doesn't have to hide them for very long," Cara said quickly. "I'll tell Eve what happened. I just need a little time to prepare her."

"Whatever. At least, you don't still sound like a frog. I'll do anything you want me to do." She was suddenly smiling brilliantly. "I'll be *so* good while I'm here that you'll want to convince your Eve and Joe to adopt me."

"You may not even want to stay for the week. We live very simply at the lake cottage. It's principally just being with family."

"I'll want to stay," Darcy said quietly. "I've seen your face when you talk about Eve and Joe. Why do you think I jumped on the chance of coming down here? Families are an endangered species as far as I'm concerned." Then she was smiling again. "So I'm here trying to muscle in on yours. Okay?"

"Okay." Cara smiled back at her. "How can I refuse? I muscled in on Eve's life. It wouldn't be right if I was selfish enough to keep her to myself." She'd found her suitcase and lifted it off the baggage claim. "But I thought you had a mother and father who lived in Nice."

"Oh, I do. Well, my mother, Felicity, and stepfather, Raoul, husband number six. She's only stuck with him because there are certain conveniences to having a husband, and he never interferes with her other 'amusements.' Maybe I fibbed a little because I was pumping you so much, and it seemed more natural if it was an exchange of information. I haven't seen Felicity or Raoul for the last five years." She pulled out the handle on her suitcase. "Endangered species," she repeated. "Now where are we supposed to meet this Officer Haverty?"

Five minutes.

Eve only had five minutes. Cara had called and given her a heads-up as they'd exited the freeway.

She hurriedly put the computer and camera equipment away and ran a quick comb through her hair. No time to start boxing Sylvie for Joe to take in to Forensics tomorrow.

But you didn't confront new guests with a skull staring at them either.

She tossed the black velvet cloth over it and headed for the front door. "Sorry, Sylvie," she muttered. "No offense."

She could hear the car doors slam as she came out on the porch. "Thanks for bringing them, Officer Haverty," she called. "We owe you."

"My pleasure." He was smiling not at Eve but at the blond woman he was helping retrieve a suitcase from his trunk. "Anytime. Just call, Darcy."

"Thank you, Bob," she said softly. "You've been such a help. But I can handle it from now on."

"Eve!" Cara was flying up the steps and into her arms. She hugged her tightly. "It's so *good* to be home."

"It's wonderful to have you home," Eve said unsteadily. "It's been too long. Can't that school arrange to have any concerts down here? We do have a modicum of culture I've been told. For heaven's sake, they sent you to Phoenix. That's clear across the country."

"It will be over soon. Just one more year . . ." She took a step back and grinned. "Then they say I'll be able to pick and choose."

"Yeah, sure. Then every impresario in the world will want their piece of you." She smiled. "They already do, or you wouldn't be used as bait to lure all those donations."

"I need the experience. And most of them are fine charities. It's win-win. Though Darcy agrees with you. She's a bit cynical about—" She turned toward the woman climbing the steps. "But she'll tell you herself. Come up here, Darcy. This is Darcy Nichols, Eve."

"I'm coming. I've been so eager to meet you, Eve. Cara won't stop talking about you." Darcy was smiling, her entire face lit with enthusiasm as she hurried up the steps toward them. "It took me a while to inveigle myself into the inner circle, but here I am. Now the first question is what can I do to make you adopt me? If you don't kick me out, I promise I'll—" She stopped. Her eyes widened in alarm. "What's wrong? Did I offend you? I'm sorry. I didn't mean to do that. I guess I'm—"

"No." Eve raised a shaking hand to halt that flow of apologies. Eve could barely get that word out. Stunned. Crazy. It was all crazy . . . and terrifying. Her gaze was clinging to Darcy Nichols's concerned face. "Not your fault. At least, I don't think it is. Mistake? I can't put it together . . ."

"Eve?" Cara took a step closer to her. "Are you okay? You're white as a tombstone." She put her arm around Eve's waist. "Let's go inside. I'll get you a cup of coffee."

"Yes, I have to go inside," Eve said numbly. "I have to see why—" She turned and went back inside the house. "None of it makes sense."

"What should I do? Someone I should call?" Darcy asked Cara. "Is she sick? Is it something I did?"

"I don't know," Cara said. "I don't think—I don't know what to think."

She had to snap out of this, Eve thought. She was scaring Cara. A reason. There had to be a reason. She stopped in the middle of the living room and took a deep breath. "I'm not sick. Something just happened that sent me—I'm just . . . surprised." Understatement. She was still in shock. "I think you'll both understand when I—"

She moistened her lips. "Coincidence. It's got to be a coincidence. God, I hope I didn't make a mistake."

Cara was gazing at her in bewilderment. "Coincidence?"

Eve knew she wasn't handing this well. She didn't know how to do it any better. Okay, just go for it, and take care of figuring out everything later. She drew a deep breath. "It's a coincidence that I've been sculpting your friend Darcy's, face for the last five days."

Eve strode over to her workbench and jerked off the black velvet cloth that was covering the reconstruction. "No, it's the same face, dammit." Her gaze was going back and forth from the reconstruction to Darcy's features. Same jaw. Same high cheekbones. Same nose. Same lips. Even the same sparkling blue eyes. "Not just a resemblance. Not a coincidence. It's the *same* face." Her hands clenched. "Do you know what that means? I made a mistake. This reconstruction is going to be useless as far as ID goes. I must have seen a photo or a TV clip of Darcy's show sometime in the past, and my memory grabbed and used it when I thought I was doing a new reconstruction. That's always a danger, but I've never made that mistake before. I'll have to break it down to the skull again and start all over."

"Maybe you won't." Darcy's gaze was fixed on the face of the reconstruction. Her face was as pale as Eve's as she moved slowly, stiffly across the room toward the worktable. "You say this is . . . a skull?"

"Yes." Eve had been so disappointed that she had failed in her attempt to bring Sylvie home that she had ignored the fact that for ordinary people, Eve's mistake would seem macabre and even frightening. "I'm sorry, Darcy. I didn't mean to involve you in—"

"That means she's . . . dead?" Darcy asked unsteadily. "Of course, it does. Who could—live without a skull. How?"

"She was shot in the temple."

"Shot." She flinched. "Would there have been—pain?"

"No. Joe believes it would have killed her instantly."

Cara was suddenly beside Darcy. "It was a mistake, Darcy. This

has nothing to do with you. Eve will fix it, and you won't look anything alike."

"Yes, we will," Darcy whispered. Her fingers were shaking as she
reached out and gently probed beneath the chin of the reconstruction. "There was an old break right here . . ."

Eve went still. "Yes, there was. It took me longer than usual to
seal it."

"You did a good job. I can barely feel it." Her hand dropped away,
and she stood there, staring at the reconstruction. "A skull . . ."

"Darcy," Cara said. "What—"

"Dead." Tears were suddenly running down Darcy's face. "She's
dead, Cara. I knew it, but she—I feel sick." She closed her eyes. "I
think . . . I have to throw up."

"This way." Cara whisked her out of the room and down the hall
to the bathroom.

Eve watched them go and turned back to the reconstruction. So
beautiful, so like that gorgeous, vibrant young woman who had stood
before her only a moment ago. "I'm very confused, Sylvie," she murmured. "But I believe we may have brought you home."

"Twins." Cara told Eve a half hour later after she'd settled
Darcy in the bedroom and come out to speak to her. "That's all
she'd say, and I wasn't going to interrogate her right now. She can't
stop shaking, but she didn't want anyone with her. I'll check on her
later. I put her to bed and left her alone to come to terms with it."
She added grimly, "Though I don't know how anyone comes to
terms with the death of a sister. I never really did, and I was only
three when my sister was killed. And Darcy just found out that skull
belonged to her twin. I don't believe she'd even been told she was
dead. It's no wonder she went into shock."

"I would have been gentler about it if I hadn't believed I'd made
a mistake," Eve said. "It wasn't as if it was a resemblance, it was ex-

act." Eve wearily shook her head. "Or maybe I wouldn't. I was pretty much in shock myself. I've been so absorbed with this reconstruction since it landed on my doorstep that it seemed impossible I hadn't gotten it right."

"But you did get it right," Cara said. "And the whole thing seems impossible." She rubbed her temple as she dropped down on the couch. "On your doorstep? What do you mean by that?"

When Eve had finished telling her of that night, Cara was shaking her head again. "You didn't tell me. Why didn't you let me know what was happening?"

"What good would it have done? You weren't involved, Cara. And you have your own life and your own problems to take care of."

"You tell me all the time that you consider me family. And then you don't tell when some nut drops a skull on your doorstep?"

"Joe and I were taking care of it. I was doing the reconstruction, and Joe was investigating to try to find out about the teeth and DNA. That was our job and not yours."

"*You're* my job," Cara said fiercely. "You and Joe and Michael. Can't you see that?"

Yes, she did see it, Eve thought. Cara had always tried to give back to her for taking her into her home without counting the cost. That was one of the reasons she had thought it best to send her to that school in New York. She needed to live life to the fullest and not think about taking care of Eve and the family. "There was no overt threat, just the skull that was delivered. It could have been possible that it was someone who wanted me to find out who the victim was so that she could be identified."

"But you didn't think that was true."

Eve remembered that blackened skull, the hole in the temple, the broken mirror. "No, I didn't think that was what was happening. But Joe has been very careful, and there's no sign that whoever delivered that box has come back. I'm sending the reconstruction to Forensics tomorrow, and that should cut my ties to the skull. If the aim was to get me to do the reconstruction, then I've complied, and my job should be considered over."

"If that was the aim," Cara repeated. "But what if he already knew? What if he was the one who shot her? And you said she'd been burned beyond recognition. What was the reason for that?" She shivered. "Ugly. So ugly, Eve."

More than Cara realized, Eve thought, remembering that charred skull. "I don't know the reason. Like you, I thought it was proof that whoever had done that to her was a monster. And monsters have to be caught and destroyed, Cara. That was what I was trying to do by finding out who she was."

"And bring her home."

Eve nodded. "But you did that when you brought Darcy Nichols into this house. And there has to be a reason why you did that, Cara. Joe doesn't believe in coincidences, and he's going to want to question her."

"No!" Cara said. "You saw her when she was looking at that reconstruction. She's practically a basket case right now. Give her a little time, then let me do it."

Eve nodded. "I understand. No one wants to hurt your friend, Cara. But we have to have answers. That poor girl I've been living with for the last five days deserves to have them."

"But Sylvie's the one who already knows all the answers," Cara said sadly. "What she needs to know is what we're going to do about it."

Eve nodded as she gave Cara a hug and rose to her feet. "I'll give you your chance. I'll call Joe and tell him what's happened and ask him to take Michael out to eat after soccer practice. It will be time for Michael to go to bed by the time he gets home. That should give Darcy the night to pull herself together. Okay?"

Cara nodded. "And it will give me time to pull myself together, too. My head is whirling. I'm jumping from thought to thought, and every one of them is wild and makes no sense whatsoever."

"Then I'll make you a cup of tea and a sandwich and we won't talk about anything but your school, and music, and Michael for the rest of the evening. Is that a plan?"

"That's a plan," she said huskily. "Only let's limit it to Michael. Somehow, he manages to make everything seem all right."

CHAPTER
5

Y ou found your way out here to the porch?" Cara stood in the doorway, looking at Darcy curled up under a blanket on the porch swing. "It's my favorite place in the entire cottage. I should have known you'd zero in on it."

"Can't have you monopolizing it. Consider it mine." She was trying to be flip, but it came out a little shaky. "Since I'm liable to be tossed out of here in the morning, I need to gather rosebuds where I may. Who said that anyway? Shakespeare?"

"I have no idea." She crossed the porch and nudged Darcy's legs out of her way to perch on the end of the swing. "But there's no need for gathering rosebuds. No one is kicking you out. Eve understood that you'd be upset."

"No, she didn't. How could she? I walk into her home and upset her, then fall apart and have to be sent to bed like a kid."

"You had reason." She leaned back on the swing. "She knows that. We just don't know what the reasons are, Darcy." She paused. "So I've been designated to find out because they thought it would be easier for you to talk to me. Is that true?"

"You know it is."

"Then will you tell me about your twin? You've never mentioned her. And I don't remember ever reading about her on your fan pages."

"You read my fan page?"

"Only when I knew you were going to room with me. I wanted to know what to expect."

"And you found me just as spectacular as you thought I'd be?"

"Absolutely." She reached out and covered Darcy's hand with her own. Darcy seemed so terribly vulnerable in this moment. Just as beautiful, but everything about her seemed infinitely fragile, like crystal on the verge of shattering.

"You're lying because you want to make me feel better."

"Well, maybe not absolutely, but close. Tell me about your twin."

"Her name is Sylvia Marie Jordan. We were born in a hospital in Nice, France. I came first, and Sylvie was born twenty minutes later." She smiled bitterly. "I always came first, you know. All our lives I came first. I was the star."

"Jordan? Your name is Nichols."

"My mother changed it when she started being a stage mother and began pushing me for auditions. Felicity thought Nichols had a better ring to it. What do you think?"

"Both are good."

"That's what I thought. Though I liked Jordan better. But what does a six-year-old know? What I wanted didn't matter. Felicity had already divorced my father and was on to number three. But number three was disappointing, too. So she decided that she'd have to concentrate on someone she could control. Someone who would do whatever she wished and not argue—who couldn't argue."

"Sylvie?"

"Heavens no, she was a disappointment to Felicity, too." Her gaze shifted to the lake. "Sylvie was very . . . slow. I told you I was first, didn't I? Sylvie had brain damage. She also developed a blood disorder that would probably have killed her before she reached adulthood."

"Dear God," Cara said. "What a tragedy."

"Sylvie didn't see it that way." Darcy steadied her voice. "She was always so happy. Everything was beautiful as far as she was concerned. I've never known anyone to enjoy life as much as Sylvie." She added softly, "Each day seemed like a miracle to her. Everyone thought I was the star, that I was the one who lit up everything around me, but it was her. It was always Sylvie."

"That must have been a great comfort to you."

"I didn't think about it. It was just the way she was. My other half, my better half." She shrugged. "Until Felicity decided that I had to earn my way. She'd been an actress and a model before she decided she preferred being supported in the way she deserved by sundry husbands. But she knew enough to know that talented child actors could be pure gold on the TV networks. I'd just turned six, and I was the right age. Oh, and I was *very* talented. I could sing. I could dance. My line delivery was faultless. I was being called a modern Shirley Temple. So Felicity took me back to New York and dedicated six months to being a stage mother until I got my big break. Then she hired a nanny for me and went back to Nice to live the good life. Needless to say, I was everything she could ask of me. I was fantastic. Of course, it was instinct driven by necessity. But it worked for her." She paused. "And it worked for us."

"Us?"

"Sylvie and me. I was a star. And Sylvie was safe."

"Safe?"

"Medical treatments are expensive. She was in and out of hospitals a lot of the time. Felicity kept talking about putting her in a charity facility. She even took me to see one." She closed her eyes. "It scared me. Sylvie was always smiling. No one was smiling there." Her eyes were glittering with unshed tears when she opened them an instant later. "But Felicity said if I did whatever the producers wanted, they'd pay me a lot of money, and Sylvie would never have to go to a place like that. She'd even set up a trust fund so that Sylvie would be able to stay at a wonderful sanitarium in Zurich where she'd be with other children with the same problems she had. She'd be so very happy. Isn't that what I wanted?" She swallowed. "Of course, it was. Only one thing wrong. Felicity didn't want any publicity about a sick little girl struggling for her life in the background. I was going to be the star of *Golden Days*. Everyone was going to tune in every week to lift their spirits and laugh and see funny, sweet, Darcy Nichols. Felicity didn't want any depressing stories hovering over me and spoiling my aura. So I wasn't to tell anyone about Sylvie. Felicity buried all the records. I couldn't even visit her." She moistened her lips. "I've seen her only a few times over the years. Once I made Felicity take me to the sanitarium to make sure it was everything she'd told me it was. The other times were when she was ill, and I thought she needed me. The last time was a couple years ago when I had to check on her myself after I heard she was having a bad reaction to a blood transfusion. I had to make sure that she was okay."

"Your mother kept her word about her care?"

"Yes. The sanitarium was a beautiful place with wonderful people, and Sylvie couldn't have been happier there." Her lips twisted. "As far as keeping her word, I made sure of it. Before I'd agree to sign a second contract when I was ten, I made Felicity do what she'd promised and set up that trust fund that guaranteed Sylvie would be protected until the day she died. Felicity wasn't pleased because that was a lot of money. But she had control of everything else I earned, so she let it slide."

"But she still wouldn't let you visit your sister?"

"No, she put that into the contract. But that was okay. Sylvie and I had already gotten around that problem."

Cara frowned. "How?"

"We're twins," she said simply. "Haven't you heard that twins have a special connection? It's true, you know. Oh, I don't mean an actual psychic connection. I don't know about that kind of thing. But occasionally I'd get pictures of what she was seeing. Or feel what she was feeling. And there was always that knowledge that she was there with me, part of me. When I first had to leave her, we were both terribly upset. But then, after we were apart for a little while, we both began to realize that we were still there for each other. Felicity couldn't take that away."

"No, I can see that," Cara said softly. "I don't believe you let your mother take much away from either of you, Darcy."

"You're wrong. But it could have been worse. Sylvie was happy." Her face clouded. "Until she wasn't. Until I couldn't feel her any longer."

"And that was when the nightmares started?"

She nodded. "A few weeks after I came to live at the residence. The first day, I could feel a kind of bewilderment from her that I didn't understand; and then I couldn't reach her. I called Felicity and she said that Sylvie was fine. She was just on a new medicine that was making her a little fuzzy. They were trying to adjust it. I called the sanitarium and they told me the same thing. So I thought it was okay." She whispered, "But I was still scared. I felt so alone without her."

And perhaps that was the reason why a strong, sophisticated, Darcy had clung to Cara during these last months. "Evidently you should have been afraid for her," Cara said gently. "You believe that's when . . ." She hesitated on how to put it. "You lost her?"

"I don't know. I couldn't reach Sylvie. My mother had told me she was going on a cruise, and I couldn't get hold of her either. But the sanitarium kept giving me reports that Sylvie was getting better. I don't know anything about this." Her hand was nervously clutching and releasing the blanket covering her. "But I've got to find out, don't I? Since I saw her this afternoon, I've been just trying to survive and face the idea I don't have her any longer . . . that I'm alone. It's . . . hard."

"I know it is."

"I never expected to have her with me always. She's been ill all her life." She looked out at the lake. "But she shouldn't have had a year, a day, not even one moment stolen from her. And someone did that, Cara." She said wonderingly, "A bullet? Why? If you could have known her . . . It would be like shooting a baby deer. There's no sense to it."

"There are crazy people out there. Sense probably doesn't enter into a crime like this."

"But I have to understand." She pushed back her hair. "Felicity must have lied to me. And so did the sanitarium. Why?"

"You don't have to deal with this now. Give yourself a little time. Once I tell Joe what happened, he'll be on it right away. He'll get your answers for you."

"Will he? You trust him, so I have to trust him. But in the end, I'm the one who has to find Sylvie's answers. I took care of her, I made certain I protected the joy that had been given to her when so much else had been taken away." Her voice was unsteady. "So I have to take care of her in this one last way." She drew a deep, shaky breath. "But maybe not just now. I seem to be falling apart again." She sat up in the swing. "I'd better go back to bed and pull myself together to prepare for tomorrow when I have to face Eve . . . and Sylvie. I have to know what happened here. Will you pave the way for me?"

"I'll be there with you."

"No, it's going to be difficult, and you'd try to spare me. I have to do it on my own." She suddenly turned and gave Cara a fierce hug. "Thank you." The words were muffled in Cara's shoulder. "I'm sorry that I've caused you so much—" She released her and jumped to her feet. "Good night. I'll see you in the morning."

She strode quickly into the house.

Cara slowly got to her feet and stood looking out at the woods. Eve had told her that the man who had delivered the skull had stood out there watching the house before he'd made his move. He was not there now she knew. She trusted that Joe was keeping him far at bay, if he was out there in the darkness at all. But the answers that Darcy was going to get from Eve tomorrow about the reconstruction were going to be as upsetting as she thought it would be.

Because it would include that man lurking in the darkness with her twin's skull occupying that gold-foil box.

But she would pave the way with Eve as Darcy had asked her to do. Tell her the tragic story of Sylvie that had not really been tragic until that bullet had taken her life. It had been the story of self-sacrifice and togetherness and finding joy in every moment. Eve would understand and be able to bond with Darcy even as she presented her with the terrible reality of Sylvie's death and the puzzle that surrounded it.

Puzzle.

But there was another aspect of the puzzle she had to confront that she'd not confided to Eve. She'd been too bewildered and uncertain that there had been any connection.

But she couldn't take the chance.

Call him now?

No question.

She took her phone out of the pocket of her robe and dialed quickly.

Jock answered in two rings. "It's three in the morning. What's wrong?"

"All sorts of things. It's not what—"

"Are you hurt?"

"No." Of course that would be his first concern after last night. "It's not me."

"Eve? Michael?"

"No. Let me talk, Jock."

"Talk."

"I just didn't want you to waste time searching for someone who was trying to kill me when maybe he wasn't."

"Cara."

"That didn't come out right. Or maybe it did. I'm tired, and my head is spinning. I'm trying to say that I might not have been the target last night. Maybe I just came into the suite at the wrong time. And perhaps when he found out that I wasn't Darcy, that was the reason he didn't finish the job and ran out."

"Darcy? You believe he was after Darcy? Why?"

"I don't know yet. And maybe it wasn't me who was being watched. You didn't find any evidence from your contacts in Moscow. It's a possibility, right?"

"Not nearly as possible as your being the target. Are you trying to find a reason why you should keep your promise to Kaskov?"

"I don't have to find a reason, the promise is the reason itself." She paused. "And I didn't even think of a threat to Darcy until I walked in and saw that skull, and even then it took me a little time to—"

"Skull?" The word came cracking through the phone.

"Sylvie's skull." She hurried through the explanation to ward off the storm she knew was on the horizon. "So you can see it would be too much of a coincidence to have a link like this to Darcy in the same week as the attack on me."

Silence. "I can also see no reason why that skull was delivered to Eve in Atlanta, Georgia, when Sylvie was presumably killed in Zurich, Switzerland. Unless Darcy's mother lied about Sylvie's still being at the sanitarium there. And why involve Eve at all . . . unless it was because you were sharing that suite with Darcy. So was she targeted, or were you?" He was silent again, and she could almost hear his mind ticking through all the possibilities. "I don't like any of it. Too many variables. Too many unanswered questions. I think I liked it better when I had the option that I could just zero in on any of Kaskov's enemies who popped up on the radar."

"I don't," Cara said. "And I don't like it that a sick woman was murdered for God knows what reason. Or that Eve is involved, and I'm not certain if it's my fault. Or that Darcy is going through the pain of losing her sister."

"And you're identifying with her," Jock said quietly.

"Yes. I'm identifying with everyone. All of them are innocent, and I want it to go away for them. Why do you think I called you in the middle of the night? You're my best friend, and I didn't want to be alone with this. Tomorrow, I'll have to be strong. Not tonight. So I'm reaching out."

"You're not alone. I'll always be here."

She closed her eyes. He had told her that before, but it was good to hear it again. Always. She wanted so desperately to believe it. She could almost see him, his face intent, smiling at her. "I know." She drew a deep breath. "And now I'll go to bed, and you'll probably do nothing of the sort since I've set your mind to working."

"Good guess. But I will wait a couple hours before I call Quinn and get together with him on contacting Sylvie's sanitarium and to try reaching her mother."

"You're calling Joe?" She paused. "I didn't tell Eve about last night yet."

"Somehow, I thought it might have slipped your mind," he said dryly. "I told you I was going to call him. There was no way I was going to let you go down there without Quinn's knowing there was a threat."

"I was going to tell Eve soon. Too much was happening."

"I'll accept that. I'll just take care of it."

"Did you identify that fingerprint you pulled from the stairwell?"

"Not yet. But I'll get Quinn to push it through Interpol, and we'll see what happens. He has a hell of a lot of contacts. By the time I get to Nice, he might have a name for me."

"Nice?"

"You said that was where Felicity Jordan lives. I'll be on a flight there this morning. That way I won't have to rely on phones or secondhand information. I have to know what's happening. I want this over quickly."

Jock was moving with lightning speed, Cara realized. Well, when

did he ever do anything else when he was motivated? That easy, almost radiant, charisma was completely deceptive, and only existed
when conditions were also easy and nonthreatening. She should have
known that he'd take control when she'd picked up her phone tonight.
And that was okay when it only concerned information gathering.

It was not okay if she had to worry about his running into men
like the one who had nearly throttled her last night. But her attacker
was not in Nice, he was in New York. Jock might actually be safer
in Nice. "You'll be careful?"

"I don't believe an overambitious stage mother will pose a real
threat to me. But I'll promise to be especially careful of her." His voice
was suddenly gentle. "Go to sleep, Cara. I'll call you later and let
you know what's happening. I'll be with you as soon as I can." He
hung up.

She slid the phone back in her pocket. She had no more information than when she'd called Jock, and he was far more skeptical than
she had been. Yet she felt warmer, less helpless, more able to cope
than before she'd spoken to him.

You'll never be alone. I'll always be here.

If she was careful, if she didn't demand too much, that could be
true.

She turned and headed for the door. And for now she still had
people who cared about her. She was far luckier than Darcy, who had
just lost the one person who had completed her.

So reach out and help her. Show Darcy that she was not alone
either . . .

There was someone in the room . . .

It was all right.

No one to fear . . .

Darcy slowly opened her eyes. The room was dim, the first rays
of dawn were streaming softly through the window and falling on
the foot of the bed and the rocking chair against the far wall.

And shining on the chestnut hair of the little boy who was sitting in that rocking chair. He smiled at her. "Hi, I'm Michael. Want to have breakfast with me? Mama's not awake yet, and she doesn't like me to use the stove if she's not around. But she wouldn't mind if you were around to help, in case I set myself on fire." He chuckled. "That's what she always says. No way are you going to set yourself on fire today, Michael."

Darcy shook her head to clear it. "I'm afraid that I'm not qualified in that department. I don't cook. I usually stock my pantry with Apple Jacks cereal." She noticed for the first time he was barefoot and dressed in blue-and-white-striped pajamas. "Shouldn't you go back to bed? Maybe it's too early for you to eat. And don't you have to go to school or something?"

"Saturday." He stood up and headed for the door. "It's not too early if you're hungry. And it's good that no one is up yet. Come on, Darcy." He smiled coaxingly at her over his shoulder. "We'll get to have breakfast with Sylvie."

He was gone.

And she was lying there in total shock. It was the last thing that she'd expected the child to say, and he'd said it with complete naturalness and eagerness. Maybe it *was* totally natural when you were the son of a forensic sculptor of the stature of Eve Duncan. And that sculptor was Darcy's hostess, whose son had just run out of here to whip up some breakfast when he'd been forbidden to do it on his own.

Not a time to lie in bed.

She threw off her blanket, grabbed her robe, and ran out of the room and down the hall toward the kitchen.

"I don't think we have Apple Jacks." Michael's head popped up from behind the counter, where he'd been going through the pantry. "Mama says all that sugar isn't good for you. We have cornflakes. Is that okay?"

"Fine." And didn't require cooking, or any fire hazard for either of them. "You get the milk out of the fridge, and I'll get down bowls and find some spoons."

"That drawer beside you." He was already at the refrigerator. "Let's sit on the couch in the living room. It will be better in there."

"Whatever you say. Though I thought maybe the porch?"

"Not this morning." His luminous smile lit his face. "Okay?"

She had an idea that women were going to say okay to this heartbreaker for the rest of his life. "I was thinking your mother might not like us to risk the mess."

"No mess. We'll be careful." He was carrying his bowl into the living room. "Come on. It's better . . ."

"Whatever." She found herself settling herself on the couch and dipping her spoon into the cereal. "How did you know what my name was, Michael?"

"My dad told me when he took me to Burger King last night. He said not to bother you because you were sad and needed some time." He put down his bowl and spoon on the coffee table. "But I knew you needed to have breakfast."

"It was nice of you to think of me." She added dryly, "At five in the morning."

"It had to be early." He was moving across the living room toward Eve's worktable. "She's beautiful with the sun touching her. I wanted you to see her."

She went rigid as she saw the little boy reaching across the pedestal toward the reconstruction. "I don't think your mother would like you to touch—"

Too late. He'd pulled the black velvet cloth from the reconstruction and tossed it on the pedestal. He turned and ran back to the couch. "See. The sunlight comes in that window and it makes her . . ." He started to eat his cereal. "You know."

Yes, she knew. Darcy stared, breathless. The diffused glow of light

was forming an aureole around Sylvie's head, highlighting every feature and making the skin appear to be illuminated from within. She
had never seen Sylvie look more beautiful or more sharply defined
and full of vitality. This wasn't the look of the dreamer or the butterfly Darcy had known through the years. This was . . . different.

"Your cornflakes are getting soggy," Michael said.

The pragmatic statement made her jerk her gaze away from
Sylvie to Michael. His expression seemed sober, but was there the
faintest hint of mischief in his face? Six years old. It had to be imagination. "How did you know that she'd look like this, Michael?"

"I came out early sometimes when Mama was working on her.
She didn't look this good all the time, until Mama fixed her, but I
liked looking at her anyway. And I think she liked me being here.
But she'll like your company better."

"Because we're twins?"

"I don't know. Maybe because she'll like you knowing how good
she's been fixed."

"By your mother?" Darcy nodded. "She's certainly done a wonderful job."

He nodded. "Yeah. I told Mama the inside was already fixed, so
all she had to do was the outside. But she matched it really good,
didn't she? Anyway, I thought that you'd like to have breakfast with
Sylvie. And maybe she'd like it, too." He scooted back on the couch
and took another bite of cereal. "Was I right?"

It was totally bizarre sitting here on this couch with this strange,
endearing child who took it for granted that she'd want to get up at
the crack of dawn to have breakfast with a skull named Sylvie. Who
spoke not of murder but of fixing, healing, and how Sylvie would
want her to know that healing had taken place. It had not even occurred to him that there could be darkness, not sunlight, in what he'd
shown her.

Because there wasn't any darkness.

"You were absolutely right, Michael." Darcy sat back and ate her

cereal, completely comfortable to be here with the sun shining brilliantly on Sylvie. For some reason, it seemed to be the right place to be
at the right time. "Now tell me what you're doing at school. And then
I'll tell you what a fantastic star I'm going to be someday. Not as big
as your Cara, but then she's really one of those once-in-a-lifetime
talents, and I've only got a terrific voice and star quality. But that
will be enough, don't you—"

"Michael, what have you been doing?" Eve stood in the door-
way with her hands on her hips and trying to look stern. It wasn't
working. She was too relieved to see that Darcy was no longer the
broken woman she'd been the afternoon before. She was still pale, but
she appeared subdued but normal. "I'm sorry, did he wake you, Darcy?
How long have you been up?"

"Only a couple hours." Darcy smiled at Michael. "We were just
getting to know each other. Only somehow it ended up with
me talking entirely too much about myself . . ." Her eyes went to
the reconstruction across the room. "And Sylvie."

And nothing was healthier, Eve thought. Bless Michael. "I'm sure
my son slipped in quite a lot about himself." She looked at the empty
cereal bowls. "I see you've had a light breakfast. Would you care to
have something more substantial? Joe is going to take Michael to
karate practice this morning, and he probably shouldn't eat too—"

"Karate," Darcy repeated. She made the connection. "Gary."

Eve chuckled. "Well, evidently you didn't completely monopo-
lize the conversation, Darcy." Eve turned to Michael. "Go take your
shower and wake up Cara, Michael. She told me she wanted to go
with you. She said she might need to pick up a few moves herself."

"*Yes.*" Michael laughed and jumped to his feet. "I was afraid I
wouldn't get to see her much today." He ran down the hall toward
the bathroom. "I can show her some moves. Dad says I'm getting
really good."

Eve turned back to Darcy when he'd disappeared. "I didn't mean to take Cara away from you today," she said quietly. "I know it must seem as if you've been thrown into a den of strangers at a terrible time in your life. But Cara said you had questions, and it seemed a good time."

"Not strangers." Her gaze shifted to the reconstruction again. "Even your son has made me feel very much at home." She looked back at Eve with a smile. "I may be disappointed when I wake up, and he's not sitting in that rocking chair looking at me with those big brown eyes."

Eve sighed. "He didn't? Oh well, it's good you get accustomed to him right away. He's a bit of an acquired taste."

"You don't believe that." Darcy grinned. "You know what you've got, Eve. He's a wonder."

Eve nodded. "I know what I've got." She grinned. "Maybe I just don't want everyone else to be green with envy." Her smile faded. "And I'm glad he had this time with you. Michael has a rather unique perspective on my work, as you've probably noticed. I assure you, it's his perspective, not mine." She paused. "But it's quite wonderful and worth considering." She turned away. "Now why don't you go take your shower and dress while I fix an omelet for you." She made a face. "I'm not much of a cook, but I can do a decent omelet. Then we'll get down to Sylvie."

"You don't have to—"

"Yes, I do," she interrupted. "You're going to need more than a bowl of flakes to get through the things I'm going to tell you." She added grimly, "And before I came out here this morning, Joe was taking a call from Jock Gavin, and that was pretty nasty, too."

Darcy made a face. "Cara said that she didn't want you to know about that just yet."

"I can believe it. Cara has always wanted to protect me. Well, Jock evidently did want us to know ASAP." Eve headed for the kitchen. "So it's all cards on the table, so we can figure out this nightmare."

DELTA FLIGHT 2482
OVER MARSEILLES, FRANCE
4:50 P.M.

"The fingerprint belongs to Rory Norwalk, born and raised in Belfast, Ireland," Joe said when Jock picked up his call. "Dalroth, with Interpol, says that he's a very nasty customer who has a record several pages long that includes everything from theft and human trafficking to drug smuggling. I'm texting you a photo right now. Ten years ago, he set up his own organization and runs a team out of Dublin. He's good at what he does." He paused. "First, you should know that according to reports, he's a psycho. He grew up working with the IRA, and the stories about the torture he inflicted while he was with them were pretty bloody. He enjoys it. He's been picked up for at least three cases of murder since he set up his organization. Never proven."

"Shit." Jock's hand tightened on his cell phone. "What connection does he have with Kaskov or any of the Moscow Mafia families?"

"None that Dalroth can trace. He doesn't work with any of the crime families. He tends to hire himself out to the highest bidder, but he sticks to his own turf. He's always confined his operations to London or Dublin."

"Then how the hell did he end up in Cara's suite in New York?" He accessed the photo of a tall, powerfully built man, wearing an olive-green windbreaker. Rory Norwalk was fortysomething, with dark eyes, a shock of thick brown hair, a square face, and thick lips. Nothing unusual. Someone you'd pass on the street and barely notice. But now Jock would notice, he'd never forget. "What's he doing in the U.S.? There *has* to be a connection."

"Cool down," Joe said quietly. "You said that Cara thinks he could be targeting Darcy Nichols. That's why you're on that plane."

"I'm here because I have to explore every possibility. I don't like the idea that Eve received that gift package of the skull of Darcy Nichols's sister. The connection is too damn clear."

"Do you think I do?" Joe asked harshly. "I'd be on a plane myself if I could justify leaving my family with that nut job running around. Norwalk got close enough once to leave that skull. He's not going to get that close again."

Thank God. And Jock was passionately grateful that Joe was there to form that protective barrier. He'd been on edge ever since he'd taken Cara's call last night. "I'll check it out. What did you find out about Felicity Jordan?"

"I texted you her current address in Nice. It's a villa on the Mediterranean. Evidently she lives very lavishly on Darcy's residuals. I've been trying to contact her or her current husband, Raoul Napier, all day, but it goes straight to voice mail. I got Dalroth to do a little checking of illegal activity with the local authorities, but they appear to be clean. If you can call her mother's appropriation of Darcy's funds clean. Raoul Napier likes to gamble and has been picked up on possession, but no serious criminal record."

"What about Sylvie's sanitarium?"

"That took longer. It has stringent privacy rules. That's one of the prime attractions to the wealthy parents who put their children in the place. Eventually, I was able to bypass the clerks and get through to someone in authority. I found out that Sylvie Jordan had been removed from the sanitarium by her mother and stepfather almost two months ago."

"So Felicity was lying to Darcy," Jock said grimly.

"It would appear so. And probably backed up by a fat bribe to the desk receptionist at the sanitarium who answers their phones. You'll have to determine that for yourself. If you can find Raoul Napier and his wife, Felicity."

"Oh, I'll find them," Jock said. "I have contacts I can tap for information in most places in the world. It's what I was trained to do. Find and eliminate. I've already called Charles Benoit, who is very,

very good at digging and providing that information. He'll be meeting me at the airport in Nice."

Joe was silent. "I hope the eliminating won't be necessary in this case."

Jock was surprised at that far-from-subtle warning. Joe Quinn was an ex–SEAL, and his instincts were often as violent and lethally efficient as Jock's. "I'll have to see, won't I? Do you think you could stop me?"

"I'd try like hell if you went off the track. Cara wouldn't let me do anything else. Which would put me up against you, and that would be the last thing you'd want to happen. Either way, you'd lose. So be damn sure, Jock."

He was right, there was no way he could ever challenge anyone Cara loved as she did Joe Quinn. "I'll be sure. Just take care of her. I'll get back to you." He cut the connection.

CHAPTER

6

I *love* this place," Darcy said as she looked down from the porch at the barbecue area directly below them where Eve, Joe, and Michael were gathered together in front of the grill. The laser lights were lit on the trees surrounding the entire area, and it appeared as if thousands of emerald fireflies were glittering off and on every branch. "And those lights are amazing. Not what I'd expect from such a bucolic setting."

"Eve's adopted daughter, Jane MacGuire, sent them to Michael last year," Cara said. "She's an artist, and she has a wonderful eye. She did that painting of Eve on the wall in the living room. She knew Michael would love those lights. She came and installed them herself to get just the right effect." She handed Darcy a glass of lemonade. "And I think Michael was happier to have her here to do it than to have the lights themselves."

"I can see that," Darcy said. "He's incredibly affectionate, isn't he?"

"He's incredible in all kinds of ways." She sipped her lemonade. "But the affection isn't that unusual when he has parents like Eve and Joe. It's all love and family here. Anything else would be truly incredible."

"I guess you're right." She looked down at Michael, standing next to Eve. "It just seems unusual to me. It's like the last scene on a family sitcom when they're wrapping up everything all touchy-feely so they'll get renewed for the next season."

Cara gazed at her openmouthed. Then she started to laugh. "Only you would make that comparison. Yes, I definitely think Eve and family will get renewed for next season."

"So do I," Darcy said. "They're wonderful. Do you know how lucky you are they took you in?"

"No question." She glanced sideways at Darcy before she asked. "You've been very quiet since we got home from Michael's karate lesson. How did it go with you and Eve?"

"How do you think it went? Eve told me I'd have to brace myself, and she was right. She didn't want to show me the photos of that skull before she started work on it, but I made her do it. I had to know everything I could about what happened to Sylvie." She shivered as she looked away from Cara. "I nearly threw up again. I'm not what you could ever call tough. The only thing that saved me was that I got so angry that it seemed to burn everything away, but what I wanted to do to the person who had done that to her."

"Eve said that the cremation had been done after Sylvie was shot," Cara said gently. "And the bullet killed her instantly."

"I know," she said jerkily. "She told me all that. But at that point it didn't help. I couldn't understand how anyone could—" She drew a deep breath. "She said she thought it was done to either make it difficult for her to reconstruct, or to inject an element of horror and shock to that skull." She moistened her lips. "I *felt* that horror and shock. Anyone who had known Sylvie would have. She was so gentle, like a leaf drifting among us, and he tried to make her into a monster."

"But Eve didn't let him," Cara said. "She brought her back. She brought her home to you."

"And I'll always be grateful to her." She looked down at Eve. "She's just as wonderful as you always told me. She was supposed to turn Sylvie back over to Forensics today, but I asked her if we could keep her here for a couple more days. She got Joe to pull strings."

"It was important to you?"

"It seemed that way. I just wanted to be able to look at Sylvie every now and then and try to understand and get my head together. I'm so filled with anger and sadness, and yet I look at that reconstruction that Eve did of Sylvie, and I think I see something I've never seen before." She shook her head. "Or maybe I saw it, and I didn't notice. Eve made her look stronger, brimming, shining, with life."

"Eve never makes her reconstructions look anything," Cara said. "She just sculpts what's there."

"Michael said she fixes them."

"But never changes them." She took a step closer and slid her arm around Darcy's waist. "I've always thought some people have a shining inside. Maybe Sylvie was one of those people, and it's only now that we're allowed to see it."

"Maybe." She smiled with an effort. "As I said, I'm only trying to understand what's happening to me. I'm not up to going very deep into philosophy or theology right now. Not that I ever am. I really like accepting the role of the dumb blonde on occasion. It's much more comfortable for me."

"And totally deceptive." But Darcy had gone through enough trauma and soul-searching for one day, Cara thought. She was still in the healing process, and Cara could see her changing with every passing hour. "But by all means, let's go down and join the family and see if you can fool them." She nudged her toward the porch steps. "Though you'll have to be very sharp to get that past Michael . . ."

A few minutes later, Cara was sitting on the bench by the barbecue pit and watching as Darcy was being drawn into the magic circle of laughter and warmth that Michael, Eve, and Joe were generating. She could see any hint of artifice and stiffness melting away from her as she threw back her head and laughed at something Joe had said. This was what she had wanted for Darcy. Cara had been given this gift all those years ago, and she knew the value. She had come to Eve almost as broken and hurting as Darcy and she had—

Her cell rang, and she pulled it out of her jacket pocket.

Jock? He'd promised he'd call her when he—

Not Jock.

She stiffened as she read the ID.

Sergai Kaskov.

She hesitated, then pressed the access. "Hello, Kaskov. I didn't expect to hear from you so soon. I'm not supposed to be in New Orleans for another week."

"And you're clearly so shocked that you forgot to call me grandfather again," he said dryly. "Though it's not surprising since I only see you for one month a year. It does tend to distance us, doesn't it?"

"I'm sorry. I did forget. But that one month is more than we were ever together from the time I was three. My mother didn't even see fit to bring me to see you until I was eleven." She paused. "So the distance was already there and established."

Silence. "I can always count on you to be entirely frank with me. Perhaps that's why I look forward to these visits so much. No one else is that brave."

"Because you'd shoot them?"

He chuckled. "I haven't shot anyone in a long time."

But he didn't mention if he'd given that order to one of his men. She wasn't going to ask him. Their periods together were too difficult without further conflict. "Why are you calling me?"

"I just wanted to tell you that I had your last concert in Connecticut recorded, and it was exquisite. You're getting better all the time. I thought you were superb when I first heard you when you were only eleven, but now you're reaching your full potential. I wanted to let you know I'm pleased."

"Thank you."

"You're welcome." His voice was mocking. "I know how little that means to you. But it does mean something to me, so I thought it would be amusing to express it. And, as it happens, I had a few other items on my agenda to discuss, so I decided I'd indulge myself."

"What other items?"

"First, I wished to tell you that I'm already in New Orleans. I got here a few days ago, and I've leased a lovely antebellum house north of the city. Very southern and old-world and very reminiscent of that film *Interview with the Vampire*. That concept always amused me. All that power and total ruthlessness."

"And dripping blood and no one really happy."

"One has to accept that vampires are seldom particularly happy. It's never written into the script. Hollywood prefers drama, not happy endings."

"And I prefer a happy solution whenever possible."

"I've noticed." He chuckled. "But that can be at great cost to you. Anyway, I believe you'll enjoy this house. It has a certain atmosphere that you'll appreciate. It may stir the creative muse. In fact, I'm think-ing you should come a little early."

She stiffened. "What? Why?"

"Why not? I'm ready for your visit, and you're no longer at school."

"I've made plans to be with you for next week."

"But you may change your mind before that time," he said softly. "And that would make me unhappy. It's a volatile, ever-shifting world we live in. I think you should come now."

"Do you?" But Kaskov had never been this insistent in any of his contacts with her. He was always smooth, reasonable, almost concil-iatory. This sounded almost like a threat. Yet she had an idea that wasn't the case. "Are you going to tell me the real reason?"

He was silent. "It appears that I am. Regrettable. I know you like the idea of my being apart from the life you lead when you're not with me, and I've tried to foster that impression. But it's really not advis-able in this situation."

"What situation?"

"The situation in which they had to call an ambulance to your suite two nights ago when you were attacked."

Shock. She drew a deep breath. "And how do you know about that?"

"The same way that I was able to obtain that CD of your concert. I have people in place to make sure that I'm not left in the dark regarding what's happening to you. You're my granddaughter, and I would not leave anything that belonged to me unattended."

People in place? For heaven's sake, first she had found out about Jock's agent, Stanton, and now Kaskov was coming up with his own men shadowing her? It was verging on the ridiculous.

Except no one had been able to stop that savage attack in the dark at the residence.

"You're not speaking," Kaskov said. "I take it you're displeased?"

"I'm thinking that it's a wonder I didn't stumble over all those 'helpful' people who were trying to keep an eye on me," she said dryly. "And, yes, I'm displeased. I don't like that you consider me your property."

"Unfortunate. You're my only living family member; therefore, it's natural that I should feel a bit proprietorial. That's why I decided that you should be removed from a potentially hazardous environment and come to where I can control what happens to you."

"And do you know why it's hazardous? Does it have anything to do with you or your enemies?"

"Was that Jock Gavin's guess? Actually, it's the answer I'd have chosen, too. He's very clever, isn't he? And so very competent. I remember I tried to recruit him at one time."

"You're not answering me."

"No, I had nothing to do with it. At least to my knowledge. I admit there are sometimes blast effects that spread havoc from my actions, but I've been careful." He added, "My enemies? They're legion. I'm investigating the possibilities now. But there's been no stirring that I've been able to detect. However, sometimes it takes time to see what's below the surface. That's why you should come and visit with me while I explore more thoroughly."

"You may not even be responsible. There's another possibility."

"Really? Is that why Jock Gavin boarded a flight for Nice early this morning? Suppose you tell me about it."

"You're watching Jock, too?" She felt a surge of panic. "Stay away from him, Kaskov. And keep your men away from him. Don't go near him."

"My, my, how fierce you are," he said, amused. "And it's my men who should be protected from Gavin. Do you think I haven't investigated who and what he is?"

"Stay away from him."

"Then perhaps you'd better tell him to stay away from me," he murmured. "I haven't mentioned the fact that he's been hovering in the background whenever you came to spend time with me. It didn't disturb me, or I would have made an issue of it."

"He's my friend. He worries about me."

"And you worry about him. I've always found that interesting." He went on before she could reply, "I'm no threat to Gavin at present. I just have to know where he's going and why. Once I get that information, I'll confine any surveillance to you. Does that make you feel better?"

"No."

"It should. I don't generally make concessions." He paused. "You won't come to New Orleans?"

"Not now." She had a sudden thought. Kaskov clearly had a handle on everything that was happening to her. "Do you know where I am?"

"Of course, I'd hardly trail after Gavin and let you wander around by yourself. I have Oleg Sakov, a very good man, on his way to keep an eye on that lake cottage, until you decide to come here. Though I understand Joe Quinn is a force to be reckoned with, I prefer my own man."

"Tell this Sakov to get away from here. Keep him away from Joe or anyone else in my family."

"But they're not your family," he said quietly. "I am, Cara."

"They *are* my family. Sometimes blood doesn't matter."

"I don't agree. But we won't argue about it. I promise you won't know Sakov is even there, and he certainly won't interact with your Joe Quinn. If you change your mind, let me know, and I'll send someone to pick you up. Have a nice evening, Cara." He hung up.

It had not been a threatening call, but that didn't keep it from being disturbing. And if Jock knew, he would definitely be upset about Kaskov's interference in her life.

But Kaskov had accepted her refusal, so the situation was pretty much status quo until it changed. However, she'd have to warn Joe that Kaskov had ordered someone to watch *his* property. He would not be pleased.

But perhaps she would wait until later tonight to tell him.

She was looking at Joe, laughing as he watched Michael concentrating on flipping a burger on the grill. Eve talking quietly to Darcy as she moved around the picnic table, setting it with plates and cutlery. Small tasks, simple tasks, homey tasks, but Cara felt a sudden rush of warmth.

She wanted to be with them, enveloped in that cozy ambience that was almost mesmerizing. In the darkness and fear that seemed to surround her, here was sunlight and comfort and love. She stuffed her phone in her pocket and moved back toward them.

Because Kaskov was wrong, blood had nothing to do with it. This *was* her family because they had chosen her to be one of them.

And choice was everything.

NICE, FRANCE

"There he is." Benoit nodded at the tall, dark-haired man who had just left the small, elegant hotel and was hurrying down the street toward the Lagazar Casino a few blocks away. "Raoul Napier.

Right on time. I told you that he'd be here. You have to admit I'm truly superb. Who else would be able to pull your prey out of the woodwork in a matter of hours?"

"Not quite superb. You haven't been able to locate Felicity Jordan yet."

"That will take time," Benoit protested. "She's not a degenerate gambler like Napier. When she's not at her villa, she travels from resort to resort, and she and Napier only come together for a week or two a year. From what I've found out about her so far, she likes money, high-fashion boutiques, and sex. The latter involves a frequent and varied change of bed partners, which Napier ignores as long as she supplies him with funds. But I'll find her." He sighed. "And I have to admit Napier was no real challenge of my skills. That's his favorite casino on the Riviera. He even checked into that small hotel so that he'd be within walking distance. He thinks it brings him luck."

"Not tonight." Jock pulled over to the curb. "Get out, Benoit. Meet me back at my hotel. You're not going to want to be involved in this."

"Right." Benoit quickly got out of the car. "Not my area of expertise. See you later." The next moment, he'd disappeared around the corner.

And Jock was cruising slowly behind Raoul Napier, watching for an opportunity. Napier was younger than he'd thought he'd be, probably at least fifteen years younger than his wife, Felicity. Well built, dark skin and eyes and a shock of dark hair that made him look even younger. Evidently, Felicity was into boy toys these days. His tuxedo was beautifully tailored and had probably cost at least nine or ten thousand.

Money that had no doubt been supplied by funds sent to his loving wife by Darcy Nichols, Jock thought. Bloodsuckers. He'd always detested the bloodsuckers of the world. Maybe he wasn't in quite so much of a hurry to get this over after all.

And Napier was now approaching an alley just ahead.

No one on the street. All the focus was on the brightly lit casino in the next block.

Jock's foot pressed on the accelerator to intersect him as he reached the alley.

Take him quickly. Get the information. Decide later just how much he hated bloodsuckers . . .

It took Napier fifteen minutes to regain consciousness. By that time, Jock had managed to get him out of the city and driven into a field secluded by tall trees.

"You . . . hurt me." Raoul Napier's eyes were wide with panic as he struggled into a sitting position on the ground beside the car. "You didn't have to do that. I would have given you my money. I'll give it to you right now. I don't have much, but maybe my credit card would be—"

"Not necessary. I need something else entirely from you." Jock knelt beside him. "Sylvie Jordan. You and your wife took her from her sanitarium almost two months ago. I want to know who paid you to do that."

"I don't know what you're talking about." He moistened his lips. "I had nothing to do with that. Sylvie's not even my daughter, she's my wife's kid. You'll have to ask her."

"I will, but I can't seem to locate her. Perhaps you can help me." Jock bent closer, and said, "But don't lie to me again. It makes me very angry. You don't want to make me angry. You both were at the sanitarium signing Sylvie out. So you definitely had something to do with it, Napier. And the next week, the casino said you appeared to be very flush. In fact, it financed a really good run at the crap tables. It didn't last long, you're currently on a losing streak." He added softly, "And tonight you're definitely on a losing streak. So you're going to tell me what happened to Sylvie Jordan and why you decided to kill her."

"Kill her? I didn't kill her." He was breathing hard, his hands opening and closing. "I had nothing to do with it. I just did what I was told."

"By whom?"

"I can't tell you that. I just owed someone a lot of money, and he said that if I did this one thing, it would all go away. All I had to do was to get my wife to take Sylvie out of that sanitarium and turn her over to him."

"And you didn't ask why?"

"You don't understand. There was no way I could pay off that debt. He would have made an example of me. So I thought maybe if I told him what a gold mine Sylvie was for Felicity, maybe we could make a deal. I didn't think he'd hurt her. Why should he? She's been a bread ticket for Felicity for years. There wouldn't have been any reason to hurt the kid. He could use her, just like Felicity did."

"Use her," Jock repeated distastefully. "And I take it your wife didn't find anything wrong with turning her daughter over to this scum?"

"She didn't like it. She said Sylvie was too valuable. I couldn't convince her to do it. But I guess *he* did. At first, he didn't think it was a good idea, but then later he changed his mind and said we could make the deal. And then I had trouble with Felicity." He added pettishly, "Nothing was going right for me. But he said he'd take care of it. He called and scared her, and she finally said she'd go along with it."

"There are too many *he*'s and *him*'s in this conversation. A name, Napier."

He was silent.

Go in another direction. "And where is your wife now, Napier?"

He didn't speak.

"Where?"

"How do I know?" He burst out. "She was pissed off that I'd gotten us both into trouble, and she didn't want to see me again. I was surprised that she was even willing to do it. She must have been really scared. She hated my gambling. The bitch never understood me. She told me that once she'd delivered Sylvie, that she was going to have to think of a way to deal with Darcy until she got the kid back." His lips twisted. "And she said my free ride was over and to expect divorce papers within a few months."

"And where was she supposed to go to deliver Sylvie?"

"After we picked up Sylvie at the sanitarium, Felicity was to drive into the hills to Paillon, a little town near the coast, and turn her over. I guess that's what she did."

"Guess? Not good enough. And I need a name."

"I can't." His face was white. "Look, he's left me alone just like he said he would after we gave him Sylvie. He even gave me a little bonus for cooperating. But I know if I talk, I'll be a dead man."

"If you don't talk, you'll be a dead man," Jock said quietly. "I'm leaning that way anyway. You're wasting my time, Napier."

"Take my money," Napier said desperately. "Maybe I can get you more if you let me go."

"I want a name. I want to know everything you know."

"I *can't* tell you."

"Can't? You'll be surprised how easy it is," Jock said. "I don't usually deal in torture. My training was in ending life, not extending it to agonizing lengths. That doesn't mean I'm not very competent at it. So you'd be wise to terminate this interview to my satisfaction."

"Take the money," Napier repeated desperately.

Jock sighed. "You're very stupid, Napier. Though to tell you the truth, your decision is very satisfying to me. It just doesn't meet my goals."

He reached and delicately stroked Napier's throat. "It's amazing how much pain can be inflicted in these muscles without actually killing . . ."

Napier whimpered, then began to groan.

LAKE COTTAGE

"**The man who was behind Sylvie Jordan being taken from** that sanitarium was Jacques Manard," Jock said when Joe Quinn picked up the phone. "He's a big-time bookie and gambling kingpin who controls a hell of a lot of the action along the Riviera. Napier owed him a bundle, and he jumped at the chance of getting out from under before he was tossed into the Mediterranean. But Napier had to have his wife cooperate to get Sylvie released, so he had to involve Felicity."

"Why the hell would Manard want Sylvie Jordan?"

"Napier didn't know or care. He'd told Manard the situation about Sylvie and her twin. He thought it might be kidnapping, or just a way to force Felicity into turning any money Darcy earned over to him."

"Too complex. And no ransom was ever asked. There was just the skull . . ."

"And what would a big-time gambling czar be doing sending a skull to Eve?"

"Why don't you ask him?" Joe suggested. "Politely, of course. And if that doesn't work, call me. I'll be glad to fly over there and deal with him in a less than polite manner. I don't like the idea of having Eve and Michael being exposed to that kind of shit on my own turf."

"Presently. Right now I'm on my way to Paillon, the little town where Darcy's mother was supposed to have turned Sylvie over to Manard. It's fairly close, and I want to check out why he chose that town to meet, then try to get information where she went from there. Then I'll go to Manard's beach house and tell him that you wanted politeness at all costs. But it wasn't Jacques Manard who left that fingerprint at the Carnegie residence. Can you see if there's a connection between Manard and Norwalk?"

"I'll get on it. But I told you that he usually limited his operations to England and Ireland." He paused. "You're thinking that perhaps the target *is* Darcy?"

"I don't know what I'm thinking. Check and see if Manard has any connection with Kaskov. None of it makes sense yet."

"If it makes a difference, Kaskov told Cara that he had nothing to do with that attack on her."

"*Told* her?"

"He called her tonight and said he thought she should come to him earlier than scheduled."

Jock was muttering curses. "Son of a bitch. What else?"

"Only that he knew you were on your way to Nice. And that he was keeping an eye on her here." He added dryly, "He's evidently filled with grandfatherly concern. Touching."

"Keep him away from her."

"She won't go anywhere without telling me," Joe said. "Right now, she's just worried about Darcy." He added grimly, "And I'm worried about whether I'll end up killing one of Kaskov's men trespassing on my property."

"Dammit, I need to get back there." With an effort, he smothered the anger and exasperation. "I'll call you after I've had my chat with Manard."

"What happened to Napier?"

"He's alive. He may not be, after I tell Manard it was Napier who gave him up. But that's his problem. I decided I really can't stand bloodsuckers." He hung up.

Don't think of Kaskov or all his machinations and wiliness that had made him one of the most dangerous criminals on the continent. He knew he'd have to go back and get a handle on any plans Kaskov might have for Cara. But he had to wrap up as much as possible here so that he could afford to put a period to what had happened to Sylvie Jordan.

Paillon should be just around the next bend. It appeared to be a nice little town with a lovely view of the Mediterranean. Evidently, the tourist entrepreneurs hadn't been able to infiltrate this area yet. He was already seeing neat houses with window boxes full of geraniums. He passed a church with a tall steeple.

He turned the bend in the road.

And he saw why Felicity had been told to bring Sylvie to this small, charming town in the mountains.

The name on the building was glowing green neon in the darkness.

PIERPONT MAISON FUNERAIRE

And down below it.

CREMATORIUM

"You heard him." Joe turned to Eve as he hung up from talk-ing to Jock. "Jock is a little annoyed about all this. It was bad enough before Kaskov interjected himself front and center."

"Not front and center," Eve said. "He's just hovering in the background and making certain that Cara knows he's there. But I can see why Jock isn't pleased."

"Nor am I," Joe said. "You're amazingly calm considering how you feel about Cara's visits with Kaskov."

"I'm not calm. I hate the idea, but I think Cara believed Kaskov when he told her he had nothing to do with that attack on her. It relieved me. Cara is nobody's fool." She smiled. "I don't even feel too upset about Kaskov's sending that guard here to the lake to protect Cara. I want all the help we can get until this is over."

"Even if that guard obeys only Kaskov?"

Eve smiled faintly. "You can get around that, Joe."

"I'd rather not have that brand of help to have to circumvent." Then he shook his head. "Okay, I'll have a talk with him as soon as he gets here and lay down the rules. He doesn't come any closer to the cottage than the far end of the lake. He has to call me for permission to make any other move. If he gives me any arguments, he's gone."

"Somehow, I don't think he'll give you an argument."

He grimaced. "And that's a disappointment." He reached for his phone again. "And now I'd better get that info for Jock before he shows up on Manard's doorstep. He'll need somewhere to start . . ."

"How are you doing?" Cara asked Darcy quietly as she dropped down beside her on the bank of the lake. "You look better today."

"Why not?" Darcy looked around the woods and lake, then to Michael splashing in the water several feet away. "It's all good here. As long as I don't think too much, I'm good, too. I know I'll have to come back to the real world soon, but not just yet." She smiled. "Hey, and I even have a great melodrama working for me." She lowered her voice to a mock hiss. "A Russian goodfella wandering around the property protecting my good friend Cara from the forces of evil."

"That's not funny."

"I think it is. But then I have a twisted sense of humor these days." She shrugged out of her caftan, revealing her beige bikini. "And believe me, I like the idea of its not being me having to be responsible for saving you again. There's no Jock around to rattle out orders."

"No one is responsible for me, but me," Cara said. "And I don't appreciate having my grandfather inserting himself in my life like this. Because it means he's also inserting himself in Joe's and Eve's life."

"But you've got to admit it would make a great movie." She was splashing her legs in the water. "I thought I was the one who had all the cinematic fireworks in her background until Eve told me about what you'd gone through as a kid. Both your parents involved in Mexican cartels that made you a pawn and put you on the run. Your grandfather, a Russian Mafia head, lurking in the background. Shades of *The Godfather*." She grinned. "You kind of put me in the shade."

"Some people would say that's a less than wonderful pedigree," Cara said dryly.

"Really?" She tilted her head. "Is that why you never told me about your background?"

"No. I'm a private person. And there were too many things that happened to me that hurt too much to remember." She met her eyes. "I don't give a damn about pedigrees or what my parents or grandfather did. Jock told me once that I was born with my own soul, and that meant I was the one who could make the choices. That changed everything for me."

"Very wise man," Darcy said. "An Adonis with a brain. Who would have thought it? I could have used a Jock in my life while I was trying to make sense of what was happening to me after Felicity made me leave Sylvie." Her smile faded. "But I'm glad that you had him. I never had many choices, or maybe I just didn't reach out and take them. Perhaps I didn't know it was a possibility. If you'd shown up on the scene a little before you did, maybe you could have told me. I guess neither of us knew what we were coming up against when that housing director threw us together at the residence." Her gaze slid away and focused on Michael playing in the water. "But I'm glad that she did, Cara."

Cara smiled. "So am I."

Darcy slipped into the water. "Well, now that we've gotten that awkwardness over, I'm going to escape and go swim with Michael. Did I ever tell you what a great swimmer I am? In one of my last episodes on *Golden Days*, the writers decided I should have a retro dream about that forties star, Esther Williams. They wanted it to be authentic, so they gave me swimming lessons galore." She was striking out in a breast stroke. "But at least it will come in handy if I have to rescue Michael."

"Have you noticed how well Michael swims?" Cara called after her. "It's more likely that he'll rescue you."

"Maybe he already has . . ." She was treading water beside

Michael and reached out and dunked the boy's head under water. "Gotcha!"

Michael came up laughing, and the battle was on.

Cara was smiling herself as she watched them. It was true that these days of being with Michael and Eve had been a healing experience for Darcy. She was still in pain, but it had temporarily been put on hold, and Cara was grateful for this blessed period of peace and healing.

Her phone rang. Jock.

She unconsciously tensed. So much for peace and healing. The call that Joe had told her about this morning had not had either of those elements. Dark. So dark.

She accessed the call. "I don't think that Joe's found out anything yet, Jock. He's still working—"

"If I'd wanted to check on those results, I would have called Joe," Jock interrupted. "I needed to talk to you, Cara."

"I told Kaskov that I wasn't coming earlier than—"

"Not that either. I'll get to that when I get back. I just thought you should be the one to handle this." He paused. "I found out why Darcy's mother was told to deliver Sylvie to the town of Paillon. It was a matter of convenience."

"Convenience?"

"One of the prime businesses in the town is Pierpont Funeral Home." He added, "Which has a state-of-the-art crematorium."

Cara felt sick. "Darcy's mother was supposed to deliver her daughter to that place to be killed, then cremated?" The sheer cold-bloodedness of the action chilled her to the bone. The vision of Sylvie, who Darcy had said was always filled with innocence and joy, being driven to her death with no idea what was awaiting her. "Monsters."

"Yes." He added, "Though in this case, Felicity Jordan might not have known what was going to happen to Sylvie. Her husband said that she'd only been told she had to deliver Sylvie, not what was going to take place there."

"She was still a monster for being involved at all."

"I'm not arguing. I just wanted to give you the entire picture when you talk to Darcy. I'm inclined to believe that Felicity had no prior knowledge of what was waiting for them. She only thought she was being forced to hand over the prize who'd been furnishing Felicity and her husband a luxurious living for the last several years."

"To be shot, then cremated," she said harshly. "I don't think that Darcy will—" She stopped as she realized how carefully he'd been phrasing his words. "Waiting for them?" she repeated. "The entire picture? What are you saying, Jock?"

"I'm saying that I've spent the last seven hours with Alan Pierpont and his son, who appear to be just as much scum as the people who hired them to dispose of the remains. It took a good deal of persuasion, but I got the entire story out of them. They were a bit annoyed that they'd had a guest staying with them for more than twenty-four hours because of the cremation of the young woman. Otherwise, they would have been done with their business in a matter of a few hours." He paused. "Because they only buried the older woman in a plot in the cemetery."

Shock.

"They killed Felicity Jordan, too?" she whispered.

"They could control her husband, but I'd bet they weren't sure about her. Mothers can be so emotional about their children."

"That hasn't been my experience," she said dully.

"I know," Jock said. "And I don't have any idea how much faith or love Darcy could still have in her mother. But children struggle to keep love alive, even when it's not deserved. All I could do was give you the facts as they were given to me."

"And Pierpont was telling the truth?"

"Without a doubt."

"And the 'guest' that stayed with Pierpont while Sylvie was being cremated? Did you get a name or description?"

"Yes, Pierpont wasn't given a name, but it wasn't Manard who met Felicity there." He paused. "I showed Pierpont the photo that Joe sent me. Rory Norwalk. Positive ID."

"So much for his not working outside England and Ireland. Then he was an accomplice to Manard."

"Or vice versa. I don't know who was pulling the strings. I'll find out when I question Manard later this evening. I've just called my man, Benoit, to confirm that Manard will be at his villa at the shore tonight and find out what I'll have to deal with when I get there. I'm on my way to his place now."

The words filled her with panic. "No, you shouldn't go. You've found out enough. Come home."

"After I talk to Manard. He's a kingpin gambler and drug dealer. Norwalk might have just worked for him. I have to make sure."

"Then call the police or Interpol or someone else to talk to Manard."

"I have a better chance of getting the information. I have no rules to worry about. Look, Norwalk killed Sylvie and her mother. Pierpont said he stayed in that crematorium and watched Sylvie's body burn but had him stop it so he could remove the head, then finished the cremation. I'd say that would require a good deal more employee devotion than most employers could expect. I'd opt for partner or even boss."

And the hideous picture he'd drawn for her frightened her almost as much as the idea of Jock's staying and dealing with Manard. "Why?" Cara asked. "Why is this happening, Jock?"

"We'll find out. Right now, we just deal with it. Or rather, you deal with it. It's not going to be easy for you to tell Darcy."

"No." She looked out at Darcy and Michael still playing in the water. Smiles. Laughter. Life. She didn't want to bring that moment to an end. "Not easy. But it has to be done." She swallowed. "I'm not going to be able to talk you into dropping everything right now and coming here, am I?"

"It's going to be okay, Cara," he said quietly.

"That doesn't mean you're doing the right thing. I hate this. Good-bye, Jock." She pressed the disconnect. Don't think about him, or the panic would start again.

And she had her own painful job to do. Her gaze shifted back to Darcy. The golden child from *Golden Days* shimmering in the sunlight, hair wet, skin beaded with water, but beautiful, vibrant, and a smile that lit up the world around her.

But Darcy had suddenly turned to face Cara and her smile was fading as she saw her expression. Darcy waved at Michael, then was swimming swiftly back toward Cara.

And the day no longer seemed golden, but overcast as Cara got to her feet and waited for Darcy to reach the shore.

CHAPTER

7

I don't know how I'm supposed to feel," Darcy whispered. "I never thought of Felicity dying. Even when you told me about Sylvie, I thought that nothing would ever happen to my mother. She was too strong, too much in control. All my life, she controlled Sylvie and me. I even thought that maybe Sylvie's death might be a terrible mistake, and my mother would pop up with some plan that would make me dance through her hoops again."

"No terrible mistake, Darcy."

She shook her head. "No, I guess not. You're . . . sure she was killed?"

"Jock is sure."

"She must have been . . . surprised."

"I don't know. Jock thinks the entire situation surprised her. It wasn't how she was thinking the situation would be going."

Another silence.

"I'm alone now. It feels . . . strange. I guess I have to see about . . . arrangements, don't I?"

"Not at the moment. You have time. All you have to do is accept what's happened. We'll take care of everything else later."

She tried to smile. "You're being very gentle and treating me like a slightly addled child. I thank you, but I don't really need that right now. I'm sorry that my mother turned out to be a selfish bitch to the very end though it's no surprise to me. Am I supposed to applaud the fact that she didn't realize exactly what she'd done to Sylvie?" She shook her head. "Mothers are supposed to protect their children. She failed miserably, and I doubt if I'll ever forgive her. Or myself, for not seeing how far she would go and protecting Sylvie from her."

"You did everything you could. Like I told Jock, monsters."

She nodded. "I'm beginning to see that. And what do you do with monsters, Cara?" She was silent a long moment, then said softly, "You hunt them down, and you kill them."

Cara felt a ripple of shock. The words had been said so matter-of-factly and with little expression. "I can see how you'd feel that way."

"Can you? Do you know what I see?" she asked with sudden fierceness. "I can see Norwalk sitting there and watching Sylvie burn. I can see him pressing a gun to her temple and pulling the trigger. I can *see* it, Cara."

And so could she. She pulled Darcy close and held her. "I know you can see it. And that may be one of the worst things this monster has done. Don't let him destroy you the way he did Sylvie."

Darcy stiffened, then she pushed Cara away. "I won't. I wouldn't let him do that to me." She swallowed. "But that doesn't mean I won't go after him. He has to be destroyed. It *has* to be done."

"You're not exactly qualified," Cara said gently.

"That doesn't matter." She lifted her chin. "I'm a quick study. You'll see." Then she took a deep breath and jumped to her feet. "But first I have to have something to study. So don't look so worried." She pulled Cara to her feet. "Come on, let's go find Eve and tell her about Jock's call. I always feel better when I'm around her." She waved at Michael. "Hit the beach, kid," she called. "Time for a snack."

As he started to swim toward them, she turned back to Cara. "Stop frowning. It's not as if I'm going to go off like Dirty Harry until I have some kind of plan. I just have to pull myself together and see where I'm heading with this." She smiled. "But Jock and Joe are being very helpful in shining a high beam on the path ahead. Have I ever told you that you do know the most interesting men, Cara?"

And Darcy was once more being light and flip and sunny.

But something had definitely changed, Cara thought, as she and Michael followed Darcy toward the house.

And what lay beneath that smile was neither light nor sunny.

NICE, FRANCE

Jock was only forty-five minutes from Jacques Manard's house on the shore when he got the call from Benoit.

"It's about time you got back to me. For a man with your credentials, I'd think you'd be a little more—"

"I had some verifications to do," Benoit said. "For which you're going to be very grateful. If it wasn't for my keen intellect and multitude of contacts, you would have walked right into it. The police are all over the place."

Jock's hands tightened on the steering wheel. "Drugs? A raid?"

"Manard should have been so lucky. He's dead. Sniper shot from a passing motorboat while Manard was basking by the pool with his current mistress."

"*Shit.*"

"I'm sure that was Manard's last thought, too," Benoit said. "You *were* at Paillon and not indulging in water sports today?"

"I was at Paillon," he said curtly. "What's the word on the sniper?"

"Very good. Very professional. He took that shot from a motorboat, for God's sake."

"Any word on who paid?"

"Not yet. But it's curious that Manard bought it on the same day that you were so eager to touch base with him. It's good that I'm so discreet . . . and trusting."

"Try to find out who took the shot. And why."

"That means I'll have to deal with Manard's men, who are less than—"

"Deal with them. Find out. I need to know!"

He cut the connection.

LAKE PROPERTY

ATLANTA, GEORGIA

He had blood on his shoes, Norwalk realized.

Strange that the blood was on his shoes and not his hands. But then he'd been careful with his hands and worn gloves. It had been after it was finished he'd been so excited and heady with eagerness that he'd ignored the blood pool as he'd walked back to his car after he'd made the kill. Or it could be that he'd been looking at Eve's pretty cottage and thinking of the kills to come.

Careless. There was a time that he'd never have been that careless, but now it didn't seem to matter.

All that mattered was that the waiting was over now. He could start moving forward. The thought was making his heart beat harder with that same excitement.

No, the blood didn't matter at all.

"Manard's dead?" Eve repeated, stunned, as Joe hung up the phone from talking to Jock. "What the hell?"

"That's what Jock is wondering. But he's on his way back here. He's not about to stick around and collar any of Manard's men for questioning. He doesn't like the fact that Manard was taken down almost immediately after Jock found out about Norwalk's connection to the Pierpont Funeral Home."

"He thinks Norwalk is eliminating witnesses?"

Joe shrugged. "Maybe. Our report on Norwalk was that he's definitely unstable, and his actions toward Sylvie and her mother confirmed that. But he may be crazy like a fox, and he does have a team he can call on in Dublin to do his dirty work."

"Or hire a sniper to do it," Eve said. "The minute he knew we'd connected him to what was happening, he began to move. Why?" Her gaze was on the reconstruction of Sylvie on the worktable. "But it all seems to be centered on Darcy Nichols, doesn't it? Her mother, her twin sister, her suite at the residence that was burglarized."

"Which was also Cara's suite," Joe said. "That's what's putting Jock on edge. Yes, everything else seems aimed at Darcy." He muttered a curse beneath his breath and got to his feet. "But we're not sure, and I don't like that any more than Jock does. I believe I'm going to go take a stroll through the woods. Where are the girls and Michael?"

"On the porch playing cards." She glanced out the window. "The sun isn't down yet. You usually wait until dark. Any reason?"

"Nothing I can put my finger on. It could be I'm a little on edge myself." He headed for the door. "Keep everyone close. I'll be in touch."

A moment later, she heard Joe on the porch laughing and talking to Michael before he ran down the steps. A lazy summer afternoon with the kids playing games on the front porch. What could be more natural or right?

Nothing I can put my finger on.

But Joe had excellent instincts, and it was making Eve uneasy that he was feeling something was not quite right. And was it natural for Darcy to be torn apart by the horror of what had happened to her Sylvie? Or right that there was that skull sitting on Eve's worktable across the room staring out of those blue eyes so much like Darcy's?

She got to her feet and slowly moved across the room to stand before the reconstruction.

So beautiful . . . Eve was always as aware of the vulnerability and wonder in that face as she had been in that moment when she had finished her reconstruction. But perhaps she was becoming so accustomed to looking at it that she was only now seeing the tiny laugh lines about the mouth, the gentleness and humor in the curve of the lips. It was almost as if Sylvie were growing, changing . . .

Imagination? Probably. After all, Eve was the one who had created this sculpture.

No, if she had created it, she would have considered she had failed. She had merely helped Sylvie come home . . .

Her cell phone rang, and she reached into her pocket.

Joe? He had left only a short time ago. It wasn't likely that he'd call before he was on his way back.

Not Joe. She didn't recognize the number. "Eve Duncan."

"Hello, Eve. Are you ever going to send that skull to the police department?" The man's voice was deep, mocking, and with a distinct Irish accent. "I know I should be flattered that you like my work so much, but there's no way it should take you all this time."

Forensics? "What? Who is this?"

"Of course, I did offer you a challenge." His voice lowered to silky softness. "But I never thought you'd keep her this long when I gave her to you."

She couldn't breathe. She stiffened in shock. "*You* gave her to me."

"Did you like the packaging? I took a long time figuring out just what to put together to make it meaningful. After all, I had to intrigue you. There wasn't any chance that I'd let you ignore her and walk away from her, too."

"Too?"

"You're so much in demand, Eve. World-renowned, the one forensic sculptor everyone wants to hire to take those poor, broken skulls and give them some semblance of life again."

This was madness. But he knew too much. And the accent was definitely Irish. She was beginning to believe him. Her hand was trembling as she pressed the record button on her phone. "That's not what I do. I just want them identified."

"But what you want and what's needed can be entirely different," he snapped, and she could sense the barely leashed anger.

"I'm not talking to you about how I work," she said curtly. "Who are you?" She paused. "And why did you bring me Sylvie Jordan's skull?"

"I think you must know who I am." His voice was calm again. "Between your Joe Quinn and Gavin, you've made great progress. But that's fine with me. I was only waiting for you to get this far along before I indulged myself by talking to you. It's going to be a great game, Eve. I was barely holding myself in check until I had all the pawns in place so that I could start the first move. But that's done now. Quinn will tell you all about it. Actually, I thought I'd have a little more time, but you have such efficient people surrounding you, don't you?"

She braced herself to say it. "Norwalk?"

"Oh, yes. And if you know my name, you must know a good deal more about me."

"I know you killed Sylvie Jordan and her mother. I know you're a murderer and a monster." She looked down at the reconstruction of Sylvie. "Why did you do it? What did they ever do to you?"

"Nothing. They were merely a means to an end."

"Means to an end? What end?"

"Why, to you, Eve. It all ends with you." He chuckled. "At least, this part of it does. All that horror and disbelief in your voice at what happened to poor Sylvie. But it was really all your fault. I might have gone another way to get to Kaskov if I hadn't been so angry with you."

"My fault? You're crazy. I don't know you. I never met Sylvie or her mother."

"But everyone chooses to reach out or not. You chose not to reach out to me." His voice was suddenly harsh. "So that's why I decided that you had to be punished. First, it was only going to be the girl,

Cara. She was the only one who was important to Kaskov. But then I realized that you were sitting there on your pretty lake thinking that you were some kind of goddess. And you'd not only cheated me, you'd helped Kaskov by taking in his granddaughter and protecting her."

"Helped Kaskov? He's *nothing* to me. Cara is the only one who's important to me." She drew a deep breath and tried to control herself. "Why did you call me? What are you going to get out of telling me this?"

"Why, satisfaction. I want you to know what's coming. My brother, Sean, never knew, and I'm grateful." His voice was low, intense, bullet fast. "But you're going to know, feel it, taste it, as, one by one, your family dies. Did you know I almost took your son that first night? But I had to keep to the plan. I wanted you to see it happen."

"Michael." She felt a bolt of pure panic. "Don't even speak his name. I'd kill you before I'd let you touch him."

"I *will* touch him. And you'll see it, Eve. I'm going to hang up now, but I don't think I'll be able to resist phoning you again. This has been such a very satisfactory call even though I'm sure you recorded it. But that's okay, I like to think of you playing it over and over. I was feeling very much alone. I feel that way all the time now. It's good to know that I can reach out, and suddenly you're right here with me."

"Wait." She had to keep him talking. She had to know more. Everything was terrifying and crazy, but he was a threat who had to be stopped. "If this is all about me and Kaskov, why Sylvie? Why did you kill Sylvie?"

He laughed. "You weren't listening. Means to an end, Eve. Tit for tat. I needed a twin." He cut the connection.

She stood there for a moment, staring down at the phone. She felt frozen. She'd been bombarded by ugliness and monstrous shock . . . and bewilderment. Is that what Norwalk had wanted her to feel? There had been so much venom in his tone. She had no doubt he'd been telling the truth about the satisfaction he'd been feeling about exposing her to that poison. How long had he been anticipating bringing her into his cocoon of horror?

But hadn't he done that when he'd handed her that skull to reconstruct? And since that night, he'd gradually been increasing the terror and tension while remaining like a macabre shadow just out of sight. But now he felt confident enough to come out of the shadows. My God, he'd almost been boasting.

All pawns in place.

She gazed down at Sylvie's beautiful face and those parted lips that made her look so eager and alive.

Means to an end. Only a means to an end.

She felt sick.

But that would mean weakness, and she wouldn't let herself be weak because of anything that bastard had said. She drew a deep breath and turned away from Sylvie and moved across the room. Her hand was shaking a little as she dialed Joe.

He answered after the first ring. "I was just going to call you."

"Come home, Joe," she said unevenly. "I need you home. Now."

"What's *wrong*?"

She'd scared him. "Everyone's safe. But we have to talk. We have to figure this out. Everything has changed. Come right away. Okay?"

"I'm on my way. I was heading back anyway. I'm calling the precinct after I hang up from you." He added grimly, "You're right, everything's changed."

"The precinct?"

"I just found Kaskov's man, Sakov, at the far end of the lake. His throat has been cut."

"Are you going to tell us what's happening?" Cara asked Eve in a low voice as they watched the officers, techs, and plainclothesmen streaming over the far bank. "Other than the obvious. But since you've never even had anything to do with Kaskov's man, Sakov, I didn't think you'd look this shaken. You're white as a sheet, Eve."

Eve nodded tensely. "I'm fine. I'll tell you more when I figure it out myself. I have to talk to Joe first." She grimaced. "I didn't get a chance to do that before this place was overrun by all his police buddies." She glanced back at Darcy and Michael sitting on the couch watching a DVD of Darcy's *Golden Days*. "I'm just grateful that you and Darcy are distracting Michael while all this is going on."

"I had to tell him what was going on out there. There was no hiding it," Cara said. "He took it well. Like you, he'd never met him, so I think it was no shock." Her brow wrinkled. "Come to think of it, I don't think I've ever seen Michael shocked. Is that a good thing?" She shrugged. "Anyway, I'll take it that way. Look, do you want Darcy and me to take Michael to Baskin Robbins to get some ice cream after he and Darcy stop making fun of her sitcom? It would get him away from—"

"No!" Eve said sharply. "He stays on the property. All of you stay close to the house. No one takes Michael away from here."

I will touch him.

"Okay," Cara said soothingly. "Just a thought. Hey, we've got that ice-cream maker Joe used last Fourth of July. We'll take it down to the barbecue area and make our own. That's only a few feet away from the porch. Is that all right?"

Eve nodded. "That's fine. Sorry."

"No problem. To hell with Baskin Robbins." She gave Eve a hug and turned and headed toward the couch. "Don't worry, we've got this under control." She looked over her shoulder. "But let us know what's happening as soon as you can," she said quietly. "You saw how Darcy was earlier today. I think it's going to be pretty hard for her to keep herself together with bodies dropping all around us."

Eve nodded. "No secrets. We just have to figure out what's happening and what to do."

"But you said Jock was coming back."

Eve smiled ruefully. "And that makes everything all right? Sometimes it makes things more difficult, and you know it."

"But it makes me feel better," Cara said. "He just walks in a room, and everything seems brighter."

"Does it?" Eve asked gently. "Then you're very lucky to have him for a friend, aren't you?"

"Yes." Cara turned away abruptly. "I'll go in and tell Michael we're going to make ice cream."

She was gone.

Eve stared after her for a moment and shook her head. Maybe she was wrong. Not now. That was the last thing Cara needed to deal with. Block it out. Think about it later. There were too many shadows hovering over them now.

Like that Russian, Oleg Sakov, who had given his life today. He might have been a criminal, but he'd been trying to protect Cara when he'd been killed. And surely that was a bright light in a dark life.

She watched as they carefully slid Sakov into the medical examiner's van and slammed the doors.

"Is that all, Eve?" Joe asked as he gazed out the window at Cara, Darcy, and Michael in the barbecue area right below them. "You haven't forgotten anything from the beginning of the conversation before you started recording?"

"No, every word is engraved on my mind. Isn't that enough?" Eve said as she handed him his coffee. "It was enough for me, Joe. It scared me to death." She had to concentrate on keeping her hands from shaking as she raised her own cup to her lips. "Michael. He threatened Michael. He said he almost killed him that first night."

"But he didn't, and even if he'd tried, that doesn't mean he would have succeeded. Michael was within yards of us that night, and he's smart. We would have heard something if Norwalk had tried—"

"Stop being reasonable. I don't feel like being reasonable. I don't want to have *cause* to be reasonable. I want Michael safe."

"He will be safe. He *is* safe. I won't let anything happen to him." His gaze was on Michael, laughing as he churned the ice cream in the red-and-blue container. "No way. Because I'm going to gut the bastard before he lays a finger on him." He turned back to her. "But it would help if we could figure out what the son of a bitch's game plan is, so I can take him down."

Eve nodded jerkily. "I know. I've been trying to make sense of what he said for the past few hours. But every time I'd remember what he said about Michael, it would stop me cold. Which was probably exactly what he wanted. Besides, a lot of it was disjointed and obviously aimed at bringing me the most pain in the briefest time."

"Another excuse to slice him to ribbons," Joe said grimly. "That's why I'm questioning you. I know that he blew your mind."

"No, he didn't. I couldn't let him. He was enjoying it too much. But he might think he did. That would be good because it will encourage him to call again." She took a sip of her hot coffee, but it didn't make her feel less chilled. "And I needed to talk to you to get it all clear in my head. Norwalk wasn't hesitant about talking, but it's not as if he was drawing us a picture. I think he wanted to dangle some of the loose ends over my head to torment me." She moistened her lips. "Because I believe he truly hates me, Joe. I don't know why, but he kept saying things about my choices and cheating him. He threw in our taking care of Cara and helping Kaskov, but I think it was more that he had this conviction I'd cheated him."

"How?"

She shrugged. "I have no idea. But I'd better find out." She frowned. "And you can forget all that fine logic that I was spouting about Darcy Nichols being the target. From what Norwalk was saying, the main targets are me, Kaskov, and maybe Cara. Sylvie and her mother were just collateral damage, and Darcy is lost in the mix. I think that somewhere in the depths of Norwalk's particular lunacy, he has this grand plan going. He kept talking about pawns and games."

She held up two fingers. "He hates me, he hates Kaskov. And just killing either of us isn't going to be good enough for him. He wants to hurt. He talked about my family. He talked about Cara because he thought killing her might hurt Kaskov."

"And he wanted you to know you were a target."

"It was important to him. He said he wanted me to see it coming." She remembered something else. "Because his brother, Sean, hadn't seen it coming. Do we know anything about this Sean?"

"No. Norwalk's personal history was sketchy. Interpol's records were principally concerned with his IRA and drug activities. I'll dig deeper." He frowned. "But why kill Sylvie Jordan?"

"That's what I asked him, remember? He said he needed a twin."

"It doesn't make sense."

She made an impatient gesture. "I don't know what that means, either. Maybe it made some kind of sense in that twisted brain of his. What we do know is that he killed Sylvie with no more conscience than if he'd swatted a fly. She was nothing to him. A means to an end." Her lips tightened. "How am I going to go tell Darcy that?"

"With difficulty and sadness," he said quietly. "And assurances that he'll pay for it."

"That's not good enough." She looked down at the sculpture. Beautiful, gentle Sylvie, who had loved life and found joy in every moment of it. "I want to tell her how and when."

"We've just started, Eve. We'll get there."

"I don't want to just plug along. I *won't* do it." She could feel the sudden anger searing through her. "I want giant steps, Joe. He threatened Michael. He threatened you and Cara. He's feeling so confident and cocky because he was able to kill that poor woman who never hurt anyone. He killed Kaskov's man today just to show us he could do it. He probably could have killed Cara when he attacked her, but he preferred to make it a taunt and a warning." Her voice was shaking with rage as she thought about what Cara had gone through that night. "Norwalk has been sliding around in the slime like the viper he is, and now he's ready to come out? Good. I'll cut his damn head off."

"Laudable ambition," Joe said grimly. "I applaud it. Shouldn't we discuss it? How are we going to go about it?"

"By not letting him keep control of his damn game. And we can't do that until we know where he's heading and why. So that we can be there waiting for him." Her hand was no longer shaking as she set her coffee cup firmly down on the counter. "I want to know *everything* about him. Not just what he wants us to know. And I want to fill in all those blanks superfast."

"I told you I'd call Interpol right away and also get Jock on it as soon as—"

"Not fast enough." Joe was being logical and smart, but she couldn't forget Norwalk spitting out all that ugliness that had struck her to the heart. She cast a last glance down at Michael in the barbecue area. Radiant and sweet and wonderful. How dare that son of a bitch threaten her son? Did he expect her to cower in terror and fall apart because he'd told her that she couldn't stop him? Did he think she wouldn't do anything she had to do to protect him? "I know a better way." She took her phone out of her pocket. It might or might not be a better way. It had risks. She would have to maintain a constant wariness and control to survive the fallout.

Joe would not like it. Jock would hate it.

Too bad.

It would be faster and more in depth than any other way to dig out Norwalk before he found and struck down anyone else she loved.

"Eve." Joe's gaze was narrowed on her face. "Who the hell are you calling?"

"Haven't you guessed?" Her eyes were blazing with anger and recklessness as she finished punching in the number. "He wants to help her? I'm going to let him do it and help us at the same time. And if he doesn't want to do it my way, I'm going to see that he does it anyway. He's going to fill in all the blanks and give us our chance at Norwalk."

"Oh, shit," Joe murmured. "Kaskov?"

She nodded. "Kaskov."

It took Eve fifteen minutes to break through the circle of three "assistants" to get through to Kaskov, and by that time she was more on edge than ever. But after expressing her displeasure to someone called Nikolai, Kaskov came on the line.

"What a surprise, Eve," he said. "How long has it been? Sorry to keep you waiting, but you caught me at a bad time."

"I'm sure you know exactly how long it's been," she said. "Because that's how long you've been using the fact that you helped to save my life and that of my son to pressure Cara into those visits with you."

"Pressure? Cara will tell you I exerted no pressure. It's just that she understands that debts must be paid, and she possesses that rare quality known as honor. I have no idea where she acquired it." He added mockingly, "Certainly not from me."

"But you've taken advantage of it."

"I believe you realize that I will always seize the advantage to get my way. I have a certain reputation to uphold. Cara understood that from the night she asked me to help you." He paused. "But I don't believe that you called me to discuss either my practices or morals, did you?"

"No, but I think my call caught you off guard, and you were scrambling to find out any information you could to maintain the upper hand. That's why you kept me waiting."

"Quite right." He sounded amused. "You're very important in Cara's life, and I wanted to be prepared. You've kept yourself very distant from my arrangement with Cara."

"No, I didn't," she said bluntly. "I tried to talk her out of it."

"She never told me that. But then she's very protective of you, and she doesn't really trust me."

"Imagine that," she said dryly. "So what did you find out while you were keeping me waiting?"

"Not enough. Oleg Sakov hasn't reported in to Nikolai since early this morning. All was well at that time. It made me a bit uneasy. But Joe Quinn is far more competent than Sakov, and I'm not really concerned about Cara." He paused. "But this call indicates something disturbing that I should probably address."

"You're damn right," she said. "We found Sakov with his throat cut earlier today. I received a call from the man who did it and attacked Cara. You told Cara you had nothing to do with that attack, but you did."

"You're wrong," he said quietly. "I told her the truth."

"Oh, you had something to do with it," she said curtly. "And so did I. Cara believes you, so I have to do it, too. But that wacko who's responsible has targeted both of us, and that means we both did something to piss him off. It's logical that it's tied together."

"You and I?" he said mockingly. "What good company I'm keeping. However, since Cara will surely blame me if you get hurt or killed, it would be wise for me to remove you from the equation."

"That's not going to happen since my family has been threatened, and so has Cara," she said grimly. "So we're going to continue to keep company until we catch that son of a bitch and my family is safe." She went on quickly before he could reply. "I'm going to play my phone call from Norwalk for you now. You listen and see if you recognize the voice or if anything he says strikes a chord."

"As you command. I'll record it, too, for further review."

She started the recording and leaned back in her chair. She glanced at Joe, sitting across the room. "I know you want to jump in and talk to him yourself."

"You bet I do."

"Not now. I'm right, Joe. He understands targets and also that Cara will be upset if he doesn't listen to me."

"I know." He smiled. "I'll have my turn."

"No question." The recording had finished, and she went back on the line. "Did you recognize his voice, Kaskov?"

"No. Heavy Irish accent. I would have remembered it. But I'll let my men listen to it and see if they recognize it." He paused. "Crazy. You're right, he's wacko. He'll be dangerous to handle. He won't care."

"And I think he has some kind of master strategy or something. He's been planning this for a long time." She sketched in the connection with Sylvie and Darcy. "That's what I was asking Norwalk about."

"And the reason Jock Gavin hopped a plane for Nice," Kaskov added. He was silent for an instant. "You handled this poorly, Eve. You let him see how frightened you are. Men like Norwalk drink fear in like blood. It excites them, and it's addictive. They want more and more."

She knew he might be right. She'd been able to sense Norwalk's intense pleasure as he'd threatened her. "He made me angry." Admit it. "And, yes, he frightened me. Michael, Cara, Joe . . . No one is safe from him. He *will* do it, Kaskov."

"Yes, he will. I have no doubt of it. So what do you want from me, Eve?"

"I want you to find out what he's planning, and why, and how I can stop him."

"The stopping is easy," he said coolly. "I'll kill him. The finding and trapping is what's difficult. Norwalk has a head start, and he's not stupid. He managed to confuse the issue, and hide his agenda for quite a while." He was silent. "And as far as you're concerned, he wins every time he takes out anyone you care about."

"And wouldn't he win out over you if he took out Cara?"

"Yes, but you can see I have a much narrower target area."

Yes, she could see that. "But then you have a much narrower life."

Silence. "It's a matter of opinion, isn't it? Your situation may prove complicated for us both. I suppose you wouldn't consider sending Cara to me for safekeeping?"

"I've already been considering it." She saw Joe stiffen and put up her hand to stop him from interfering. "It was my first thought when I realized she'd be in danger. You're not the guardian I'd choose in a million years, but I believe you could keep her safe at that place in New Orleans. Jock said that estate where you live in Moscow is almost impregnable."

"He should know. I believe he was planning an invasion at one point. So send her to me." Silence. Then he added, "You have my word I'll send her back to you when the threat is over."

"Your word? I have no idea what that's worth."

"Neither do I. It ebbs and flows with the situation. But I think that I'd be forced to keep it in this case. Cara can be so difficult."

"Yes, she can. Which is why I can't send her to you. The minute she finds out what's happening, there's no way that she'd leave us. She considers us family."

Another silence. "So I've been told. As you say, difficult. Will Quinn permit me to send another guard to the property? That will have to do until I find a way to persuade Cara that her allegiance should be with me."

"I don't see any reason why not. Except that you've already lost one man, and it may not do any good. Norwalk evidently had no problem taking him out."

"And I don't like that. Norwalk must be very good. Oh, well, I'll find out."

"You'll do it?" she asked quickly. "You'll find out what I need to know?"

"My dear, Eve, it's also what I need to know, remember? It's that advantage thing again. I'll know everything there is to know about Norwalk in twenty-four hours. And hopefully neither of us will be dead in that time, and neither will anyone of importance to either of us. Will that be satisfactory?"

"I'm not certain. I don't know if I can trust you to call me and tell me what's happening. I believe your instinct would be to take care of Norwalk yourself."

"Quite right. That might be the most efficient way."

"*Your* way. I don't want him disappearing and not be sure what had happened. I need to know my family is safe. I don't trust you or anyone else. Do you think we're going to stop going after Norwalk because I've brought you into it? I want you to contribute, not dominate. You find the information, you call me, Kaskov. Understand?"

"I understand you may be every bit as difficult as Cara," he said dryly. "I'm not at all sure that your influence on her should continue to be tolerated. I'll have to think about it."

"You do that," Eve said. "In the meantime, you get your ass busy gathering the information that might keep her alive. We'll expect that call from you in twenty-four hours."

Silence. "And what would you do if you didn't get it?" he asked silkily.

She could hear the edge, and she should back down. She knew he was one of the most dangerous men on the planet. But she was tired and scared, and he had to know that she would go to any lengths to stop Norwalk. "I'd go after you. I'd find a way to make you do it," she said wearily. "It's the only thing I could do. I need you, Kaskov."

He didn't answer for a moment. "Yes, you do." Then he added crisply, "So speak with more courtesy to me the next time we talk. You mustn't hurt my feelings. Most people find that an exceptionally foolish thing to do."

"I can see how they might. Do you want me to apologize? You probably deserve it."

"No, I believe we'll chalk it up to stress. I'd judge you're much more diplomatic in the usual way. I recall even when your life and that of the child were on the line all those years ago, you behaved well. We seem to come together at periods that aren't in the least usual."

"Don't count on my behaving in a civilized manner right now. And there's no way you'll see diplomacy when we find Norwalk. He said he was going to kill my son." She had to get off the phone. Stressed wasn't the word for what she was feeling right now. "Good-bye, Kaskov. I'll expect your call."

"And you'll probably get it." He paused. "But I'm not certain what else you might get, Eve. I don't take orders, and I don't remember the last time I wasn't in control. You should keep that in mind."

A warning? Who could be sure? Kaskov was always an enigma. "I'll remember." She pressed the disconnect.

She looked at Joe and made a face. "I didn't handle that well. Do you think I'm on a hit list?"

"I think you were skating on extremely thin ice," he said quietly. "But I don't believe I'll have to go take him down to keep him from turning loose the big dogs on you. There were a few moments where it came close."

"But you believe he'll do what I asked?"

"Yes." He got to his feet and came across the room. "But if something changes, I don't know which way he'll jump. No one knows with Kaskov." He reached down and pulled her to her feet. "But what I do know is that there wouldn't have been those few harsh words if you hadn't been stretched to the limit." He took her in his arms and rocked her back and forth. "And I believe that's why Kaskov didn't blow. No one speaks to Kaskov that way, particularly if they're asking favors."

"It was to his advantage to do—" She nestled her head in the hollow of his shoulder. "Advantage. There's that word again. If he really cares anything about Cara, he would have wanted to do it anyway. But who the hell knows what he's feeling?" She lifted her head. "What do we do now, Joe?"

"Oh, I finally get asked my opinion?" He smiled down at her.

"You've been exploding on all cylinders and making outlandish decisions since I walked in that door. Now I get to join in?"

"Not so outlandish. And it was Michael . . . and Cara."

"And your maternal instincts were turning you into a female terminator. I could see it happening before my eyes. Maybe Kaskov could sense it, too." He kissed her gently. "It's okay, Eve. I believe it's dangerous dealing with Kaskov on any level, but it could be a smart move. I just wasn't prepared to roll the dice anytime soon."

"He's a target. Even if Cara wasn't involved, he'd have reason to go after Norwalk."

"But he's had decades of making deals and looking the other way if it was to his ultimate advantage. He's a brilliant man and not driven by revenge or violence unless it suits him."

"Well, I did roll the dice," she said grimly. "And I just have to hope we don't end up with snake eyes."

"We'll hedge our bets." He checked his watch. "Jock should be arriving at the airport any time now. We'll see what he has in mind." He turned her toward the door. "In the meantime, let's go down and sample Michael's homemade ice cream. Or rather, *I'll* sample it. I'll keep Michael occupied and you can have some later. I think it's time you played that recording for Cara and Darcy."

CHAPTER

8

BELLE GRACE
MORGANA, LOUISIANA

"The woman was not respectful," Nikolai said quietly. "Do you wish me to do something about it?"

"No." Kaskov smiled as he gazed down at his phone. Nikolai had been with him for many years, and he was sometimes even more conscious than Kaskov of the dangers of his being thought weak by the people around him. There were rules that must be followed, or the organization could disintegrate into chaos. And since he *was* the organization, that meant he would disappear when that chaos occurred. "It will not happen again. Eve Duncan was disturbed. She didn't realize there would be consequences. Nothing must happen to her." He met Nikolai's eyes. "Nothing."

"I only asked," Nikolai said. "Brazoff was also in the room and recording that phone message. He's not been with you long enough to realize that sometimes you have agendas that supersede the rules."

"Then make certain he does realize it." He smiled. "Which I'm sure you were going to do anyway, my friend." He moved toward the window and gazed out at the gardens, which gave way to the lush shrubbery of the bayous a short distance away. "You heard Sakov is dead. Find out if he has family and send him home to them."

"Yes, sir," Nikolai said. "Do I have your permission to increase the guards around this property? There seems to be a threat to you."

"When isn't there a threat?" He added mockingly, "Yes, by all means make it even more of an armed camp than it is already. I can't have that madman take me down. It would be a terrible end to my illustrious career."

"My thought exactly, sir." Nikolai was smiling faintly. "And we should find this Norwalk and not wait for him to pounce? It would be more efficient to set a trap."

"Yes, it would." He turned and pressed the remote button on his stereo. "But that would mean I could lose more than I gained." The strains of the Tchaikovsky concerto Cara had played at the concert in Connecticut swept through the room. "We'll do both. Find him, then I'll make up my mind whether to do it the safe, efficient way or keep my word to Eve Duncan."

ATLANTA AIRPORT

Jock's phone rang as he was coming down the jetway.

Joe Quinn.

He waited until he'd reached the gate area before he answered the call. "I just arrived. I should be at the lake cottage in thirty minutes. Is Cara okay?"

"Probably not as well as before Eve told her about the call she received from Norwalk," Joe said. "We were trying to spare her until we had a handle on what to do, but that usually doesn't work with Cara."

"What call?" Jock asked harshly. "And why the hell didn't you phone me?"

"You were on a plane heading here anyway. We had enough to do without bothering to keep you in the loop. Kaskov's man, Sakov, was killed today, throat cut. Bloody footprints leading to a car parked near the freeway." He paused. "And it's no coincidence that Eve got that call from Norwalk later on the same day. I'm sending you the recording, and you'll see what I mean. Check it out while you're on the road here. I want you up to speed by the time you talk to Cara . . . and Eve. Eve made a few decisions that—" He broke off. "Later. She'll tell you herself. Just get here, and we'll talk about possible damage control. The important thing to realize is that Norwalk isn't hiding in the shadows any longer. He's on the attack."

"How can I realize anything until you let me hear that damn call that—" He stopped as his phone buzzed. "Hold on. I'm getting a text." He punched the button for text access. "It's from Benoit. I'll be—" He started to curse. "Son of a bitch!"

"What's wrong?"

"What could be wrong? Certainly not with your estimation of the current situation," he said through his teeth. "Yes, Norwalk's def-initely on the move, and taking no prisoners. Benoit just got a report that Raoul Napier was found shot in his hotel room in Nice last night. And this morning, the Pierpont Funeral Home was blown up, taking father and son and any evidence that might remain with them to the Pearly Gates."

He was here!

Cara was waiting on the porch when the headlights of Jock's rental car speared the darkness of the risers of the steps as he pulled into the driveway. But she couldn't wait anymore. She ran down the steps as he got out of the driver's seat.

It seemed forever since she had said good-bye to him at the air-port in New York. Just a few days, but too much had taken place in those days. She had been worried and sad and empty inside without—

"Jock!" She threw herself into his arms and held him with all her might. "I'm so glad you're here. So many bad things . . . Joe said he told you, but there's Darcy and Silvie and now Eve . . . Is it my fault that Eve's going through all—"

"Shh." His hand was over her mouth. "None of it is your fault. Norwalk is a crazy son of a bitch who wants to hurt Kaskov by hurting you. It was what I've been afraid would happen for years. As for the rest with Eve, I haven't a clue. But we'll find out and make it right." He took his hand away and smiled down at her. "I promise."

He was making it right just by being here and smiling that smile, she thought. She drew a deep breath. And it was okay that she wanted to touch him. He was touching her with affection and tenderness as he always did. Nothing had really changed. Best friends, she repeated to herself. Best friends forever. She took a step back and smiled at him. "I knew that. I just wanted to hear it from you." She took his hand and pulled him up the steps to the porch. "Except about Eve. It could be that her taking me in caused Norwalk to target her, but she believes it's something else." She made a face. "I hope she's right. It may be wishful thinking on her part, too. I'm in good company."

"Yes, you are."

"Eve wants to see you right away. But I wanted to see you more, so I waited out here until you came roaring up the driveway." She chuckled. "I knew you wouldn't be in any mood to give me anything but frowns after she talks to you about Kaskov."

He stiffened. "Kaskov?"

She nodded. "She told Joe that telling you was her responsibility. But I'd bite the bullet for her if she'd let me. She's had a really bad time with Darcy after that damn call from Norwalk." Her lips tightened. "He killed Sylvie for nothing, Jock."

"Or to make a statement."

She shook her head. "It sounds like nothing to me. And I don't need to tell you how it sounded to Darcy. She loved her, Jock."

Jock's gaze was on the door. "What's it have to do with Kaskov?"

She nodded. "And you can't get that out of your mind, can you?

Go on. You're not going to like it, but she was right, Jock. And don't you give her a hard time, do you hear me? I'm not the only one that she has to worry about, that we all have to worry about."

"She was *right*?" He repeated as he was heading for the door. "If you're that defensive, I don't think I'm going to agree."

The door closed behind him.

She didn't think he would agree either, she thought as she turned back to look at the lake. Particularly since he'd been proven right about the threat being targeted at her and Kaskov. Yet she could see how Eve would go to any lengths to make sure Michael was safe after that hideous threat to him. Cara felt the same way. She'd do anything to keep that monster who had killed Sylvie away from Michael.

"Cara."

She turned to see Darcy coming out the door. "Hi, come and keep me company. Are you hiding out from all the flak flying around in there? Do I need to go in and throw Jock out?"

"No, Eve can take care of herself." Darcy came out and stood beside her as she added absently, "Though I can see why you'd feel so protective of her. You love her. Defending her is also a way of defending your life with her. It's almost a form of self-defense."

"Good God." She shook her head as she stared at Darcy. "Where did all that come from?"

"I took a few courses in psychology here and there. I was pretty messed up, and I had to learn how to sift through the bullshit." She smiled without mirth. "Though I may have to take a few more lessons to see my way through what's happening now. I'm having big-time trouble understanding that beast, Norwalk."

"There's no understanding. As you said, beast."

"But I *have* to understand," Darcy said fiercely. "I have to understand everything about him. You heard what he said on that call. Sylvie didn't really exist. She was nothing to him. I'm nothing to him. But there had to be a reason that two people whom he thought had no value were still important to him. I've been thinking about that ever since Eve played back that call. I couldn't think of anything else."

Cara could see that. She had never seen Darcy so intense. She had been afraid that callous call might break her, but instead it appeared to have caused her to strengthen, totally focused. And Cara had to focus, too. Help her find an answer. "Twins," Cara said. "He said he needed a twin."

"But why?" Darcy murmured. "I was so upset and angry the first time I heard it that I couldn't think of anything other than that Sylvie had been nothing to him. But then I played it again, and a few lines jumped out at me. When he was saying good-bye to Eve, Norwalk was telling her that talking to her made him feel like he was no longer alone. And that he always felt alone these days."

"So?"

"That's how I felt when I lost Sylvie," she said simply. "I may have mentioned it to you. She was always with me, then she . . . wasn't."

Cara went still. "Because you were twins."

She nodded. "Twins." She looked out at the lake. "I know it sounds weird, but what I told you about the bond between Sylvie and me wasn't limited to just us. Look it up. It's been medically documented. There have been all kinds of tests, zillions of explanations why it occurs. The result is that nobody really knows why, it's just *there*."

"I wasn't doubting you," Cara said. "I didn't understand, but I know that there's too much going on in this world for me to question anything if I trusted the person saying it. I trust you, Darcy." She paused. "So what are you saying?"

"I'm saying Norwalk needed a twin for his master plan, so he killed Sylvie. What did he say? Tit for tat?"

"That's what he said." Cara was gazing at Darcy's face. "And that could mean because he'd lost a twin, he was taking another one away as some kind of revenge?"

"Sick. But that's what he is, right? I don't know why he did it. A statement? Whatever. But it meant something to him. A twin always *means* something. You have no idea how powerful that pull can be. Since Norwalk is clearly a psychopath, it might be a completely different dynamic than that between a normal set of twins, but the loss would still be mind-blowing."

"Like yours?" Cara asked softly.

"Yes." She glanced back at Cara. "But this isn't about me and Sylvie right now. It's about Sylvie and that devil who killed her. That's what I'm trying to focus on now."

She nodded. "And if he's lost his twin, does that mean his twin is dead?"

"That's what it meant with me."

"Did you tell Eve?"

She shook her head. "Not yet." She swallowed hard. "I've just been piecing it all out after I recovered from listening to that damn call. And it's just guesswork right now. But it makes sense to me."

"It makes sense to me, too." She was mentally going over Norwalk's call. "Sean. He mentioned a Sean. His twin?"

Darcy shrugged. "Possible. I don't know. I've given you all I have. I thought it might help to track Norwalk down."

"I don't believe Interpol said anything about Norwalk's having a twin brother."

Darcy's lips twisted. "But no one knew I had a twin either. Check it out." She moved over to the swing and sat down. "But I'm still confused about all this. It seems like the tip of the iceberg. Maybe this Kaskov will be able to find out more. Eve seemed to believe he could." She stared Cara in the eye. "What do you think?"

"Eve's very smart."

"That's no answer. You know your grandfather better than Eve, better than anyone. Can he help me?"

"Me?" she repeated quietly. "This isn't only about you, Darcy. We're all in this fight together."

She was silent. "I know that." Her lips twisted. "But I sometimes forget. I spent all my life being number one. Number one in the spot-light. Number one in responsibility. Number one behind the eight ball." She wrinkled her nose. "Though that last doesn't make much sense, does it? You know what I mean."

"Yes, I do." She sat down beside her and took her hand. "And number one when Sylvie was left behind. You don't want her left behind this time."

"She can't be left behind," Darcy said fiercely. "I won't let that happen." Her hand tightened on Cara's. "So tell me about Kaskov."

"You're expecting more than I may be able to give. Can he find out the information we need to know? Probably. If he chooses to do it."

"Will he choose to do it? You're a target. He must care some-thing about you, or he wouldn't want you to spend a month with him every year. That's sort of sentimental, so he can't be that tough."

Cara looked at her incredulously. "Sentimental? Kaskov doesn't know the meaning of the word. Tough? He walks in the room, and everyone else fades away."

"Do you fade away?"

"Not when I'm playing for him, but that's the only time I know I have any value for him. It's the music. It's always the music."

"Why?"

"He grew up in a work camp in Siberia. His mother was a vio-linist. Kaskov was going to be a musician. But one of the guards smashed the bones in his hands. It ruined his chance of a career as a performer." She grimaced. "So he told me that he went in 'another direction' to reach the top. Evidently, he reached that goal when he was in his twenties and never let go. In Moscow, he's not only a pre-mier crime boss, but he controls a good many of the political parties that come and go. He's a contributor to the arts, and he even funds scholarships to various music academies. He's extremely clever, com-pletely ruthless, and he never lets down his guard." She moistened her lips. "Which makes it almost laughable that Norwalk thinks he can take him down."

"Unless he can strike at an Achilles' heel. Does he have any other family?"

She shook her head. "Just me. His mother died years ago. He had two children—Natalie, my mother, and his son. They're both dead now. I'm not sure how his son died, but I heard a few years ago that my mother had been killed in a helicopter accident."

"You *heard*?"

"We weren't close. Never." She made an impatient gesture. "Enough. Norwalk won't find any weakness in Kaskov as far as family is concerned."

"I'll take your word for it," she said. "And I'll back off, Cara. I haven't forgotten my promise. I just had to know. I might—We might need to use him."

"Eve is already going down that route. I gathered she wasn't entirely sure she'd handled it right."

"I received the same impression." She was frowning. "Would you mind if I seduced him?"

"What? Who?"

"Kaskov. I could probably do it. And that would solidify any chance we might have to—"

"Yes, I would mind," she said in exasperation. "First, you're going to seduce Jock, and now Kaskov? That's playing with fire, Darcy. I thought I'd made that clear. That's crazy."

"No, it's Sylvie," she said quietly. "Sex is only a fun game to me, and I wouldn't use it ordinarily. But all the rules are off now. However, if it upsets you, we'll have to find another way."

"It upsets me," Cara said positively. "And besides, the last I heard, Kaskov has a mistress who's a diva in the Bolshoi Opera."

"No problem. I could overcome." She smiled. "But I can't overcome you, Cara. I've never had a friend like you." She released her hand. "And now that I've thoroughly rattled you, why don't you go inside and be referee between Eve and Jock, while I sit here and think more about Norwalk's call."

"Are you trying to get rid of me? You said that Eve didn't need me."

"That doesn't change the fact that you have a need to help her."

And that Darcy might need to be alone to recover from the agony of that call, an agony that she'd managed to submerge while she tried to find something of value in the message. "True." Cara got to her feet. "I'd hate to prove all your psychological mumbo jumbo about my relationship with Eve is a total fallacy." She moved toward the door. "I'm off to the rescue."

"Cara."

She looked over her shoulder.

Darcy was smiling curiously. "You said that when Kaskov walked into a room everyone else faded away . . . Did Jock Gavin fade away?"

Kaskov standing warily at the bar in the anteroom of his box at the theater in Moscow, tall, broad, powerful with his gray-streaked hair and that aura of total dominance and power.

Jock standing looking at him, slim, sleek, lithe, his silver eyes glittering with intensity. Eager, ready, his entire body like a stiletto poised to strike.

She shook her head. "No, Jock didn't fade away."

"I didn't think so. And what did Kaskov do? What was his reaction?"

"He wanted to own Jock. He tried to hire him."

"Now that's a truly intelligent man . . . and even more dangerous than anything else you've told me about him." She smiled. "Or maybe not. Don't we all want to own Jock? Don't answer that." She looked back at the lake. "That was a little too close to the edge . . ."

Yes, it had been, Cara thought as she opened the door. Not because Darcy had reminded her how desirable Jock was in so many ways. Because it had brought back memories of that night that Jock had risked everything to guarantee that Kaskov would keep his word to save Eve and her child.

"I was wondering when you would show up to check casualties," Jock said, as she came into the house. He was sitting at the kitchen bar with a glass of whiskey in his hand. "I would have come to you after I had a drink. I needed it."

"Where's Eve?"

"Putting Michael to bed, and probably telling Joe that I was more civilized than she'd thought I'd be." He lifted his glass to his lips. "All an act, Cara. I'm not feeling at all civilized."

"And Eve would realize that. She wasn't looking forward to your reaction." She paused. "None of us were."

"Because you all knew I'd have found a way to have prevented it if I'd been here."

She shook her head. "No one could have prevented it once Eve made up her mind. Even Joe couldn't have done it."

"I'd have found a way." He took another drink. "It's what I've been dreading for years." His hand tightened on the glass. "Hell, I could *see* it coming. And now she's joining forces with the devil who could destroy you?"

"Eve thinks he can help." She came closer to him. "And the reason everyone was afraid for you to know was that they were afraid you'd do something that would make that impossible."

"And is that what you thought?" His lips twisted. "Am I going to do that, Cara?"

"No, you're going to hate it, but you'll find a way to do what you think has to be done without damaging what Eve has set up with Kaskov." She met his eyes. "Because you wouldn't want to take the chance that she might be right, and you'd run the risk of spoiling a way of winding this up quickly." She smiled faintly. "Is that what you told her?"

He was silent a moment. "No, I wasn't that generous. I was too pissed off. I told her what she'd done was dangerous, and it might be hard to pull her out of the fire."

She nodded. "But she'd recognize that as a tacit acknowledgment that you'd accept it and be ready to do the extraction." She added, "So she felt comfortable about leaving you and going to put Michael to bed." She nodded. "And you thought a stiff drink is what you needed to bring that frustration and anger down to a low simmer. Too bad MacDuff isn't here. He's your favorite drinking partner. He would have been glad to join you."

"You think you can read me so well?" he said softly. "In this particular situation, I'm finding that particularly annoying."

"Of course I can read you. Not as well as you can read me. You sometimes say one thing and mean another. I'm clear as glass, and I never try to hide anything from you."

"Yet I've been feeling lately that you might be trying to do that." His gaze was narrowed on her face. "I believe I mentioned that before. Now isn't the time for secrets, Cara."

She suddenly couldn't breathe. She wanted to reach out and *touch* him. She had made a mistake and blundered into that area that was causing her to—

Back out. Don't reach toward him. But don't run away, that would be worse.

Distract him.

"Hiding something? Because I know that you and MacDuff usually have a drink when you're together?" She looked at his whiskey. "Though how the two of you can stand that stuff, I'll never know. Perfectly foul, Jock. The one time I ordered one, I nearly choked."

"Ordered one?" He tilted his head. "Just where did you order a whiskey?"

"Phoenix. We went out after a charity concert to a party at the home of one of the benefactors, and I ordered one from the bartender. So it was kind of legal."

"Were you with Darcy?"

"No, that was before I knew her. She doesn't drink much anyway. But she does believe in experimenting. So I should probably go with her if I try anything else. Right?"

"You could wait awhile. You're only eighteen."

"But I told you, it was almost legal. These days there are all kinds of exception laws about liquor in private homes." She looked at the whiskey again. "I have to find out what I like, and I don't like. Experimenting is important. The older I get, the more aware I am that I should experience everything. Don't you agree that—" She stopped as she met his gaze. She had been rattling on, but she suddenly realized she was in deep waters. She inhaled sharply. Too far? "Jock?"

"Not the time for this, Cara," he said quietly. "I don't know quite what you're doing, but I believe that you're playing me. You know I'm very protective, and what you said would send up red flags. If you recall, my own experiments when I was even younger than you almost destroyed me. I want everything for you, but I prefer a controlled environment." He tossed back the rest of his whiskey and set the glass on the bar. "We'll discuss experimentation later." He moved toward the door. "But right now, I intend to set about 'doing what has to be done' to safeguard us all from Kaskov."

"Now? You just got here," she said. "And I meant to tell you that Darcy thinks that Norwalk had a twin who perhaps was killed. We were going to tell Eve and Kaskov."

"Don't bother with Kaskov. I'll tell him myself."

The door shut behind him.

Kaskov?

She stood there a moment, her hands clenched into fists. She had rushed forward with the first thing that she thought might distract him from seeing too much, and it could have been the wrong way to go. He'd been in an explosive mood anyway, and she might have driven him to be more reckless.

No, she knew he would do whatever he intended to do anyway. And when he did it, there would be no recklessness, just cold, precise efficiency. The exact response she had been hoping never to see in him again.

But it had been a foolish hope in a situation like this, she thought wearily. The trigger was there, and Jock would pull it. All the more reason to get this over and everyone safe.

The twin.

She started across the living room and down the hall. She had to tell Eve about the twin who might have been the reason for all this madness.

And break the news that Jock was going to see Kaskov to inform him himself.

BELLE GRACE

MORGANA, LOUISIANA

4:40 A.M.

The last move.

Jock slid out of the secret compartment in the hall wall and closed it behind him.

He glided silently down the hall toward the bedroom.

No security alarms on the bedroom door itself.

But it was Kaskov who was behind that door, and that was always the principal danger, Jock thought.

He soundlessly opened the door and slipped inside into darkness. He could see the king-size bed across the room. And the shape of a man beneath the covers in that bed.

Enough.

He had reached his objective. He dropped into a brocade chair beside the door. "Kaskov," he said softly.

The man on the bed was instantly awake. His body language changed, became tense, ready. "You're dead, you know."

"No, I don't know." Jock turned on the lamp on the table beside him. "But the attempt might have been enjoyable enough to be worth it. Hello, Kaskov."

"Gavin." A little of the tension left Kaskov's muscles. "I should have known." He sat up in bed. "I'm glad we found the means to keep you entertained. How did you get into the compound?"

"With difficulty." He smiled. "And I have no intention of telling you how. I might need to use it some other time. But you'll be glad to know that your men were all alert and fairly competent. I only had to put one down, and I didn't have to make it permanent."

"Thank you," he said dryly. "Since I had Nikolai put on extra guards today, I wouldn't want to feel the effort was wasted." He paused. "The man you put down wasn't Nikolai by any chance?"

"No, I remember from our former encounter that you have a fondness for him. I didn't want to start off on the wrong foot."

Kaskov stared at him, then chuckled. "You don't think invading my turf . . . and my bedroom is starting off on the wrong foot? Nikolai would say that such a show of disrespect could have only one ending."

"But I didn't kill you," Jock said. "He might agree that you should grant me a pardon." He leaned back in the chair. "And I'll let him know most of the weaknesses in his compound defenses, and that should please him. You can tell him that I was just doing a test run."

"You locked him in the trunk of my limo in Moscow. He's not likely to believe me."

"We were on opposite sides at the time." He met his eyes. "I understand that's changed."

Kaskov gave a low whistle. "You're angry. That's what this is about." He studied him. "You don't trust me. You don't like the power I can wield. You're afraid I'll take a step too far and get Cara killed."

"All of the above," Jock said. "Or get in my way and keep me from stopping that son of a bitch from killing her."

"Serious concerns." He was silent. "I wish to get out of bed. I have a gun in the drawer of the nightstand and a knife in that drawer in the table you're sitting beside. Those are my most obvious weapons. The others I will have more difficulty getting to. May I get a cup of coffee from my automatic coffeemaker across the room on that buffet?"

"Of course. As you can see, I have no weapon."

"Is that supposed to make me feel secure enough to attack? You are angry." He was shrugging into his robe. "And you *are* the weapon, Gavin." He strode across the carpeted floor to the buffet. "And you'd like nothing better than to remove my troubling presence from Cara's life. But your unique skill isn't enough in this case. As long as she feels a debt, she won't permit you to do as you wish. And I shall continue to find ways to increase that feeling of gratitude. So it appears we may be stuck with each other for the foreseeable future." He turned and smiled. "Coffee, Gavin?"

"No, I believe that we'll be disturbed in about three minutes, and I want to have my hands free."

"Because you were compassionate and didn't kill that guard."

"Compassion had nothing to do with it. I want you to have a full complement of men when Norwalk goes after you. He's the enemy . . . at the moment."

"Yes, at the moment." He took a sip of his coffee. "How often during the last three times when Cara was visiting me have you been tempted to breach my walls to show me you could do it?"

Jock didn't answer.

"But this was different," Kaskov said softly. "You felt that it wouldn't cause the ripple of disturbance and make Cara feel you were interfering. And it let me see that the threat was always there." He tilted his head. "Now why else did you come tonight?"

"To tell you that Norwalk probably had a twin, and it might have had something to do with the targets he chose. You and Eve specifically." He got to his feet. "And to ask if you had any information you haven't told Eve yet."

He shook his head. "Though I assure you I'm being very proactive. And I'm certain you have a few ideas on the matter you'd like to share?"

"Norwalk has to have had something to do with you."

"I never dealt with him. He never crossed my path."

"Yet he attacked Cara. That was quite pointed." He smiled faintly. "Maybe, like me, he wanted to show you that you're vulnerable. But he went to a great deal of trouble. He wanted you to know he could take her, kill her, and you could do nothing about it." His smile vanished. "And he was right, he came damn close. Next time, he'll try to go all the way. But why go to all that trouble just to make a point?" His gaze was narrowed on Kaskov's face. "Why, Kaskov?"

Kaskov's face was without expression. He repeated, "I had nothing to do with him."

"But you might have a hunch?" he murmured. "Something I said triggered something. I believe I might want to stick around while you think about it."

"Not a good idea," Kaskov said. "I prefer that your expertise be leveled at protecting my granddaughter. I might let you know once I've firmed up—"

"They're at the end of the hall," Jock interrupted, his head tilted as he listened. "At least three men trying to be quiet. Probably your Nikolai is with them. What are you going to do?"

"I should ask what you're going to do."

"If attacked, I leave the house and the compound. I always have an exit plan. But first, I'd kill Nikolai, then you. My problems would be solved."

He chuckled. "And very efficiently." He finished his coffee. "But I prefer a more peaceful solution today. I shall invite you to breakfast, and you'll discuss the fallacies in my security arrangements with Nikolai. However, I agree that you should let him believe that it was totally my idea." He was heading for the door and glanced back over his shoulder. "By the way, you should never have been able to breach those defenses without extensive research and time. How did you do it?"

He shrugged. "You invited Cara to New Orleans three months

ago. When I was in Moscow on my 'hunting' trip, I delved into your possible rentals in New Orleans. There were only two that would have been suitable for your needs. I researched the history of the houses and the architectural plans and studied both of them."

"Just in *case* you needed them? You were trained well."

Jock's lips twisted. "Oh, yes, exceptionally well." He moved across the room. "You'll notice I'm directly behind you. If you change your mind when you open that door, I can break your neck before you take another breath."

"Not before breakfast." Kaskov smiled as he threw open the door. "I'm always hungry when I'm forced to wake this early."

CHAPTER
9

"Can't sleep?" Eve was standing in the hall gazing at Darcy, who was sitting at Eve's worktable staring at Sylvie's reconstruction. "Neither could I." She tightened the belt of her robe as she came toward Darcy. "I kept thinking about Norwalk and . . . You know what I was thinking about." She reached out and touched the cheek of the sculpture with her index finger. "All the time I was working on her I felt as if every stroke I took was taking away the horror he was trying to make of her."

"And you did it," Darcy said. "She's beautiful now." She leaned back on the stool. "And I was thinking about how Norwalk told you how alone he felt . . ."

"Because you thought he also had a twin."

"Yes, and how I've been feeling that way, too, for the past few months." Darcy's gaze never left Sylvie. "He probably wanted me to feel that way, and I don't know why. If he does have a twin, he knows about the emptiness. He said Sylvie and I weren't important, so does he want the whole world to feel that emptiness?"

"It wouldn't surprise me."

"Then I think that he's going to be disappointed." She touched the delicate curl of Sylvie's lower lip. "At least as far as I'm concerned.

I've noticed for the last couple days that I'm not feeling . . ." She stopped and moistened her lips. "I don't feel that emptiness any longer, Eve. I know you probably don't realize what that means . . . I'm not sure I do, either. But it's gone . . ."

"I don't know what you mean. How could I?" She touched her shoulder gently. "I hope it's because you know that we all care about you. And that we won't let you be alone."

She nodded jerkily. "Yes, I know that, and I've never felt more . . . it's very strange and wonderful for me. But that's not what this is about." She looked down at the bright blue eyes of the sculpture. "I feel as if she's coming . . . closer to me. It's as if she's just out of reach but coming closer all the time. Crazy, huh? Sylvie's dead. You showed me what he did to her. But it doesn't seem to matter. I can *feel* her."

"Not so crazy. Unless you don't want it to happen." She was silent a moment. "Did Cara tell you about my daughter, Bonnie, who died when she was only seven?"

"Yes," she said unevenly. "Not very much, but I wanted to know all about her family, and I kept at her. I can be pretty determined."

"I've noticed. And strong, very strong, Darcy." She paused. "I wasn't that strong when I lost Bonnie. She was my whole world, and all I wanted to do was go to her. I was heading down in that direction when she decided to come to me instead."

Darcy's gaze flew to her face. "Come to you?"

Eve nodded. "Call it hallucination. Call her a ghost. She started to come to me in dreams; and then the dreams were no longer necessary. I *saw* her. She visited me, and it was all love." She added simply, "She saved my life. It's not what I wanted at the time. I would rather have been with her all the time. But we worked through it together. And then I found Joe and my work, and now I have Michael. Bonnie was right, and I was wrong."

"You believe she actually came to you?"

"I know she did. But no one else has to believe it." She smiled. "They can think I'm crazy. Bonnie and I know better."

"You're not crazy."

"Then why doubt yourself? You and Sylvie started off with much more than is usually given to any of us. Don't you believe that she'd be allowed to still be part of the person she loves the most?"

"Allowed?"

Eve shrugged. "I don't know how it works. I only know from my own experience that sometimes there's special dispensation. Or maybe it happens to most people, and they don't realize what's happening. I think the best thing to do is just grab it, then give back as much as you can." She smiled. "And that's my last bit of advice. I just thought I'd try to save you the months of self-doubts I went through when I started to dream of Bonnie." She gazed at her inquiringly. "Do you dream of Sylvie?"

"No, not yet. I just feel her."

"Is it a bad feeling?"

"No." She thought about it. "It's kind of . . . glowing. But different than when . . . stronger." She was silent, trying to find a way to make her understand. "I remember when we were both very little, Sylvie loved butterflies. She used to wake me up very early, and take my hand, and we'd run out in the garden when there was dew still on the flowers. She would sit there and watch as the butterflies touched the blossoms. She thought they were sort of like us. She said I was like the very brightest, scarlet butterflies, and she was like the gold-orange and brown Monarchs. She loved them all, but she wondered if we'd ever change, if we could be different. She said brown and orange was pretty, but it would be nice to be a scarlet butterfly, and shine like me sometimes." She reached out and gently touched Sylvie's cheek. "It's sort of like that. Stronger . . . and brighter . . . and scarlet."

"And it makes you happy?"

She smiled. "It makes me happy."

"You're sitting in front of my sculpture. Do you feel closer to her here?"

"No." She frowned. "I don't think it has anything to do with it. I felt closer to her on the porch, and I just wanted to see if—" She said, "You're asking me questions you think I should be asking myself, aren't you?"

"Just getting you started." She bent and brushed a kiss on the top of Darcy's head. "Try to go to bed and get some sleep if you can. That's what I intend to do. But it's difficult when we keep thinking of how we're going to get rid of that monster. Everything about that conversation keeps going around and around in my mind."

Darcy nodded. "Me, too. I was so full of the ugliness that I had to come in and see that she wasn't really like that. She was still Sylvie."

"And maybe Sylvie wandered through your mind and helped a little?"

"Maybe." She looked up at her. "And maybe my friend, Eve, wandered in and helped quite a lot. I know that telling me about your Bonnie wasn't easy for you. Thank you."

"It wasn't that hard. You needed her. And as I said, what's given, you try to give back." She was heading across the living room toward the hall. "Good night, Darcy."

"Eve."

She looked over her shoulder and saw Darcy sitting there in the strong beam of her work light in front of Sylvie. Both beautiful, both glowing with vitality, the same, and yet not the same. Darcy's face was changing, gaining in maturity, and Sylvie's face that should have seemed frozen in time, appeared to be subtly changing, too. A trick of the light? Blooming . . .

Blooming. Where had that word come from?

"I wanted to ask you a question," Darcy said. "If you don't want to answer, I'll understand."

"Try me."

"Do you ever see your Bonnie these days? You have so much. Is she still with you?"

"She's still with me. She doesn't come as often. Hey, maybe they keep her busy. Since Michael was born, perhaps she thinks I don't need her as much." She smiled. "Though I've tried to tell her that's not true. I'll always need her just as you'll need Sylvie. But Bonnie's always there when it's important for me. Even though I may not know it's important. She never really leaves me." She tilted her head. "Anything else?"

"Nah, though I'll probably think of something else later." She grinned. "Cara probably told you I was incurably curious."

"She did mention something of that nature." She took one last look at that pool of golden light surrounding those two radiant faces. "But we can all learn to live with that. There's always the word no."

"Which you didn't use tonight," she said softly.

"I didn't, did I?" She turned and started down the hall toward her bedroom. "See you at breakfast, Darcy."

Had she helped? She thought she had, but who could know at moments like this? In the end, everyone had to face their own angels or demons. And perhaps there were both on the horizon for Darcy.

"Everything okay?" Joe asked when she came into the room.

"As okay as they can be." She took off her robe and tossed it on the chair. "Darcy is having a few problems." She crawled into bed and into his arms. "Or maybe not. Maybe she's having problems solved. I'd like to think it's the latter."

"And that means?"

"Sylvie." She cuddled closer. "I told Darcy about Bonnie. I thought it might help."

"That's unusual. You seldom talk about Bonnie."

"I thought it would help both of us." She put her cheek on her favorite spot on the hollow of his shoulder. "I miss Bonnie. I don't see enough of her."

He didn't answer. His hand just stroked her hair.

"I told Darcy Bonnie would always be here for me. But I get scared that she might think Michael is enough and go away entirely."

"Not likely."

She was silent a moment. "He's so special. Do you know sometimes I think that Bonnie had something to do with how—"

"I know you do," Joe said. "But stop thinking and wondering and just enjoy him. Michael is what he is." He kissed her. "And you are what you are. You gave a little too much to Darcy tonight, and it's having an aftereffect."

He was right. It had been a disturbing and horrifying day and, as she'd told Darcy, her mind was still working at top speed. It appeared that her emotions were also in a similar state. "Yes, I am what I am." She relaxed against him. "And it's good that you're around to remind me that doesn't always involve clear thinking."

"You do exceptionally well in that department. Though I believe that bringing in Kaskov might have been an exception to prove the rule."

"I think he might help. We need help. Norwalk was spitting out information right and left, but we couldn't quite grasp it. Except Darcy, she just applied her own experience and came up with a possibility. If I could just try to do the same thing . . ." She was thinking, going over Norwalk's words. "I told you I thought he hated me, and it wasn't because we'd taken in Cara. It was something I'd done to him. Or not done. He said something about not reaching out . . ."

"What?"

"Remember, he said I had a choice to reach out or not. And I'd chosen not to reach out. It was when I was telling him that he was all wrong about what my job is. That all I wanted was to ID and bring the victims home." She was thinking back, trying to remember nuances. "It made him angry. He said what I wanted and what was needed were entirely different." She was attempting to get facts in a row. "It had to be all about my job. I didn't reach out when I should have reached out. That might mean I refused to do something he wanted me to do."

"And that it probably wasn't in your job description."

She nodded. "But I do get lots of requests that don't always pertain to establishing ID. Mostly from funeral homes or those who are paid to reconstruct the deceased."

"I don't recall your accepting them."

"No, I refer them. I regard bringing a victim home as far more important. That's principally cosmetic work."

"And have you referred any recently?"

"I don't remember. There are so many, Joe. Have you seen my backlog file?"

"No, but I'm beginning to think I should."

She sat upright in bed. "I'm thinking that, too." She swung her legs to the floor. "Come on. Let's go take a look."

"May I suggest morning?"

"No, neither of us would probably sleep anyway." She slipped on her robe again and headed for the door. "We need to find out why Norwalk hates me so much . . ."

After more than three hours of going through backlog requests and isolating the ones from private individuals and funeral homes, they had two that they considered possibilities.

Joe tossed the first one aside. "Only one request to you. No drive. No obsession." He held up the second file. "Six requests. The money escalating with every offer. The first two offers were made by George Phillips Funeral Home in Syracuse, New York, a request to do facial reconstruction on one of their clients who'd suffered a mishap at a construction site. An explosion had made it very necessary before they could possibly have an open casket. However, they refused to send you photos."

"Because explosions make reconstruction virtually impossible," she said grimly. "Bone, muscle, and flesh go everywhere. It was doubtful that even an experienced forensic crew would have been able to retrieve the necessary pieces. As you see, I did refer them to the best person in upstate New York to make a try at it. But it would have taken entirely too much of my time. But I remember that they kept sending me requests. After the fourth one, I didn't open the envelopes any longer."

"And you didn't reach out," Joe said softly.

"You're thinking this was the job Norwalk was talking about," Eve said. "You believe it might have been his twin?"

"We should explore the possibility." He looked at the date. "Five months ago. That would have given him ample time to put his grand plan together and start integrating the pieces." He tapped the file. "And place you squarely in the crosshairs."

"We could be wrong."

"Absolutely. That's why George Phillips Funeral Home is going to receive a call from me as soon as it gets daylight." He looked out the window. "Which won't be too long. Well, maybe I'll wait until after nine." He pulled her to her feet. "In the meantime, we go back to bed and get a little sleep. Okay?"

She nodded. "But it could be Norwalk, Joe. It kind of fits together. It does make sense."

"It could be." He pushed her gently down the hall. "And that face they were so desperate for you to reconstruct could be Sean Norwalk. But right now, it's all supposition. We'll just have to wait and see."

GWINNETT SQUARE

ATLANTA, GEORGIA

It was almost amusing, Norwalk thought as he drove through the crowded intersection. One telephone call, but he knew it had sparked an explosion of activity in that pretty house on the lake.

And in Kaskov's armed fortress near that bayou in Louisiana. He'd not been able to tap the phones at the lake cottage due to Quinn's interference, but he'd made preparations for Kaskov. Lucky. He hadn't counted on Eve Duncan's calling on Kaskov for help. That had not been amusing at all. He had counted on a certain amount of time to enjoy her frustration and fear before he struck hard and deep.

Oh well, he could make adjustments. He gazed around the pleasant little square with its shops and restaurants. It reminded him of one of the squares in Belfast where he'd grown up. They'd rebuilt the square in the last few years, but it wasn't the same. It had only warehouse stores now instead of the intimate shops that had been there before.

But he remembered them every time he drove through Belfast. He hadn't seen how Sean could have wanted to lose touch with that glorious time in their lives.

Adjustments. Always adjustments.

He might have to move faster, but it would not be any less exciting or satisfying.

He pulled over to the curb and took out his notebook. Fast, but thorough and detailed. He began to make a list as he waited . . .

You see, Sean? You were always too impatient. That's what I tried to teach you. This is the way to do it.

"George Phillips was killed in an automobile accident four months ago," Joe told Eve after he'd hung up. "His brakes failed, and he went over a cliff. Convenient."

"Another loose end tied." She shivered. "But it might prove that we're going in the right direction. Were there any records about this 'client'?"

"No paperwork. The funeral home was taken over by his nephew, Matthew Dalks, who was his assistant before his death. Dalks says he remembers his uncle talking about the job, but he never met the client. He only knows that the client's name was Bellings and that his uncle wanted to be through with dealing with him. He said the guy was nuts and wouldn't take no for an answer. His uncle had examined the remains himself and told him there was no way they could be restored. The client said that Eve Duncan could do it, and it was his uncle's job to hire her and make her do the reconstruction." He looked at Eve. "Obsessive. Nuts. We're definitely on the right track."

"Yes." She was frowning. "Did he know where the body came from? What construction site? What city?"

"Bellings arranged for the transport of the remains. He said the accident took place at a construction company near the Canadian border. He told Phillips the local coroner in Buffalo had released the body to him, and he'd arranged for a refrigerated coffin for transport."

"Buffalo?"

Joe shook his head. "I'll check, but I'll bet it wasn't Buffalo. Phillips had been in the business a long time and was familiar with where to obtain refrigerated containers. The plaque on the coffin indicated it was sold primarily in southern Connecticut or Queens, New York. Both of them very far from Buffalo. That's why Phillips was eager to walk away from the job in spite of the fat fee. He didn't want to become involved in anything definitely illegal. Shady, he'd accept, but he just wanted to get rid of those remains and forget Bellings existed."

"And he did get rid of him and died less than a month later."

"Evidently, Norwalk didn't forget him," Joe said grimly. "He was pissed off, and he had to get rid of evidence. So Phillips had to be eliminated."

"Connecticut or New York," Eve murmured. "If his brother was killed in one of those places, why did he feel he had to whisk the remains that far away? Why not pick somewhere closer?"

"Interesting question," he said. "But first I have to check and see where and when that particular refrigerated coffin was sold. There was a serial number in the funeral-home inventory files that was entered when the coffin arrived. That was separate from the files that Norwalk stole after Phillips was killed." He got to his feet. "I'm going down to the precinct and see what I can access on the computers. I'll pick up Michael on the way home."

"I didn't want him to leave this morning. You're sure he's safe?"

"I arranged for a squad car outside the school totally assigned to Michael. That squad car will be with him every minute unless he's home with us. And I spoke to the principal and told them that only you or I can pick him up." He met her eyes. "And I had a talk with Michael on the way to school. I told him bad things were happening, and they mustn't happen to him or you would be unhappy. I told him it wasn't the time to try anything new or different, and he had to be careful. He understood."

Eve was sure he did, but it still made her angry. "He shouldn't have to understand. What if he's afraid?"

"He wasn't afraid, Eve."

"Well, I am."

"I could go get him. He just wanted to be at soccer practice today. Their first game is on Saturday. He's really excited about it."

And Norwalk was trying to ruin that for her son, too. He would love it that she was so terrorized that she was taking away one of the pleasures of Michael's childhood. "Just make certain that those men in the squad car know that I'll murder them if Michael gets so much as a skinned knee while they're watching him."

"I'll pass that along." He got to his feet. "But it wouldn't hurt that you keep Cara at home. Norwalk seems very adept at sleight of hand. Making us think he's going for one target when he means to hit another. Cara could be the immediate target." He added tightly, "Or you, Eve."

"I believe I'll be last on his list. He wants to make me hurt first."

"I don't care what you believe," he said roughly. "The son of a bitch could change at a moment's notice."

"Not the venom. He wants me to feel it." She held up her hand.

"I'll see that Cara stays here. It would be easier if Jock hadn't gone to see Kaskov. Have you heard from him?"

He shook his head. "But I'm sure I will after I text him this info about the refrigerated coffin. He's probably busy intimidating Kaskov and company." He headed for the door. "I'll call you when I know something."

She watched the door close behind him.

Dammit, she wanted to be going with him.

She felt helpless and on edge, and the last thing she wanted was to stay here with doors locked against that bastard. She went over to the worktable and took out the FedEx box she used for transport. She could at least pack up Sylvie and get her ready to send back to Forensics.

"Is she on her way?" It was Darcy standing in the hall, her gaze on Sylvie. "I knew you'd have to do it, but I'll miss her."

"Too much?" Eve frowned. "I thought from what you said last night that maybe the skull wasn't as important to—"

"It's not," Darcy said quickly. "And I don't think I need a crutch any longer. Maybe I never did. Do you want me to help you package her?"

She shook her head. "I'm accustomed to doing it. You know that you can request she be returned to you when Forensics finishes all their paperwork? It's mostly red tape anyway." She added, "And if you want me to wait, I'll do it. Say the word."

She shook her head. "I won't say that word. I'll think about the request. Right now, I don't believe I'll want to be thinking about that wonderful job you did on Sylvie. I need to focus on something else."

Eve grimaced. "Then focus on keeping Cara in the house or very close to the property. I promised Joe I'd keep her safe. He's worried about sleight of hand."

"Is he?" She smiled bitterly. "Oh, yes, like the time Norwalk confused you all by dangling the possibility that he was going after my totally unimportant self? I can see why Joe might be worried about his doing that again. Don't worry, Eve. I'll keep Cara busy here at the cottage." She turned back toward the bedrooms. "And the first thing I'll do is remind her that with all the turmoil yesterday, she didn't get in her practice so she needs to do double today. We'll go from there."

"Master stroke," Eve said. "Very good."

"You just have to find out what's important to someone and offer it to them." She paused. "Or threaten to take it away, depending on the circumstances. You could do the first, I don't think you'd be comfortable with the second. But with Cara, that wouldn't be necessary."

Eve grinned. "Since you appear to have it under control, I'll leave it to you. Anything I can do to help?"

"Maybe. Do you have a gun I could borrow, Eve?"

Eve felt a ripple of shock. "What?"

"Just a thought." Her smile had never faltered. "I didn't mean to upset you, but I did want to make sure that you and Cara are safe. I do know how to shoot a gun. I learned when I did an episode of *Criminal Minds* when I was fifteen. Bad show, but I was pretty good in it."

"I'm sure you were," Eve said. "I do own a gun, but I prefer to keep it for my own use. You can talk to Joe about getting one when he comes home tonight."

"That will be fine. As I said, I didn't mean to upset you." She took a last look at Sylvie. "No, I don't need that sculpture any longer," she said softly. "I won't ever need it. She's back with me now . . ."

BELLE GRACE
MORGANA, LOUISIANA

"Why am I still here, Kaskov?" Jock said as he looked down at the chess board. "Some kind of bluff? Did I make you uneasy about the break-in, and you want to show a little muscle?"

"I don't believe in bluffs," Kaskov said. "It's much more effective if you don't see even a hint of a threat coming. No, I don't often have the chance to play chess with someone who's not afraid to beat me." He moved his knight. "And you did beat me twice so far. I admit it did irritate me. If I hadn't won that last game, I would have told Nikolai, 'Off with his head.'"

"I don't believe that. But you would have found a way to make me suffer."

"So you let me win?"

"No, my ego wouldn't have permitted it." He leaned back in his chair. "Four hours. Why am I still here?"

"I hadn't had a chance to observe you at close range. It was an opportunity." He smiled. "You appear to dominate Cara's life, and I had to know the best way to go if I had to extract you."

"You wouldn't waste four hours on me."

"Oh, but I would," he said softly. "You invaded my turf. The challenge you issued was very clear. Since Cara insists that you're her best friend, my options are limited. I have to either remove you or learn to deal with you. Either way, I have to know gains and losses."

"Not by playing chess."

He smiled. "Perhaps not. That might have been a bonus advantage." His gaze went to Nikolai, who had just entered the study. "And here comes my friend, Nikolai, and if I'm not mistaken, you'll be able to spare me losing another game and get on your way."

Nikolai was handing Kaskov a file. "Very efficient. They did well. Anything else?"

"Not at the moment. Thank you." He opened the file and scanned it. "Yes, very thorough."

Nikolai smiled and left the room.

"Here's your copy, Gavin." Kaskov handed him a sheet from the file. "It's only Norwalk's initial background history, but it might help to put things together. I had one of my people in Dublin dig deep and fast. He found a source who had been in the IRA with Norwalk and later in his organization. He squeezed him with a great deal of enthusiasm."

RORY NORWALK

Jock glanced up from the paper. "And this is what I've been waiting for?"

"Of course, your trip here was an explorative venture on many levels on both our parts. Norwalk is perhaps the only puzzle that we can solve, so I urged ultimate speed." He was scanning the report. "Rory and Sean Norwalk were born in Belfast. Mother, Rosalie Shea, prostitute, father, Ryan Norwalk, peddled drugs and was a petty thief until he became involved with the IRA. That's where he was taught the art of explosives, a skill that was valued by the IRA. Rory and Sean were brought up to serve both their father and the organization. They were very close during those years. It was as if they belonged to a secret club. Rory told everyone they were special and didn't need anyone else. He was always reading books and stories about twins and searching out passages that said that they were stronger and smarter and had special powers. He *was* smart, he was the fair-haired boy of his cell, and was given his own assignments when he was only twelve. Sean was less talented and a little lazy, and jealousy reared its head."

"Trouble in twin paradise?"

"Big time. Rory tried to tell his brother what to do, and Sean exploded. Conflict. Fights. Bitterness. Their mother had already died of a drug overdose. That year their father was blown up in an explosion he'd set at a police station in South Belfast. That left the twins alone at fifteen though they'd never paid attention to anyone but each other anyway. But they split immediately after their father's death. Sean left Belfast and headed for Europe. He was still bitter and cut all ties to his brother. He even changed his name. Rory stayed in Ireland, kept his contacts, and did well for himself as he moved into organized crime. The fact that he was bloodthirsty and ruthless as hell didn't hurt his rise to the top."

"Sounds familiar," Jock murmured.

"Not at all. I've never been bloodthirsty. I do only what's necessary." Kaskov glanced down at the report again. "Sean never returned to Ireland as far as it's known. But Rory made several trips to Nice and Madrid, where his twin had set up shop during the next twenty years. But only after a decade or so had gone by. He probably had to bury his pride to be the first one to make an approach. But he'd always been the one who was dazzled by the twin mystique and thought he needed Sean to complete himself. He never mentioned his brother to any of the men in his organization. But once he was seen with Sean at a casino in Nice."

Jock went still. "Which casino?"

"Which one do you think?" Kaskov asked softly, "Lagazar Casino. Sean spent a lot of time there. As you can see, a connection emerging. It appears that Rory wanted to reunite with his twin, but Sean was still reluctant. Rory had done too well, and Sean wasn't about to fade back into his shadow. He made Rory come to him."

"And would Sean have been put into the shade?"

Kaskov nodded. "He never rose above the role of enforcer or occasional assassin after he left Ireland. He would have felt humiliated if he'd had to face comparison to Rory again."

Jock was quickly reading his own copy of the report. "And he preferred to work for Jacques Manard and a few other crime bosses where he felt he had at least a little prestige."

"Presumably." He put the report down on the table. "So now we have a peek at the inner workings of the minds of the brothers Norwalk. I hope you found it interesting and worth the wait."

"Interesting. Far from complete." Jock was still reading the report. "Sean changed his name to Marc Sanford?"

"So it says."

Jock glanced up at Kaskov's expressionless face. "And you've never seen this report before?"

"Never. I told Eve that I knew nothing about Rory Norwalk." He smiled. "Now we do. A first report, but quite informative. Do you wish to call Eve or should I? She should be pleased."

"I'll do it." He was still gazing at Kaskov's face. "She might be pleased, but you're not. There's something . . . bothering you."

"Is there? Mind reading? Or just being a good chess player?"

"I think your mind is operating at warp speed, and I'm wondering what you're trying to work out."

"Well, I'm afraid you'll have to wonder somewhere else." He rose to his feet. "I've enjoyed our little get-together, but I have to start to work. I believe it's time you left the property. Do you need a car?"

"I have one parked down the road." He got to his feet. "I'll see you soon, Kaskov."

"I imagine you will," he said dryly. "But please not at such an early hour. I know you only wanted to make a statement, but I might find a second time more disturbing."

Jock started for the door, then stopped and looked back over his shoulder. "You told Eve you knew nothing about Rory Norwalk. You never said you knew nothing about a Marc Sanford."

"Do you wish me to say it?"

"No, I imagine you lie exceptionally well. Now that you're on guard, I wouldn't be able to tell the difference." He smiled. "But it's something to think about it. I'll find out for myself. But that means I'll also be able to use it any way I please."

He turned on his heel, and a moment later, he'd left the columned mansion.

He called Joe Quinn the moment he got into the car. "I'll call Eve with the rest of the info I got from Kaskov, but I wanted to give you the name Sean Norwalk used from the time he and his brother parted ways. Marc Sanford. And he was working for Jacques Manard at least a good part of that time. Got it?"

"I'll check it out," Joe said. "I'm glad you managed to gather something of value from that trip to Kaskov's lair. You've been gone a long time, Jock. Eve was getting nervous. What the hell were you doing there?"

"Not much." He started the car. "Just playing chess, Joe."

CHAPTER

10

C *hanges.*

Cara stopped playing and gazed out at the lake. The water was still, but she could hear the wind in the trees. Soon it would touch the crystal smoothness of the lake surface and bring it to life. And the storm would follow the wind. She could *feel* it coming. She could feel *him* coming.

Just as she could feel those changes coming, as haunting and unable to escape as the sonata she had just played. Dear God, how desperately she had tried to escape it. But in the end, she had to face who she was, who she had become, even if that meant that she could no longer be what Jock wanted her to be. Yes, everything would change, and she might not weather the storm.

She fought off the fear at the thought. Choices. Her own soul, her own choices. And the music. She had the music. She could weather anything. She lifted the bow and started to play again.

It had started to rain by the time she saw the headlights of the gray Toyota Jock had used the last time he'd been here. She stopped playing as she felt the relief sweep through her. Eve had told her that Jock was fine and on his way back to Atlanta, but she was always on edge when Jock and Kaskov were anywhere near each other.

And she had known that she couldn't hide any longer.

She got to her feet and moved to the top of the steps as she heard the car door slam.

"I heard you playing as I drove up the road." Jock was running around the car, raindrops catching in his fair hair. "Magnificent welcome." He smiled up at her as he took the steps two at a time. "Relax. I'm fine. Were you staking out the porch to check me for battle wounds? Both of us survived without incident."

"I don't believe that. Eve told me that you found out some information we needed about Norwalk, but Kaskov might have given that to Eve without your going after him."

"True. But perhaps not as quickly. And with much less satisfaction on my part. I was very frustrated when I left here, and I needed an outlet."

"And did you get it?"

"Aye." He looked beyond her at the door. "I need to see Joe. On the plane, I was going over the timeline of what had been happening, and I made a few phone calls. I think I have an idea of what's been going on."

She tensed. "What? Tell me."

He moved toward the door. "Sure. Right after I talk to Joe and get his—"

"No. Now." She moved between him and the door. "I want to know now." First test, don't worry about anything but being who she was and not what he wanted her to be. "I don't want you to pat me on the head, I don't want you to put me aside or set me on a shelf in some kind of crystal showcase. That's what you do all the time, Jock, and it's got to stop."

He went still. "You're being weird again. I know you've been upset by all that's been going on, but this isn't the time to get temperamental on me."

"Temperamental?" She laughed incredulously. "I guess that's an apt description of who you think I am. Just an artist, a musician, a dreamer, with all the emotional hang-ups that traditionally go along with it. Just a kid you have to protect because you think I can't protect myself. You've done that ever since the day we first met."

"You *were* a kid then. What did you expect?"

"Nothing. I suppose you're not that different from anyone else. Darcy and Eve have been hovering over me all day."

"Good for them. You're a target, dammit."

"But I'm no longer a kid," she said fiercely. "I have to accept responsibility for myself. I can't let you or Joe or Eve wrap me in cotton wool. For God's sake, even Kaskov treats me like a doll he takes out to play with and puts away when I bore him. Perhaps I bore you, too, Jock. That's too bad. I should never have let you go tearing down to New Orleans to see him."

"You had no choice."

"Yes I did. I could have gone with you. I could have refused to let you put me back on my shelf where you like to keep me. But I didn't want to upset you or make you angry. You were always too important to me. But that's a child's excuse, and I won't use it any longer." She moistened her lips. "You have to stop it. I'm not going to sit on that damn shelf and watch you get yourself killed. Temperamental? Hell yes. You haven't seen temperamental, Jock."

Jock was silent, gazing at her. "I believe I may have just gotten a sample. Wrong word?"

"Yes." She met his eyes. "But not all your fault. I allowed myself to be treated like that because it's what people seemed to want of me. I guess somewhere down deep I thought if I gave what was wanted, I'd never be alone again. You came into my life when I'd lost everyone, friends, family . . . so I was particularly vulnerable to you. And you were wonderful to me, you enriched my life. I just wanted to hold on to you. Not fair to you, Jock."

"The hell it's not," he said roughly. "Shut up, Cara. This is tearing me apart."

"See?" Her smile was shaky. "Not fair to you. That's what I'm trying to change. I can't be that kid you felt you had to take care of any longer. I thought I could pretend, but I don't think I can. It's too dangerous for you and too scary for me. I have to be on my own." She paused. "Even if it means that you find you don't like me that way."

"Shh." His hands were suddenly cupping her face. "Hey, best friends, remember. You're always reminding me. I'm not sure what you're going through right now, but we'll work it out."

She loved his hands on her. She loved his silver-gray eyes shimmering down at her. She loved his lips, which were smiling that wonderful smile. She loved the way he was trying to soothe away the hurt he sensed she was feeling.

Too much.

"Best friends." She took a step back so that his hands fell away from her. "Good friends. Friends that are honest with each other." But maybe not totally honest right now. Tonight she had taken the first steps, but she found herself clinging desperately to the comfort of the past. It would take time. She forced a smile. "And if we can't work it out, we'll be honest about that, too." She turned around to face the lake. "So what did you want to talk to Joe about? Timeline you said."

"We're back to that?" He went to the porch rail and leaned against it, his gaze still studying her. "It's not as if I'm trying to keep anything from you, Cara."

"No, you just don't want it to get too close to me. Timeline?"

"It was over five months ago that Norwalk contacted Eve about doing reconstructive work on Sean. That means that it was probably shortly before that he was killed in that explosion. Joe pinpointed the coffin purchase in Connecticut or New York. But Sean Norwalk worked out of Nice for Jacques Manard and any other crime organization who would hire him. What was he doing in the New York area?"

"You think he was on a job? Eve said he was an enforcer and assassin."

"I thought it likely he was sent to do what he did best. So I called Benoit, my agent in Nice. He couldn't find out details, but he did verify that Sean was sent to New York on a job around that time. Benoit couldn't definitely confirm, but it was presumably contracted by Jacques Manard."

"A job for Manard? Then it must have gone wrong."

"Obviously," Jock said dryly. "Since Sean ended up in pieces. I have to tell Joe to narrow down that search on those caskets to Manhattan. And then we have to figure out why Manard sent a hired killer to New York and got him killed."

Her gaze was searching his face. "But you have an idea or two on that, don't you?"

"One. Singular. Because it fits in with the timeline. That was also about the time that Stanton told me you were being followed, and we found that your place was bugged. I thought it might be Kaskov or someone targeting you because of him, and I flew off to Moscow to find out. But it might have been Sean Norwalk. He could have been the man Stanton saw tailing you."

"After me?" she whispered. "Manard sent him to kill me? Why?"

"I have no idea. I could be wrong. But it fits."

"If he was sent from Nice . . . It could still be because of Darcy."

"Not according to Rory Norwalk. He was the only one using Darcy and Sylvie for his own purposes." He shook his head. "I'm thinking Manard sent Sean after you. I'm having Benoit try to probe deeper and come up with an answer why. He said that Manard had never been at odds with the Russian Mafia. Yet that doesn't make sense to me. I'm betting that Benoit is going to find a feud between Kaskov and Manard."

"But you said Norwalk was working with Manard."

"Until he wasn't. I'd bet that sniper who took him out was financed by Norwalk." He straightened. "That's all I have in mind. Most of it is guesswork. I'll let you know more when I do. Okay?"

"It has to be." She grimaced wryly. "However, I do appreciate knowing that I'm still tops on the hit list." She added, "Better me than Eve."

"I knew you'd say that." He paused. "Do you want to come in and talk to Joe with me?"

"How accommodating you're being now." She shook her head. "Thanks for the courtesy, but I never said I wanted to take over any-thing. I know how valuable and experienced you both are. I just don't want to be left out. And when I'm needed, I want to be there."

His lips tightened. "I can't promise you that."

"I know. I'll have to do it myself. But I had to give you fair warn-ing." She made a shooing motion. "Go talk to Joe. I'll see you later."

"Dismissed?" He was smiling curiously. "That's another change, Cara. I'm not certain I like it."

Changes . . .

"I'm not certain either." She turned around and looked back at the lake. "I guess we'll both have to get used to it and see how we feel as time goes by . . ."

Changes.

A presence in the darkness.

But she knew that presence very well now . . .

"Hi, Darcy," Michael whispered. He was standing beside her bed. "I was sitting in the rocking chair, but my feet are getting cold. Can I climb into bed with you and cover up?"

"What are you—" She shook her head to clear it of sleep. "Mi-chael, it's after midnight. What are you doing out of bed? And don't tell me you want me to go have breakfast."

"I just thought you might be lonely. Sylvie went away this after-noon." He smiled. "And then my feet got cold. Can I come to bed?"

"Why not?" She lifted the cover. "But only for a little while. Your mom won't like you wandering around."

"She won't mind if you don't." He jumped into bed and cuddled close to her. She could hear the rain pounding rhythmically on the roof. The scents of lemon shampoo, Dial soap, and Michael suddenly surrounded her. Her arms instinctively went around his small, warm body. "Mama always listens when someone needs her to do it."

"Yes she does." She paused. "And your mom did the right thing sending Sylvie away. It was time for her to go. I'm not upset about it, Michael. Though I'm glad you decided to pay me a visit."

"Yes, time for her to go . . . Always a time . . . Not upset . . ." He yawned and cuddled closer. "But maybe a little lonely because things are different and sometimes it gets confusing . . ."

"Different?"

"You know . . . Sylvie's like you now, but still herself. She didn't lose anything. You'll get used to it . . ." He was dozing off. "She did . . ."

Sylvie. Still herself, all the joy and gentleness. Like Darcy, all the strength and clarity. How wonderful it would be . . .

As wonderful as this little boy who had come to her in the middle of the night because he'd thought she might need comfort.

"No, Sylvie didn't lose anything," she whispered. She brushed a kiss on his head, her arms tightening around him. "And we didn't lose each other. You're right, we just have to get used to something a little different. It's just a sort of change . . ."

Changes.

"I think that Michael's probably paying a visit to Darcy," Eve said, as Joe came into their bedroom after his last check of the property. "I took a peek after I left the bathroom, and he wasn't in his room."

Joe stiffened. "What?"

"Don't panic. The house is perfectly secure. He was in his room earlier, and I think I heard his voice talking to Darcy. I expected he might go see her tonight or tomorrow morning."

Joe relaxed. "Okay. Though I'd expect he'd go visit Cara instead."

"She's not having the same kind of problems Darcy is having. He thinks Darcy needs him." She thought about it. "And I don't think he could really identify with Cara's problems at the moment. He's only six. Maybe in a few years . . ."

"What in hell are you talking about?"

"Nothing. Just thinking out loud. If we don't hear Michael go back to bed, I'll go get him. He's got his first soccer game tomorrow afternoon, and he should get his rest. Come to bed. No sign of a problem on the property?"

"No." He was already stripping off his clothes. "I have a hunch that Sakov's murder was a swan song on Norwalk's part, a last statement before he initiates phase two. He'd know that there would be police and state troopers all over those woods from now on. I'll still be on the watch because he's a tricky son of a bitch." He slid into bed and took her in his arms. "I was hoping you might get another call from him. Though Jock seems to be getting close to finding out the big picture. But we need to know which direction he's going to jump next."

"Hell would be nice." She cuddled closer. "He'd feel comfortable there. Jock would be delighted to show him the way."

"So would I. And at least Jock's free to go on the hunt for him."

Eve stiffened as she heard the barely repressed impatience in his voice. She had been sensing that raw edginess since Norwalk's call. She said quietly, "And you're *not* free. I know it's frustrating you. All your life, you've been a warrior of some sort. SEAL, FBI, police. It's your instinct to go on the attack, and it's probably driving you crazy to have to sit here and just play defense." She was silent trying to find the words. "It's a completely unnatural role for you, and I've been wondering lately if you're regretting that day you came knocking on my door and let yourself in for it."

"What? You're the one who drives me crazy when you talk like that," he said roughly. "Hell yes, I want to go after Norwalk. But so do you. And are you running out and leaving Michael and Cara to do it? What about it, Eve? Would you rather have not opened that door and devoted your entire mind and heart to all those skulls?" He got up on one elbow and stared down at her. "I know the answer to that because I know you. And you should know me well enough not to worry about me like you do the rest of the people you love. I have a special status." He suddenly smiled down at her. "I'm the guardian at the gates. Can't you see my shiny armor and mighty shield?"

"Yes, I can see it," she said unsteadily. "All the time, Joe."

"I thought you could. And that's what keeps me from mounting my trusty steed and going out in search of demons to conquer." His index finger gently traced the line of her upper lip. "Who needs glory? I've been there. It's not so great. Everything changes, Eve. And every change connected to you and Michael is beautiful. Okay, right now some of those changes are causing a lot of upheaval. Sometimes we don't know what we're going to face next. But every day offers a chance to keep what I have intact by just guarding those gates. I'd be a fool to give it up." He settled back beside her again. "So stop trying to make trouble. Unless you decide to give me my walking papers, you're stuck with me. But I'd advise against it, you don't see a gate guardian with my qualifications very often."

"Never," she said thickly. "It appears you're irreplaceable. So I guess that means no walking papers. We'll just have to get through this as we have everything else."

"Together."

Her arms tightened around him. "Guarding the gates or beyond. Together, Joe."

CHAPTER
11

Y ou're sure, Benoit?" Jock asked. "No mistake?"

"You insult me. A man of my experience and stature never makes mistakes. Occasionally, I have a slight omission in information, but never a true mistake. It was Manard who made the mistake. Arrogance can sometimes blind one to one's limitations. I struggle constantly with my own, but Manard evidently did not." He paused. "I hope you're not planning on doing anything with that information. Even Manard was clever enough to avoid direct confrontation."

Jock didn't answer. "Concentrate on any movement of Norwalk's men and get back to me if they head this way." He hung up.

Timeline completed. Picture in place.

And to hell with avoiding confrontation.

He punched in the number on his phone.

This time Kaskov himself answered within three rings. "I've been waiting for you to get in touch with me. You took a little longer than I thought you would."

"Perhaps your contacts are a little better than mine since they crawl on the underbelly. That avoids all kinds of traffic problems. But I did get there." He paused. "A huge arms shipment to Pakistan by Robert Akim. Sound familiar?"

"Go on."

"Manard was to accept a major percentage of the selling price to settle a gambling debt Akim owed him. He even invested some of his own money in the project. It would have been a fairly peaceful transaction until Akim got greedy. He decided to risk muscling in on territory some of your people had already established with the Pakistanis to get a bigger fee to make up for what he had to pay Manard." He paused. "Very stupid. Your organization would never permit that to happen. It had the expected result. Akim and his men were shot, and the cargo disappeared into the mountains."

"That often happens, doesn't it? Pakistan is still such a primitive country."

"But Manard wasn't that philosophic. He'd lost a bundle when your 'associates' hijacked that shipment from Akim. He found out you were the kingpin in the background, and he was mad as hell. He wanted revenge."

"Unfortunate. But it was unlikely I'd even know who Akim's investors were nor would I care . . . if any of my associates happened to be involved. Strictly small potatoes. Nikolai approves of statements, and it seems as if a statement had been made and a transaction completed."

"I believe you probably didn't know about Manard. As you said, small potatoes. You'd just keep an eye open for any fallout. And there was no immediate fallout. It came a few months later. Manard wasn't about to take you on, but he wanted his revenge. So he did some research and found Cara. He sent his favorite hit man to see if he could cause you a little pain and suffering and still keep his ass intact. Sean zeroed in on her like a true professional, but he wasn't all that good. That's why he had left Dublin; he didn't want to be compared to his twin. Even my man, Stanton, spotted Sean, and he thought he might have scared him off." He paused. "But that wasn't it, because someone else also evidently spotted him. You mentioned to Cara that you'd had someone watching her. And when it was reported back to you that Sean was a possible threat to her, you decided elimination was necessary. Of course, nothing close to Cara's school. There was a car-bomb explosion in Harlem the next day. Very big explosion and vaguely designated as gang-related. But there was not even enough evidence to identify the victim."

"The C-4 was Sean Norwalk's," Kaskov said. "He was planning to set off an explosion in Cara's suite at the residence." Kaskov added softly, "Only a touch of poetic justice. Tell me that you wouldn't have appreciated that poetry, Jock. Though you would probably have pre-ferred using your hands. The thought of Cara's being blown to bits would have been difficult for you to handle."

"Yes, and I'm not arguing that Sean Norwalk wouldn't have died whether you'd been involved or not."

"I regret robbing you of the pleasure. But I admit I thoroughly enjoyed giving that order."

"And why didn't you go after Manard?"

"I wasn't sure he was involved. I didn't know that much about Norwalk. He was going under an assumed name, Marc Sanford, and he wasn't under an exclusive contract to Manard. There were at least four other organizations who used Norwalk's services in France and Spain. I didn't even know about Manard's connection to Akim at the time. So I decided to watch and investigate and be certain. Only fools act hastily. I thought the immediate threat was over, and Cara would be safe now that I'd issued a statement."

"Until she almost got choked to death," Jock said harshly.

"I was watching Manard. I didn't know Sean Norwalk even had a brother. As I said, he'd changed his name when he left Ireland. Yes, there were reports a Rory Norwalk visited Manard during the time I had him under surveillance after I'd disposed of the threat to Cara, but I didn't see a connection." He added, "But after the attack on Cara that night, I let you look for connections for me. You did ex-ceptionally well, Gavin."

"Always pleased to serve," he said ironically. "It didn't occur to you that you could have been a little more open."

"It's not my nature. I did give you considerable information. That's not my custom, either. However, I will tell you that Rory Norwalk did me a favor in disposing of Manard. If he wasn't such a totally erratic psychopath, I might have decided to let him live."

"Really? Not likely. It was inevitable that he'd kill Manard. He had his own share of responsibility, and Norwalk is getting rid of everyone connected with his twin's death. He probably went to Manard, crying vengeance, and pressured him into doing what he wanted. It wouldn't have been that difficult. Manard had to know what a nut job Norwalk was from his visits to his brother during the preceding years." He added, "And Cara is on that list. It's a wonder he didn't kill her that night. But we both know why he didn't, don't we?"

"He wants me to see her die," Kaskov said without inflection. "And probably in the most painful and bloody way possible. It's the customary ending in a situation like this."

"Aye, so it is. But it's not going to have a customary ending. Because you're going to use yourself as the bait to trap Norwalk. It's the only way to keep him away from her."

Silence. "Oh, am I going to do that? It sounds like a fine plan, but I believe Nikolai would have objections to its effect on my many enterprises. Along with damage to my rather vulnerable body. Besides, there's also the fact that I make my own decisions, Gavin."

"I'm sure you do. So do I. That's why I thought that I'd give you a chance to think about it before I made any overt moves. Give me some other way to get it done, or that's the way we go." He cut the connection.

How's that for confrontation, Benoit?

"Shit," Joe said. "Did you have to sign your own death warrant, Jock?"

"You may be exaggerating. It's a practical way to go," Jock said. "Norwalk wants Kaskov more than anyone else. If we dangle Kaskov in front of him, he may forget about Eve or Cara."

"Dangle? No one dangles Kaskov." Joe was silent. "Though I can see how tempting it—"

"No, Joe," Eve said firmly, as she handed Jock his cup of tea. "What can you be thinking, Jock?"

"I'm thinking I have to get Cara out of the crosshairs." He shrugged. "Oh, I'd try not to get Kaskov killed." He smiled. "I thought I'd give him a chance to sacrifice for his beloved grand-daughter. Of course, if he refused, it would look very bad for him, wouldn't it? Do you think Cara would be so upset, she wouldn't think she had to keep her promise to him? Pity."

"No, she would not expect anyone to sacrifice themselves for her. You know that."

He nodded regretfully. "It would only be an unexpected bonus. I didn't really think Kaskov would go for it, but I wanted to throw it out and see if he could come up with anything else. He's smart, and he likes challenges . . ." He added, "And he *might* care . . . some-thing . . . about Cara."

"That's a huge admission for you."

"I didn't say what he felt. I'm just exploring every option." He was silent. "I want this over. I don't like what's it's doing to Cara. She's not the same."

"You can't expect her to stay the same," Eve said gently. "She's growing up, and all this stress is forcing it to escalate at warp speed."

"Then we have to get rid of the damn stress." His lips tightened. "She has a right to enjoy these years. She had a nightmare childhood, and I thought when she was safe, she'd be able to live the life she should have."

"I think she was living that life," Eve said. "She had her music, she had us." She hesitated. "She had you. But sometimes it's a ques-tion of shifts and balances, and it all has to come from her."

"No, it doesn't. I'll change the balance when I kill that son of a bitch," he said recklessly. "Then she can go back to enjoying her life again." He set his cup down on the coffee table. "Though she'll probably argue about that, too. She seems to always be on edge with me these days." He turned to Joe. "I want to take a look at that box that Sylvie's skull was in. Can you take me down to the precinct today and get me into the evidence room?"

"Not today. Eve and I have to go to Michael's first soccer game this afternoon." He smiled at Eve. "Some things are too important to put off. Eve's worried that Michael's being cheated by all this ugly business. You should identify since you're so concerned about Cara's missing anything. But I'll call ahead and get you permission to look at it on your own."

"That will do." He headed for the door. "Now that we know why Cara was a target, the only missing link is how Darcy and Sylvie fit in all this. I have Benoit looking into it, but maybe I can figure it out on my own if I examine that gold box." He had a sudden thought and stopped as he opened the door. "Who's going to be here with Cara and Darcy?"

"You mean besides half a dozen police officers milling around within calling distance?" Joe asked dryly. "I think that would be enough protection for our three-hour absence. I thought about it, Jock."

"Aye, probably." He frowned. "Still, maybe I'll take them with me."

"Why doesn't that surprise me?" Joe asked. "You don't trust any-one but yourself."

Jock smiled. "Not true. I'd trust you, but you're going off to play soccer."

He swung the door shut behind him.

SATURDAY

4:40 P.M.

"We were pretty bad, weren't we?" Michael was frowning up at Joe as he walked with Eve and Joe back to their car after the game.

"The coach said we sort of fell apart, but we'll be better the next time."

"I'm sure you will," Eve said. "I thought you were fine. You just have to become accustomed to all the action that's going on around you. It's distracting. Don't worry. You'll pick it up, bit by bit."

"I'm not worrying. It was kind of fun. It didn't matter if we lost."

"Now that attitude does bother me," Joe said. "Winning is important because competition always makes you perform better. And people should always reach the highest peak they can manage."

"Says the ex-SEAL." Eve chuckled. "So much for soothing his bruised ego."

Joe looked down at Michael. "Climb the highest peak, or be satisfied with the roller coaster at Disney World?"

Michael thought about it. "Both."

Eve laughed. "And I'm not going to delve into that. We might get in too deep. You did great, Michael. Next time, you'll do even better."

"I know," he said absently, his gaze on a tall, sandy-haired child in soccer uniform running toward him. He was suddenly straightening, moving protectively closer to Eve. "It's going to be okay, Mama."

"I know it will." Her gaze went to the boy. Freckles, pale skin, huge blue eyes, dressed in the same red-and-gold soccer uniform Michael was wearing. And Joe was right, he was almost a head taller than Michael. "Gary?"

He nodded. "I thought I made him understand, but maybe he's not—" He took a step forward. "Hi, Gary, do you need something?"

"Nah, I just wanted to see her." He was standing there, gazing at Eve. "Michael says you bring people like my dad home."

"It's a little more complicated than that, Gary," she said gently. "I'll be glad to explain myself later if your mom says it's okay."

"I don't think there's going to be time. But I think maybe my Dad wanted me to know about you." His eyes were fixed intently on her face. "He knew I was scared."

"There's no reason to be scared, Gary," Eve said. "No reason at all."

"I know that." He smiled. "Michael told me. But I still had to see you. He said it would be better." He turned to Michael. "Coach said to tell you that he's going to take the whole team to Pops Ice Cream Emporium on the square. He said we can't celebrate a win, but we can practice for the win next week. Can you go?"

Michael's face lit with eagerness as he looked at Joe. "May I?"

He nodded. "Why not?" He got in the car and waved the squad car on duty to follow them. "We'll drive you to the square and wait in the car until you're done. We wouldn't want to intrude." He looked at Gary. "Need a lift?"

He shook his head. "I'll go with the rest of the guys in the coach's van. See you, Michael." He was dashing back toward the field.

Eve was gazing after him as she got into the passenger seat. It had been a strange few minutes, but she supposed it was positive. "I take it you and Gary have straightened out your differences. You told him it would be better if he saw me?"

"No. That wasn't me." Michael was buckling up his seat belt. "I wasn't the one who told him that." He leaned forward to talk to Joe. "Isn't this cool? Do coaches always buy ice cream after a game? You said you played football. Did you get—"

"No, I don't recall ever being offered ice cream for making touchdowns." Joe was grinning. "But then I could be mistaken . . ."

Joe pulled into the square at the same time as Coach Wilkes and parked the next row down from him. The boys poured out of the van and ran toward a shop with "Pops Ice Cream Emporium" in ornate red script on the frosted windows.

Michael jumped out of the backseat of their car and was streaking after the other boys. He caught up with them at the red swinging doors. He gave Eve and Joe a brilliant smile and a wave, then disappeared inside with the rest of the red-and-gold-uniformed boys.

"I believe he might be a little excited," Eve said as she leaned back in the seat gazing through the frosted windows at the boys running around the ice-cream shop. "That poor coach is going to earn his money today."

ATLANTA POLICE DEPARTMENT

ATLANTA, GEORGIA

"I've been in a police station before but this is much different," Darcy told Cara as she stared with interest into the offices they were passing as they made their way toward the evidence room. "No one's paying any attention to me. The last time I was only ten, and we were filming in a police station in New York. I was supposed to have run away from home, and the cops brought me to the station until they could convince me I should go back to my family."

"What an amazingly original script," Jock murmured.

"Hey, don't knock it. The ratings went off the charts for the episode. I even got an Emmy nomination. I was touching, funny, and I even sang a wistful little song to those cops. It wasn't like 'Somewhere Over the Rainbow,' but it hit square on dreams and family values so it—" She stopped and drew a shaky breath. "I'm talking too much. Sorry. I guess I'm kind of nervous about this."

"You don't have to do it," Cara said. "Go back to the car and wait for us."

"I do have to do it. He put Sylvie in that box. I've seen the rest of what he did to her. I have to finish it." She smiled determinedly. "And I will. It's not so bad. Come to think of it, I did get some attention as we came into the station. Maybe they thought I was a hooker. No, at least a high-class escort. The first is Academy Award material, but I'm not ready for that yet and I—"

"Hush." Jock was showing his pass to the policeman in the wire cage. "We'll be out of here soon. I don't really expect to find anything unless something just strikes a note. It just needs to be checked." He took the gold-foil box from the policeman and placed it on the table. "Joe said it was a double-sided mirror with the top mirror intact and that the mirror facing down to reflect the skull was broken." He was carefully opening the lid. "I just wondered about the mirror that was left unbroken. It's been nagging at me. Norwalk has been planning this down to the last detail. The broken mirror was to reflect Sylvie's death. What was the other mirror meant to reflect?"

"Me?" Darcy whispered, gazing down at the box. "One broken, one intact. One twin dead, the other one left alive. It makes sense, doesn't it?" She moistened her lips. "Open that box. I want to see it."

Cara took a step closer to her. All she could do was offer silent support. She knew what strain Darcy was under, but she also knew that in her place she would have had to do the same thing.

Jock opened the lid. "Quick look, and then we'll be out of here. It's not necessary to— What the hell!" He started to swear.

Glass. Shattered mirror pieces spread all over the interior of the box. No intact mirror reflecting their faces. Jagged splinters. Total destruction.

Cara stared down at it stunned. "You said it was— It's not supposed to be like this, Jock."

"Tell me about it."

"Maybe one of the police clerks was careless?"

"It has a fragile tag. Police know how to care for evidence. It can make the difference between a murderer's going free or being convicted."

"He was here." Darcy's face was pale. "Or he paid somebody to do it. That could happen, couldn't it, Jock?"

"It could happen," he said quietly. "But he'd have to have a good reason to go to all that trouble."

"He's crazy." Her voice was shaking. "I think that's probably a good enough reason for him. But let's take it a step further. He wanted to prove he could do it and make us feel helpless. And he wanted to tell us that there's going to be another death, that he wasn't done." She was staring at the glittering shards of glass. "That there was still another twin who had to die."

Cara grasped her arm. "He's wrong. We won't let him touch you."

"I'm saying what he intends. Not what's going to happen," Darcy said. "I won't let him kill me. He butchered Sylvie. I won't let him do that to—"

"What's that scrap?" Cara had stiffened and was looking down at a bit of colored material on the bottom of the box that was half covered in glittering mirrored shards. "I've seen that—" Then she realized what it was. Her heart lurched. "No!" She couldn't breathe. "*My God. No!*"

Eve's phone was ringing.

"Cara. She was worried about how Darcy would take that visit to the precinct." She accessed the call. "How did it go? Is she—"

"Michael," Cara gasped. "Do you have Michael with you?"

She stiffened. "Easy. He's only about twenty yards away inside the ice-cream shop."

"Go get him. The mirror was broken. You have to get him."

"Calm down. Tell me."

"There was a scrap of the material they use in the soccer uniforms in the bottom of the box. Red and gold. Don't ask questions. Go get him. Red and gold."

"Right." She dropped the phone. "We've got to go get Michael, Joe." She was out of the car. Her heart was beating so hard she could barely breathe. She could see the boys inside the shop as she started running toward it.

Red and gold.

Red and gold.

Red and gold.

And then there was only red.

The blast knocked her to the ground.

She could see the flames leaping high as the second blast ignited and blew what was left of the shop into the sky.

She *screamed*.

Joe was running toward the building.

He was going to go get Michael.

She had to help him.

She struggled to her feet.

Another blast!

She was knocked down again as the shops on either side of the Ice Cream Emporium blew up.

Joe was tossed several yards back onto the parking lot and lay still.

Then two more blasts.

The entire square was in flames.

But she had to get to Michael.

Michael was in there. Maybe there was air near the floor. He could be alive. He had to be alive.

She had to get to Michael.

She was on her feet and moving toward the shop.

"No." Joe was on his knees. His clothes in tatters, his face bleeding. "Not you. I'll do it."

What was he saying? Michael was in there. She had to get him out. Fire . . . So much fire. Joe always wanted to do it, wanted to do everything. But he was her son. She couldn't let him—

Another explosion.

She was on the ground again. But not from the explosion, Joe had tackled her.

"I'll *do* it." He was staring down at her. "Stay here. I'll do it." He was trying to get to his feet. "Stay here."

"You can't go in there." It was one of the police officers who had been in the squad car who had grabbed Joe. "Neither of you. Suicide. The entire square is going up."

"My son . . ." Eve was struggling to get up. "Don't tell me that. I have to get my son."

"I understand. God, I'm sorry, ma'am." He nodded to someone over her head. "It's too late. We have to stop you. I can't let you—"

"Don't you *hurt* her." Joe tore free from the officer's hand. "I'll take care of it." He was kneeling beside her. "You can't help, love." His hand was on her neck. "Just go to sleep for a while . . ."

Darkness.

Noise.

So much noise.

Screams. People crying. Sirens. Helicopters.

Crackling. Something was burning . . .

She opened her eyes. Ambulance. She was lying on a stretcher in an ambulance.

Joe.

But not Joe. His head was bandaged and his face was black with soot except for the streaks on his cheeks. Tears. Joe had been crying. She reached out and touched his cheek. "Joe? Okay?"

"Hi." He took her hand and raised it to his lips. "Not okay." His voice broke on the words. "You're going to remember in a minute. I had them give you a sedative, but it's not going to do much good. So I'm going to tell you what's happening while you can still process it. Norwalk did what he does best and wired the entire square to blow. Not just the ice-cream shop, the whole damn square, so he could have his fantastic 'statement.' Thirty-six shops and they don't know how many victims yet." His voice was a little unsteady. "Together with the ice-cream shop, they're guessing at least fifty victims."

"Ice-cream shop," she repeated. There was something to recall about the ice-cream shop, but it wasn't coming clear. "Norwalk . . ."

"You'll remember him very soon. What you have to know is that he's very good at what he does. Those blasts were superefficient. When they went off, no one inside could have survived. It wouldn't have mattered if we'd managed to get inside. We wouldn't have found anyone alive. There were a few bodies blown out by the explosion, but even they didn't survive." His hand tightened on hers. "You have to understand that. There was *nothing* you could do once that explosion went off. There was nothing I could do."

He sounded so desperate, she realized vaguely. Poor Joe, why did he sound so sad and desperate? Why was he pleading with her to understand? She always understood that he did his best. Always.

Explosion?

What had he been talking about?

But the mist was clearing now.

Red and gold. Red and gold.

Red!

She screamed!

Joe grabbed her close, holding her, rocking her back and forth in an agony of sorrow. "I know. I know. Hold on to me. I can't make it right, but just hold on to me."

"Michael!"

"I know." He kept repeating it. "I know. Hold on to me."

"He didn't get out?" She couldn't believe it. "Of course he got out. It's Michael. Michael couldn't die. God wouldn't let Michael die."

"I didn't think so either." The tears were running down his face again. "Not Michael. We need him too much. It shouldn't have happened."

"There's some kind of mistake. I lost Bonnie. I can't lose Michael, too." The pain was unbearable. She had to get away from it. She was thrashing back and forth, trying to escape.

Red and gold. Red and gold.

Fire.

Had Michael felt the fire?

No, Joe had said it had happened when the explosion went off.

Michael had died when the explosion had gone off.

No!

Red and gold.

Death was like sleep.

Michael curled up in bed, asleep, with her bending over him.

Red and gold.

"Eve." Joe holding her tight. "Let me help. Let me do something."

What could he do? What could anyone do?

If Michael was gone, what could anyone do?

Empty. The world was empty.

Red and gold.

Don't let the red come again.

Please don't let it come.

It was a monster, like Norwalk was a monster.

The pain was increasing. She could feel herself curling in a fetal position to get away from it. Go away. Go away. Go away.

Yes, that was what she had to do. Go away and never come back.

Red and gold.

Red and gold.

If she went away, that monster red would never come back. There would only be the dark.

Red and gold . . .

Darkness.

No, not really darkness.

Swirling gray mist, cold against her hot skin.

Why was it hot?

Fire.

"No, Mama. No fire. Not for me," Michael said. "Don't cry. I'd never leave you. Not even like this."

Red and gold.

But she could see him now. Red-and-gold knee socks. Red shorts, gold jersey. Not smiling. Sad. So sad. But it *was* Michael, and she could feel the agony of his worry for her.

"Michael?"

"Please don't hurt like this." His eyes were moist with tears. "I can't stand it. I don't know what to do about it. I want to come to you, but I can't right now. You might have to come to me."

"Then I'll come to you. Just tell me Joe's wrong." But he might mean something else. "Or if he's right, tell me how I can come to be with you there."

"No, you mustn't think about that!"

"Then tell me your dad's wrong."

"Is that all it takes to make you stop hurting? It's true. Dad's wrong, Mama . . ."

Cold mist.

Darkness . . .

And then the overhead light of the interior of the ambulance.

Joe's face above her.

"Don't do that to me," he said unsteadily. "I can't lose you, too."

"Not fair," she murmured. "I know I'm not being fair. I should be stronger for you. But it's Michael, Joe. I couldn't stand that I—" She drew him down and held him tight. "But maybe we won't have to do it. Just hold me for a moment and let me . . ." Hallucination? Survival in the only way left to her? Or Michael? Oh God, let it be Michael. "Just give me a little time, then we'll talk . . ."

CHAPTER

12

"There's such a thing as wanting something so desperately that you will it into being," Joe said in a low voice as he stroked her hair. "I don't know whether it's mental or the real thing. But there's no doubt you want Michael back so badly that you could refuse to accept reality and make up your own scenario."

"I know that I could do that," Eve said unsteadily. "But I'm hoping that I didn't. It *felt* like Michael, Joe. You know that from the moment he was conceived, I could feel him, sense him. I could tell what he was thinking. Later, as he grew older, it faded away. But this was *him*, Joe. He was upset because I was hurting so badly, and he couldn't get to me. He said I might have to come to him." She paused. "I imagine you know what I thought he might mean."

"Yeah, I know."

"And he knew also. But he said, 'No,' and then, 'Dad's wrong.'"

"I want to believe that," he said thickly. "Lord, I want to believe it."

"I think I have to believe it," she said unevenly. "I'm not certain I won't turn catatonic again if I don't. Michael wouldn't like that." She pushed him away and sat up. "So now I have to act like a coherent human being instead of an emotional wreck. If it's true, there's a chance that Michael might need us." She brushed the hair away from her face. "How badly hurt am I?"

"Not bad. Severe bruising. Your cheek looks swollen and purple like a truck hit you. But the EMTs weren't worried about your physical health."

"No, they thought I was heading for a nervous breakdown." She hoped they were wrong. If she had purpose, if she had a miracle, if she had a chance for Michael, they would be wrong. She was barefoot but she was dressed in an oversized blue man's shirt and loose khaki pants, "What happened to my clothes?"

"The same thing that happened to mine. Blast. We were too close. But they scrounged a pair of pants and shirt for me, too, from one of the merchants in another shopping center."

"Call Cara and tell her I need—" Her gaze flew to Joe's face. "Cara?"

"She's outside. She and Darcy and Jock got here about thirty minutes ago. I told her she couldn't see you until after I told you."

"I'll have to see her right away. She loves Michael. She must be devastated."

"Everyone loves Michael. But she has Jock and Darcy. She's not alone."

"But sometimes it seems that way, doesn't it? One person goes away and it seems like the whole world is—" She stopped. "Okay, you go out and talk to them while I pull myself together." She smiled. "Be sure to let them know what great delusions I'm having. It will save me from explaining, and I really don't want to go through that craziness."

"They'll understand regardless, Eve." He headed for the door. "Take your time before you decide to come out. What you're going to see will make you want to turn around and run back inside."

Joe was right, Eve thought sickly, as she opened the vehicle door and stepped outside. The formerly small, charming, square looked like a postnuclear disaster site. The shops were almost all totally leveled and on fire. The fire department had been called, and some of the fires had been put out on the end units, but the ones burning in the middle were still feeding each other.

Red and gold.

Red.

Red flame, eating away everything it touched.

Fifty dead. It had touched at least fifty, Joe had said.

TV cameras. Police. Yellow tapes encircling the entire square.

Her gaze was drawn toward the place where the Ice Cream Emporium had stood, but she could no longer tell where it had been. The raging fire had made everything along that stretch one huge flaming conglomeration.

"Eve!" Cara was running toward her, tears running down her cheeks. "I'm so sorry. Maybe if I'd seen that scrap of material sooner. Maybe if I'd—" She was in Eve's arms, holding her close. "I should have been here for you. Maybe if I—"

"Shh, if you give me one more 'maybe,' I'll be very upset with you." She held her tight an instant longer, then stepped back. "We could all play that word game into infinity and it wouldn't help. No one is to blame but Rory Norwalk." She was still staring in horror at the scene before her. "And no one could ever forgive him for it."

"For nothing." Darcy was suddenly beside her, her gaze fixed on the inferno, her voice harsh with bitterness. "Like Sylvie. All those people died for nothing. It wasn't only Michael, he wanted to show you how powerful he was, what he could do."

"And he did it." Eve tore her eyes away from the flames. She felt as if she were being pulled into that inferno, devoured in the sorrow of it all. She couldn't allow that to happen. Not if there was a chance that Michael was still alive. She had to look for him, find him, figure it all out. She forced herself to look at the makeshift morgue at the far end of the square, where she could see the bodies lying on the ground.

"I have to look at the bodies that were blown out of the shop. Joe said that none of them were Michael, but I have to see for myself."

Cara shook her head. "Eve, you don't want to see—"

"No, I don't," Eve interrupted fiercely. "I don't want to see any of it, but I have to be certain. If Michael's not one of those boys, then I can eliminate that possibility. Yes, he could be in that inferno or blown to bits, but if I have no evidence, then I can still believe that somehow he's still alive. I've got to believe that to keep me going, Cara."

Joe stepped forward, and said quietly, "Don't argue. Just let her go, Cara."

Cara nodded jerkily. "I'll go with you, Eve."

Eve shook her head but didn't answer. She was already walking toward those tarp-covered bodies. Not only the three boys from the emporium, but six other bodies that had been tossed out like broken dolls from the blast.

A police officer was coming forward to stop her, but Joe waved him aside. "The ones on the end, Eve," he said quietly as he stepped in front of her. "One quick glance should show you. Don't let yourself look any longer than that."

"It's not that I don't trust you, Joe," she said hoarsely.

"I know. It's just that you have to be able to trust yourself, what you're feeling." He lifted the first tarp. "Smaller than Michael. Blond hair."

She flinched. "Right."

He lifted the second tarp. "About the same height but very dark hair."

She nodded.

He lifted the third tarp. "Much taller than Michael."

She inhaled sharply. The boy's face had been almost destroyed, but she knew who he was. "Gary."

"Yes." He dropped the tarp. "Done?"

"Done." She said shakily. But it could never be done until Norwalk paid for those atrocities. She turned away. "Thank you, Joe."

"For giving you new food for nightmares?" He took her arm and drew her away from the bodies. "I want to get you away from here. Will you come home with me?"

"Soon." She stood looking at the fire. "He's not there, Joe. Michael's not there. It's *not* my imagination."

"God, I hope it's not." His eyes were glittering with moisture. "It will be hard for anyone to verify who was killed in that explosion for a long time."

"Maybe not." Eve's gaze never left the flames. "Not if he tells us."

"What?"

"Norwalk told me he wanted me to see, feel, taste the pain. I believe this qualifies, don't you? But maybe he thinks it's not enough, not as close-up and personal as he wants." She had to say it. "It could be he has other plans for Michael."

Joe was silent. "Torture?"

"I'm trying not to think of that." But it was hard not to think of that possibility. "But whatever he plans, he'd want me to see it. He'll get in touch with me. But it won't be before he believes I've received the full measure of agony from this monstrosity." She swallowed. "So I'll stay here for a little while longer and stare at his handiwork in case he has someone here watching me. I'll pray for those poor victims, and I'll pray for Michael." She paused. "And I'll pray that God gives us a way to strike down that monster and send him straight to the depths of hell."

Eve managed to stay almost an hour and thirty minutes longer before she let Joe help her back to the car.

"You look like you're about to collapse," he said roughly as he tucked her into the passenger seat. "You should have gone right home. It took too much out of you."

She nodded wearily. "I felt as if I were bleeding. But so did those other parents who were standing and watching that fire. At least, I have hope to hold on to."

"I wanted to catch you before you left." Jock was suddenly beside the car. "One of the TV stations got an interview from the wife of the owner of the Ice Cream Emporium. She said that the coach usually took the boys of his sports teams to the shop for ice cream if they won their game. But last week, one of the fathers dropped by the shop and offered to pay for a gift certificate to offer the coach to buy treats for the boys regardless of whether they won or lost."

"And the father resembled Rory Norwalk?" Joe asked.

"General description. Irish accent." His gaze shifted to Eve's face. "What can I do?" he said gently. His eyes were glowing with sympathy. "I don't need to say what I'm feeling for you, do I?"

She shook her head. "Just keep on doing what you're doing. We have to find him, Jock." She saw his eyes wander back toward the fire. "He's not there. Believe me."

He smiled. "I believe he's a wonderful lad. I believe that you believe. I'll be there when you need me." He lifted his hand and moved away. "And when Cara needs me. I'll take her and Darcy home now. They wouldn't leave until you did."

She watched him go as Joe pulled out of the parking lot and got on the road. "Very diplomatic answer. He probably doesn't believe me."

"He might. He's a Scot. Even if he doesn't, as he said, he'll be there for you. He'll be there to rejoice or to comfort." He paused. "Or to go to war for you. Can't ask more than that, Eve."

"No." She looked back at the fire, now in the distance. "It's a horror story, Joe. All those little boys who had everything to live for, all those innocent people just going about their day. We've got to stop him from ever doing anything like that again." She leaned back on the headrest and wearily closed her eyes. "But first, we've got to get our Michael back from him. We can't let him win that battle."

"You're already on your way to winning it," Joe said gruffly. His hand left the wheel to cover hers on the seat. "I saw you start when you came back to me after I thought I'd lost you. I don't know if it was Michael, I hope it was, but I'd never seen a despair like that. But you came back, and I'm going to keep you here until we find Michael. No matter what it takes."

"You're what it takes. You and Michael." She closed her eyes again. "I'm not even sure that you believe me, Joe. That's okay, except that you'd know there was hope. That's what's keeping me going, and I want to share it with you . . ."

"Then I'll try to share that with you. You may have to help me a little."

"I'll help you. We may all have to help each other." Even with her eyes shut, she could still see that inferno she'd just left. Still feel the panic that Michael had wanted to save her from. I'm holding on, Michael, she told him. I'll find a way to get to you. But it's a horror story . . .

Dense leaves hiding the sky, cypress roots reaching deep into the water clutching like giant teeth. A small hand reaching into those dark waters as the canoe passed those roots. Michael's hand . . .

Eve gasped and jerked upright in bed. "Michael!"

Joe was beside her, holding her. "I'm here, Eve."

She drew a shaky breath. "So was Michael." She ran a hand through her hair. "Or it might have been a dream or a nightmare, but he could *feel* the water on his hand. He was curious about the water underneath the tree roots and wanted to—" She stopped. "You know how curious he is, Joe."

"Yes, I know." He was holding her. "But you also know it's natural for you to have dreams about him right now. Try to go back to sleep, Eve."

"Not right now." She swung her legs to the floor. "I'm going to go get a breath of air. I won't be long, Joe." She shrugged into her robe and put her hand up as he started to get out of bed. "Don't come with me. I'll be fine. I just want a little time to myself." That was the truth. After they'd reached home last night, Joe had helped her to bed and held her until she'd gone to sleep. So loving, so protective, but she could feel both his pain and her own, and it was overwhelming. If she wanted to stay sane and controlled, she had to let herself face whatever was in store and not be protected.

It was almost five in the morning and still dark as she went out on the porch. The lake was rough this morning, not like the still, murky water she'd just dreamed about.

If it was a dream.

If it wasn't Michael trying to reach her.

"Eve?"

She turned to see Cara standing in the doorway. "Are you okay? Can I help? I'll go away if I'm a bother."

"You're never a bother." She held out her arms. "Come here."

Cara ran into her arms. "I won't get in your way. You seemed to want your own space, and that's fine. I just want you to know that whatever you want me to believe or do, I'll do it."

Eve smiled ruefully. "Even to the point that Michael told me he's alive?"

"Whatever." She leaned back and looked at her, eyes glittering with tears in the moonlight. "You're a wonderful woman, and Michael is Michael. Why shouldn't God give you a break? I want so *badly* to have him back, Eve. If you tell me that it's going to happen, it's going to happen."

Cara. So full of love and youth and faith where there should be no faith. Eve kissed her cheek. "Thank you, Cara. All I can tell you is that I don't believe Michael died back at that square. And we'll get him back because we have to do it. I don't think any of us can stand to lose Michael. We'll just have to go from there."

She nodded. "Whatever you say. But don't try to do everything yourself. We can't afford to lose you, either." She hugged her quickly and turned toward the door. "I'll let you have your space. Call me if you need me. Anything, Eve."

"I know. The best thing will be to try to be normal, and just hold ourselves together. Because if—" She instantly corrected the word. "Since Michael is alive, it's because Norwalk wants him to be alive, and I'll have to wait for him to call." Eve turned back to look at the lake. "But right now, I just need to think."

Think about still, murky water, jagged tree roots disappearing below the surface.

And a small curious hand dipping down into the water near those roots to explore . . .

The call came at noon that same day. Eve was still sitting on the porch, but Joe had come to be with her and was standing looking out at the lake.

No ID.

Her hand was trembling uncontrollably as she reached for the cell phone.

He's alive. He's alive. He's alive. She was saying it over and over again to herself as a desperate mantra as she accessed the call and pressed the speaker button.

"Hello," she said. Even to herself the word was only a breath of sound.

"You're answering your own phone," Norwalk said. "You're stronger than I thought. I was afraid you might have collapsed, and I'd have to go through Quinn to make you take my call."

She saw Joe tense to rigid attention.

"Norwalk. What kind of monster would do that?" Her voice was shaking as badly as her hands. "Innocents . . . Children . . ."

"There are no innocents in the world, Eve. There are just people who haven't had opportunity to reach out and grab. I learned that as a child myself."

Tell me he's *alive.*

She couldn't ask him. It might be a weapon she could use. He had to believe he was totally in control, that she was as without hope as he'd wanted her to be. He'd use anything to twist the knife.

"They'll catch you," she said harshly. "It's not only Michael, over fifty people died in that square. Every law-enforcement agency in the country will be after you. They'll hunt you down and kill you. There's no place you can hide."

"Do you think I'm an amateur? I'm very good at hiding, and I've had a long time to plan. No one will catch me." He paused, and said softly, "And I have no intention of going on the run until I finish what I started. Sean would never forgive me. The square was just the opening shot, Eve. Did you know I had a few choice photos taken of you on the scene and sent to me? No, of course, you didn't. You've been devastated by all this, haven't you? You looked as if you were being tortured on the rack. I enjoyed those photos enormously."

"Bastard."

"Now you mustn't make me angry with you. Be polite. I hold all the cards, Eve."

Tell me he's alive. Why didn't he say the words?

"The game's over as far as I'm concerned," she said hoarsely. "All I have left to do is to bury what's left of my son and find a way to help the police hunt you down."

"You don't want the police involved. That would be a mistake. And the game is far from over, this move was just to position all the players conveniently in place."

"Fifty-two deaths?"

"You're being overemotional, Eve. You mustn't fall apart like this. Your son has much more control than you do. I wasn't expecting that, but it's far more convenient for me."

She went rigid. She couldn't breathe. Was it coming? *Tell* me. "Are you insane? My son is dead. You murdered him."

"Did I? Then I wonder who's staring at me right now with those huge brown eyes. He doesn't talk a lot, but he stares at me all the time. It's beginning to annoy me."

"You're lying."

"But there's the *tiniest* bit of hope, isn't there?"

Dear God more than that. She was dizzy with hope. "No, because I realize that you want to bring me up so that you can crash me down."

"True. But that comes later, after you've gone through hell trying to get this fine lad back to your loving arms."

"You have to be lying."

"No, I was in the back of the Emporium watching all the joy and frivolity. When the time came to put an end to it, I knocked the boy out with an injection and took him out the back way. We were out of the square a few minutes before it blew." He added regretfully, "I didn't really get a good look at my handiwork. It's lucky that I have the photos."

Now she could say the words she'd been keeping back. "He's really alive?"

"Would I lie to you? Yes, I would, but not at the moment. You have to know what you have to do to keep the boy alive. Michael and I are together and will stay together for the foreseeable future. Your next move in the game is to come after him and try to get him away from me before I get impatient enough to dispose of him. Of course, there would be considerable pain before I got to that point. You wouldn't want that to happen. Your son appears to have great affection for you. As I said, he seems very controlled for a child, and the only time I saw him cry was when I showed him those photos of you at the square."

She could see how those photos would have hurt and disturbed Michael. "That was terribly cruel."

"He deserved it. I wanted him to stop—" He broke off and said, "I'm in charge of him. I can do whatever I like. So come and get him, Eve. No police. No FBI. That would mean his immediate death.

Step into my parlor. Positioning. I want you here. I want Cara Delaney here."

"I won't take your word for it that Michael is alive. Prove it."

"I'm sending you a photo now with the usual boring newspaper to verify date." He added, "And now I'll let you talk to the little bastard."

An instant later, Michael was on the line. "Mama, it's okay," he said in a rush. "No, it's not okay, but don't worry about me. Don't let it hurt you. I'll be all right. There has to be ways—don't worry."

"I'll try." She tried to keep her voice steady for his sake. "I'm coming for you. Keep yourself safe. I love—"

"Touching." Norwalk had come back on the line. "Just exactly the interchange that will bring about what I need from you. Goodbye, Eve. I'll see you soon." He hung up.

Joe grabbed her phone and was trying to check on the possible trace he'd set up.

Eve collapsed back on the swing. She felt weak and dizzy . . . and grateful.

Thank you, God. Thank you, God.

Michael.

"No trace," Joe said curtly. "But it was Michael?" He fell to his knees in front of her. "It was really Michael?"

She nodded jerkily. "You heard. It was him, Joe."

"Hey, then why are you crying?" He touched her wet cheek. "You knew it all along, right?" His eyes were also wet. "Just a confirmation . . ."

Yes, a confirmation.

And the answer to a prayer.

She went into his arms and held him tight for a moment. "And he was worried about *me*," she said brokenly. "Yes, it was Michael . . ." She drew a shaky breath. "The photo. We need to see his photo." She took her phone back and accessed the photo.

Michael still in his gold jersey and red shorts. He was standing in front of a tree and holding a newspaper. She zoomed in and enlarged it. "*Times-Picayune*. Today's date."

"*Times-Picayune*." Joe said. "New Orleans newspaper. Unless Norwalk's trying to lay a false trail."

"No, he's not trying to lay a false trail." Eve was still gazing feverishly at Michael. He looked pale, there was a bruise on his cheek, but he didn't look frightened. She hated the idea of that son of a bitch scaring him. "He's telling us where to come."

"New Orleans?"

"No, not New Orleans, but probably near there." She tossed him the sketch she'd made last night. "If we believe Michael somehow managed to reach me to let me know he was alive, I have to believe that dream meant something. Swamp, bayou, those cypress trees. We've been down there in those swamps, but we've never taken Michael. Naturally, he'd be curious about a bayou."

"Naturally," Joe said absently. "There are a hell of a lot of bayous and swamps near New Orleans."

"But maybe not that many close to Kaskov." She met his eyes. "He kept saying the word positioning. He wants all the targets in a row so that he can pick us off in the most painful and efficient way possible. But he has to have Kaskov because he's the one who gave the order to kill his brother. So Norwalk is bringing us down to Kaskov so that he can also use us to get to him. He knows Cara might be useful since Kaskov killed Norwalk's twin to protect her." Her lips twisted. "And we both know why I have to be there. He wants to kill Michael in front of me."

Michael. She couldn't think of him right now. She was getting too shaky. There was too much to do, and it all had to be done at top speed.

"But that's not going to happen." She got to her feet. "I'm leaving for New Orleans today. We have to start right away to make certain we kill Norwalk before he gets too 'impatient.'"

He nodded. "But you have to know that this is going to spark a massive manhunt. Homeland Security might even become involved if they think terrorists could be involved."

"And I'd be grateful if I didn't think it might get Michael killed. Michael will die the moment that bastard feels cornered. We have to find Norwalk before they do." She headed for the door. "Now I'll go tell Cara and Darcy that I'm not crazy and that Michael is still alive. They'll be relieved on both counts. Will you call Jock and tell him we have to know everything possible about Kaskov's estate down there and the surrounding area? Particularly any swamps or bayous?"

He nodded. "And one of Norwalk's men was taking photos of the disaster last night. He's probably not still in town, but if we can find out who he is and a description, it may help to find him."

She looked over her shoulder. "And I believe that either you or Jock would be able to make him tell anything he knows about Norwalk, don't you?" She added grimly, "If not, I'd be glad to do it myself."

She shut the door behind her.

BLACK POOL BAYOU

The damn boy was staring at him again, Norwalk thought with annoyance. He'd expected talking to his mother would upset him, maybe make him break down in tears. Why hadn't it done that?

"Stop looking at me." He grabbed Michael's shoulder and shoved him toward the canoe. "You're going to die, you know. I wouldn't even have to do it myself. There are so many ways to die in this swamp. Drowning. Coral snakes. Some say there's even a swamp monster sighted around here called a Rougarou. And what about alligators? How would you like to be eaten by an alligator, brat?"

"I've never seen an alligator except on TV." Michael looked at Norwalk as he got into the canoe. "They look ugly and mean, but maybe they're just hungry. Do they really eat people?"

No fear. Why wasn't the kid afraid? Since the moment he'd regained consciousness on the plane, Michael had not behaved like any normal kid. He'd started to fight and struggle, but when he realized it wasn't working, he'd stopped and just stared at Norwalk as if he were some kind of puzzle he had to solve. Even Norwalk telling him what he'd done to the other boys in that ice-cream shop had not caused him to break. He'd just seemed to draw into himself and gotten very quiet.

Now the boy was staring at him with those clear brown eyes that held only curiosity and something else that was once again filling Norwalk with frustration and uneasiness. He instinctively struck out. "You'll find out. Maybe I'll let you watch me feed your mother to the alligators first, you weirdo. Yes, I think that would be a great idea."

"Mama?" Michael tensed as he looked down at the murky waters. "No, I don't think I could let you do that." He raised his eyes to meet Norwalk's again. "Though I would like to see one sometime."

"Oh, you definitely will." Norwalk started paddling through the swamp with long strokes. "It's only a question of when."

"I guess you're right. A question of when." Michael looked down at the waters again. "Alligator . . ."

LAKE COTTAGE

"**Kaskov?**" Cara repeated, staring at Eve. Then she nodded her head. "I can see how Norwalk would think any attack should revolve around him. He'd be the best protected, the hardest to target." Her lips twisted wryly. "And if he wants us there, it appears the ball is in his court."

"No real choice. He has Michael," Eve said. Cara and Darcy had listened quietly as Eve had told them about Norwalk's call, but Eve had been able to tell that Cara was thinking, eagerly searching to put together a plan. "You don't have to be involved in this, Cara," she said. "I don't *want* you in it. Yes, I know Norwalk will want to use you to bait Kaskov. But I might be enough for him."

"And you might not," Cara said. "As you say, he has Michael. Who knows what that monster might do to him to convince you to do exactly what he wants. How could I take that chance?" She added impatiently, "Of course I'll be involved. I wouldn't think anything else. I'd be with you regardless of what that son of a bitch wanted. We've had a miracle, Eve. Michael's alive. We just have to follow through to make sure that we get him back." She smiled. "And that I don't end my promising career while I'm playing bait."

Eve gave her a quick hug. "That won't happen."

"Of course it won't." Darcy broke her silence as she got to her feet. "I don't have that many friends. I won't lose you, Cara." She looked at Eve. "I'm going with you."

"No."

"Oh, yes." Darcy's smiled sardonically. "Though as usual, I haven't been given an invitation. Norwalk regards me as unimportant, a nonentity, perhaps just a statement. Do you know, Eve, when we opened that gold box and saw the broken mirror, I thought it was a warning for me? But it wasn't, he's through with me. It was to tell you that he was going to kill Michael." Her lips tightened. "Well, I'm not through with him. I'm not going to let him hurt that little boy as he did Sylvie."

"I don't know what you can do," Eve said quietly.

"I'm very talented and innovative. I'll find a way to make myself useful. When do we leave?"

She could tell that Darcy would not be dissuaded. Who would have more reason than her to want Norwalk destroyed? "Sometime today." Eve got to her feet. "Jock and Joe might want some more time here. But regardless, I'll be in New Orleans by late tonight."

"I'll start packing." Darcy looked over her shoulder. "But I believe it's time for you to ask Joe to get me that gun we talked about. It could help if innovation doesn't work."

Guns, Eve thought as she felt a ripple of shock go through her. Weapons and danger and these two young women who might have to contend with both. All to help her and Michael and rid the world of Rory Norwalk. But it was going to be such a dangerous path. It wasn't fair to them. What could she do to make it safer? She could think of only one way.

"Eve?" Cara was studying her. "Okay?"

"It will be." She reached for her phone. "As okay as I can manage right now."

She dialed quickly. Kaskov answered in three rings.

"I've seen the CNN report about the explosions, Eve," he said quietly. "You have my deepest sympathy regarding your son. I hope you're not calling because you have some misguided notion that I had anything to do with it."

"I don't want your sympathy. I want your help. And I'm going to get it. You probably started most of this, but we're caught in the middle of it. So I'm going to tell you what's been happening and what I need you to do. And you *will* do it, Kaskov."

The embers of the fire at Gwinnet Square were still flaring to life occasionally, but the search and recovery teams were at work when Jock and Joe reached the disaster area. So was a police command center, several police officers and plainclothesmen, and two television crews.

"I'll go check and see if any of the officers who worked that night noticed anyone suspicious," Joe said. "Cops know pyromaniacs often like to stay and watch their destruction, and someone taking photos should have attracted attention. You go check with the TV crews and see if they noticed any paparazzi ghouls at the scene. Most reporters wouldn't want to share their big story."

"Ghouls is right," Jock said grimly as he gazed at the wreckage of the square. "But whoever took those photos wasn't focusing on the disaster, he was after the human element. That should have set him apart." He strode toward the ABC TV truck. "I'll nudge their memories."

"Gently," Joe said.

"As long as it's quick," Jock said. "I'm going to have a lead before Cara gets on that plane for New Orleans. I'll get them to play me their footage from those first few hours after the explosion. I may be able to spot our ghoul myself." He glanced at Joe. "You persist in thinking that I might go off the rails. Newspeople don't respond well to violence. I'd tend to get the wrong result. I don't get wrong results."

Joe watched Jock as he approached the TV truck, smiling at the young journalist who was gazing speculatively at him.

No, Jock would not get a wrong result this time either. He'd do whatever he needed to do to get the job done. So forget him and go about your own business, Joe thought. He headed toward the Officer in Charge at the Police Command Center.

"Got him," Jock said as he strode toward Joe three hours later. He handed his phone to Joe. "Their cameras caught shots of this guy moving in and out of the crowd watching the fire. He wasn't too concerned about the explosion, he was taking shots of Eve, Cara. Even you, Joe." His lips tightened. "Norwalk didn't miss a thing by skipping out when he did. He got everything he could want to satisfy him."

Joe scanned quickly through the photos. A tall man in a black windbreaker, thirtysomething, dark hair in a crew cut, hooked nose. "I'll check the Interpol database and see if I can ID him. There wasn't anyone else who could be a contender?"

Jock shook his head. "Some people were taking photos, but it was all about the disaster for them. Run these and see what you get. In the meantime, I'll send them to Benoit and see if he can connect them to anyone in Norwalk's organization in Dublin." He headed for his car. "And I'd make a bet this particular ghoul headed for New Orleans the minute he'd finished doing his duty for Norwalk here. You might see if you can check the airlines and see if anyone recognizes him."

"Not likely. With the thousands of people who pass through that airport, faces are just a blur to them." He held up his hand. "I'll check it. But I have a better chance with Interpol." He gazed at that face again. He remembered how agonized Eve had looked last night, and this scum had taken her photo when she'd been at her most vulnerable. "I'll do anything I can. I *want* him, Jock." He got into his car. "I'm going to the precinct and work on this. It may take a little time. But Eve called me, and she's going to be on a flight leaving in two hours to New Orleans, with Cara and Darcy. She's not waiting for anything. Who can blame her? She's going to Michael." He looked at Jock. "I don't want them alone there. Not for a minute. I don't think you do either."

"Two hours." Jock turned away and headed for his own car. "They're not going to be alone. Call Eve and tell her I'll meet them at the airport."

CHAPTER

13

Their Delta flight landed in New Orleans at 11:40 P.M.

Jock stopped Cara for a moment while they were waiting for the doors to open. "What the hell is wrong? What did I do? You have barely looked or spoken to me since I met you at the airport."

She still didn't look at him. "You haven't done anything."

"That's not good enough. Look, I know you're traumatized by what happened. We're all going through hell. Is it something you think I did wrong? I thought you wanted to be with Eve and Joe. It wasn't because I didn't feel your pain and was ignoring you."

"I know that." The doors were open now, and Cara moved quickly forward after Eve down the jetway. This was so terribly difficult, she thought. But she had promised. And it was a little thing compared to what Eve was going through.

Eve.

Support her.

Protect her.

She moved closer to Eve in that silent support as they moved toward the exit.

Jock glanced at the taxis and shook his head. "I made reservations for you at the Windsor Hotel and reserved a car. Give me a minute, and I'll bring it around."

"No." Eve stepped forward as a black limousine slid to a stop before them. "I believe we have transport."

Jock went rigid as he saw the driver get out of the car. "Nikolai?" He muttered a curse as his gaze shifted to Eve. "You expected him?"

She nodded. "I expected him. Kaskov prefers not to expose himself unnecessarily."

"And Nikolai is extremely capable," Jock said between set teeth. "Kaskov trusts him implicitly."

"Thank you," Nikolai said as he opened the passenger door. "It's good to have the trust of one's superiors. Are you going to accompany us to the compound? I was told to only pick up the three ladies."

"Oh, I'll be going to the compound," Jock said. "But I'll pick up my rental car and be right behind you." He looked at Eve. "I assume this is your choice? No manipulation by Kaskov?"

"My decision. My choice," Eve said quietly. "Any manipulation was on my part. I knew you wouldn't like it, so I thought I'd face you and Joe with a fait accompli." She got into the limousine. "I wasn't in any shape to face a struggle." She gestured to Cara and Darcy, who had followed her into the limo. "They were going to come with me no matter what I said. I had to find the best way to protect them."

"Best way?" He shook his head as his gaze met Cara's. "Major mistake, Eve." He turned on his heel and strode toward the rental-car lot.

Nikolai slammed the door and moved around to the driver's seat.

Eve looked at Cara. "He thinks you betrayed him by not telling him what I was going to do," she said wearily. "I just didn't know what else to do. As I told him, I'm rationing strength right now."

"He'll get over it," Cara said. "And if he doesn't, I'll face it then.

I know he's been too important to me. I can't let what he thinks run my life."

"Hey, Jock isn't going anywhere." Darcy smiled and reached for Cara's hand. "You did what Eve wanted, and he'll come to terms with it. If he doesn't, we'll send him on his way, and I'll show you how to live life like you're in the middle of a tornado. Of course, we'd have to change the destruction for sensuality, and add a really sexy rock star to the mix. You haven't lived until you've had a rock star or two. There's something about their rhythm that translates to—"

"Please don't." Eve was smiling. "Let her find her own way, Darcy."

Darcy grinned. "Only if she lets me come along for the ride."

"No question," Cara said. Darcy had managed to lighten the heaviness of the moment for both her and Eve. She was ready to face both Kaskov and Jock now. She squeezed Darcy's hand, then released it. "You're here for the long haul, Darcy. I'd have no idea how to handle that rock star."

Eve braced herself as Nikolai drove the limousine through the guarded gates of Belle Grace and up the sweeping driveway to the huge, columned mansion. Jock had told them that it was a compound, but the outbuildings were so graceful and well built and that no one would guess the men inhabiting them were criminals. Light was pouring out of the open front door, and she could see Kaskov silhouetted against the brightness. It was one thing to fire orders to Kaskov over the phone, but entirely different to come face-to-face with him. She remembered how intimidating he could be.

But no one was more intimidating than that monster who was holding her son.

Cara sensed that tension and leaned forward. "It will be fine. I'll stay with you."

Eve shook her head. "I'm not afraid of Kaskov. I'm just wondering how to handle him." Nikolai was opening the door and helping her out. "I'll work it out."

"Pleasant flight?" Kaskov was coming forward to meet her. "Welcome to Belle Grace." His voice was deep, silky. "I do hope you'll enjoy it since you were obviously so eager to come."

"I don't believe either one of us is going to enjoy my visit," Eve said. "All I can hope is that it's successful. It *has* to be successful, Kaskov." She turned to Darcy, who had just gotten out of the car. "Darcy Nichols. Sergai Kaskov, Darcy."

Darcy smiled. "I've heard interesting things about you, Mr. Kaskov."

He chuckled. "And that's an interesting way of greeting me." He looked at her critically. "Fantastic-looking. You may be worthwhile just for decoration." He turned to Cara and took her hand. "Here you are at last. I told you that you should come early. I'm sorry that it was this tragedy that brought you."

"I'm sorry, too. I know our coming will turn this place upside down." She looked him in the eye. "But I'm glad that you're going to help Eve. Michael is very important to me."

"I remember. After he was born, you couldn't be pried away from Eve. I had to wait a long time." He gestured toward the open door. "Come in. May I offer you all something?"

"We had a snack on the plane," Eve said as she followed him into the house. "We need rest more than food. None of us have slept much in the last twenty-four hours. If you could get Cara and Darcy settled, I'd appreciate it."

"Everything is prepared . . . as ordered." He turned to Nikolai. "You know what rooms to give them. The first three in the west wing. See that Cara and Miss Nichols are comfortable." He turned back to Eve. "I'll give you a glass of wine before you retire for the night if you don't mind?" He gestured to the lavish parlor. "Our conversation was so hurried when you called this afternoon. I'm sure we'll both sleep better to have everything clear."

"I think that's a good idea." She waved for Darcy and Cara to follow Nikolai upstairs. Kaskov's voice was silky smooth, but she could hear the thread of steel running through it. She had expected to meet nothing less. "A glass of wine always makes one more relaxed in difficult situations."

She followed him into the parlor and watched him as he went to the small cherry bar and poured two glasses of wine from a crystal decanter.

He brought her glass to her. "You look exhausted." His gaze was studying her face. "Strain. Shadows. Determination. Endurance." He took a sip of wine. "But no panic. No desperation. I thought you might be desperate since you called and spoke to me as you did."

"The desperation might come later. I have to keep it at bay right now. It would interfere with my thinking and making decisions. I can't let that happen." She lifted her glass. "And I'm sorry if you thought I wasn't polite to you. That was the last thing I was worried about when I decided I needed your help." She met his eyes. "Jock says you have an armed camp here, and that's what I need to protect Cara and Darcy. Under usual circumstances, I'd try my best to keep them away from you and your men. But I can't do that now. I'm going to have to rely on you to keep that son of a bitch from killing them. He's going to try. He's positioning us all for the kill."

"So you told me. But you're still here."

"Because we have to position *him* for the kill," she said simply. "It's the only way I can get my son back."

"Now that's an answer I understand." He smiled. "Particularly said with total ruthlessness and determination. You're very intimidating at this moment, Eve."

"He has Michael. No one can stand in my way." She took another sip of wine and set the glass on the table. "So we find Norwalk, we trap him, we kill him. You know a lot about all of those things, so I'll accept your help if you'll give it. If you don't want to help, then I believe you'll at least protect Cara." She tilted her head. "Won't you?"

He nodded. "If you'll recall, all of this started because I was protecting Cara from Sean Norwalk. Nothing has changed in that regard. I won't promise you anything else."

"I didn't expect any promises from you. I don't know if I'd believe them. But you do have some kind of feeling for Cara, and just living in an armed camp will make it safer for Darcy." She smiled without mirth. "And I'll use your armed camp. We need a place where we won't be vulnerable to launched attacks after we find my son. And don't be too confident about being able to stay out of the fray, Kaskov. You're the prime target."

"I never said I wanted to stay out of the fray. I just said that I'd make you no promises. I take care of my own business in my own time." He finished his wine and smiled. "But by all means, use my place as your own, and I'll instruct my men that I consider you all family. Amusing . . ."

"Not at all amusing." She rubbed the back of her neck. "Now I think I'll go to bed if you think I've been 'clear' enough. I'm very tired, and I've got to get over it."

"So that you'll have strength for the battle to come?" he asked softly. "Yes, that's what I'd do. We may be more alike than you dream, Eve."

"We're nothing alike." She turned and headed for the grand staircase. "I don't kill people."

"Except when it's important to you. You'll have no problem at all killing Norwalk to save your son." He lifted his glass to her. "Good night, Eve. Sleep well."

"Good night." She started up the stairs. She *would* sleep well. She had to rest and gain strength. Kaskov was right, there was a storm brewing and a battle on the horizon and she had to be ready.

I'm here, Michael. I'll never leave you. Hold on, I'll come to you . . .

Kaskov was sitting in a beige brocade easy chair in the parlor, his eyes closed, listening to Cara's concert CD when Jock walked into the room. He didn't open his eyes. "I really wish you'd have the courtesy to announce yourself, Gavin. I know you're probably annoyed, and there's a certain amount of power-satisfaction about being able to come and go as you please, but I'm beginning to find it irritating."

"You're right, I am annoyed. I didn't like being caught off guard, and I don't like anything that's happening between you and Eve. She thinks it's safer, but it's setting up everyone in one place for Norwalk."

"Then you'll have to talk to Eve." Kaskov opened his eyes. "She appears to be running the show. I'm just a poor lackey, doing her bidding."

"As long as you let her."

"I can't help myself. She's an indomitable force at the moment. A mother with a child in danger. There's no one more dangerous on the planet." He smiled. "Refreshing. I'm quite enjoying her."

"You'll not enjoy Cara's reaction, if you do anything to get in Eve's way. Nor my response, if you make my job harder."

"Oh, I'm well aware of all the land mines. Why do you think I waited up for you instead of going to bed and have you pay me a visit in the middle of the night again? I knew that you'd want to come and threaten me and so forth. So I put on Cara's newest CD to soothe me and keep me from being tempted to kill you. It was quite a wonderful concert, wasn't it?"

"Fantastic. She's always fantastic."

"And therefore worthy of being kept alive and producing fantastic music."

"She's more than her music."

"She *is* her music. It's an integral part of what some people call the soul. I could see it the first time she played for me when she was eleven years old." He smiled. "You've always been worried that I'd hurt her in some way. But there was never a chance of that. I would always protect the music."

"If you could manage to do it without her getting in your way."

"I will manage. Why do you think I haven't interfered with you hovering over her? What better protection could she have than you, Jock Gavin? If I'm not there, you would be." He met his eyes. "Perhaps in time, we might come to terms. Until then, I wanted you to know that if you see a threat you can't handle, you have only to call me. On this subject, we're on the same page."

He meant it. And there was no way that Jock would reject that offer. The power potential was too impressive. "I'll remember. I don't expect it to be necessary, but we both know that expectations aren't always fulfilled. Eve thinks that your security will be enough, but I managed to get through."

"But you're remarkable. Norwalk will not be that good."

Jock made an impatient gesture. "I'd rather not take the chance. I went over some of the weaknesses with Nikolai, but tomorrow I'll go and show him a few more."

"I thought you'd probably leave a few for you to slip into the property again."

"And the house isn't that safe either. Every house has its secrets. I'll look that over, too."

"We're at your disposal. I suppose you're staying here?"

"Not in the main house. You have a summerhouse on the grounds. It's close, and I'll be able to monitor your security guards and yet be here in a few minutes if it's necessary."

Kaskov smiled curiously. "And did you have that possibility in mind when you scoped out the property the last time you came?"

"Not consciously. It's an automatic response from my wicked, misspent past."

"I don't regard it as misspent. When you become an expert at anything, the time is well used."

"But then look to whom I'm talking." He turned and headed for the front door. "You might let Nikolai know I'm moving into the summerhouse so that he won't try to shoot me." He glanced back at him. "We might all get along if you give the order to everyone to stay out of my way, Kaskov."

"Warning received, noted, and under consideration." He leaned back in his chair again. "I've already given the order not to interfere with you, Gavin. Now run along and let me hear the end of Cara's concert. I think a Tchaikovsky encore comes next . . ."

It was Jock.

Cara could see him moving quickly down the path, through the rose garden, toward a small, but elegant white summerhouse near the huge hedge that led down to the bayou.

She took a step closer to the window as she saw a huge shadow near that hedge. Nikolai.

But he wasn't moving toward Jock she realized with relief. He was just standing there, watching him.

But Jock had stopped on the path. He was not confronting Nikolai but turning around and looking up at her second-floor window. He slowly nodded, then turned on his heel and continued down the path. The next moment he had disappeared into the summerhouse. It didn't surprise her that he'd known she was watching him. Not only had he been trained to the hunt, but they had always had a connection.

"Jock?" Darcy asked from her chair across the room.

Cara turned to look at her. "How did you know?"

"Body language. I'm really good at it. Why do you think everyone thought I was such a primo actress? Expressions are only part of creating a character. A lot of it is what happens with the body." She made a face. "And you're easy. Every time Jock comes within view you tense, change." She chuckled. "Besides, I hate to destroy my mystique, but we were expecting him to follow, weren't we? That's the reason I came in to keep you company until he showed. I knew waiting was making you edgy."

"You said it was because you were on edge," she said dryly. "I thought it was odd, but Kaskov has that effect on people."

"I can see why," she said. "He'd have to be carefully handled."

"I wouldn't know, I've never tried."

"And that's probably one of the reasons why you're safe from him." She smiled. "Along with the fact that I believe he might care about you."

"It's the music."

"Maybe." She shrugged. "What do I know?"

"Sometimes quite a bit," Cara said quietly. "But you're probably wrong about this. And I'll ask you not to try to handle Kaskov for any reason, Darcy. It might . . . complicate things."

"Ominous." She made a machine-gun motion, firing all around the room. "Rat-a-tat-tat. Rat-a-tat-tat. Rat-a-tat-tat."

"Darcy."

"I know you mean it. I'm not stupid."

"But you're deliberately not answering." She frowned. "I didn't want you to come here. But I knew I couldn't stop you. You'd have found a way. And Eve thought by putting us into this fortress, she could keep us safe."

"It wasn't a bad idea."

"As long as you didn't do anything that would rock the boat. She doesn't know you as well as I do. Rocking boats is your specialty." She came toward her, her voice pleading. "Look, Darcy, none of this was your fault, you should never have been pulled into it. There's no way you should be a target. Norwalk isn't even after you any longer." She fell to her knees in front of her chair. "Let me put you back on a plane and get you out of here."

Silence. "But I *was* pulled into it, and so was Sylvie." Darcy met her eyes. "And so were you, Cara. You're the closest friend I've ever had except Sylvie. He took her away. Do you think I'm going to let him do that to me again?" Her eyes were suddenly glittering with tears. "And what about that sweet little kid I was cuddling the night before

Norwalk decided to tear his life apart? Even if we manage to get him away, how is Michael going to cope with what happened in that square?" She shook her head. "Rocking his damn boat is the least I want to do to Norwalk. You go after him your way, I'll do it my way." She reached out and gently touched Cara's cheek. "But I'll be careful with Kaskov. I've even agreed not to seduce him. Though I won't promise not to use him if the occasion comes up."

It was all she was going to get from her Cara could see. She'd had little hope in persuading Darcy to leave, but it had been worth a try. "Be careful with everybody. You're my friend. I care about you." She jumped up, pulled Darcy to her feet, and shook her. "And I want you around when we find Michael. You could always make him laugh. That's a talent we're going to need to cultivate and encourage."

"Hey, I'm not only a natural, I'm an expert," Darcy said, as Cara led her toward the door. "You're kicking me out of your room?"

"Out with you. You need your sleep, and you've finished offering me comfort for the night." She added grimly, "Jock is safely stashed and surrounded by some of the worst criminal elements in the world. Why should I be worried now?"

"You shouldn't." Darcy opened the door. "But you will. Try to sleep. Good night, Cara."

Cara watched her until she went into the next room down the hall and closed the door. Then she locked her own door and leaned back against it.

Weariness was creeping into her every muscle. All the tension, the worry, the horror of the last days were assaulting her.

Michael.

No, don't think of Michael out there tonight and what he might be going through with that psychopath. How could she help but think about him? She felt the panic rising. But Norwalk would have to be careful with Michael, she told herself frantically. He was valuable to draw Eve.

Calm down.

Don't think. Try to plan.

But if she was this sick with fear, what was Eve feeling? Maybe she should go to her so that she wouldn't be—

No, Eve was exhausted and hopefully asleep. She might wake her. Cara should go to bed herself and hope for sleep and not nightmares.

She crossed the room and looked down at the garden again. There was no light in the summerhouse. Jock was surrounded by darkness. But then Jock often moved from sunlight to darkness. As close as she'd been to him through the years, she hadn't realized that until lately. Perhaps it had come with the same maturity that was causing her such upheaval . . . and making her want to go to him tonight and help him banish that darkness.

Foolishness. It would be a mistake. She was too aware of him. She couldn't be with him without wanting to touch him. One thing might lead to another, and there could be betrayal and disaster. Would she be willing to risk everything to enter into that darkness?

She couldn't take her gaze from the summerhouse. She could almost see him before her. She could feel the heat . . .

She turned away from the window. The answer was coming closer and closer every day. There would come a time when she wouldn't be able to push it away, when Jock would be able to see it. It had almost come tonight.

But tomorrow she wouldn't be as tired and sad and discouraged. There would be plans to make and people to help.

Tomorrow would be easier.

"I have a name," Joe said when he called Jock at six the next morning. "Our photographer is Donal Macvey, and he's worked for Norwalk for the past three years. But not as a photographer. Enforcer."

"Surprise. Surprise," Jock said sarcastically. "Have you been able to find out how long he's been in the country?"

"According to his passport info, he entered Kennedy four weeks ago. I've been checking credit-card info, and he's had charges in Atlanta . . . and New Orleans."

"What's he buying?"

"Liquor. Gas. Building materials. Hammers, nails, lumber, tarps. That kind of stuff. No explosives. That would have to be an undercover purchase. Or maybe Norwalk bought it himself. Anyway, Macvey was definitely brought over to aid and assist." He paused. "And Interpol says that four more of Norwalk's men headed for the U.S. in the last week."

"He's pulling together a team."

"That's what I figured," Joe said. "And he's getting close to zero hour, or he wouldn't have blown that square. Did Macvey leave for New Orleans right after the blast?"

"The night coach at midnight."

"Then he might have been the last of Norwalk's pieces to put in place. Building materials . . . Give me the address where he bought them, and I'll try to gather info about what he was doing."

"Home Depot. Canal Street."

"And the liquor store?"

"Mardi Gras Pete's on Magazine Street. I'll e-mail you the rest."

"Right. I'm on my way." He paused. "Do you want me to tell Eve, or are you going to do it?"

"I'll do it later. She phoned me last night and told me from where she was calling. Needless to say, I'm not pleased. And I'd just as soon she doesn't try to tag along with you while you're doing hunting and gathering. I don't like the idea of her being with Kaskov, but she's safer there than running around the French Quarter. I'm catching the next flight to New Orleans. I should be there by this afternoon." He added dryly, "Tell Kaskov I'll bunk with my wife. He won't need to provide me with a room, too." He hung up.

It was clear that Joe was as irritated with the situation as he was, Jock thought. Well they'd both have to live with it for the time being and just get on with business at hand.

And his particular business was to track down Norwalk's men and the reason that they'd purchased all those building materials. He headed for the front door.

But his phone rang before he reached it.

Joe, again?

No, Jim Stanton. New York.

He accessed it. "I'm in a hurry. What do you have, Stanton?"

CHAPTER

14

I'm here." Darcy was sweeping gracefully down the grand staircase of the main house fifteen minutes later. "I feel as if I should be wearing hoops and corset, but I wasn't prepared." She stopped before Jock. "So why am I here? I know I'm irresistible, but I haven't had breakfast, so the allure is fading away as we speak."

"Come for a drive with me. I'm heading for New Orleans to do some checking on some purchases made by Macvey, but I'll circle around and drop you back here." He was heading for the door. "Ten minutes, Darcy."

She hurried to catch up with him. "Why? And you told me not to tell Cara. I don't like keeping things from Cara."

"You can tell Cara when you get back. I just didn't want you to have to keep up the wisecracks or stiff upper lip until you came to terms." He opened the passenger door of the Mercedes rental car he'd parked in the driveway. "You'll probably want to tell her since it concerns both of you."

"Now I know I'm not going to like it. And I thought stiff upper lip was a British term, not a Scot's." She was silent as he drove down the driveway and out onto the road. "Bad, Jock?"

"You've gone through worse. It may be a relief. It's just something you have to know." He looked away from her. "I got a call from Jim Stanton this morning, the guard I hired to watch over Cara. You were told about him."

She nodded. "You were furious that he didn't stop that attack on Cara."

"But he was still a good operative. So I told him to dig up as much as he could about everything concerning the circumstances of the attack and try to find who had done it. I'd already found out most of what I needed to know about the attack from Benoit and Kaskov by the time he called me this morning, but he fed me some additional info. He'd thought it was odd that Norwalk told Eve that he needed a twin, and Cara just happened to be rooming with one. I've always thought coincidences are very rare in this world, and so does Stanton."

"No coincidence." Darcy moistened her lips. "A setup?"

Jock nodded. "It was true there was a shortage in living accommodations, but there was a bribe put in place to the housing director to put you with Cara."

"Why?" she whispered.

"Part of his master plan. He knew you were at the school in New York. He just made the next move."

"How did he know I was at Carnegie Tech? How did he know anything about me?"

He was silent. "He had a very personal contact."

"What the hell do you mean? *Tell* me."

"Your mother and he were lovers."

Her eyes widened in shock. "What?"

"For at least six months before his twin was killed, Rory Norwalk spent several nights with Felicity whenever he visited his brother in Nice."

"My mother?" she whispered. "He slept with my mother."

"From what you told Cara, it wasn't unusual for her to sleep around."

"But not *him*. He's a monster. Why would she—" She closed her eyes. "But I can see it happening. She always got bored easily." She shuddered. "He would be . . . different." She opened her eyes. "And she wouldn't even see what made him that way."

"Stanton said that it was probably Sean Norwalk who introduced them. He knew how obsessed his brother was about the twin concept. Raoul Napier and Sean both worked for Manard, and Napier might have mentioned that his wife had twins by a former marriage. So it amused Sean to give Rory something he knew would please him. A beautiful woman who was also the mother of twins."

"And my mother told him all about me . . . and Sylvie."

He nodded. "They were lovers. He must have been very persuasive."

She still couldn't believe it. "She gave him *Sylvie*."

"Napier might have had something to do with it. Yes, Felicity must have told Rory Norwalk details about both of you. But Napier was scared to death of Manard and probably didn't even know the orders were actually coming from Norwalk. Everything changed when Norwalk started pulling the strings after Sean had been murdered."

"You don't have to tell me that," Darcy said bitterly. "And my mother was one of those strings. They must have had a fine time together until Kaskov took out his brother, and he decided that he needed a twin to complete his plan." She could see it unfolding. "He knew about me and Sylvie, and we were so very convenient. He threw me and Cara together, then went about getting Sylvie's skull to give to Eve."

Jock nodded. "That's what probably happened."

"Not probably. I can see him doing it. Ugly. Ugly. Ugly." She was shaking, her voice hoarse. "And wasn't it a plus that Cara and I became so close, and she took me into her family? What a great setup that Eve and Cara were there to have to deal with me when I fell apart when I saw Norwalk's handiwork. Maximum pain all around."

"As much as he could inflict." He pulled over to the side of the road and turned to gaze at her. "He wanted to break you and have Cara see it. But he didn't succeed. You might have fallen apart, but you put yourself back together, and the bond between you and Cara just strengthened."

"Bullshit." The tears were suddenly running down her cheeks. "I might have put myself back together, but I have scars, and I resent every one of them."

"Shh." He pulled her into his arms. "We all have scars. Accept them and let them heal. They won't fade away, but in time you'll be able to bear them more easily."

She didn't speak for a moment, her face buried in his chest. Then she lifted her head and stared up at him. "At least you didn't give me any of that soothing, comforting nonsense," she said unsteadily. "No lies about everything going to be fine and back to normal someday." She wiped her eyes, then straightened away from him. "I would have socked you if you had."

"I thought I *was* being comforting." He was smiling down at her. "Truth is comfort to someone like you, Darcy."

"Yeah." She drew a deep breath. "And you're very smart to realize that, Jock. And you were very smart to realize that my stiff upper lip might dissolve a little when you told me to what lengths Norwalk went to destroy Sylvie and me. And I thought that my mother couldn't hurt me anymore, but she managed to reach out and do it. It does . . . hurt. You had to get me away because you knew what it would do to Cara to see me like this."

He went still. "Not entirely. I knew it would hurt you, too."

She nodded. "And I appreciate it. But we both know that Cara is the center, and the rest of us just revolve around her."

"Is she?"

"Of course." She gestured impatiently. "And I'm not going to dive into this and invade your privacy. I'm too grateful that you let me cry on your shoulder and made me feel as if I wasn't too much of a wimp."

"You'll never be a wimp, Darcy."

"Right." She straightened in the seat. "So what are we going to do today to prove it to the world? What's next, Jock?"

"Next, I take you back to the compound, and you can tell Cara what I told you."

"Wrong. You said you're going to check out some purchases by Norwalk's men at the stores in New Orleans. I'm going with you."

"No."

She looked away from him. "I have to keep busy today. I'm not ready to go back over all this again with Cara. She'd be sympathetic and giving, and I'd really break down and make a fool of myself. I'm very delicately balanced these days. Give me a little time." She turned back to him, and a brilliant smile lit her face. "And you have no idea how persuasive I can be if I put my mind to it. Clerks and cashiers literally fall at my feet to give me information. You'll be amazed."

"I'm sure I would be," he said dryly. "You're playing me."

"A little." Her smile never lost any of its wattage. "But it's also true. Take me with you, Jock."

He looked at her silently for a moment. Then he started the car and pulled out onto the road. "Okay. But if no one falls at your feet begging to give me what I need, you're in deep trouble, Darcy."

BLACK POOL SWAMP

"That alligator is twelve feet long." Norwalk pushed Michael closer to the bank of the island that was really more of a huge mound in the dense stand of cypress trees. He pointed to the alligator basking in the sun of another island, several hundred yards away. "There are two more on that island but he's the biggest. He could swallow you with one gulp. It would take a little longer for your mother. He'd have to chew her up."

"He won't do that." Michael kept his eyes fixed on the alligator.

"He *could* swallow me. Why do you keep saying things like that? Do you want to make me afraid?"

"You are afraid," Norwalk said roughly. "You're just pretending you're not. Why shouldn't you be afraid? You jump in the water and try to get away, and the alligators will get you. I had a steel net put up to keep them away from the waters near this island. But all I'd have to do is have those guys lift it and let them in." He nodded at the four men with rifles on either side of the island. "Or maybe my men will shoot your head off. Either way, you're dead and will never see your mother again. And see that box of explosives over there by the shack? I might decide to tie some dynamite to you and set it off. Like all your little friends that I blew up in that shop in the square. All alone and stone-cold dead." His gaze narrowed on Michael's face and his eyes lit with satisfaction as he saw him blinking back the tears. "Ah, that got you, didn't it?"

"They're not alone." He moistened his lips as he looked out at the bayou. "But I'm lonely for them. We're all lonely for them."

"You'll be able to join them soon. But not before I'm ready. That's why I brought you out of that shack to show you how stupid it would be for you to try to escape."

Michael shook his head. "That's not why. I bother you. You're beginning to wish that you hadn't had to take me. You think that if you can make me afraid, you'll feel better about it."

He could see the anger flare in Norwalk's eyes even before he felt pain as Norwalk brutally struck him in the face. He dropped into the mud of the bank. "Stupid kid. What do you know? Yes, you bother me. How do you like the way I'm dealing with it now?" He jerked Michael to his feet and shoved him up the slope toward the shack. "Keep your eye on that alligator. You're going to become very close in the next few days."

"I was totally magnificent," Darcy said as she swept into the parlor where Eve and Cara were sitting that afternoon. "Of course, I

did a little shopping for myself." She tossed several boxes on the brocade couch. "But I devoted most of my efforts to saving Jock's ass
while he was questioning those poor clerks at Home Depot." She
turned as Jock followed her into the room. "They didn't actually
kneel to me, but they went the extra mile, didn't they? And all you
had to do was stand there and look slightly threatening."

"So which worked?" Eve asked. "Charm or threats?"

"Charm." Jock's lips twisted. "By the time she'd spent three minutes with them, they couldn't even see anyone else."

"Standard operational procedure," Cara said. "She never fails. I'm
glad that she came through for you." She looked at Darcy. "I could
have wished for a little more than that short text message to tell me
why you took off with Jock. It wasn't like you."

"No one is behaving as they usually do," Darcy said. "We're all
just trying to survive as best we can. I'm falling back on automatic."
She smiled. "And, as I said, my automatic is magnificent." She looked
around the room. "Where's Kaskov?"

"In his study, trying to pretend that we aren't here," Eve said.
"We'll try to pretend that, too, until it's necessary that we don't." She
looked at Jock. "Tell me that you've found something to let us know
where that bastard is holding my son."

He shook his head. "The description matched Macvey's photo.
And we got a description of his truck and maybe the dock where he
loaded the wood to be shipped. He had to have it delivered, the bed
of his truck was too small to carry it all. It's a dock on the north side
of New Orleans. Near Lake Pontchartrain. I'll head out there right
away. Have you heard from Joe?"

"He should be getting in about an hour from now," Eve said.
"Wait for him." She grimaced. "I could tell when I talked to him
that he was holding on by a thread. He needs to do something that
doesn't involve being behind a desk or doing detective work. Michael
is his son."

"I'll wait. I have to talk to Nikolai anyway." He looked at Cara. "You're okay?"

She nodded. "Sure, it's just been a long day. I would have felt better if I'd been able to go with you and done something valuable." She smiled faintly. "But that wouldn't have worked out. No one is going to fall on their knees to please me."

He met her eyes. "I wouldn't be too sure."

"Yep, it only takes the right audience," Darcy said as she started to gather up the boxes she'd thrown on the couch. "But take a couple of these boxes up for me, will you, Cara? I need to wash up and change. I bought a gorgeous peacock-colored maxi skirt that's perfectly stunning. But being magnificent in this muggy climate is a chore. We can talk while I change." She glanced over her shoulder at Jock, and said quietly, "Thanks. I'm ready now." Then she was flying out of the parlor and heading for the staircase. "Come on, Cara. I *need* you. I can only manage to be strong and magnificent for so long."

"All that trouble, all that planning," Cara said bitterly. "Just to bring you and Sylvie into his grand scenario." She went to where Darcy was sitting on the couch at the foot of the bed and dropped down beside her. Then she drew Darcy's head down to rest on her shoulder. "Even bribing someone to arrange us to room together? Crazy."

"Sure. Maybe crazy like a fox," Darcy said unevenly. "Look at you, rocking me like a mom with a hurt child. He threw us together and hoped that we might become friends, so that it would be painful for you when you saw me suffering when I found out about Sylvie." She lifted her head. "And it worked, didn't it? His twin was killed, so he used another twin to twist the knife in you, Cara, the person who was the reason for Sean's death. This whole damn nightmare has been about twins. He even slept with my mother because the concept intrigued him. He might have even thought there was some mystical reason he and Felicity had been brought together to show him a way to use Sylvie and me to help avenge his brother."

"You know, you could be right about that," Cara said. "As obsessed as he was with twins throughout his life, it could be the answer why he chose the two of you in particular."

"It's as good a guess as any. Other than that, it just goes back to the fact that he didn't believe us to be of any importance. No, perhaps as a symbol. He's into symbols. Look at those mirrors in the gold box." She added, "But even then, he didn't use that second mirror to reflect me. Michael was more important to him."

Cara could feel her pain and bitterness, and it was hurting her. She reached out and gently touched her cheek. "He may have thrown us together to eventually hurt me, but he failed, Darcy. He gave me more than he took. He probably never even realized how valuable friendship can be."

She nodded jerkily. "I can believe that. I think he's a hollow man with only a corrosive poison inside." She drew a deep breath and forced a smile. "Okay, that's over. This hit me hard, and I had to work my way through it. It was very personal to me. He used me, and he used Sylvie." She was silent a moment. "And he used my mother to try to destroy both of us. It came as a shock that he went to such extraordinary lengths to use me to hurt you, completely ignoring how it would also hurt me." She got to her feet. "And it was good that I had this day with Jock to come to terms with the initial shock, wasn't it? I didn't behave too badly. You must be bored with me falling apart all the time."

"Don't be ridiculous. When you're hurting, you come to friends to help. That's the way of it," she said. "And I'm glad that Jock was with you. He has a kind of shining inside that sometimes makes— He helps." Darcy was looking at her curiously, and she rushed on, "You must have noticed it today."

"I noticed that he was there for me," Darcy said. "And that he's probably as unique as I always thought him. I was a little too upset to notice any shining."

"You will. Anyway I'm glad he could help you." She smiled. "He's always been there when I needed him."

"That's been evident from the moment I found out he existed in your life. I'm happy you let me borrow him for today. I had a moment when I wasn't sure I should hijack him, but I needed him so I decided to take the chance."

Cara frowned. "Chance?"

"I was afraid you might think I was— Look, I told you I was backing off from Jock. And I did it, didn't I? Do you think I'd blow it now? Before it was just a trial balloon set up to test the weather." She made a face. "Not that I could have seduced him anyway. Anytime you're anywhere near, I don't resonate with him."

"Of course you do."

"Have it your own way. I shouldn't have brought it up." She headed for the bathroom. "I'm going to go take that shower and change. None of this is—" She suddenly whirled. "No, I *should* have brought it up because you're the most clueless girl on the planet where Jock is concerned."

"What?"

"You heard me. You're smart, you're empathetic, you're kind, you're giving, but you don't *see* anything." She shook her head. "Maybe I shouldn't expect it. Jock has always been your whole world, and between your music and him you don't have any experience in the way to play the game. You're a virgin, aren't you? Nothing wrong with that, if you want to take your time. I never did. I was always afraid that someone would grab the brass ring before I did. But you probably can't see the signs, and with Jock, even I have trouble."

"Where did all this come from?" Cara was staring at her in bewilderment. She had been completely caught off guard. She could feel the heat flushing her cheeks. "We were talking about you, not me, Darcy."

"Because I've been so damn subtle and tactful. Not at all like me. But I've been watching you, and I don't like what I've been seeing. I think I triggered something that night at the residence, so it might be my fault. I guess I have to straighten it out." She looked her in the eye. "You and Jock are best friends? Maybe. But you also want to jump him. Who wouldn't? And you don't know what the hell to do about it."

"I can't talk about this, Darcy."

"Fine. I'll talk about it. I'll tell you what to do about it. You jump him."

"It's not that simple. I know you mean well. I'm . . . not like you. And Jock . . . he doesn't . . ."

"He doesn't what? Like sex? Oh yes he does, and you know it. You told me how many women he'd had. But I'd bet he was careful about keeping them entirely separate from you. I can't read him all the time but I've noticed sometimes he's guarded around you. He might just be a better actor than I am. At any rate, you're in a special place."

"Exactly."

"Then get out of it. He's probably a hell of a lover. Life's too short to waste time hemming and hawing and worrying about what Jock will think. You won't know that until after you've gone to bed with him anyway."

Cara smiled crookedly. "And that could be too late."

"Could it?" She took a step closer, her voice intense, urgent. "Listen, Cara, the only things that are too late are the things you wish you'd done. I might have saved Sylvie if I'd moved faster, if I'd followed instinct instead of believing Felicity. I *lost* her. I'm not going to make that mistake again. And I don't want you to lose one minute of what you should have. If something happened to Jock, how would you feel? Would you tell yourself, isn't it lucky that I didn't open myself up to feeling more than I do right now? I don't think so."

"That's not fair," she said unsteadily. The mere thought of anything happening to Jock was terrifying.

"I don't have to be fair. I'm an actor, a communicator. All I have to do is make my point and move on." She scanned Cara's expression. "And I think I've made it." She gave her a quick hug, turned, and headed toward the bathroom. "Now I'll escape and drown myself under a cool shower. And let you ponder my words of wisdom and take them under advisement. Subject closed." She glanced over her shoulder with a hint of mischief. "Unless you'll be generous enough to confide in me if Jock is as good as I think he is." The door shut behind her and a few minutes Cara heard the sound of the shower.

Cara slowly crossed over to the window. She felt as if she'd gone through a tornado of emotions in that short period when Darcy had turned on her and let loose that hail of words. How could she resent it? Her friend had done it with love and with a passion of caring and wanting to share. It was just that sharing had tapped into what Cara had been going through for the past days and shined too bright a beam.

Coward. Had she been a coward about facing how to handle this disturbance that . . .

Of course she had.

What if something happened to Jock?

Fear tightened her chest again. She instinctively tried to bury the thought.

Coward, again.

Bring it out, face the possibility.

She couldn't do it.

Darcy, what a very wise and very cruel person you are.

Eve was standing in the driveway when Joe drove through the gates. She only waited until he'd parked before she ran down to him. She went into his arms and buried herself there. Safety. Strength. Love.

"How are you doing?" he whispered. His arms tightened around her. "Holding it together?"

"Barely." She looked up at him. "And you don't look like you've had any sleep at all."

"I've been busy." He kissed her and stepped back. "And hoping to be even more busy now that I'm here."

"Really, Quinn. Such a display." Kaskov was standing outside the front door. "Not a sight I want my men to see since I don't allow them to have women while they're on the property. I welcome you into my home, and you cause instant disturbance."

"I'd be glad to leave," Joe said. "Say the word."

"I don't believe Eve would like that," Kaskov said mockingly. "And how can I refuse her? So I suppose I'll have to accept your behavior." He gestured for them to enter. "Actually, I find your presence here amusing. It's not often that I have such a prestigious law-enforcement officer as a guest in my home. I imagine you might have a few explanations to make if anyone knew you were here."

"And I'd make them without reservation."

"Yes, I heard you were that rare individual, an honest cop. People like you have always made my life difficult." He entered the foyer. "Which is why I felt it necessary to greet you personally. Nikolai and a few of my other men are very protective of me where the law is concerned." He inclined his head. "So consider yourself greeted. If you confine yourself to the business to which Eve tells me you're committed, you're welcome here. You'll forgive me if I continue to conduct my affairs from my study, as I've been doing since I've been bombarded by Eve and company." He raised his brows. "I promise it will not involve murder or mayhem while you're all on the premises."

"You're enjoying this," Joe said bluntly. "I won't forgive you anything. But I know that you won't do anything that will incriminate you while you're here in the United States and don't have your crooked hierarchy to protect you. And you might have an interest in helping to protect Cara, if not my son. So I'll take what I can get."

"Good." He nodded to Eve. "I probably will not see you for the rest of the evening. I've sent a message to Cara that the music room is hers to use to practice, and I will not be in attendance . . . until I have her full attention later in the month." He turned back to Joe. "And you should know that there have been no strangers or anyone suspicious within at least a distance of twenty-five miles since they arrived. Nor any electronic monitoring of any sort within that same area." He turned and headed toward the study. "Good evening. Enjoy your dinner."

Eve watched him leave before turning to Joe. "And it will be a good dinner. He has a Cordon Bleu cook in residence who's been preparing buffet meals we can eat at our convenience. She specializes in Cajun. Nothing formal. And no one else is in the house. He's obviously been trying to keep us at a distance from his men . . . or himself."

"Surprise."

"We always knew he was a surprising man. Yet he's been very cooperative."

"He's brilliant, but that only makes him more dangerous," Joe said grimly. "But I'm relieved that he's keeping his men away from you. All the snakes around here aren't in that bayou." He looked at the grand staircase. "Now suppose you show me where I can leave this suitcase. Jock phoned me right before I landed and told me that we have a trip to make to a Lost Cypress Bayou. I want to get going."

Eve nodded. "He's staying at the summerhouse. I'll call him and tell him to come up here." She took out her phone. "Our room is the first one to the left at the top of the stairs. I'll tell Jock we should leave within the next five minutes."

"We?" He stopped on the stairs to look back at her. "No Eve, Jock and I can handle this. I don't want you running around where you might be picked off by some sniper, like Manard was. You're the one who arranged to stay here against both Jock's and my judgment. Now stay inside these gates, dammit."

She shook her head. "I came here because it was the only place that I could be sure that I'd satisfy Norwalk's desire to 'position' us for extermination and still have a chance to keep Cara and Darcy safe. That doesn't mean I can stand to just sit here and do nothing." She added gently, "You told me once that you were the guardian at the gates. But somehow through no fault of your own those gates were breached, and our boy was stolen. So you've got to let me help get him back. I've been going crazy all day waiting for Norwalk to call again and give us something else to work on." She tried to steady her voice. "You've got to understand, I don't matter anymore, Joe. Michael's the only one who matters."

"The hell you don't," Joe said hoarsely. He drew a deep, harsh breath. "But I do understand that I can't budge you. Okay, but you'll do what I say?"

She nodded as she smiled faintly. "I promise I won't be careless. I have to take care of myself if I'm going to be able to take care of Michael. I don't think that Norwalk is ready to take me down yet. He wants to see me hurt more." She turned to go to meet Jock on the driveway. "Besides, I believe you'll be able to keep an eye on me."

"Count on it," he said grimly as he started back up the stairs.

"Oh, I do. There isn't a minute of my day I don't count on you, Joe."

Cara really was extraordinary, Darcy thought as she came down the staircase. The music pouring out of the music room was both poignant and intoxicating, singing through the house and making every note Cara's own. She was always good, but perhaps the emotional trauma she was going through was freeing hidden depths. It was no wonder the critics thought she was a genius. Darcy would have liked to listen to her, but she had no time. She had to take advantage of this time with Eve, Jock, and Joe out of the house.

She went to the couch and retrieved the small pouch she'd tucked beneath the arm cushions where she'd tossed the boxes and packages when she'd come back from the city this afternoon.

She paused a moment, listening to the music as she tried to brace herself. Then she straightened her shoulders and sailed out of the parlor and across the hall.

I hope you've mellowed him, Cara. I might need it.

She knocked on the door of the study, but didn't wait for an answer before she opened it. "I'm sorry to intrude, Mr. Kaskov." She smiled at him as she swept into the room and shut the door. "I just wanted a word with you."

"Did you?" His face was expressionless as he leaned back in his chair. "Now I wonder why? Because it is an intrusion, Miss Nichols. I'm sure you realize even after being here for such a short time that I generally don't see anyone without an invitation. You're either very bold or very stupid. And your motivation is a mystery." He looked her up and down. "You could think that I might want a new mistress. You're exceptionally beautiful, but I'm quite satisfied with my present arrangement."

"Are you? That's nice for you." She moved a few steps closer. "But that's not why I'm here. I knew this wouldn't be a good time for you, so I'd better get this over quickly." She cocked her head, listening to the music pouring out of the speakers around the study. "Your auditory connection to the music room here is wonderful. I thought it would be. You wouldn't want to miss one note. You offered Cara her space and avoided any awkwardness, but you wouldn't be cheated."

He nodded slowly. "True." His gaze narrowed on her face. "Have I underestimated you?"

"Probably. Most people do. It's the blond hair and the big blue eyes." She took another step closer to his desk. "But I'll get out of here and let you enjoy Cara." She pulled the pouch from the fold of her skirt. "I just wanted to show you—"

"Don't move." He was pointing a gun at the center of her forehead. "Drop it."

"Oops." She instantly dropped the pouch to the floor. "I made a mistake?"

"A big one." His eyes were ice-cold. "Nikolai will be walking through that door in two minutes, and we'll discuss remedies."

"Did you think I was going to shoot you?"

"It occurred to me. Or anthrax or a stiletto wielded by someone accustomed to being able to get close to people."

"Well, I can use a gun, but I know nothing about knives. However, most people do like me to get close to them." She swallowed. "And I don't know anything about anthrax. But evidently you do."

He nodded. "Two years ago I had a visit from a delivery boy younger than you who tried to toss an envelope full of it in my face."

"Risky. He must have been very brave."

"Yes, but then so are you."

"No I'm not. I'm scared to death."

"I know. That means nothing." He looked beyond her shoulder as the door opened behind her. "Just a precaution, Nikolai. Don't hurt her yet. Check that pouch on the floor."

Nikolai moved swiftly past her. "A weapon?"

"No," Darcy said. "It's just a— Oh, for heaven's sake, see for yourself."

"I will." Nikolai cautiously slit the doeskin material of the pouch. "Something . . . black, sir." He spread the sides of the pouch and examined the interior. Then he carefully lifted the mound out of the pouch. "Very soft . . . and malleable." He frowned as he shook it out. "I don't see any threat."

"It's a *wig*," Darcy said with exasperation. "No anthrax, no gun, just a wig. I just wanted to show it to you. I've always believed in show-and-tell to get what I want. Maybe it wasn't such a good idea this time. Now will you stop pointing that gun at me?"

"What shall I do?" Nikolai asked, holding the wig gingerly. "She's one of *them*. And she doesn't appear to necessarily be a very—"

"You can leave," Kaskov said. "As I said, just a precaution. Give her the wig, Nikolai."

Nikolai handed Darcy the wig. "It was not wise," he told her soberly. Then he was gone.

Darcy expelled the breath she'd been holding. "You made a big fuss for nothing." Her fingers were digging into the thick black mass of the wig. "Though I guess I might have deserved it, considering who you are."

"You were overconfident and it might have come from that beauty and charisma. But as Nikolai said, it was not wise. We've seen too many threats clothed in both of those qualities." He put away his gun. "Now either leave or tell me why you have that wig in your hand."

"I'm not about to leave after I've gone through all this." She was swiftly and skillfully tucking her blond hair beneath the brunette wig. "Show-and-tell." She smoothed the dark hair back and tidied it. "Long, dark, shiny. I wouldn't fool anyone close-up, but we're about the same size. From a distance it could work."

"What could work?"

"Cara. If the hair's right, you'd be surprised how many people would accept that I was her. The makeup would have to be just about perfect. But I've had lots of experience with that."

"And?"

"You could use me," she said simply. "You're sitting back here and waiting and watching until the time is right to make your move. Then you'll go after Norwalk yourself. From what I've been told, you like to be in control, so that won't be long. I don't believe you'd ever use Cara as bait, but it would be one way of trapping him. He wants to kill her to hurt you. I could put myself into a vulnerable position and let him find me."

"And risk him blowing you away before I blow him away?"

"It is a risk, particularly since you don't care if he does it. But Cara would care, so I might be okay. You seem to value what she thinks."

"Bait." He savored the word. "Why come to me? Why not go to Quinn or Gavin?"

"They wouldn't let me do it. They care if I live or die. And Eve only wants to protect and heal me. So it has to be you."

He was silent. "You must want this very much. Why?"

"You know why." She met his eyes. "I may seem to be the least important person in this game Norwalk's playing, but I'll bet you know everything that's happened to me just in case it might prove useful. Well, I've given you a reason to pay attention to me. I *can* be useful. Set it up, and just give me the chance. I won't fail you." Then she was suddenly smiling as she tore off the wig and fluffed her hair. "Now I'll let you go back to listening to Cara. She's wonderful tonight. I'm sorry that I took so much of your time, but part of that was your fault. I had no idea you were so paranoid."

"Don't push it," he said dryly. "You were very close. Get out of here."

"I'm gone." She opened the door, then stood there, staring straight ahead, not looking back at him. "I can't let him go on living," she said in a low voice. "Please, let me help."

Then she was out of the study and running down the hall toward the staircase.

It was done.

Now all she could do was wait for Kaskov or for some other opportunity to present itself . . .

CHAPTER

15

LOST CYPRESS BAYOU

PIERRE LADEAU SWAMP TOURS

FEED THE ALLIGATORS

E ve gazed up at the crudely painted sign nailed to an ancient oak tree. And then looked at the broken-down shack several yards away. "Not exactly a high-class operation. What are we doing here, Jock?"

"I have no idea." His gaze went to the dock, where an airboat and two motorboats were anchored. "But those boats are in good condition. And this is where Donal Macvey had those Home Depot supplies delivered. It's obvious that they weren't used here, and Ladeau isn't trying to hide." He gazed out at the dark waters of the bayou that stretched into the distance, then turned and headed for the shack. "Let's see if we can find this Pierre Ladeau and ask him."

"Ask me what?" A stocky man with curly dark hair and round face stepped out of the trees a few yards away. He was thirtysomething and wearing jeans and a red short-sleeved tee shirt with an alligator on the front. He smiled cheerfully. "You want to go on a tour?" His Cajun accent was as broad as that smile. "It's a little late in the day, but I can set you up for tomorrow." His voice lowered dramatically. "Or if you pay me extra, I'll think about a night tour. Did you know that the alligator eyes show up as pure red in the dark? It's something to tell your kids when you get home."

"No tour," Joe said. "You took delivery of a shipment of supplies from Home Depot a few weeks ago. It was purchased by a Donal Macvey, but you accepted the merchandise a few days later. Tell us about it."

Ladeau's smile faded. "No tour?" He looked at them in disappointment. "Are you cops or something? I thought that guy was a little shady." He added quickly, "Not that I did anything illegal. Strictly business, you understand."

"No, we don't understand," Jock said. "Make us understand. Tell us about him."

He shrugged. "This Macvey just showed up one day and said that he'd pay top dollar if I'd accept a delivery for him and rent him my airboat to transport the shipment into the bayou. What could I say? It wasn't as if I was accepting drugs or anything like that. It was Home Depot for God's sake."

"Where did he take those supplies?"

"How do I know? I helped him load, but I didn't go with him." He frowned. "And maybe you don't have any right to question me anyway. Show me your ID."

"We have the right," Eve took a step closer to him, and said fiercely, "It's you who don't have the right to say no to us, Ladeau. You're helping to protect a monster. I want to know where Macvey went in the bayou that day. You *will* tell me."

Ladeau looked taken aback, but he managed to smile at her. "I don't have to tell you anything pretty lady. My cousin, Philip, is a lawyer on Canal Street, and all I have to do is give him a call and—"

"That's assuming that you have fingers left to punch in his number." Jock was suddenly between him and Eve. "Look at me. What do you think your chances are that will be true if you don't tell me what I need to know?"

"Threats? My cousin says that's—" He broke off as he met Jock's eyes. He moistened his lips. "You're no cop."

"I never said I was. I'm someone who needs information. Where did Macvey go?"

"I don't know. An island on one of the swamps out there, I guess. Why else would he need all that wood? But how could I know which one? Do you know how many bayous can be reached from this point? That's why I set up my business here. Some of them are pure wilderness, nothing but winding waterways, alligators, and snakes. You can start off going into one bayou and end up in another."

"Where?" Joe repeated.

He hesitated, then pointed to the west. "But it won't do you any good. Like I said, he could have doubled back and around before he brought my boat back."

"But you'd probably know all the ways he could do it," Jock said. "And if we take you with us, you'll be able to show us all that you know."

He swallowed. "Maybe."

"No maybe. You'll do it."

"Not likely. Macvey said that someone might be showing up and he told me—" He suddenly ducked back into the trees from where he'd appeared. "Screw you!"

A shot!

"Down!" Jock was next to Eve, and he was pulling her to the ground as another shot rang out. She felt Jock flinch, then he was on top of her.

"Eve?" Joe said as he pulled his gun.

"She's okay," Jock said. "Get him. The shot came from those trees. He must have had a rifle stashed there."

"Watch her!" The next instant, Joe had disappeared into the thick shrubbery.

"Get off me," Eve said as she pushed Jock away. "Go with him."

He shook his head as he shifted to the side. "No way. I believe

Ladeau might have been firing wildly to discourage us from follow-ing, but he might also have been told to get rid of you if you showed up. That second bullet came close to you, Eve."

She inhaled sharply. "It came closer to you." She was looking at the bloodstain on the lower right side of his shirt. "You're hurt?"

"Just grazed me. I'll take care of it later." His gaze was on the trees. "But I don't like the idea of your being out here in the open. Let's get you back to the car."

"I'll get myself back to the car. Go after Joe."

"And take the flak from him later?" He shook his head as he got to his feet. "Ladeau isn't a big threat to Joe. He's an amateur. He was scared, or he probably wouldn't have even used that gun against us. He was about to break, and he panicked."

"Go after Joe," she repeated. "Now."

"I'm here." Joe was coming out of the woods. "Stop nagging him, Eve." He turned to Jock. "Why didn't you get her back to the car?"

"I yield to your greater persuasiveness. Ladeau got away?"

He nodded. "It's like a jungle once you get into those trees, and Ladeau must know every inch of it. I didn't even get a glimpse of him after the first minute or so. He disappeared without a ripple."

"Everyone makes ripples," Jock said. "We just have to find out where the ripple begins." He looked to the bayou to the west, where Ladeau had pointed. "But we won't start there. We'll go in the op-posite direction."

"And we'll start first thing in the morning," Eve said firmly. "I don't think we'll see anything in the dark but the red eyes of those alligators Ladeau mentioned."

Jock shook his head. "The dark doesn't bother me. I'll go after him now. You and Joe go back to Belle Grace. I can handle this by myself."

"No one goes alone," Joe said flatly.

"I do. It was how I was trained. I'll be able to find him," he said quietly. "It will even be easier since there's not a kill at the end of the hunt."

"Unless he fires at you again," Eve said. "No, Jock. Tomorrow." She was looking at the blood on Jock's shirt again. "And *now* we'll go back to the car so I can take a look at that 'graze.'"

BELLE GRACE

"Jock was shot?" Cara went rigid. "How bad, Eve? Why didn't you tell me that right away?"

"Because I knew you wouldn't hear anything else after I told you," Eve said wearily. "You were asking Joe and me all kinds of questions the moment we walked into the house. I wanted to give you the big picture."

"How bad, Eve?" she repeated.

"Not bad at all. He was telling the truth when he said it was just a graze. I cleaned it up in the car. Very little bleeding. He wouldn't even stop at an urgent care place on the way back here."

"You should have made him stop. What if it gets infected?"

"He said he'd take care of it. He'll be fine, Cara. He's been trained to take care of wounds. Do you think I'd let him go without hospital care if I thought there was danger? He was shot protecting me."

"No, of course not," she said quickly. She swallowed. "It was just such a shock. Where is he?"

"He said he was going directly to the summerhouse." She smiled. "He probably knew he'd face this reaction from you and wanted to avoid it. He was annoyed that I was insisting on 'fussing' as he called it."

Cara nodded. "Yes, that's probably it." She looked away from her. "He wanted to spare me. It's what you do with kids, isn't it?"

"He wouldn't mean to hurt you," Eve said gently.

"No, he's always kind." She turned away. "Come on and get something to eat. When Joe comes downstairs after changing, you both need at least a sandwich and coffee before you go to bed. I'll make some decaf. Kaskov's cook always brews it Cajun black and strong. That's the way Kaskov likes it, and he's the only one who matters to her."

"I've noticed." Eve could tell that Cara was making conversation to avoid letting her see the rejection and hurt she was feeling. But the only thing she could do was to go along and try to ease her through it. She followed Cara from the parlor to the huge kitchen. "Where's Darcy?"

"I haven't seen her since I started practice tonight. I'm not surprised. It was a long practice session. I needed it. I'll tell her what happened to Ladeau in the morning." She looked up from searching through the cabinet for coffee to look at Eve. "In a way it's good news, isn't it? You found out that Norwalk is probably on an island in one of those swamps. It's a start."

"Yes, it's a start." And a tiny glimmer of hope in the darkness. "But it could be a nightmare trying to find out where that island is located."

Before Michael was hurt.

Before Michael was killed.

"We'll find it," Cara said, sensing her pain. "We're all here for Michael. We all love him, and that love has to make a difference. We'll find him, Eve."

She *had* to believe it. She had to believe that faith and love could transform a world that seemed so dark right now.

Eve nodded. "We'll find him."

The summerhouse was just ahead. Its soft white stucco walls and beveled-glass windows gleamed in the moonlight, but the interior was dark. Cara had thought Jock was too often in the dark, she remembered as she stopped before the front door. But that didn't matter now. If he wanted to stay in the dark, it was his choice.

She knocked on the door. "Open the door, Jock. I need to talk to you." She didn't wait for an answer but opened the door herself and walked into the living room. Empty. She could vaguely see a gray brocade couch and chairs in the dimness. "Jock?"

"I'm here. I'm just throwing on some clothes. I wasn't expecting you." He was coming out of the bedroom pulling on his shirt. "And you'd better have a good reason for coming down here in the middle of the night," he said roughly. "If one of Kaskov's men had decided to knock you down and rape you, I might not have even heard you."

"I had a good reason." She turned on a lamp beside the couch, and she could see his tousled fair hair, his naked chest beneath the open white shirt, and the coldness of those silver-gray eyes. Even in this moment she felt the impulse to do anything to rid him of any coldness toward her. Block it. It was a habit instilled by all those years with him. It was the past, not the present. "My reason was that I've been lying there in bed thinking since Eve told me about your being hurt." She lifted her chin. "I was shaken but not really surprised that you didn't come and tell me yourself. But it did serve to bring everything together for me. It defined what I'll always be to you." She sat down in a chair and looked at him. "And I didn't think I could bear to let it go another hour without telling you. I've waited too long as it is."

"I wasn't really hurt," he said quietly. "I didn't want you getting upset. You seem to be constantly on the edge these days. I know it's Michael, but I thought I could spare you worrying about me."

"Yes, it's Michael. I think about him all the time." She paused. "And it's you. I'm going to lose you, Jock. I could see it coming, and I was fighting so hard against it. But tonight I decided that I was losing more than you by trying to give you what you wanted from me."

"That's bullshit," he said roughly. "No one is losing anybody. Nothing's changed."

"Everything's changed." She forced a smile. "Not your fault, Jock. Probably not mine either. It just kind of snuck up on me. You're used to feeling this kind of thing, but it caught me off guard."

"You're not making sense. What kind of thing, dammit?"

"Sex," she said simply. She turned her hands over and looked down at her palms. "I want to touch you all the time these days. I want you to touch me."

"Oh, *shit.*"

She looked up at his face. Shock, anger, intensity, and something else she couldn't define. "I thought that's what you'd say. Do me a favor and don't feel sorry for me? I've always known that would never be my role in your life. I still know it. You have other women for that. I was best friend, a kid to protect. This just kind of happened but I know it ruins everything."

"No it doesn't. Sorry for you?" His eyes were blazing in his taut face. "I'm mad as hell. Why did you even bring this up? You're only eighteen, and you don't know what you want. Next month it will have gone away."

"You'd like to think so. I know better. I've been living with this for a while. It might go away, but I'm not going to change back to what you want me to be. Somewhere along the way, I grew up, Jock." She had to go on, say the words. "Even though I know it's probably going to be the end of what we were together. I'm tired of pretending that nothing has changed and that I'll always be the young girl you met and saved all those years ago. It's too hard, and it makes me feel like a liar. We've never lied to each other."

"Haven't we?" he asked hoarsely.

"I didn't think so." She had to end this quickly. She got to her feet and moved toward the door. "So I think that it would be better if we didn't see each other for a while. I know it would be awkward for you, and it would just confuse me more than I am right now. I'm so used to wanting to please you, and I have to get over that." Her lips twisted. "I might find myself falling back into that same pattern. I won't do that. I'm going forward, Jock."

"Without me."

She flinched. "I think it has to be that way. Though Darcy would probably think I'm stupid. She thinks it's so simple. I should just jump you and let the cards fly where they might. But nothing is that simple where we're concerned. We've known each other too long. We've been too close." She looked him in the eye. "And there's no way that you'd want that to happen."

"You're damn right I wouldn't." He was across the room in seconds. His silver-gray eyes were glittering down at her, and a muscle was jerking in his left cheek. "Not after all I've done to keep it from happening." His hands grasped her shoulders and he shook her. "Forget it. Get *over* it, dammit."

"I will." She stared at him in bewilderment. She had never seen him like this. "I told you what I thought I had to do. Why are you being so—"

"Because I thought I had it all under control. I didn't think I'd be dealing with you, too. I thought you'd find some young guy at your school, and maybe— No, I didn't let myself think that, but that's what should have happened."

"What are you talking about?"

"I'm telling you that there's no way I should ever be anything closer to you than what I've been during these last years. So get over it."

"You keep saying that."

"Because it's true." His hands tightened on her shoulders. "I know you, and I know myself. You may have just stumbled on this page, but I've got it memorized. I've worked too hard to let you—"

"Shut up a minute." She was gazing up at his face. "I'm confused, but I have to get this straight. You're not like this with me. You're usually not—" She was thinking back about what he'd said. There was something there, something to which she should pay attention. And then put it together with what she'd known about him through the years.

And then it did all come together. She stiffened in shock. She gazed up at him in disbelief.

"Jock?" But she had to be sure. She slowly reached up and pushed open his shirt. His body was so beautiful . . . every muscle defined, the lines full of grace and power.

"No." His eyes were glaring down at her, his face tense. "No, Cara."

"But I have to know." She spread her fingers and put the palms of both her hands on his naked abdomen.

A long, shudder racked his body. She could feel his muscles tighten, twist beneath her fingers. She couldn't breathe. She could feel his tension, and it was becoming her tension.

"How long?" she whispered.

"I don't know," he said jerkily, his gaze dropping to her hands on his body. "Far longer than you, I'm sure. I'm a man with the usual urges, and all of a sudden you weren't a kid anymore. It shocked the hell out of me." He pushed her hands away from his body. "Why do you think I've stayed away from you for the past couple years? I knew where it could end up, and I wasn't going to allow it. I thought I could just keep us on an even balance, and you'd gradually just drift away from me as your career took precedence."

"You had it all planned," she said wonderingly. Her hands were no longer on his body. Why could she still feel the vibrant, tingling smoothness of his muscles on the skin of her palms? "But then you always did think ahead."

"And you blame me for that?" His voice was suddenly harsh. "One of us had to look ahead. You wandered into my life all full of dreams and music and faith that I could do anything. But we both know what I do best, and there was no way I was going to let you stay too long or too close to me."

Her lips twisted. "But I pulled the rug out from under you, didn't I?"

"Maybe. It's not going to work out like that now. We may be left with nothing. I didn't want to lose you entirely." He took a step back from her. "But perhaps in time I might be able to salvage—"

"*You* might be able?" She was suddenly angry. All the worry, the hurt, the helplessness she'd felt was hitting home. "You didn't hear anything I said except about the sex. Maybe you thought that was all that was important. It was for me for a while because I thought it would destroy what we had together since that wasn't what you wanted from me. But I told you I'd grown up, Jock." Her hands clenched into fists at her sides. "And what you want from me isn't going to matter any longer. I have my own choices and decisions. I've been going through hell trying to come to terms with the most important relationship in my life, and I didn't even have all the facts to do it. I was feeling desperate and inadequate, and I *hate* feeling like that." She turned and opened the door. "So don't try to tell me what you're going to do. You left me entirely out of the decision process before. That won't happen from now on. I'm upset, and I don't know what I'm feeling right now. But I do know this. If there's any salvaging to be done, it will be a joint venture. Providing I decide it's worth my while to do it." She slammed the door behind her.

Jock threw open the door and stood there on the step watching Cara run down the path toward the main house.

Son of a *bitch*!

His hands clenched into fists at his sides. He had screwed everything up tonight. He should have been cool, understanding, and big brotherly, convinced her that it was entirely natural for her to have certain feelings that would fade soon. But she had caught him off guard and blown him out of the water. He had tried so hard for so long to keep this from happening, and having it come from her instead of him had been too much to handle.

No, it hadn't been too much, *she* had been too much. He had tried to keep her a child, keep her safe from the world . . . and from him. But he had been blind, and she had slipped away.

And put her hands on him.

He drew a harsh breath, his muscles clenching as the heat seared through him. It had nearly killed him not to reach out and take in that moment. But he hadn't been able to not let her feel that need.

And he wasn't in much better shape right now. He knew that house like the back of his hand. He could follow her, convince her, seduce her, take her, show her, make her give what he—

And destroy everything he wanted for her? Yeah, great idea, and the reason that he'd been fighting this battle.

And losing it.

And tonight he was very close to losing it. He was burning. His body was tense, ready, and he couldn't stop feeling her hands on him. He wasn't going to be able to lie all night in that bed in the summerhouse when he knew how easy it would be for him to get to her. The very skills that made it impossible for him to allow himself to get any closer to her would make it simple for him to reach her, touch her. As he had told Eve, he could reach out and find anyone.

Catch 22.

Screw it.

He turned on his heel and strode back into the summerhouse. He damn well couldn't stay here tonight, so he might as well do what he did best and go after Ladeau right now, he thought recklessly. He was on edge, and the frustration would only fuel the hunt.

And it would keep him from showing Cara how right he'd been to stay away from her.

Darkness.

The air was thick and so suffocatingly close Eve could hardly breathe. It was as if she were breathing in water. Dampness all around her.

And the darkness seemed to be pressing in on her, causing her heart to labor and—

"But darkness is good, Mama. Everyone is asleep, and it's easier for me to get to you. They kind of interfere . . ."

Michael!

"I can't see you, Michael. I can't see anything. Are you all right?"

"I'm fine, Mama." Soothing. Anxious to calm. Loving. *"I miss you. But we'll be together soon."*

"Yes, we will." She paused. "Is Norwalk hurting you?"

"I'm fine, Mama."

"You didn't answer me."

"Only a couple times. I got hurt worse when I fell down at soccer practice. Remember that?"

"Yes, I remember." And she was also remembering those young, joyous, exuberant boys who had been playing with him when he had taken that fall.

"Me, too." Sadness. Bewilderment. Hurt. Terrible, terrible, loneliness. "He shouldn't have done it. I don't know why, Mama. I've tried to see, but I can't. I guess I'm not smart enough."

"No one is smart enough to know why anyone would do something that wicked, Michael. We just have to try to keep them from doing it. That's what your dad does every single day."

Silence. "And when they do it anyway, they just have to go away?"

"Yes, so they won't ever do it again."

"That's what I thought. He has to go away." A pause. "I'm crawling outside the shack now. I want you and Dad to be able to see this island where I am. That will help, won't it?"

"Michael, it's too dark. Even if it wasn't, I can't see what you see."

"Yes, you can. If you think hard, and I think hard, we can do it. We were able to do it before. We just didn't need it anymore."

"He lets you move around this island? He doesn't tie you up?"

"He showed me all the bad things to scare me. I bother him . . . I think he wouldn't mind if I tried to get away. He keeps talking about the alligator on the other island. The one that could swallow me."

Fear. Panic. Desperation. "Don't try to get away. Don't go in the water. We'll come for you."

"I know. Don't be afraid, Mama." Comfort. Warmth. Infinite love. "I'm outside the shack now. You have to try to see. It might not be easy, since we're not used to it anymore. And I don't know how long I'll be able to stay with you."

"It's too dark, Michael."

"No there's moonlight, you'll see it soon. Think about it, we'll see it together . . ."

"I'm trying hard." She concentrated, desperately focusing. "What am I supposed to be seeing?"

"I'll tell you, but I want you to see it. You need to remember. It's important. Today he kept talking about something happening tomorrow. It's tomorrow now, Mama."

"I'm trying, Michael," she said frantically. "I don't know if I can—"

"You can do anything, Mama. And you're not alone. They'll help you."

"Who will help me?"

"You know."

Yes, she knew. The desperation was suddenly gone, sliding away as if it had never been.

As the surrounding darkness was beginning to fade and slide away.

And then she could see the moonlight.

Alligators.

Snakes.

Rougarou.

Eve sat up straight in bed, her heart pounding. "Joe!"

Joe was instantly awake. "What's wrong?"

"I hope something's right. Maybe not enough . . ." Eve jumped out of bed. She glanced at the clock as she turned on the bedside lamp. 3:40 A.M. "I have to find my sketchbook." She saw it across the room with her overnight case, and the next moment, she had reached it. "I have to get it all down. There was so much . . . Michael said I have to remember it. He said that Norwalk mentioned something might happen today."

"Michael." Joe threw the cover aside and swung his legs to the floor. "What the hell are you talking about? Tell me, I need to—" Then he stopped. "Or maybe I don't. Michael?"

"Call it a hallucination. Call it a dream. Call it stress. Call it wishful thinking." She was flipping open the sketchbook as she dropped into a chair close to the lamp. "But you went along with me before, Joe. Go with me now. I saw where they were keeping him."

"That's all I need to know," he said quietly. "I'll go with you to the end of the line, Eve." He got up, grabbed her robe, and brought it to her. He tucked it around her. "What can I do?"

"Just let me draw what he showed me while it's fresh in my mind." Her pencil was flying over the page. "He saw a lot, Joe. Norwalk was trying to frighten him." Her pencil hesitated for an instant, and she had to steady it. "I believe he thought it was safe because Michael would die before he'd be able to tell anyone." Then she was drawing swiftly again. "He won't die. We're not there yet, but we're on our way."

"Just one question. How is Michael doing now?"

Her eyes were filling as she glanced up at him. "Hurting. Sad. Wonderful. Michael. Even that son of a bitch couldn't change him."

He nodded and turned away. "Get to work," he said gruffly as he headed for the door. "I'll make some coffee and bring it up to you."

5:05 A.M.

"That's all I can remember." Eve tossed the final sketch on top of the others lying on the floor. "I think it's everything. I didn't forget anything." She smiled faintly. "Michael would be proud of me."

"Three small islands in that swamp?" Joe was sitting on the floor going through the sketches."

"They're more mounds than islands," Eve said. "The one where Michael is being held is the largest, and that's where Norwalk built the shack. His four men occupy sleeping bags on the four corners of the island." She indicated the four muddy banks overgrown with shrubbery and cypress trees. "And most of the time that's where they stand guard. Norwalk doesn't take chances." She pointed to another small mound a short distance away. "No guards, but three alligators call it home. Norwalk wanted Michael to be sure to see them." She tapped a large metal box jammed against the shack. "He told Michael it contained explosives like the ones he used to kill his friends." She drew a long shaky breath. "What's all this doing to him, Joe? Even when we get him home, how can he ever be the same?"

"We'll worry about that later. You told me yourself that he might be hurting, but he was still Michael." He picked up the sketch with the box containing the explosives. "Not a great defensive weapon. He probably needed the explosives for another attack of some sort."

Eve felt sick. "Another Gwinnet Square?"

"That attack had a purpose. Huge amount of damage and horror factor, Michael, and luring everyone down here." He was still looking at the sketch. "Not a public shopping square. Maybe a compound?"

"Here? You think he's going to attack Belle Grace?"

"I don't know. I believe it's possible if he's figured out a way to get those explosives in place."

"Bribery?"

"I'm just guessing. Our best bet is to prevent any attack here by going after Norwalk and taking him out in that swamp." He frowned. "All of these sketches are just of where Michael is now. How did he get there?"

"He couldn't tell me. He was in a canoe, and it was night. You know how impossible it can be to keep track of directions when you're traveling in a bayou or swamp." She moistened her lips. "And he's a little boy. He managed to tell us so much, but I told you it might not be enough."

"We'll make it enough," Joe said. He was bundling up the sketches. "You have sketches of all three of those islands and the trees and animals surrounding them. Someone who knows the swamps should be able to recognize the location from them. And who do we know who's very familiar with the Louisiana swamps? "

"Ladeau? But we're not even certain he's not working with Norwalk."

"Then it's time we found out. One way or the other, he might be able to tell us how to reach Norwalk." He stood up and pulled her to her feet. "Get dressed. I'll call Jock and get him up. He said he could find Ladeau. We're going to give him his chance."

"You need Ladeau right away?" Jock asked Joe. **"I'll try to** accommodate. Would fifteen minutes be too long?"

"What the hell?"

"At the moment I'm sitting in front of Shari Damar's place in Jefferson Parish. She's a bartender at a club on Bourbon Street and she and Ladeau have been sleeping together for about two years. After I tracked Ladeau through the bayou, I saw that he'd doubled back. So I broke into Ladeau's house and found letters, photos, and an address."

"That doesn't mean he's there."

"He's there. I checked. He was in bed with her, but now she's in the shower. It looked like a long-term relationship and who else would he go to if he thought he was in danger? And evidently he cares more about his own skin than endangering this woman. You didn't answer, is fifteen minutes okay? No, on second thought I'll go in now. I was getting annoyed with waiting while he was jumping her. I'll take him while she's still in the shower."

"You weren't even supposed to go after him until this morning. I suppose you got bored and ignored everything we asked?"

"Not exactly bored. That's not the word I'd use," he said curtly. "Do you want him at Belle Grace or back at his place."

"His place. We may want to use his boat if we get the information we need."

"We'll get it. I'll meet you at Ladeau's." He cut the connection.

BELLE GRACE

"Did Eve talk to you before she ran out the door?" Darcy asked Cara. "I was on my way down to breakfast when she told me that they were headed out toward that Ladeau's place again." She made a face. "I was not invited along, but I thought you might be."

Cara shook her head as she went to the buffet. "She woke me to give me a kiss, tell me that there might be a breakthrough, and she'd call me later. Then she was gone." She took eggs and bacon that she didn't want, and a cup of coffee that she definitely needed. "But any breakthrough is good news. I just hope she calls soon." She sat down at the table and took a small bite of egg. "And who can blame her for leaving us behind? She's frantic about Michael, and she's only accepting Joe and Jock on the front lines. It's not what I'd like, but I'm not about to give her a hard time." She made a face. "I think she's forgotten that I've been with Michael since the day that he was born, and I'm also hurting. And that's okay, she'll get any support she needs from me."

"Hey, I'm grateful just to be here," Darcy said. "As far as I'm concerned, this is the front lines. It's up to me to get anywhere beyond it." She smiled. "But I'm working on it."

"I'm sure you are." Cara took a drink of her coffee. Cajun strong brew, as usual, but today she needed it. She hadn't got to sleep for hours after she'd returned from the summerhouse. Not that those hours had been of any benefit. She had been so disturbed and bewildered that she had not been able to think, only feel. And those feelings had caused a whirlwind of emotion. "And at least you were able to help Jock yesterday." She took another sip of coffee. "And that's helping Michael. I told you that I envied you."

"Jock . . ."

Cara held up her hand. "Drop it. I'm not talking about Jock right now." She finished her coffee. "We're here for Michael and for Eve." She pushed back her chair. "And now I think I'll try to keep myself busy by practicing until I hear from Eve."

Darcy gave a low whistle. "Have I missed something? Oh well, I'll catch up later. You're obviously a little too on edge for me to go into it now."

"Excellent decision." Cara smiled. "Sorry, Darcy, I didn't mean to be sharp with you."

"You wouldn't know how to be sharp. I'll have to give you lessons."

"You could be mistaken. I've seen signs that I might have potential." She headed for the music room. "I guess I'm just tired, and want all of this to be over. I thought that caffeine would do its job, but maybe it's going to take more than that. I'll let you know when I hear from Eve."

CHAPTER
16

E ve and Joe were almost to Ladeau's dock when Eve got the call.

She tensed.

No ID.

Norwalk?

She drew a deep breath. "Hello. Norwalk?"

"I'm so glad that you decided to accept my invitation, Eve," Norwalk said. "I hope that Kaskov has been making you welcome. I thought that you'd go running in his direction. In fact, I planned on it."

"Did you? You could have been wrong. There was a good chance I would have distanced myself from him."

"But I wasn't wrong." His voice lowered silkily. "Because I know you, Eve. I may know you better than anyone you've ever met. I had months to study you and the people around you, and how you'd re-act to every situation."

"Then you know the only thing important to me is to get my son back." She paused. "Is he still alive?"

"Yes. He's a little worse for wear because he's managing to rub me the wrong way. But I'll get through to him before I send him to join his friends."

"What can I do to get you to send him back to me?"

"Well, I was thinking I might return him to you in another gold box as I did Sylvie, but I really don't have time for that kind of elaborate send-off. So I'm content to let you come and see him die. I understand you and your loyal pack have been running around New Orleans trying to find me. I expected that, and it doesn't worry me. I was very careful. It will all be resolved before you get near me."

"You said that it's me that you want. Release Michael, and I'll come anywhere you say."

"But that's not the way I planned it, Eve. I want your son to have the comfort of his mother's arms before he dies. And perhaps to see the expression on the little bastard's face when I kill you. It's such a hard decision who to kill first. I never thought I'd have that conflict until I spent time with your Michael." He paused. "But I may be able to make a compromise since I've arranged for him to have someone else here to comfort him. I'll have to consider it."

She stiffened. "Someone else?"

"Of course, I told you that she was high on the list. It's time she was put at the very top. I have to say good-bye now. I have to prepare to receive her." He hung up.

She whirled to Joe. "Cara! He has to be talking about Cara."

"Bluff?"

"No, that's the reason he was calling me." She was frantically punching in Cara's number. "Michael said that he was planning on doing something today."

Cara wasn't answering.

After six rings, it went to voice mail.

She called Darcy.

Her phone was turned off.

"So much for their being safely tucked under Kaskov's wing," Joe said grimly as he screeched to a stop and turned around to go back to Belle Grace. "What the hell could have happened?"

"Norwalk happened." She was dialing again. This time to Kaskov. "But whatever he did, it had to have just been done. I saw Cara right before we left."

"Over an hour ago. A lot can happen in an hour."

A lot could happen in seconds, she thought desperately. That's all the time it had taken for Norwalk to blow up that entire shopping square. And Cara and Darcy were only two young women.

And *why* wasn't Kaskov answering?

Two more rings, and he picked up. "Good morning, Eve. How delightful to hear from you. I suppose that you have some other demand that I haven't yet—"

"Where's Cara, Kaskov?"

Silence. "I have no idea. I heard her practicing earlier."

"Find her. I can't reach her, and I can't reach Darcy."

"I'm certain that she's safe. I told you, I gave orders."

"Don't tell me that. Go find her. I heard from Norwalk."

He asked no questions. "Hold on. I'll check on her." She heard him speak to someone in the background. Probably Nikolai, she thought. Then she was put on hold.

One minute.

Two minutes.

Four minutes had passed by the time Kaskov came back on the line. "She's gone," he said tersely. "Nikolai found Darcy Nichols unconscious on the couch in the parlor. Probably drug-induced. We found the cook jammed into the pantry off the kitchen. Dead. Throat cut. But no sign of Cara."

"How could she just disappear from the damn place? How could anyone get through those gates?"

"I'm checking." He paused. "But am I checking for the living or the dead? What did Norwalk tell you?"

"I don't think he's planning on killing her yet. He mentioned taking her to Michael."

Silence. "And you still think your son is alive?"

"He's alive."

"Then I'll assume that he didn't intend to have Cara share his grave. Very well, then we'll go retrieve her. Where are you?"

"On our way back to Belle Grace. We're an hour away."

"Then I'll have more information for you by the time you return." He hung up.

"Cara," Eve whispered. "We tried so hard to keep her safe, Joe. And he just walked in and took her."

"We don't know that," Joe said. "Kaskov may find out something. She may still be on the property."

She nodded. "But Norwalk said he had to prepare for her. He must have had word she'd been captured or he wouldn't have felt it safe to call and gloat."

"We'll have to see." He covered her hand with his own. "But if you're right, it was a bold move, and it made Kaskov angry. He'll go after Norwalk with guns blazing."

"That's not much comfort. We don't know where he is yet." She was shaking. "And it's Cara . . ."

"I know." His hand tightened on her own. "And now you've got to call Jock."

"Dear God." She'd been in such a panic that all thought of anyone but Cara had flown out of her mind. "Jock . . ."

"Wake up."

Her head ached, Darcy thought vaguely, and her lids felt too heavy to open. But that voice was cold and demanding and would not accept excuses.

She slowly opened her eyes and saw Kaskov sitting in a chair next to her. Wrong. That was all wrong. "Wrong . . ."

"Without question," Kaskov said crisply. "The entire situation is wrong. But I'm here to determine if you're one of the elements that made it so. I've very angry, Darcy. You will answer what I ask immediately and with detail, or I will turn you over to Nikolai. He's very upset and feels humiliated that Cara could be taken on his watch. He will not be gentle."

"I don't know what you're talking about." She shook her head to clear it. Then one sentence he'd said tore through the haze. "Cara was taken? What's that supposed to mean?"

"That's what I want to know. Did Norwalk pay you to set her up? Where was she taken?"

She lifted her shaking hand to her head. "Pay me?" Then it hit home. She struggled to sit upright. She was on the couch in the parlor, she realized. She vaguely remembered feeling tired and sitting down for a moment. "Are you crazy? Why would anyone pay me to do anything?" Cara. He had been talking about Cara. And nothing and no one would make him look like this but something bad. "She's hurt? No, you said . . . taken?" She reached out and grabbed his arm. "Stop threatening me and tell me what's happened, damn you."

He looked down at her hand on his arm. "Remove your hand."

She ignored him and shook his arm. "You *tell* me. Is she hurt?"

He was silent, studying her face. "I have no idea. Is she?"

"How should I know? The last time I saw her, she was going to the music room. She was fine. And now you ask—"

"Remove your hand. Or I'll be forced to break it."

"Do what you have to do. Just tell me what's happening."

He was still studying her. "Perhaps I will. You're supposed to be a very good actress, but I don't believe you're acting now." He took her hand off his arm and put it on her lap. "Briefly, my very competent chef was murdered this morning. Throat cut. We found you unconscious on the couch. Cara was nowhere to be found. We've searched the house and the grounds." He paused. "But one of my men, Alex Brazoff, drove out of the main gates forty-five minutes ago. He was on a very plausible errand to pick up supplies that Niko-lai had approved yesterday."

"And you can't get in touch with him?"

"No answer." He smiled coldly. "But there's no doubt that I'll get in touch with him."

She tried to mask the shudder as she looked at him. "No doubt at all. You're sure this Brazoff turned traitor and took a bribe from Nor-walk? He wasn't working on his own to kidnap Cara?"

"No one would be that stupid. He'd have to receive an excep-tionally fat bribe to be able to get him to a country where he'd have a chance to escape me." He leaned back in his chair. "And besides, Norwalk called Eve today telling her that Cara was going to be taken. It was what caused her to phone and alert me. You didn't see Brazoff?"

"I wouldn't have recognized him if I had. You evidently gave orders that your men be invisible." She shook her head. "I had break-fast with Cara, then she went to practice. I was feeling a little tired, so I sat down on the couch." She motioned with her hand. "I guess I went out like a light."

"Drugs. Did you and Cara eat the same thing?"

She shook her head. "The only thing that was the same was that Cajun coffee." She made a face. "That stuff is so strong that I wouldn't be able to tell even if anyone put cyanide in it."

"I guarantee it would become immediately obvious," he said dryly. "But evidently the drug Brazoff used was weaker and more subtle. You came out of it in a remarkably short time." His expres-sion hardened. "But once Brazoff got Cara away from the property, he'd probably give her another injection to keep her out."

"And because the dose I was given wasn't that strong, you thought I might have been an accomplice?"

"It wasn't unreasonable. You're appealing, and you have a certain boldness. Norwalk might have bribed you to inveigle your way into my home. You're a twin, and that would have pleased his hunger for statement. You could have been part of his master plot of which he's so proud."

"Yes, I could, and I would have done it well. You're right, I'm a very good actress." She looked him in the eye. "But I would never have done it. There are only two people in the world whom I've ever cared about. One was my sister, Sylvie, the other is Cara, who is like a sister to me now. Norwalk killed my sister, and now he wants to take Cara away from me. I'd burn in hell before I'd do anything to help him."

He nodded slowly. "I believe you would. I was afraid you'd managed to con me. I'm glad that I can tell Nikolai that you are not involved."

"I'm glad also. I don't need to be dodging Nikolai while I try to get to Cara. You've sent people after Brazoff?"

"Immediately."

"But you don't expect them to find him."

"He had a head start and is working on Norwalk's plan. Norwalk has been very efficient so far. But we'll still find him eventually."

"Eventually sucks," she said flatly.

"I agree. So I'll work on a way that doesn't suck."

"I already gave you a way." She swung her legs to the floor. "You should have done what I told you to do. We could have pulled it off. Then Cara wouldn't have to go through—" She broke off as her eyes filled with tears. "You should have done what I told you. Don't you screw up again."

"I'll endeavor to keep from doing that," he said quietly. "Though I believe you'd think leaving you out of the equation would be a screwup, and yet I find I'm tempted to do it."

"Don't you *dare!*"

He shrugged. "Why should I argue when you might end up giving me what I need?"

"You shouldn't argue. Just let me be with you when you go after

Norwalk." She wiped her eyes on the back of her hands. "But you'll do it now because you feel guilty about—"

"Guilty?"

"I know you probably consider yourself above guilt or below it. But I can't walk on eggs around you right now. Maybe when I feel better. Did you call Eve and Joe? When will they be here?"

"Shortly." He got to his feet. "And I left it to them to notify Jock Gavin. I have things to do, and I have no time for the explosion."

"You might have to make time," she murmured. "We might all have to make time to deal with Jock."

"Repeat that," Jock said softly. "I don't believe I heard you correctly, Eve."

"You heard me," Eve said. She had liked neither the silence when she'd told Jock nor this icy softness. It was far worse than any outburst of anger. She'd seen him like this before, and it meant he had reverted back to the Jock he had been when he'd been that beautiful boy who had been taught by Thomas Reilly to kill without remorse. "And I can't talk to you right now, Jock. We can't meet you at Ladeau's. We've turned around and are heading back to Belle Grace to see what we can find out. We'll finish questioning Ladeau later."

"That's all you know? Just that she's gone?"

"Right now. Kaskov will know more by the time we get back there. He was very angry."

"Was he? It's too late for anger. It had to be an inside job. No one could get onto the grounds. I made sure that Nikolai had plugged all the holes."

"We'll find out when we get back. You can't be sure of anything. Don't make any rash decisions. You're coming right away?"

"I'll be there soon. There are a few things I have to do first." He hung up.

Pure ice. If ice could burn.

Joe glanced at her. "It could have been worse."

She shook her head. "No, it couldn't. Cara and MacDuff have been fighting for years to keep him from spiraling back down to that violence level, and he's—" She stopped. She'd as much as told Jock she couldn't deal with him right now and yet she was trying to do it. "It probably couldn't be worse. But neither could Norwalk's having Michael and Cara." Her voice was suddenly fierce. "So I don't care, Joe. Let Jock do whatever he wants to do as long as I get them back."

"You can't do this," Ladeau said defiantly as Jock came back in the room. "Untie me. I told you, my cousin knows all about the law, and he'll find a way to lock you up for the next ten years. I didn't do anything that was illegal. I just leased my airboat. A simple deal between two businessmen."

"Nothing simple about it. Or you wouldn't have run and put a bullet in me."

"I didn't mean to hit you," he said quickly. "I just wanted to scare you off. Macvey warned me that I couldn't talk about our deal. Not that it was crooked. But he's not someone I wanted to offend."

"So you chose to offend me." He leaned back against the wall and gazed at him. "Not a wise choice, Ladeau."

Cara sitting beside him at the lake playing her violin.

Cara in the summerhouse last night.

Cara staring up at him in bewilderment and wonder.

Cara gone.

Don't think about it. Don't think about her. Push it away. Coldness was better. Get the job done as Reilly had taught him. It was the only way he could function right now. The pain was too great.

Kill Ladeau?

Not now, later perhaps. Ladeau could be of use.

"I won't answer any questions," Ladeau said defiantly. "I don't know anything."

"I hope you do. Because it will be a very uncomfortable time for you if you don't give me the answers I need." He straightened away from the wall. "I found all sorts of maps and charts in those cabinets over there. I'm going to put them on that desk one by one, and you're going to look at them and tell me where Macvey took those supplies."

"I don't know. He didn't want me to know."

"But you're very familiar with all these swamps and bayous. It's how you make your living. I imagine you can make a good guess."

He shook his head. "There are so many rivers and bayous. It could take weeks to find the right area."

"I don't have weeks." Jock moved toward him. "I doubt if I have twenty-four hours. So we're going to study those maps, and you're going to tell me where I have to go."

"I can't do it." He nervously moistened his lips. "I *won't* do it."

"You will," he said softly. "You'll tell me everything you know." He stopped in front of him. "Because you may be stupid, but you're not suicidal."

"I didn't mean to get mixed up in this," he said desperately. "You don't know what kind of man Macvey is. I think he would have killed me if he hadn't thought he might need me later." He broke out, "And the son of a bitch said he'd cut off my dick if I said one word."

"And you'd miss that dick with your pretty little bartender." He looked him in the eye. "I wouldn't do that to you. That's such an ugly, quick solution to my problem. I was taught extended pain is always better. And I know so many ways to make certain you're telling me the truth as we go forward step by step."

Ladeau was staring at him in fascination. Jock could see the horror and the realization beginning to dawn in him as he realized what he was facing.

Give him a moment, Jock thought. Let him see that he meant it.

Let him see the ice and the disconnect and the fact that he'd do any-thing . . . and everything.

Yes, give him a moment.

"Cara. Wake up. I *need* you!"

Michael?

But she couldn't wake up, she wanted to tell him. She was too far away, and she couldn't come back. She might not be able to ever come back.

"Yes you can. I need you, Cara."

Michael needed her. She had to come back to be with him. She fought desperately, and finally her lids lifted.

Michael's face above her. Michael's brown eyes staring down at her.

A dream. It had to be a dream. Michael couldn't be here. But miracles did happen, didn't they?

"Hi," she whispered. "Awfully sleepy, Michael. Can't keep my eyes open. Maybe we should both go back to sleep . . ."

He shook his head. "I don't think that's a good idea, Cara. Nor-walk was mad that you didn't wake up. He told that Brazoff man it might mean he'd given you too much, and it might kill you."

"Norwalk . . ." She was suddenly jarred to full awareness that something was terribly wrong. She glanced around her. A crude wood shack, the smell of wet grass and peat. Michael? She tried to think, to fight through the haze.

"Where's . . . Norwalk now?"

"Outside on the bank yelling at Brazoff. He said he wasn't going to pay him for you. He only came in to fasten that vest on you."

Vest?

She looked down at her body.

She inhaled sharply, her heart jumping to her throat. The canvas vest was tight, and had neat pockets in which cylinders had been inserted. She suddenly couldn't breathe as she realized what those cylinders must contain. She had never seen one before except in movies, but she knew what this vest was, what it had to be. In the movies, it was usually an explosive suicide device.

No dream.

A nightmare.

But she was not alone in this nightmare. Michael was here. She glanced quickly at his body. No vest, she realized with relief. Deal with anything else later. But he'd said he needed her, and that was the only thing important at this moment. "Come here." She held out her arms to him. "I don't know what's happening, but I'll find out about that later. I need you, too, Michael. I've been so worried about you. Let's just hold each other right now."

Then she inhaled sharply. What was she doing? She was telling him to get close to her when she was a walking bomb? How cruel of Norwalk to have her make the choice of comforting Michael or trying to push him away from her for his own safety.

Not that there was anywhere in this small shack where he would be safe if Norwalk set off these explosives. They would both die, so there was no real decision to be made. But the choice was a torture in itself and worthy of Norwalk.

"I've missed you. I've been lonely." Michael came into her arms and nestled close. "And I'll tell you all I know about this place, and that might help keep you awake. Right, Cara?"

"I'm sure it will." Her fingers were gently stroking the silky hair on his nape. So dear, so *alive*. After all the frantic worry, he was here in her arms, and she was going to have a chance to bring him home to Eve in spite of that damn vest. And until she found a safe way to distance herself from him, she would give what she could—love, comfort, a companion to keep away the loneliness. "But Norwalk was wrong, I'm not going to die, Michael. And neither are you. It will be—"

She stiffened as a gunshot echoed from somewhere outside the shack.

He was yelling at Brazoff. He said he wasn't going to pay him for you.
Except with a bullet?

"Cara?"

"It's going to be okay." She held Michael closer. "We're together now, and we just have to figure out how to help each other get away from here . . ."

BELLE GRACE

"What else do you know?" Jock asked Kaskov as he strode into the parlor two hours later. He glanced at Joe and Eve standing by the window before he added, "I talked to Joe while I was on the road coming here and he told me about Brazoff. The bastard is your man, you must have an idea how to get your hands on him."

"I'm working on it." Kaskov's lips twisted. "Nikolai is definitely motivated. All of my cars have LoJack and he's been able to trace the car he took from the property to a pier on Lake Pontchartrain. But the car was abandoned, and there was no sign of Brazoff or Cara." He paused. "But one of the boat owners on the next pier said they saw a motorboat leaving the pier earlier this morning."

"No definite direction, Jock," Eve said. "Brazoff was heading east, but that could be anywhere in those bayous."

"The bayous again," Jock said. "I was concerned that Norwalk might be leaving a false trail, but not this late in the game. He'd know that Cara's disappearance would bring Kaskov front and center into the mix."

"Joe told you that I was sure that's where Michael was being held," Eve said quietly. "I can't expect anyone else to have any confidence that it's true, but I believe it, Jock."

"I'd have more confidence if you could tell me how I could get to them," Jock said harshly. "I've seen amazing things happen while I've been around you, Eve. And Cara has told me about how close you are to Michael. I'd like to believe you. You gave Joe descriptions on how the camp is set up, but it's no good to me if I can't find it in those swamps. I'll believe black is white if you tell me that."

"She can't do that," Joe said. "Give her a break."

"I don't have time." He glanced at Kaskov. "Norwalk is going to want you there when he kills her. That means that he'll call you and set it up. I want to know when that happens."

"That's entirely possible."

"And you're going to go where he tells you to go. You're not going to sit here in this antebellum mansion and send Nikolai."

"I'll do what I wish." Kaskov met his eyes. "As I always do. And if I didn't see how upset you are, there would be a reckoning for your insolence."

"I am upset," he said softly. "You have no idea. I'll use you if I can. If I can't use you, I won't permit you to get in my way. I won't let Cara die." He turned on his heel. "If neither of you can help me, I'll have to go back to using Ladeau. I brought him with me. I have two maps in the car that Ladeau selected as possible sites for building a shelter in the swamps that would have the total isolation Norwalk needs. I'll bring them in, and we'll take a look at them."

"A cooperative effort?" Joe said dryly. "What a surprise."

"I'll use anyone I can," Jock said. "You were a SEAL. You know about operating in swamp terrain, and that could prove valuable. Eve might find a detail in the maps that could trigger something. Kaskov is intelligent and may know more than he's telling us. And eventually he should know where he's going to have to go to meet with Norwalk." He headed for the front door. "I'll be right back."

"I don't believe I've seen this Jock Gavin," Kaskov said as he gazed after Jock. "He's always been innovative and lethal but not this . . . reckless."

"He's not reckless." Eve could see how he might mistake the total focus and icy concentration. "He just doesn't care. He's driven.

He'll do anything he has to do and nothing must get in his way. And he's incredible in what he does." She looked at him. "Don't you get in his way, Kaskov. Ordinarily, I'd try to stop him. Cara would be very upset with me that I didn't. She hates it when anything twists him like this. So do I. But if anyone has a chance of getting Michael and Cara back, it's Jock." She gazed directly into his eyes. "*This* Jock."

"I told you once that you'd kill for your son." He smiled faintly. "And now you're willing to use Jock as the weapon."

"No, I'm not. Because I'll be there beside him when he finds Norwalk."

"If he permits it. Everything appears to be ebbing and flowing at the moment." He shrugged. "We shall see."

"Two possibles." Jock was back and unrolling the first map on the coffee table. "This one is Green Cypress Swamp. Both of these swamps are off the beaten routes of any of the swamp tours because the waters are too difficult to negotiate, and it's too easy to get lost. Once lost, you're in bad trouble. Ladeau says nothing lives in either one of them but snakes and alligators. Very prehistoric."

"Are there islands?" Eve came over to look down at the map. "I don't see any islands."

"Ladeau said he thought he remembered seeing a couple, but he was there only once. No reason to go back when it would have been foolish to try to take any tourists back there. But, if they exist, this map doesn't show them." He unrolled the second map. "Black Pool Swamp. Same scenario. Ladeau knows there was at least one island there because he tried to set up a tour through this swamp once and thought he might be able to use it as a rest stop. But once the interest faded, he thought it would be a lost cause to keep it on his agenda." He pointed to the first map. "He thinks the chances are that it's either one or the other. But they're halfway across the state from each other. We can't afford the time to try to wind our way through both those swamps. We have to guess right."

"Not much information," Joe said. "Can't you go back to Ladeau and dig deeper?"

"I could. I have him tied up and locked in my car outside right now. But it would be useless. Ladeau told me everything he knew."

Joe frowned. "You're certain?"

"Everything," he repeated with emphasis. "These were the only two options he could see that would afford Norwalk the isolation he'd need. I only brought him with me because I'll need to take him along to act as guide when I make a decision." He turned to Eve. "Joe's right, neither choice is good. Do you see anything? Do you have any . . . hunches?"

He meant could she relate anything she was seeing to what Michael had told her. She shook her head. What could she see? Two dense swamps that Jock had said were almost prehistoric in nature. One that had perhaps only one island when Michael had shown her three. The other might not have possessed even that. Nothing on the map.

Snakes and alligators.

Michael had mentioned those, but both swamps had them. Probably every swamp in Louisiana had them.

Think. Was there anything else that would set one apart? Anything Michael had told her that could help.

Help me remember, Michael.

But Michael had helped her all he could, it was her responsibility now. She gazed at the second map with the island where Ladeau had been going to set up his rest stop. But he had abandoned that idea when—

She stiffened, her gaze flying to Jock. "You said Ladeau decided not to set up a tour when the interest faded. What interest, Jock?"

"He was going to set up Fright Night tours. Alligators with glaring red eyes, snakes hanging from the branches of the trees, creatures howling at the moon. He thought it would be a perfect setting and make him a bundle."

"Creatures? What kind of creatures? No, let *me* tell you. *Rougarou.*" Her eyes were wide with excitement. "A mythical werewolf, half man—half beast that's supposed to live in the swamps. Superstitious stories abound of sightings in the Louisiana swamps."

Jock nodded. "*Rougarou.*"

She tapped the second map. "And there was a supposed sighting in this area?"

Jock nodded. "But only one or two reports, then the interest faded."

She tapped the first map. "But none in this swamp?"

Jock shook his head. "Ladeau said only Black Pool Swamp."

"And Norwalk mentioned a sighting of a *Rougarou* monster in the swamp where he took Michael to frighten him." She pointed to the island on the second map. "Ladeau's 'rest stop' might be where we can find Michael and Cara." She drew a deep breath. "It's all guesswork. But if I have to choose, I'll choose Black Pool Swamp."

"Good enough for me," Jock said as he grabbed the map. "I'm on my way to check it out. I'll be in touch."

He was gone before Eve had a chance to even reply. She started to follow him.

"No," Joe said. "My job, Eve." He headed for the door. "As Jock said, I know my way around swamps. And you're also a target, and I can't afford to worry about you. Sorry, you might get in the way." He glanced at Kaskov. "And I want someone here to make certain that he doesn't do anything to spoil our play. Watch him."

Then he was also gone.

"Frustrated?" Kaskov was looking mockingly at Eve. "And so unfair when you appear to have been the one to tell them where Norwalk could be found. Of course, I find it very hard to believe that you could be right about that swamp."

"I don't care what you believe. And, yes, I'm frustrated. But not enough to take a chance on blowing the opportunity of freeing Cara and Michael." She met his eyes. "So I'll do what Joe told me to do and watch you. Jock and Joe may be able to get in a position to ambush or rescue, but you and I are still the targets Norwalk wants to put down. You're going to get a call, and I'll be here to know what's happening and how it will affect the people I love." She smiled grimly. "Or I'll get the call, and I'll make very certain to share with you, Kaskov. Because then, whatever happens won't be up to Joe or Jock, it will be up to us."

CHAPTER
17

"What a tender sight," Norwalk said sarcastically as he stood in the doorway, looking at Cara and Michael curled up together on the blanket on the dirt floor. "It's not your mother, Michael, but obviously she's a good substitute."

"It's Cara," Michael said. "And I heard you say that something that man did to her could have hurt her. You shouldn't have let him do that."

"I didn't mean it to happen. Brazoff was a fool. I took care of it. But if you don't shut your mouth, I'll—"

"Hush, Michael," Cara said quickly. "Don't talk to him. I'm fine now."

"Yes, you are." Norwalk was studying her. "A few hours ago I wouldn't have given a dollar for your chances. Brazoff was so scared of Kaskov that he was a little too careless with sedating you. But you've bounced back." He smiled mockingly. "You'll be in fine shape for my grand finale."

She looked down at the vest she wore. "I'm sure you've planned something as horrible as what you did at Gwinnett Square." She tried to keep her voice steady. He would like it if he saw the fear. "I don't believe you'd set it to go off at a certain time. You'd want to be able to control it."

"Quite true." He pulled out a small black control device and showed it to her before slipping it back into his pocket. "Does it make you feel helpless?"

She didn't answer. "And all because my grandfather is Sergai Kaskov? We're not that close, you know."

"Close enough. You see him every year." His lips thinned. "Close enough so that he blew my brother to kingdom come because Sean had been sent by Manard to take you out. The son of a bitch must care something for you."

"Have it your own way. But if you're planning something special for me, then that must mean that you're going to bring Kaskov here to see it. That would be very stupid. He wouldn't come alone. He may not come at all."

"Even if he cared nothing for you, he'd have to make an appearance. Otherwise, his men would think he was afraid. And that could be the end of him. Strength is everything to the families. I just have to give him the foolish idea that he might have a chance."

She shook her head. "He's smarter than that. You're stupid to think otherwise."

"That's the second time you called me that, bitch." He was across the shack in seconds. His face was twisted with rage as he struck her with all his strength on one cheek, then the other. Then he did it again. And again.

Pain.

Darkness.

She was vaguely aware of Michael crying out and throwing himself across her. He mustn't do that, she realized dazedly. He'd get Norwalk's attention. Dangerous . . . She managed to push Michael aside and get in front of him. "Did that feel good, Norwalk? As good as how you felt when you killed all those poor children?"

"Maybe better." His eyes were blazing down at her. "If you'd died that night, Sean would have walked away, and I'd still have him. But I have a chance to make it right now. Did you know that Sean was planning on blowing you up in your suite that night? But Kaskov used his own C-4 to kill him. Can you guess how you're going to die, Cara? Don't you think it fair that Sean be able to put his plan into effect at last?"

"I'm sure that you do."

"Oh I do. And even if your Eve Duncan was alive, she'd never be able to put you together again. Poor Cara."

"Since I seem to be the main attraction, could I talk you into sending Michael back to Eve or Joe?"

"Of course not. I want it all, Cara. I'll have it all." He turned away. "And I'll see that no one follows Kaskov and keeps me from keeping to the main plan." He smiled. "But I think it's only fair I give you something to think about until it's time to phone Kaskov. When I was sitting watching the flames cremate sweet, gentle Sylvie, I was reading about the Vikings. I found one of their customs very interesting. Can you imagine why?"

Yes, she could, and it was sending a chill through her.

But he didn't wait for an answer. The next moment he was gone.

"Cara." Michael was running from behind her. "He hurt you." Tears were running down his cheeks. He reached out and touched the bruise on her left cheek. "I tried to stop him . . ."

"I know you did." She pulled him close again. "You were very brave, but you mustn't do that. Because I couldn't stand it if he hurt you. That would be much worse than being hurt myself. So we'll both just have to be careful." She paused. But that last threat of Norwalk's had filled her with sick dread, and she had to prepare him. "But in spite of what Norwalk said, you have to know that everyone loves you and they *will* be coming to get you, Michael. Nothing will stop them. Your mama and your dad, and Jock, and probably other people." She had to keep her tone calm and unafraid, or he would sense that fear. "But Norwalk may separate us before that happens, and whatever you see, you must not fight back, you have to stay here and wait for your mama. Will you promise me?"

His arms tightened around her neck. "I won't leave you, Cara."

"No, it will be me leaving you. But only for a little while. Promise?"

He was silent. "You shouldn't go away. It's Norwalk who has to go away."

"Well, if I do have to go, will you promise?"

He nodded. "But it won't happen, Cara. We can't let it."

"Right, we'll do our best." She had his promise. "Now let's sit here and talk about your mama and dad and all the fun things you'll do when you go home to them."

"I can't take you any farther, Gavin," Ladeau said. **"The river** ends here, and the bayou runs right beside the swamplands for the next seven miles. It almost splits the swamp in two. Any boat would be spotted by anyone on guard." He moistened his lips. "If you expect there to be guards with guns?"

"Oh, I expect it," Jock said. "And that island is five miles?"

He nodded. "Five or six. I don't remember."

"Remember," Joe said. "Precisely."

"Five miles. When are you going to let me go home?"

"When it's over," Jock said as he took the paddle and rowed the speedboat off the bayou and deeper into the marshy swampland cove. "But we won't ask you to go any farther, we'll leave you here in the boat and make you as comfortable as possible. You'd just be trouble from here on." He jumped out of the boat, and his boots sank into the deep peat mud. "But you'll be in very deep shit if I get to that island and find it's not where you said it was. Or that it's not the place Norwalk would choose to put his shack."

"I didn't say for sure. How could I?"

"Talk to Joe Quinn about it," Jock said. "Norwalk might be

holding his six-year-old son on that island." He looked at Joe. "I'll go and check it out. Will you tie up Ladeau to make sure he doesn't decide to give us any grief? And then set up a base camp for us?"

Joe nodded reluctantly. "Though I should go with you, dammit."

"And if you saw Michael, would you be able to stop yourself from trying to go after him?"

Joe didn't answer.

"I didn't think so." Jock turned and headed through the shrubs. "I'll be back before dark. We've just got to hope that Eve was right about this being the place. I'll call you as soon as I know. If it is, I'll try to put up a couple cameras and audio feeds around the island and find a place to take my shot."

"Shot? Only one? Eve said there were four men beside Norwalk."

"If Eve's intel from Michael is accurate. But he's only a little boy, and we can't be sure that Eve wasn't having a dream."

"I'm sure."

"And I'll be sure after I take a look and see how close she came. Besides, Norwalk is the one who gives the orders. I blow his brains out, and his great plan falls apart."

He didn't wait for an answer but plunged into the brush.

Keep moving.

Five miles, and he'd know if Eve had guessed right.

Five miles, and he'd see if Cara and Michael were still alive.

Five miles, and he'd see who he'd have to kill.

Keep moving.

BELLE GRACE

"Nikolai says I have a call, Eve," Kaskov said as he lifted the phone from his ear to look at her. "I imagine it's our mutual adversary. Would you care to listen?" He smiled. "Never mind, I know the answer. Put him through, Nikolai." He spoke into the phone. "What do you have to say to me, Norwalk? I'm a busy man."

"Not that busy. You took the call, and you let Eve Duncan talk you into protecting her and the pretty girl I'm looking at right now. I'd say that you have an interest in what I'm going to tell you."

"I'm mildly amused by all this furor. But it's gotten out of hand. I stopped your inept twin from killing Cara because it was a question of family pride. But as you must know, I'm a man who never goes too far without stepping back and looking at the big picture. And I certainly have no intention of sacrificing myself for a granddaughter whom I have only known for a few short years. However, I might be persuaded to offer a ransom."

"Not an option."

"Too bad. Good-bye, Norwalk."

No! Eve sat up straight in her chair. He couldn't cut this connection. She wouldn't let him—

"Bluff," Norwalk said. "You may care nothing for the girl, but you wouldn't want your reputation to suffer because you'd allowed me to take her away from you . . . and be killed in a most unpleasant way. All the crime families of Moscow would come after you with blades drawn to cut your empire into digestible pieces. You have to make the attempt."

Silence. "Go on."

"I'll send you directions to where you can find your Cara. I'm sure you've discovered that she's somewhere in the bayous, but that's such a very large area. It would take you weeks, months to search for me. But I'm willing to help you. I'll even send her halfway to meet you."

"Generous."

"Yes, but you can't have all your very competent men with you. I realize that you won't come alone, but I'll permit only two boats, your boat and another occupied by no more than three other men. That will allow you a certain amount of security."

"Not much. And allow us to be picked off?"

"Possibly. But that's your challenge. When Cara joins you, then you whisk her away . . . if you can. Then you turn the tables on me and maintain your sterling reputation."

"And you'll have a number of dirty surprises for me along the way."

"Without doubt. Just as you did when your men killed Sean. Dirty wasn't the word for it. I not only couldn't tell he was my twin, I couldn't tell he was a human being. Is Eve there?"

"I'm here, Norwalk," Eve said.

"I just wanted to assure you that I'm not leaving you and your son out of my plans. But you can see how I have to concentrate on Kaskov at the moment. However, I'll permit him to bring you along if you so choose."

"So that you have the chance to get two instead of one?"

"Actually, I'd rather deal with you individually, but I'm a practical man. And I'm remembering that you wouldn't help me to put my brother back together after this bastard blew him apart." His voice lowered to deep malice. "I'll even try to arrange to make sure that you'll get the opportunity to see your son one more time while we reminisce about it." He paused. "Kaskov, I'll put the directions on your phone in four hours. If you come, you have a small chance. If you send someone, Cara and the boy die. If anyone follows you, they die. And I'll know if that happens. You've noticed I do make preparations." He cut the connection.

"He sounded very satisfied, didn't he? But he's no fool. He picked out a way that he thought would force me to get in the crosshairs. He has obviously studied me extensively."

"And was he right about you?"

"Yes and no." He looked at her. "But he was right that it's to my advantage to go after Cara. Providing that he made it a possibility that I'd survive."

"He'll not let you live. He won't let Cara live. You know that's true. It's better to wait until we hear from Joe and see if they've located Norwalk's island."

"Perhaps. It depends entirely on what they find there. I'll be interested in hearing from them." He turned and headed for his office. "In the meantime, I have some advance preparations to make in case I decide to let Norwalk lure me into his trap."

She went rigid. "Preparations? But Norwalk told you that if you made any move at all, Cara and Michael would die."

"Then I mustn't let him see them."

"And if he does?"

"I've already answered you. I don't lose, Eve. I won't go there without having—"

Her phone rang. Jock.

She tensed as she quickly punched the access. "Yes or no?"

"Yes. Black Pool Swamp. I saw the camp, and it was very close to those sketches Joe showed me on the trip out here."

"Michael and Cara?"

"No, I didn't see them. They must have been in the shack. But I saw Norwalk and all four of his guards. Plus a corpse that was floating in the bayou about fifty yards from the island and furnishing lunch for a couple alligators. Norwalk has put up a metal-link fence to protect the bayou waters around his island from gators, so he must have tossed Brazoff to them. Norwalk would have been finished with him after he delivered Cara."

"Good," she said fiercely. "Let them all kill each other."

"We can't hope for that. But it will get done." He paused. "There are a lot of explosives on that island, Eve. Some of it's packed around the door of the shack. We'll have to get around it before we can get to Cara and Michael. I'm on my way back to Joe to figure it out."

The explosives Michael had mentioned. Of course, it was practically Norwalk's trademark. But the thought of it that close to Michael and Cara terrified her. "Get back to me as soon as you can. Call

Kaskov later, he may be thinking of doing something that could be a problem."

"No, he won't," Jock said grimly. "No one gets in the way when we're this close." He hung up.

"So you were correct?" Kaskov said, as Eve turned to face him. "How very interesting . . . and helpful."

"And it might eliminate Norwalk's trying to find a way to kill Cara and you at the same time. That sounded like a losing proposition. You're damn right it could be helpful. We might have a chance of going in and getting them off that island."

"Or not." He gazed at her quizzically. "You're excited. I take it that you're not going to accept Norwalk's concession to accompany me to his deluxe ambush?"

"No, and neither should you. I'm going to leave for Black Pool Swamp right away to join Joe. If Norwalk's not going to give you the directions to the swamp for another four hours, I'll have time to get there before he suspects that we know where he is and heightens security. Will you arrange to get me a speedboat?"

"Of course. Whatever you like."

Her eyes narrowed on his face. "But you have no intention of going with me?"

"I prefer to be the backup plan. I admit Norwalk's proposition is intriguing me." He lifted his hand. "But you needn't set Jock on me. I will not endanger your son or Cara unless it becomes necessary."

"You will not do it at all," she said harshly.

"The backup crew sometimes has to make its own rules." He took out his phone. "But if you all do a superb job, and I'm not needed, then the point is moot." He dialed Nikolai. "You'd better get down to the dock. Nikolai will have that speedboat at your disposal within five or ten minutes, and it appears you're on a four-hour time constraint."

Eve gazed at him in frustration mixed with suspicion. But she would not stay here when she had a chance to go to her son. She had to be there if he needed her. She turned and walked quickly toward the French doors. "Don't do it," she said curtly. "Let us get Cara out. He'll kill you."

"I'm touched that you'd care." He inclined his head. "I'm sure we'll be in communication. Be safe, Eve." He spoke into the phone. "Nikolai, you have a small job to do in the matter of obtaining a speedboat . . ."

Kaskov stood at the French doors and watched as Nikolai helped Eve into the speedboat. Nikolai stepped back and waited while Eve gunned the engine and tore down the bayou toward open water. Then he turned, lifted his hand to Kaskov, and started back toward the house.

"Am I allowed to come out now?" But Darcy had already come out of the office and was standing at the doorway of the parlor. "Has she left?"

"Yes. Off to the rescue." He smiled mockingly. "And I'm certain that you would have erupted out of that office if you'd wanted to do so. I just gave you a place and the ability to observe and listen without having to interact. Isn't that what you told me you wished?"

She shrugged. "It was what was best. It was better that I fade into the background where Eve would like to keep me. She's having enough stress." She met his eyes. "And don't you make fun of her because she's willing to do anything to save the people she loves. She's one of the good guys."

"You're being impolite. I wonder why I put up with your lack of respect."

"I don't know why either. But I can't let it matter to me. There's no time to tiptoe around you."

"Even though I'm not one of the good guys?"

"Compared to Norwalk, you're not so bad."

"Oh, you're so wrong, Darcy." He suddenly chuckled. "But I find being compared to Norwalk is not pleasing to me. It makes me want to destroy the object of that comparison." His gaze narrowed on her face. "Was that your aim?"

"Maybe. You're thinking all the time. You're very smart, very reasonable. I don't want you to be reasonable about Norwalk." She added simply, "Because then you might not help me kill him."

He tilted his head. "Have I been demoted to a secondary position in this endeavor? That's not how I operate."

"You know better. Everyone else wants to keep me safe and away from Norwalk. I have to rely on you to take me to him. You're going to do it, aren't you?"

He was silent. "I believe I am."

"Why?"

"Does it matter? You'll get what you want."

"I think it does matter." She was frowning. "I'm not sure why. I'm very persuasive, but I don't think that would sway you."

"It might." He smiled faintly. "Or it might be that you're wrong about how reasonable I am. Perhaps I have a deep passion for revenge and feel a certain kinship for you. Or it could be that I understand the value of family and that it has to be protected at all costs. But that would reveal a weakness of which Nikolai would disapprove." His lips twisted. "So we'll have to discard that possibility. Suppose we leave it to the fact that I am as ruthless as Norwalk, and it amuses me to see you risk that very beautiful neck."

"Okay." She drew a deep breath. "Then let's get to it. If you're going to take me along, then you must be planning on substituting me for Eve. Right?"

"It occurred to me when Eve decided that she wasn't going to accompany me."

"Me, too," she said. "And I knew it would be the first thing you'd consider since I tried to convince you that you should use me as bait for Cara." She made a face. "But that wonderful black wig won't work now. I'm sure that Nikolai will be able to get me a red-brown one that will do the job. He appears to be able to pull anything out of his hat. Eve is a little taller, but I'll wear dark clothes, and that always increases the look of height." She turned toward the stairs. "But the makeup will be more difficult. I'm too damn good-looking. It will be hard to get rid of that impression and just be very interesting and attractive."

"I'm afraid you don't have time for plastic surgery."

"Tell Nikolai to get a wig that will hang straight and shadow my cheekbones. I'll manage the rest." She was taking the steps two at a time. "I have almost four hours . . ."

BLACK POOL SWAMP

"Cara, I think someone—" Michael whispered as he rolled closer to her. "Someone's . . . near . . ."

"Shh." She drew him into her arms. "Try to sleep, Michael. We don't want Norwalk to come back in here." All that poison and ugliness he'd spat at her earlier had upset Michael, and it had taken her almost thirty minutes to quiet him. "I won't let anyone hurt you."

"No. That's not it." His voice was a breath close to her ear. "Not hurt . . . Good . . ."

"What?"

"Someone's close . . . Help. I thought maybe . . . earlier. But now very close . . ."

She went still. Eve had been sure that Michael had reached out to her the night of Gwinnet Square, and Cara had told her that she would believe anything that Eve wanted her to believe. But now she was faced with believing Michael himself. "It could be a dream, Michael."

"No, don't be scared." He cuddled nearer. "Close, Cara. He's so close . . ."

"He?" She paused. "Who?"

He shook his head. "I don't know. But I thought I'd tell you so that you wouldn't be afraid."

She was trying not to begin to hope, but it was all they had right now. And wasn't it reasonable that someone would come after them and not stop until they found them? "Sometimes you can talk to your mama. Maybe it's her?"

"No, not yet." He reached out and touched her cheek. "But she loves you and me, she'll want to be—"

"On your feet, Cara." Norwalk was standing in the doorway. "I want to show you off to the subjects of your kingdom. They've been waiting for you for a long time."

Michael stiffened, and his arms tightened around her.

She had to get away from here quickly, or he might try to protect her. She gave him a quick kiss on his temple. "I'll be right back," she whispered as she pushed him aside and got to her knees. "It's okay, remember?"

He shook his head. "Not safe. Just close . . ."

"Get out here!" Norwalk was cursing as he strode across and jerked her to her feet. "You've already caused me too much trouble today." He pushed her out into the darkness only lit by the light affixed to the cypress tree rooted in the waters off the island. "Everything was supposed to go smoothly, then Brazoff screwed up." He was shoving her down to where the stagnant water was lapping against the bank. "Nothing goes right with you. Sean died, and now this Brazoff—"

"I can hardly be blamed that the man you hired to kidnap me almost killed me," she said dryly. "That's unreasonable even for a maniac like you, Norwalk."

"Very brave when the boy isn't around," he said between set teeth. "You're very careful around him I notice."

"Because I don't want him frightened. I'm not brave. I just know that nothing I can say or do will change what you intend to do to me." She turned to look at him. "Why did you bring me out here, Norwalk?"

"I told you, I wanted to show you what's in store."

"I think that you've already made that clear." She looked down at the vest around her body. "What did you say? I'm just a toy that can be broken whenever you press that button? You've blown your punch line. I don't believe you can think up any threats that would scare me more than that."

"You underestimate me. Let me try." He pointed to the island several hundred yards away. "You see those red eyes glowing in the dark? Alligators. They're restless tonight. They've already had a very satisfying breakfast, but they're always looking for fresh meat."

Don't let him see the fear. He would enjoy it too much. "You can't have it both ways, Norwalk. Are you going to throw me to the alligators or blow me up?"

His hand tightened on the remote control. "Arrogant bitch. You're just like that weird kid. But when it comes down to that last minute, you'll both know that I was the one who made it happen."

"That 'weird kid' has more strength and courage than you'll ever have. And I think you must know it, or he wouldn't disturb you so much." She met his eyes. "And I'm not trying to be arrogant. I told you that I'm not brave, and I'm just trying to get through this."

"So young and talented," he said mockingly. "So much to live for. I hear everyone thought you were going to be famous. Too bad all that music is going to go to waste when you end up in more pieces than Sean."

"You'll be disappointed there," she said quietly. "You might be able to destroy me, but not the music. Just because I'm not here to play it doesn't mean that there's not going to be someone else out there who will be able to hear what I heard and let it flow out of them. I don't believe the music ever goes away."

"And what if I break these fingers?" He reached out and grabbed her hand. "I can take it away from you in one second."

She tried to stifle the panic. "And what good would that do? It just proves that you can't make up your mind. You said you were going to blow me up anyway." Distract him. "Or have you decided on the alligators?"

He threw her hand down. The next instant his fist lashed out and struck her jaw. "Do you think I'd let you spoil my plans?" He was breathing hard, his eyes wild as he watched her drop to the ground. "I was just playing with you. No, you're still going to face your fate in the true Viking tradition. The alligators aren't for you, they're for the boy. I've been saving him for them."

She shook her head to clear it. The bitter taste of blood was on her tongue from her split lip. "When I saw that you hadn't given him one of these vests, I didn't think that you meant him to join me." She raised herself on one elbow. "And he told me that you kept talking about the alligators. He's not afraid, Norwalk."

"But you're afraid for him. That will be enough for right now," he said. "The fear's coming to all of you." He jerked her to her feet. "And Sean and I are the ones who are bringing it. Now go back and cuddle that little viper for the next few hours. It might be the last opportunity you're going to have. And it will make it harder for him when I tear you two apart. He'll feel so alone. Like I feel without Sean."

Next few hours.

The words echoed in her mind as he roughly pushed her back up the incline. Not much time left. How to get Michael free before that time ran out?

But Michael had said that someone was close who could help.

Close enough, she thought desperately. And was it only hope and imagination ignited by the horror and stress Michael had been going through all this time?

She involuntarily cast a glimpse over her shoulder at the darkness of the surrounding swamp across the bayou.

He?

Jock? Kaskov? Joe?

She wished she could feel something, anything that Michael had felt. But she was only aware of that murky darkness and the silence broken only by the sound of the swamp creatures.

"Taking a last look at those alligators?" Norwalk asked mockingly. "They're still there, waiting for the boy." He pushed her inside the shack. "By all means, think about them."

She couldn't bear to think about them. Instead, she would think about Michael and all the joy he brought them. And she would try to think of a way that she could save him.

And wonder if that fragile hope that Michael had sensed was close enough to do them any good.

Control.

Jock's hands dug into the stock of his Remington until they turned white.

Then he forced himself to slowly release his grip. No killing. Not now. No quick ending.

But he had *hit* her.

And Jock had seen the blood.

Breathe deep.

Forget how Cara had looked in that moment.

Embrace the ice as he always did.

Impossible. He was hot, he was burning. He had come back here by himself to scope out the shack where Cara and Michael had to be held because Joe wanted to be available to guide Eve to their location. He was already searching for a way to stop Norwalk's attack on Kaskov. But Jock had brought the Remington because he'd thought he might even be able to stop Norwalk in his tracks with a single bullet.

Until he'd seen the belt of explosives around Cara's body.

He still felt the shock that had torn through him. It should not have done that to him. There had always been that possibility. Optimism had nothing to do with reality. Admit that he'd not thought about it because he had known he'd have this reaction. Then seeing the son of a bitch hitting Cara had compounded the response.

Don't think about it. Think about what he'd learned tonight. Think about how to make it work for them.

He took out his earpiece, shimmied down from the cypress tree where he'd been setting up the shot, and moved away from the island. He had to phone Joe. He had to plan and function. He wasn't going to be good for anything else until he got his head back together.

He had *hit* her.

"Eve just got here," Joe said as soon as he picked up. "Tell me it's going to be easy to take Norwalk down so that I can keep her out of it."

"Cara has a vest of C-4, and Norwalk has a remote he's carrying around with him."

"Shit." He paused. "Michael?"

"I didn't see him, but I don't think so. Cara said something about her being the only one."

"You spoke to her?"

"No, but I'd already set up the audio in the trees in the swamp across from the island. The bayou is very shallow and narrow there, and it's only twenty or thirty feet from the swamp to the island dock. I was lining up my shots when Norwalk brought her down to the bank of the bayou. I was able to hear pieces of the conversation she was having with him."

"Then we'll have to take that vest into consideration. I was hoping that—"

"*Screw* hope," he said harshly. "We should have assumed that Norwalk would do it when I saw all those explosives. We just didn't want to think about her being that helpless, about *us* being that helpless. Well, it's here, and we've got to deal with it."

"And we will," Joe said quietly. "And the first thing to deal with is that Eve said we can't trust Kaskov not to meet with Norwalk and try to take him out. He's not going to trust anyone but himself."

Jock muttered a curse. "Then maybe I should take Kaskov out before he gets here. I can't let him interfere."

"And cause Norwalk to press that remote button because he has no reason not to do it if Kaskov is already dead?"

Jock knew that was the truth. He just wasn't thinking straight. "Then call and tell Kaskov about that vest so he can be prepared not to do anything that might get her killed." He added bitterly, "Providing he gives a damn."

"And in the meantime, we try to take care of business ourselves," Joe said. "Anything else Kaskov should know?"

"Norwalk won't attack him while he's in the swamp. He'll do it on the primary bayou where the waters are broad and deep. Probably right before he actually goes into the swamp."

"How do you know?"

"He was taunting Cara. Something about the Vikings. You're familiar with how the Vikings prepared to go to their Valhalla?"

"Sure. They're sent out to sea in a boat while their bodies burn on a funeral pyre on deck," Joe said.

"And how better to destroy Kaskov than to have his only granddaughter sent out to meet him in a boat that will explode and kill both of them as soon as Norwalk judges her close enough to cause maximum damage?"

Silence. "Twisted as everything else about Norwalk." Joe paused. "But I'd judge Kaskov should be on his way by now. That means that he should be here in four or five hours. You're coming back here?"

"I'm on my way. We have to come up with something to work around that damn vest. And I'll need more weapons to take down those guards. I left my automatic rifle at the boat because I hoped that I could concentrate on Norwalk." He hesitated. He knew Eve was there listening, and he didn't want to hit her with another horror prospect, but he had to prepare her. "And then we need to talk about Michael."

"What about Michael?" Joe said quickly. "You said that he wasn't wearing that damn vest."

"He isn't." Later. "I should be back there in another twenty minutes." He hung up.

And by the time he got to Eve and Joe, he had to have a plan that would keep Cara and Michael alive.

Explosives.

Detonator.

Use all that Reilly had taught him about killing and try to make it work for him.

Clear your head and come up with an answer.

What destroyed bombs?

Explosions that also killed.

Discard.

Think. Review. What else?

Detonator?

Remove the hand on the button.

And that could still press down and kill just as a reflex action.

Discard.

Or not . . .

Examine.

He had heard of one way that might be possible.

Slim. So damn slim.

Grab it.

No time for any other choice.

He reached for his phone and dialed Kaskov. "Listen, before you leave for Black Pool Swamp, there's something you have to do."

"You persist in giving me orders, Gavin."

"Do you want me to beg you? I'll do it, Kaskov."

Silence. "No. I might go into shock. What do you want, Gavin?"

CHAPTER
18

FIVE HOURS LATER

You're sure it will work?" Eve asked Jock as she waited for
Joe to finish packing the weapons to take to the island. It was
an idiotic question, she realized. But it had been terrible waiting
here for these last nerve-racking hours after Jock had told her what
Norwalk was planning for Michael. "Sorry, Jock. I know there aren't
any guarantees. We'll just do the best we can and hope that we can
all survive."

"We have a chance," Jock said curtly. "With you and Joe on his
side, the odds on Michael may be better than for Cara. Remember
to remind Joe he has to get Michael out of that shack right away. It's
primed with explosives, and we don't know what orders Norwalk has
given his men if the camp is attacked."

"Joe could hardly forget it," she said dryly. "He knows what he's
doing, Jock."

"I know. I'm just hoping Kaskov does." He grabbed his rifle and
checked it. "I'll go around to the north side of the island and take
out the two guards there. That will leave you and Joe with only the
two on the south side. Their absence shouldn't be obvious to Norwalk when he takes Cara from the shack and puts her in the boat. It's
dark, and there will be no sound."

"Damn him," Eve said shakily. "And we have to stand there and watch him and not do anything?"

"Unless you want to watch *him* press that button on the detonator," Jock said. "But one way or the other, I promise he's not going to live long, Eve."

"No, he's not," she said quietly. "As I told my son, he has to go away." She saw that Joe was ready, and she turned and started to follow him. "I'll see you at the island."

Jock let the guard fall to the ground and wiped his knife on the front of his shirt.

One down.

He moved silently around the edge of the north bank, using the cypress trees for cover.

The other guard was using earphones, probably bored and listening to music. Not good discipline for a sentry. But he wouldn't have to worry about it soon.

Jock stepped behind him, and his arm snaked around his neck. Quick. No sound. End it.

He broke his neck.

He dropped him on the ground.

Done.

Now go closer to the shack and make certain Norwalk wasn't changing plans at the last minute.

"It's time. Are you ready, bitch?"

Cara couldn't see anything in the doorway but Norwalk's dark silhouette behind the brilliant, glaring beam of the flashlight he was holding. "It wouldn't matter, would it?" She got to her feet and turned to Michael. She had been preparing herself for this moment, but it was still difficult. "I have to go. Remember, I told you it might happen?" She put her arms around him. "Don't worry, I'll be—"

"Touching. But it's not according to my plan," Norwalk said as he grasped Michael's shoulder and jerked him across the room and out the door. "He's going with us."

"No!" Cara ran after them. "You said I was going alone."

Michael was looking over his shoulder as Norwalk pushed him down the incline toward the dock. "It's okay, Cara. Don't be scared."

"Oh, do be scared," Norwalk said mockingly. "That's the entire purpose." He stopped beside the motorboat tied at the makeshift dock. "You were being entirely too calm and disgustingly brave. I needed to see the panic." He smiled at her as he quickly tied her hands behind her. "No, I haven't decided to make him accompany you. I just wanted to bring him out here to bid you good-bye." His waved at a man standing a few yards away. "Macvey here will keep him company until I call and tell him it's time to bid him good-bye. Then he'll toss him over that metal gate and send him to meet those alligators who want so desperately to welcome him." He glanced at the other island. "Which will be at the exact moment when you meet your fate with Kaskov. I thought it would increase the pain enormously for you to know that was happening." His gaze raked her face. "Yes, I can see it starting now. Mission accomplished. You may say good-bye to the boy now."

She wanted to strike out. She wanted him to *die*. She could do nothing unless she wanted him to start the death cycle right now. At this moment, she was bitterly aware of the helplessness he'd wanted her to feel. The only thing she could do was to hide that fear and panic as much as possible. "I'll do that." She fell to her knees in front of Michael. "You're going to be fine, Michael," she whispered. "Don't be afraid. Like I told you, I can't believe that they won't come for you. As for me, it's only for a little while. And if it stretches out to be a little longer, then you just play my CDs I sent you, and when the music starts, I'll be there. Understand?"

He nodded. "But I'm not afraid." His dark eyes were shimmering in the light. "Don't you be afraid, Cara. I tried to tell you . . ." His arms were suddenly around her neck, and he was holding her tight. "No one's going to hurt me." He whispered in her ear, "They're not close, they're here. Mama's *here*."

She stiffened. Oh, God, make it so. Whatever miracle you have to perform. Keep him safe.

"Enough," Norwalk said. "Into the boat."

"Do whatever you have to do, Michael," she whispered. "No one must hurt you. Your mama wouldn't like it." She kissed his cheek. No good-byes. "See you later." She turned and got into the boat. She glanced at Norwalk as he jumped in and started the motor. "You don't look pleased. Wasn't my response satisfying enough for you?"

"Not entirely. But you'll make it up later when it comes home to you how many deaths are going to be triggered by you when you do your Viking bit." He was guiding the boat carefully through the shallow waters of the bayou. "Including that kid back there. I can hardly wait to stroll back from bidding you farewell to see that big alligator finish him off."

She looked back over her shoulder. Michael was standing on the dock, his legs parted, looking after her. An eager smile lit his face. Then he turned and gazed into the thick, impenetrable darkness of the cypress trees of the swamp across the bayou.

Oh, God, protect him, she prayed.

Let it be true.

"You can change your mind," Kaskov said as he glanced at Darcy standing beside him at the wheel of the speedboat. "If you're seen, you probably won't survive."

"And you sound so concerned," Darcy said as she gazed out at the darkness of the water whipping in front of the powerful white boat. "I'm surprised you're trying to talk me out of it. I'm your ace in the hole, Kaskov. What would you do without me?"

"I usually manage. But I'm also surprised that I'm offering you a choice at the eleventh hour." He looked at her. "You'd better live up to all that PR you gave me. It's got to be done right or not at all."

"I always live up to my PR," she said. "And I won't be cheated, Kaskov. I can do this. I *will* do this." She tensed as she saw the lights of a small boat appear from the jutting edge of darkness of the swamp ahead. "Is it showtime?"

"We shall see." He cut the engine. "Let's have Norwalk tell us. I imagine he'll give us a proper greeting." He looked at Nikolai coming up behind in another speedboat, with two men on board. "Be ready," he called.

Nikolai raised his hand and cut his engine.

"Is she there?" Darcy asked, her eyes straining on the boat. "It wasn't a lie? It's Cara?"

"It's Cara." He handed her the infrared binoculars he'd used. "Much worse for wear. But she must not have your talent and access to makeup."

Darcy quickly focused the binoculars on Cara. "That wasn't funny," she said. "That *bastard*."

"Just your usual, garden-variety sociopath. But I admit I'm having problems with what he did to her. I'm getting quite anxious for the action to begin." His phone rang. He murmured, "And that must be the bell to signal the start."

"Welcome, Kaskov," Norwalk said. "Do you know that until this moment, I wasn't positive you'd actually accept my invitation? You must actually care something for Cara. That will make the prospect to come much more entertaining."

He was practically salivating, Cara thought bitterly. All the malice and ugliness had come to the forefront in these final moments. He believed only triumph was ahead. She could only pray that he was wrong.

"I have a certain sense of family," Kaskov said. "And as you said, it was a move that was politically correct. I believe it's your move. What's next?"

"I told you, it's very simple." He jumped back on the shore. "In a few minutes, I'm going to start the motor on this boat and send Cara toward you. If you wish to help her, you can try to retrieve her. In which case, I will press the button, and she will blow you away. Or when you think she's getting close enough to be a threat, you can fire off that heavy artillery I'm sure you're carrying at her boat and save yourself. That's probably what you'll decide to do. But it will mean that you'll kill Cara yourself. Which will be very satisfying for me."

"I'm sure it will. But not totally satisfying. How do you dispose of me then?"

"Did I forget to mention I have pretty heavy artillery myself?" He gestured to a white tube on the ground at his feet. "A small surface missile by some standards, but heat-activated, and big enough. The moment you start to run, I blow you and your men in that other boat out of the water. Are you getting nervous, Kaskov?"

"Terrified," he said dryly. "Is that what you want me to say?"

"That's what I want you to feel. And you will. Is Eve Duncan there?"

"Right beside me. I couldn't keep her from coming. You said that you'd let her be with her son. She still thinks she can save him."

Cara went rigid. "Eve?"

Mama is here. Michael had said.

But not if Eve was on that ship. Michael was wrong. And there was no way Eve would be able to save him.

"I want to see her face," Norwalk said. "Turn on the boat lights. And I want to talk to her."

The speedboat lit up, and Cara could see Eve standing there, red-brown hair windblown, every muscle appearing tense, strained. She took the phone from Kaskov. "Where is my son?"

"Hello, Eve," Norwalk said. "It's so good that you showed me how much power I have over you. I'm sorry that you appear so stressed." He smiled. "But I'm afraid that I've changed my mind. The boy will be alligator food by the time this little standoff is over."

"No!" She grabbed an automatic rifle from the seat and began firing at Norwalk. "You can't do that. You can't kill my son! I won't let you—"

"You *fool*. I make the rules here." Kaskov grabbed the rifle, swung it, and hit Eve's head with the barrel.

She fell backward over the rail, into the water.

Cara screamed!

She leaned forward, trying to catch sight of Eve in the water.

Not *Eve*!

Nothing. No sign. Nothing.

She must have been unconscious when she hit the water and sank immediately out of sight.

Cara felt sick, her gaze still frantically searching.

"A fine way to begin," Norwalk said. He had his binoculars lifted and was also scanning the water. He lowered the binoculars. "I was looking forward to doing that myself, but I'll accept being the cause of it." He bent forward and started the motor. "And now I'm eager to see the rest of it." He shoved the small motorboat in the direction of Kaskov's speedboat. "There you go, Kaskov. Choose which way you want it to happen."

Cara could feel the movement of the water beneath the boat, she could see Kaskov's speedboat in the distance, but all she could think about was Eve's terrible cry as she reached for the automatic weapon and her face as she plunged off the speedboat into the water.

The tears were running down her cheeks as she remembered Michael's excited whisper.

Mama is here!

Norwalk's face was lit with hunger and a feral joy as he watched the motorboat chug slowly toward Kaskov's huge speedboat.

Jock was feeling that same hunger as he gazed down his sights at Norwalk from the branches of the cypress tree above him.

Not yet.

Something could still go wrong.

Hell, something might already have gone wrong.

He didn't want to think about that possibility.

Focus.

Don't look at Cara's small motorboat that was already too close to Kaskov's speedboat. Soon, Norwalk would decide that she was close enough to allow him to take down both boats with that detonator.

Move Kaskov!

And Kaskov *was* moving, he was starting to reverse, backing away from Cara's boat.

And Jock could see Norwalk stiffen, his entire attention on Kaskov's apparent defection.

Now!

She was going to die.

She was too close to Kaskov's speedboat, Cara realized. The blast was going to come soon. What would it be like to die? What was out there? Music? Surely there would be music . . .

But there were so many things that she had left undone. Jock . . . Michael . . . Darcy . . . Eve . . . They were all there before her as she saw that white speedboat in the bayou ahead.

And Kaskov. Was there something left undone there?

She didn't know, but there might have been.

And if she was going to die, she didn't want to give Norwalk the satisfaction of using her as a weapon to destroy him.

The only way she could keep that from happening now was to work her way to the edge of the boat and roll into the water. Her hands were tied, so that would mean a good chance of drowning, but the alternative was giving Norwalk what he wanted, and he'd already taken too much from the people she loved.

She moved a little closer to the edge.

She started to rock the boat. If she tilted the boat, she might be able to slip over the side into the water and that would—

"No! For God's sake, don't do that, Cara. You're going to screw up everything!"

She froze, her gaze flying to the water several feet away. "Darcy?"

"Well, I'm not a mermaid. Listen, don't ask questions. Just do what I say, okay?"

She nodded dazedly. "Okay."

"Keep on the edge of the boat, but get up as far as you can and draw up your legs. Quick. Kaskov can only keep Norwalk distracted for so long."

Cara was already moving, curling up at the top of the boat. "Darcy, I don't want you to—"

"Be quiet. I have a job to do." She was pulling out a plastic-wrapped object that looked like an oval ball and was hurriedly unwrapping it. "I'm going to toss this grenade into the bottom of your boat, and I can't jerk you into the water until it goes off. You have to be close to it for it to work. So expect an explosion . . ."

"Grenade? How much of an explosion?"

"I have no idea." She pulled out the metal grenade. "Just brace yourself." She pulled off the safety and tossed the grenade into the boat. "He said no more than a minute until—"

The bottom of the boat exploded, rocking Cara almost into the water.

"That wasn't too bad." Darcy was swimming toward her. "You're not hurt?" She didn't wait for an answer, but jerked Cara the rest of the way into the water and was pulling her away from the sinking boat. "I'll check you later."

"Darcy, get away from me." Cara was struggling, trying to push her away, but her hands were still tied. "Norwalk will have seen that explosion. He's going to press that—"

"Let him. I'm not leaving you. What do you think this is all about? I've got to get you out of this stinking bayou."

"I'll go with you. Let me try to swim. Just don't get close to me."

"It's okay," Darcy didn't let her go. "I'll explain later, but Norwalk must have pressed that damn button already. And you're still in one piece. I think the bastard is probably in a tearing rage and going to focus on Kaskov instead." She started to swim toward the bank. "Jock will take care of it. I've done my part."

Yes.

Jock watched the smoke rise from the sinking motorboat before he swung back to see Norwalk's reaction. Rage. Frustration. Confusion. Wild rejection. Norwalk was looking at Cara's head bobbing in the water, and he still couldn't realize what was happening. He had the detonator in his hand and was pressing the button over and over in disbelief that it wasn't exploding Cara's vest.

No way.

But there was still a small danger, and he couldn't permit Norwalk to continue to press that button. It might trigger some random response in that bomb.

Jock quickly aimed carefully and pressed the trigger. He blew the fingers off Norwalk's right hand. The next shot exploded the phone he was holding in his other hand. Norwalk screamed, looking wildly around and up at the trees as he dove instinctively for the missile at his feet. But Jock had already targeted the missile, and he blew the firing mechanism.

Now for the head shot, Norwalk . . .

But Norwalk was no longer there, he'd rolled into the shrubs at the side of the path.

Son of a *bitch.*

Jock was climbing down the tree even as he called Joe. "Cara's safe, but Norwalk's still on the loose. I'll be there as soon as I can. But I have to get Cara out of that damn vest. Go get Michael. *Now!*"

He jumped the rest of the way to the ground and ran to the edge of the water, where Darcy was now struggling to help Cara onto the bank. He took Cara away from her, lifting her onto the mossy shore.

He took out his knife, cut her out of the vest, and hurled it into the bayou. Then he cut the ropes that bound her wrists. "Is she okay, Darcy?"

"Well, we didn't blow her up if that's what you mean." Darcy boosted herself out of the water. "But I wasn't expecting that big of an explosion."

"Neither was I." Cara was looking dazedly up at Jock as she tried to get her breath. "But then I wasn't expecting any of this."

"You should have expected it," he said roughly. "Do you think I'd ever let anyone take you away from me?" He glanced at Darcy. "Make sure she's really okay. I have to go after Norwalk."

Darcy went rigid. "I heard a couple shots. I was hoping we weren't going to have to worry about him any longer."

"Well, he has no fingers. I wasn't sure how foolproof that grenade was, so I made certain that he wasn't able to keep pressing that damn button. And I made sure his phone was out of action so he can't contact his men. But he rolled into the brush before I could finish him. If he's not bleeding to death, he's probably trying to get back to camp."

"No!" Cara jerked upright. "He can't go back there. Michael!"

"Joe and Eve are already there," he said curtly as he turned and started wading back through the high grass. "And I'll be there after I take care of Norwalk. Watch out for her, Darcy."

The next instant, he'd disappeared into the trees.

"Watch out for me?" Cara repeated in disbelief as she gazed after Jock. "I'm *fine*. It's Michael who's in trouble when Norwalk gets word to his men to throw him to those damn alligators." She began to struggle to sit upright. "I can't stay here and let you pamper me because Jock made a bad shot. I have to get back to the island."

"I'm not arguing," Darcy said as she helped Cara to her feet. "There's no way I want Michael hurt or that bastard to get away. But we don't have a boat, so we'd better start moving." She looked her over appraisingly. "You look like hell, but you'll make it with a little help from your friends."

"You're the only friend I have on hand right now."

"As usual, I'm more than enough."

"Yeah." Cara was frowning. "But you look . . . funny. Something's wrong with your hair . . ."

"Nothing's wrong. It stayed on, didn't it? I did a damn good job of being Eve. What do you expect when I ended up in that bayou?"

Cara's eyes widened with hope. "Eve's alive?"

"I told you how good I was. Never mind, I'll explain on the way." She took Cara's elbow and nudged her deeper into the swamp. "But you should know that wasn't a bad shot Jock made. He had to make sure that he took out that detonator, just in case the grenade wasn't foolproof. We didn't know what to expect. That was an electromagnetic-pulse grenade that I threw into the boat. It was designed to destroy the electronics used to activate roadside bombs and improvised explosives."

"What? I've never heard of anything like that."

"Jock says the Pentagon has been trying to design a good EMP grenade for years, but the best one that he knew about was an experimental model created by a lab in Mobile. But the lab couldn't get the Pentagon to pay their price, and they were considering selling it to the highest bidder." She paused. "So Jock set Kaskov on persuading the CEO to give him a sample grenade to use. It was amazing how quickly he got him to agree and deliver it. Well, not amazing. I think fear had a lot to do with it. We only had to take an hour's delay before we got under way."

"I agree, not so amazing." And not so amazing that Jock had known where to go for any weapon in the world's deadliest arsenal. "Well, I'm glad it turned out a success since I was the experiment."

"It wasn't an easy decision for any of us," Darcy said quietly. "Jock didn't see any other choice. I've never seen him scared before, Cara. He was scared when he asked Kaskov to go get that grenade."

She nodded soberly. "And I'm grateful that he did. I'm grateful that you were all there for me. I thought it was the end, Darcy."

Darcy shook her head. "No one was willing to give up on you or Michael." She added grimly as she increased her pace through the swamp, "And Norwalk isn't going to be allowed to take one more life, Cara."

"Cara's safe!" Joe ran back to where Eve was standing. "But Jock says Norwalk may be on his way back. We have to get Michael out now. You know what to do."

She nodded, her heart pounding. Her hand tightened on her rifle as she moved forward out of the darkness to stand just to the rear of the cypress tree across the bayou from the dock. "You're going to take out that other man on the west bank. Then you blow up the shack as a distraction, and I cover that Macvey man Norwalk assigned to watch Michael. If he turns on Michael when the shack blows, I shoot him."

"Right. Ten minutes." Joe was gone.

Eve drew a deep breath as she gazed out over the shallow waters of the bayou that separated the island from the swamp where she stood. Michael was sitting on the dock, still in his soccer uniform, which was dirty and torn, his face bruised, his hair tousled. Yet he was calmly sitting there, his arms linked over his knees, as he stared into darkness.

He knew she was there, watching him. She could feel it. But he was not making any sign that would alert Macvey, who was only a few yards from him with his rifle in hand. Not that Macvey appeared to be particularly alert at all, she noticed. No one would consider a six-year-old boy a threat, would they? Fair game to shoot or throw to those alligators, she thought bitterly.

Soon, Michael. You'll be safe soon.

Warmth. Serenity. Love.

Four minutes.

Six minutes.

Seven.

Everything appeared to be still and perfectly normal on the island. But Joe was very good, and that did not surprise her. He should have taken the sentry out by now. He might have even—

Kaboom!

The shack blew up! Wood speared the sky, flames climbed to catch fire on the branches of the surrounding trees.

Her rifle was trained on Macvey. But he never even looked at Michael as he started running up the incline toward the burning shack.

Yes.

Michael was alone on the dock.

Not for long.

She was wading across the bayou, her rifle held above the chest-high water. She could see Michael jumping to his feet, his eyes widening with excitement as he ran toward her. She glanced up the hill and saw that Macvey had almost reached the burning shack.

And Joe was moving toward him from behind.

Then she was on the dock, kneeling, her arms holding her son.

"Mama." He buried his face in her neck, and she could feel his warm tears. He whispered, "I'd like to go home now, please."

"Right away." She pushed him away from her. "Not quite done. I'm going to carry you across this little bayou to that pretty cypress tree, and then we'll—"

"Step away from him, Eve."

She froze. She didn't have to turn around to know who was behind her. She knew that voice, it had echoed in her mind and every nightmare she'd had since he'd appeared in her life. "I won't do that, Norwalk. I'm never going to leave my son again while you're alive."

"Then I'll shoot right through you."

And he would do it.

She looked into Michael's eyes. "I'm going to stand up, and I want you to get behind me. Don't be afraid."

"I'm not afraid. Why should I be?" He smiled at her. "It's our time to go home." He paused. "And it's his time to go away."

"Get away from him," Norwalk said. "I have to see your face. But first put down that rifle."

She gave Michael a kiss on the tip of his nose. "I think it's time you took a swim to the other bank," she whispered. "The cypress tree. On *Go*." Then she got to her feet, put the rifle down, and turned around. Norwalk was standing on the bank over twenty feet away. He was dirty, his face pale and racked with pain. He was pointing a Magnum revolver at her with his left hand. His right hand was clumsily wrapped in some kind of cloth and bathed in blood. "Hello, Norwalk. You kept telling me what a mastermind you are, but you don't seem to be doing so well tonight."

His eyes were staring dazedly at her face. "I had to see that it was really you. I saw you drown. But you're really here . . ."

She had no idea what he was talking about, but she might as well capitalize on this weakness. "Perhaps I'm a ghost. Or it could be that you're going a little more crazy than you were already." She took a step closer to him. She had a sudden idea, and her voice lowered to a hiss, "Or did I forget to tell you I'm a twin, too? That should make you feel very close to me."

"You're lying."

"Am I?" She held his eyes as she took another step. "What other explanation is there? Twins rule your world, don't they? I'm sure your brother, Sean, would say it's fate. Why wouldn't I be—*Go, Michael!*"

As she dove for Norwalk's Magnum, she heard the sound of Michael's splash behind her. A bullet whistled past her as Norwalk knocked her aside. But her attack caught him off balance, and he toppled backward into the water. She leapt back on the dock and grabbed the rifle she'd put down.

Another bullet whistled by her ear, and she whirled and shot blindly before he could fire again.

He screamed.

Blood was pouring from a wound in his throat, and he was trying to lift his gun again.

Another shot.

Blood blossomed on Norwalk's chest.

Joe was walking down the hill, his gun aimed at Norwalk.

He shot him again.

Norwalk collapsed slowly back into the water, his eyes wide with horror as he saw Eve walking toward him.

"Is Sean waiting for you?" she asked him softly. "You'll have to tell him you failed. But Sylvie didn't fail, and neither did all those other children you killed. We're all sending you straight to hell, Norwalk."

"No!" It was more of a gurgle than a word because of the wound in his throat as he managed to turn in the water and started to frantically swim away toward the metal-wire barrier. For an instant, she was tempted to let him get beyond the fence, where the alligators waited. Death by alligator seemed fitting for a monster like Norwalk.

No, she thought regretfully, as she started to follow him down the bank. Michael was too close, and she wouldn't want him to either see it or learn that particular lesson.

"Eve." Joe was coming toward her. "I'll do it."

"No." She didn't glance away from Norwalk. "Mine." She raised the rifle. "Norwalk!" she called. "Look at me. I want you to see my face."

He looked over his shoulder, his eyes wide with panic. "Go away! This isn't how it should be."

"You're wrong, it's exactly how it should be." She aimed carefully. "Sylvie!" She fired and took out his right eye. "Gwinnet Square!" She took out the left eye. He was starting to sink below the surface, but she had time to aim one last time at the very center of his forehead. "Michael!"

Norwalk's skull shattered, and splinters flew as she blew his head off.

Michael was waiting at the cypress tree when Eve and Joe crossed over the bayou a few minutes later. He ran toward her, and his arms slid around her waist. "I'm still all wet, but I swam good, didn't I? Why didn't you come right away?"

"We had something to finish." She paused. "How much did you see, Michael?"

"Nothing." He tilted back his head and looked up at her with those wise, clear eyes. "You didn't want me to see, did you, Mama?"

"No." She bent down and brushed his forehead with her lips. "Not because I felt it was something to hide, but it's hard to explain. Perhaps when you're older."

He nodded. "Whatever you say." He looked at Joe. "Did you cause that big fire? It's still burning. Are we going to have to put it out?"

"Not this time. We'll get someone else to do it." He reached for his phone. "Right now, I think I'll call Jock and give him an update. He'll be annoyed to know that we didn't need his help. But I do have to ask him exactly what happened with Cara—"

"You can ask her yourself," Jock said as he came out of the brush and jerked his head back toward the trees in the swamp behind him. "She's right behind me. As usual, she didn't do what I told her to do. And she had Darcy aiding and abetting." He looked at the blaze. "Norwalk?"

"No." Joe nodded at the bayou. "There. The explosion was a distraction."

"And we're not talking about it at the moment," Eve said firmly, her hand on Michael's shoulder. Her gaze was searching the trees behind Jock. "Cara's okay, Jock?"

"As good as she can be considering what she's been through." His lips tightened as his gaze shifted to the blood on the water. "Joe is right. I'm disappointed."

"So was he," she said quietly.

Jock's gaze narrowed on her face. "Really?"

She nodded jerkily. "Why the surprise? He was going to kill my son." Then her chin lifted as she caught sight of Cara and Darcy coming out of the trees. "Look, Michael, there's Cara. She looks very tired, doesn't she? I bet she'd like it if you ran to meet her."

"And Darcy!" Michael was already running through the brush toward her. "Cara, it's all right now. We can go home!"

Eve smiled as she saw Cara kneel down as Michael rushed into her arms. "That's the first thing he asked me," she said. "It's very important to Michael." She looked at Joe. "There's no way anything is going to be normal for him for a long time to come, maybe never. Once the media gets wind of what happened here, they're never going to let it go. But we have to go home right away and start to try."

Joe slipped his arm around her waist. "Then we'll make it happen."

"No, I'll make it happen," Jock's lips twisted. "Have you forgotten how efficient I am at cleanup?" He turned to Joe. "The alligators will take care of Norwalk and friends, but the fire's going to attract attention. And I'll need information from you about any other aspects of the scene that are also going to arouse curiosity. No way do we want Michael to have the paparazzi asking him questions about what happened to him. He was never here." He looked from Joe to Eve. "None of you were ever here."

Joe nodded and turned to Eve. "Go take everyone back to the cove and get ready to go. I'll be with you as soon as I'm through with Jock."

She nodded as she turned to go. "Thanks, Jock."

"No, we all have our parts to play. You just have to take care of her." Jock's gaze was on Cara and Michael. "She won't let me do it. But just look at her, Eve."

Eve was too busy looking at him at the moment. Cara was not the only one in pain. "I'll take care of her." She started toward Cara, Darcy, and Michael. So much pain to be healed. It was difficult to know where to begin.

Love.

Start with love.

She took Cara in her arms. "I'm so proud of you. I love you. We're all going to get through this."

"I know." Cara's arms tightened around her. "Otherwise, he'd win, wouldn't he?" She drew a deep breath. "Even though Michael said that Norwalk went away and wouldn't come back. Is that true?"

"Michael always tells the truth." She released her and turned to Darcy and gave her a hug. "You look . . . different." She took a strand of her hair and looked at it. "Red-brown? And the shape of your eyes . . ."

"*Your* eyes. Waterproof makeup." She made a face. "And I had to practically glue that wig in place so that it wouldn't come off in the water. But I had help from those old Esther Williams movies."

"Esther Williams? I'm . . . confused. Why did you come, Darcy?"

"Why did *you* come?" Darcy asked. "Norwalk. Cara. Michael. Kaskov was the only one offering me an opportunity. But I had to pretend to be you to take advantage of it." She waved her hand dismissively. "I'll tell you all about it later." Her gaze went back to the burning island. "It was worth it. I did help with Cara. My only regret is Norwalk. I promised Sylvie I'd make him pay. I didn't do it."

"I think perhaps you did," she said gently. "Or maybe Sylvie helped a little." She was remembering Norwalk's wild eyes and confusion as he'd stared at her during those last moments. And what had prompted Eve to bring up that claim that she was also a twin that had so upset him? It had all come out of nowhere. She reached out and touched the sodden, red-brown hair clinging around Darcy's face. "Joe said we should all head for the boats." She took Darcy's arm and nudged her down the path. "Suppose you and I go ahead and lead the way. There's something I should tell you . . ."

CHAPTER
19

LAKE COTTAGE

Dad says he's going to barbecue tonight," Michael said.
"Sort of a welcome home. Isn't that a good idea?"

"A very good idea," Eve said. "Is Cara with him? I haven't seen her since we got home." But then they had only arrived a few hours ago. They'd taken a flight out of New Orleans immediately after they'd arrived at Kaskov's dock. Only Darcy had decided to stay behind to take time to get rid of the remnants of the wig and makeup, and told them she'd join them the next day.

"She was down by the lake." He went to the railing of the porch. "There she is." He waved at Cara. "She has her violin."

And she was starting to play. Mendelssohn.

Eve stood there, listening.

Beauty to sing to the spirit and free the soul.

"She'll be better now," Michael said as he went to the porch swing and dropped down on the cushions. "It was bad for her, Mama. She doesn't understand ugliness. It hurts her. But the music will make her all well again." He smiled. "It's doing it now. Can't you feel it?"

"Maybe not as well as you can." She sat down beside him and

put her arm around him. "But, yes, I feel it." Jock had asked her to take care of Cara, but she was already taking care of herself. She was reaching out to the one source that she knew could make her whole again. That's what they were all doing. Joe was going back to the small, wonderful tasks that made them a family. Eve was holding, watching, keeping guard.

But what was Michael doing? He appeared perfectly normal and loving, but she had been at her most vigilant in watching him. Yes, he was unusual and unique, but he was also a six-year-old child. "Do you want to go down and help your dad?"

He shook his head. "I'll go down later. I'll stay with you for a while."

Because he knew that she needed him? Was he trying to heal her, too? "It's nice sitting here and listening to Cara. She's delayed her visit to Kaskov and she'll be going back to school next week." She paused. "And so will you, Michael. Your dad and I have been talking about it, and we've decided that maybe you should go to another school. We're going to tell everyone that we were mistaken about your being in that ice-cream shop, that a relative had picked you up. But things might still be—it could be sad for you."

He nodded. "It is sad for me." He laid his head on her shoulder. "But it will be more sad for everyone else. I'd remind them, wouldn't I, Mama?"

The only survivor from that terrible tragedy? "Yes, I'm sorry, but that's true."

"And families need to remember them all alive and happy. It's going to be hard for them to go on if they don't. It's like what you do with the skulls. They have to believe they've come home to them."

"I guess it's something like that," she said huskily. "So is it okay with you if we sign you up in another school?"

He nodded. "But maybe not right away? Is it all right if we go to London to see Jane? I haven't seen her for a few months, and you said she was busy with her paintings. Maybe I could even go to school there for a little while."

She looked at him in surprise. "I guess we could. If that's what you want."

"That's what I want. Then we'll find a great new school here. Maybe I'll even play soccer again."

And maybe he wouldn't. But he'd slip seamlessly into the new regime after giving everyone a chance to forget who he was and start their healing. Her arm tightened around his shoulders. "I think that's a very good idea. Anything else on your wish list?"

"Just one." He was silent for a moment. "Remember that last day when Gary came running up and said he wanted to see your face because he'd been told it would make him feel better to know who you were."

She nodded. "And your dad and I thought it was you who had talked to him."

He shook his head. "Not me. But I was wondering . . . Would there have been a reason for Gary's mom to want you to . . . help her with him?"

She remembered Gary's terribly damaged face, which she'd looked at when she'd been searching for Michael. "It's possible."

He looked soberly up at her. "Then will you call her right away and ask if you can help? I think maybe that would make Gary and his dad feel better if his mom was happier."

"I'll offer," she said gently. "Almost a week has passed. It may be too late."

"I don't think it is. Maybe when real bad things happen, we sometimes get a break." He leaned back against her, his eyes on Cara. "She's switched to the Tchaikovsky. I like that better. She says it soars, Mama. What do you think?"

"I think she's right," she said unsteadily as she pressed her lips to the top of his head. "I believe there's definitely some soaring going on, Michael."

BELLE GRACE

Kaskov was back.

Darcy drew a deep breath as she saw the huge white speedboat pulling up at the dock. It was almost nine at night, and she'd thought he'd be here earlier. But what did she know about what Kaskov did or didn't do? He was careful to make certain that no one really knew him and made it clear he didn't appreciate her attempts in that direction. And that was fine with her. Their encounters had been filled with tension, and even danger, and she wanted no more of it. She wanted peace and good times and to be totally in control of her life.

Well, she was almost through with dealing with him, and she wouldn't have to think about it for much longer. Or would she? Cara's connection to him would almost assure that she would also have some kind of connection. Because she would never give up her friendship with Cara. But that would be okay, she assured herself. Darcy would see that Kaskov would be a very *distant* connection.

Worry about it later. Right now, she had to finish what she had on her list and move on. She tidied her hair and swept majestically down the grand staircase. She would miss the feeling of cloning Scarlett O'Hara after she left this—

"Much better," Kaskov said dryly from the foyer, looking up at her. "I like Eve's look, but I much prefer you as a blonde." He looked at her peacock-colored maxi skirt and purple halter top. "Is this all for me? I think I told you I was content with the arrangement I have."

"Don't be silly. We both know you'd never seduce any of Cara's friends. Besides, you find me a little disruptive," she said as she reached the foyer. "I just wanted to leave a lasting memory on this old house." She grimaced. "And after trekking in that stinking swamp, I needed to remind myself who I am."

"I don't think you have to worry about lasting memories," he said dryly. "Though I wasn't sure you'd still be here. Eve said you wanted to stop here and clean up, but I thought you might want to leave before I got back."

She shook her head. "I had a couple things to finish up with you before I left." She smiled. "But I'll get out of your hair as soon as I take care of them." She swept past him into the parlor. "It may be my last chance since you'll probably have all your defenses up the next time we get together."

"I beg your pardon?"

"See. It's starting already." She turned to face him. "First, you have to do something about Norwalk."

His brows rose. "I believe something quite permanent has already been done about Norwalk."

"And that's fine. I wish it had been me, but Eve says that maybe it was, and I have to accept that she might—" She broke off. "That's not what I meant. It was too permanent, too efficient. You have to fix it."

He leaned against the French doors and crossed his arms across his chest. "Elaborate."

"Jock took over the cleanup on the island. Knowing Jock, any trace of what went on there will have vanished as if it had never been. Absolutely no answers. He had to protect Cara and Michael and Eve and Joe. He wouldn't want to make one mistake."

"I agree. He's exceptional. I'm getting impatient, Darcy."

"But there *have* to be answers," she said simply. "Norwalk killed too many people. He hurt too many families. He left them bewildered and angry and frustrated . . . and empty. Just as I was when he killed Sylvie and my mother. I had to have a reason. I had to have revenge. It was tearing me apart."

"I know." His eyes were narrowed on her face. "What are you saying?"

"Give those families what they need. You can't give them Norwalk, but you're very clever. You can set up an entire scenario. There are so many scumbags in your world that the human race would be much better without." She moistened her lips. "You'd have to choose well to give the ultimate in satisfaction. Really, really, bad people, Kaskov. Maybe even worse than Norwalk. No, that's not possible. But find someone just as bad. Then you prove they were at the square and did that horrible, horrible thing. And then provide a truly spectacular ending that would give final resolution to all those poor families. That's just good theater."

He suddenly chuckled. "You're incredible. A colossal frame-up? And then you want me to remove them from this earthly plane?"

"I told you, only if they're monster caliber."

"And why would I go to all that trouble?"

"Because you started it all by killing Norwalk's twin."

"And saved Cara from being blown up."

She nodded. "But it's like dominos, they keep falling. But you can help put an end to it." She paused. "If you'll do it. It will be very complicated. But you can look on it as a challenge. You might en- joy it."

His smile vanished. "You have the nerve to think you know me that well?"

"I wouldn't presume. If I did, you'd go the other way to prove me wrong. I only know how it hurts not to know, to be helpless, to have justice just out of reach." She lifted her chin. "And I know that you'll never tell me if you're going to do it or not. But I had to try."

"Are you finished?"

"No, just going on to item two. I thought I'd give you a reward if you took item one under consideration." She met his eyes. "I got to Cara just in time to stop her from rolling out of that boat when it was heading toward you. She had her hands tied, and she knew she'd probably either drown, or Norwalk would immediately blow her up. But she wasn't going to let you die because of her."

"Indeed?" His face was without expression. "And that's supposed to mean something to me?"

"Yes, it does. I don't know what you want from her, but it means you have a chance." She turned toward the front door in a whirl of peacock skirts. "That's all. Would you call Nikolai and ask him to take me to an airport hotel?" She stopped at the door to look over her shoulder. "Good-bye, Kaskov. It's been quite intriguing."

"Yes, it has. Almost . . . entertaining." His tilted his head. "But I'm not going to let you run away before I'm finished, Darcy. I have a question to ask."

"What?" she asked warily.

"You're a singer, I'm told. Are you good?"

"I'm fairly spectacular. Not the talent of the century like Cara. But I have so many other talents, that would be overkill. But I'm a very, very good singer." She frowned. "Why?"

"Jock and I had a discussion about Cara, and I tried to convince him that she *was* her talent, and that was her worth to me. And, therefore, that was why I insisted on keeping her close to me. I think he might have believed me."

"Was it a lie?"

"I think I'll let you decide. I do have a certain obsession about music that might point in that direction. There could be a possibility that I enjoy being behind the scenes and pulling the strings, of controlling the artist even if I can't control the music. But, of course, that's only a possibility." He was smiling mockingly. "However, I've just decided to get a few of your CDs from that concert you did with Cara. I hope you prove just as entertaining performing as you are in real life."

Her mouth fell open. "You're joking?"

"Am I?" He turned away. "Why would I do that? I'm always interested in *new* talent. Good night, Darcy. I'll give you my critique after I listen to your concert. And I'm certain you'll want regular reports, regarding the progress of my 'challenge.'" He headed for his office. "You're so very concerned about it . . ."

Controlling the artist, if not the music? What the hell? Had he meant it? So much for keeping her distance, she thought dazedly. If he *had* meant it, that would be a constant battle to maintain her independence. No, surely he must have just been annoyed with her for trying to tell him what to do.

Maybe. But that smile . . .

Darcy watched as the door closed behind him before she managed to pull herself together.

"Holy *shit*," she whispered.

ATLANTA AIRPORT

"I saw our plane, Cara." Michael's eyes were shining with excitement as he ran back from the observation window to where she was standing with Eve in line at the gate. "They're loading our luggage. One guy was putting on a crate with a puppy. You said it was a long flight to London. Will the puppy be okay, down there?"

"Fine. It's just as comfortable for animals as it is in the passenger compartment for us." She pushed him toward Eve, who was holding the boarding passes. "But stay here now. It's time to board the flight. You don't want to miss it."

"You wouldn't let me." He was grinning at her. "Is there a way for me to get down in the cargo compartment from where we'll be sitting in the—"

"I have no idea. You'll have to ask the flight attendant. They probably wouldn't like it."

"I'll ask. People can be nice sometimes. I bet that puppy is going to be lonely."

Yes, people could usually be nice when it came to Michael, she thought. And it was wonderful that he still had that faith in human nature after the nightmare he'd just gone through. "It wouldn't hurt to ask," she said gently. "Just don't be disappointed if it doesn't work out."

"I won't." He was frowning, trying to puzzle it out. He looked at Eve, who was giving the boarding passes to the flight attendant. "What do you think, Mama?"

Eve pushed him ahead of her in line. "I think that we should worry about getting to our passenger seats before you worry about the cargo hold." Her gaze shifted to the gate lobby, then she looked at Cara. "And I think that Cara may be too busy to answer questions for the next few minutes."

Cara stiffened as her gaze followed Eve's.

Jock.

She whirled and was out of line and beside Jock in the lobby in seconds. "Why are you just standing here? Weren't you even going to come and say good-bye?"

"Maybe." He smiled crookedly. "I just got here. And the last time we had an in-depth conversation, you were telling me that you were the one in control of the situation. Yet I notice you didn't call and let me know that you were going to London."

"I knew Joe had called you."

"But Joe isn't you." He was silent an instant. "I was surprised you and Darcy hadn't gone back to school."

"Darcy did. I'll go back to New York next week. I thought I should help Eve get Michael settled with Jane. We all need family right now. Joe will be coming in a few days."

"From what I saw, Michael is doing pretty well." His gaze was still searching her face. "How are you doing?"

"All bruises healing. Who knows how the inner scars are doing? But they *will* go away, Jock. So stop looking at me as if I was still that kid you've known all these years."

"I liked that kid," he said thickly.

"Well, she doesn't exist any longer. I told you that I was grown-up that night at the summerhouse." She shook her head. "It wasn't true. But what I went through with Norwalk gave me my diploma."

"I know it did. I could see it. I *hated* it."

"So did I." She added fiercely, "But I'm not going to let him ruin one minute of what I want to take forward with me. I thought quite a bit about that when I was in that boat heading toward my personal Armageddon. I want beautiful, splendid music, and a family that will light every darkness, and all the love I can gather and hold." She punched her finger at his chest. "And I want *you*, Jock Gavin. I don't know how I'm going to manage to get you, but it's going to happen."

"No, it isn't," he said roughly. "I told you that's not possible. I'm the worst choice you could make. You might have forgotten that you're also my best friend. That's allowed, that can't hurt you." He added bitterly, "And I won't destroy my best friend because I want to take her to bed." He added in frustration, "And, for God's sake, you're only eighteen years old. Out of bounds, Cara."

"Interesting thing about age is that it keeps changing. Going up and up and up." She shook her head. "I don't know where we're going, Jock. But I know we have something wonderful that we can build on. So I'm not letting go." She met his eyes. "And I don't think you can let me go. I'll have to see. Let's do a trial run." She moved into his arms. "I don't know much about this part, but I'm a fast learner." She kissed him. "I'll ask Darcy about all the nuances." She kissed him again. "Unless you'd like to demonstrate." She looked down at his lower body. "And I think you would, Jock."

He drew a harsh breath. "Damn you, Cara."

"I'm not going to let you cheat me." She took a step back. "But I'll let you give me a little more time if that's what's bothering you. You might need a period of adjustment."

"I'm not *right* for you," he said through set teeth.

"You're the only one who will ever be right. So get used to it. Find a way to deal with me." She took another step closer, her voice shaking. "We can *do* this."

"Get on that plane. You're going to miss your flight."

"And then what would you do with me?"

"Get you on the next flight."

"But you do live a good deal of the year at MacDuff's Run, near Edinburgh. Maybe I could join you for a few days in Scotland."

"No!"

"Then take what I offered. You set the pace." She smiled. "Because today, tomorrow, or in a few years, I'm going to have you, Jock."

"The hell you are."

"You'll see." She turned and walked back toward the gate. She looked back over her shoulder at him. So golden and wonderful, so angry and grimly determined to give her what was best for her. Why hadn't he ever been able to understand that he was that best?

She knew the answer. Because she hadn't been able to make it clear, and that had to change. She smiled lovingly at him because he had to see the love. Passion was all very well, but they had so much more.

She turned and started down the jetway.

"Think about me," she called back to him. "Think about us. Because you can bet I'm going to be thinking about *you*, Jock Gavin."